Different World

Part 5
of

The Ambition & Destiny Series

By
VL McBeath

Different World
By VL McBeath

Editing services provided by Wendy Janes at WendyProof and Susan
Buchanan at Perfect Prose Services.
Cover design by Michelle Abrahall

ISBN: 978-1-9999426-0-1 (Kindle Edition)
978-1-9999426-1-8 (Paperback)

Main category – FICTION / Historical
Other category – FICTION / Literary Collections

Legal Notices

This story was inspired by real-life events but as it took place over one hundred years ago, parts of the storyline and all characterisation are fictitious. Names have been changed and any resemblance to real persons, living or dead, is purely coincidental. Although the story took place in and around the Summer Lane area of Birmingham, and Handsworth, exact locations have been changed.

Explanatory Notes

Meal times

In the United Kingdom, as in many parts of the world, meal times are referred to by a variety of names. Based on traditional working class practices in northern England in the 19th Century, the following terms have been used in this book:

Breakfast: The meal eaten upon rising each morning.

Dinner: The meal eaten around midday. This may be a hot or cold meal depending on the day of the week and a person's occupation.

Tea: For the lower and middle classes, this was the meal eaten at the end of the working day, typically around five or six o'clock. This could either be a hot or cold meal.

Tea also represents a beverage of the same name. It was made in a teapot by pouring boiling water over tea leaves and allowing it to stand (brew) for several minutes before pouring into a cup. It was commonly served with milk and sugar.

Afternoon tea: Afternoon tea can vary but would often consist of a cup of tea with a selection of cakes. Initially this was a pastime restricted to the wealthy, but as the price of tea and sugar came down, it became more widely adopted, especially by the middle classes.

Money

In the nineteenth century, the currency in the United Kingdom was Pounds, Shillings and Pence.

- There were twenty shillings to each pound and twelve pence to a shilling.
- A crown and half crown were five shillings and two shillings and sixpence, respectively.
- A guinea was one pound, one shilling (i.e. twenty-one shillings).

It can be assumed that at the time of the story £1 is equivalent to approximately £100 in 2017 (i.e. add two zeros to each figure).

Ten thousand pounds (£10,000) would be equivalent to approximately one million pounds (£1,000,000) or one million, five hundred thousand dollars (US$1,500,000) in 2018

Scouse/Scousers

Scouse (rhymes with house) is a word commonly associated with Liverpool.

The Accent: People of Liverpool have a distinct and instantly recognisable local dialect (Scouse) compared to other parts of the UK. People from outside the city who are unfamiliar with the accent may have difficulty understanding what is said.

The Food: Scouse is also the name given to a local dish.

Typically it is a stew made of meat (beef) and vegetables cooked in one pot. At the end of the nineteenth century, fish may have replaced the beef. The vegetables vary, but are generally a base of potatoes, carrots and onions. It was often a way to use up leftovers.

The People: People from Liverpool are widely known as Scousers.

Football

In the UK, football is a team game of eleven players where a round ball is kicked towards rectangular goals. It is the game that is known as soccer in some parts of the world.

Assizes Court: In the UK this is now known as the Crown Court.

For further information on Victorian England visit:
https://valmcbeath.com/victorian-era

Please note: This book is written in UK English

It is recommended that *Different World* is read after Parts 1-4 of The *Ambition & Destiny* Series

Previous books in
The *Ambition & Destiny* Series:

Short Story Prequel: *Condemned by Fate*
Part 1: *Hooks & Eyes*
Part 2: *Less Than Equals*
Part 3: *When Time Runs Out*
Part 4: *Only One Winner*

❧

Join my mailing list for further information and exclusive content about The *Ambition & Destiny* Series.

Details can be found at **www.vlmcbeath.com**

❧

The Family Tree shown on the next page represents the family at the start of this story.

For larger versions please visit:
https://valmcbeath.com/different-world-family-tree/

To Grandad and Uncle Frank
The past is gone ...
Rest in Peace

The Jackson and Wetherby Family Tree

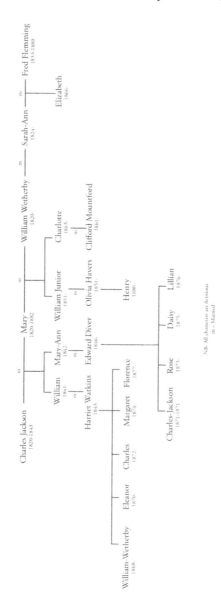

N.B. All characters are fictitious
m = Married

Chapter One

Liverpool, Lancashire. England. April 1890

Today had turned into a day of firsts. Until this morning, William-Wetherby had never travelled more than five miles from the centre of Birmingham. He had never needed to or wanted to, and yet here he was, away from the place he had called home for the first twenty-one and a half years of his life. He stood on the platform of Liverpool's Lime Street Station, transfixed by the magnificent engine that had pulled him across the country. He'd seen trains coming in and out of Birmingham's New Street Station, of course he had, but he'd never imagined travelling on one. Today had changed that and it was a thrill he didn't think he'd tire of. How did something so large, pulling so much weight, move with such speed? The train rested now with plumes of smoke spewing from its chimney, but it was about to do something he may never do again: go back to Birmingham.

With his heart pounding, he stared down the platform at the backs of his fellow passengers as they scurried from the noise and soot. He would have to follow them if he wanted his first glimpse of this new city, but his feet were like lead. Taking hold of his small travel bag, he gripped the handle and forced himself forward. His pace was slow and once he passed through the main entrance, he stopped to take a deep breath of fresh air. It smelt different. Not the choking smog of Birmingham, but something else ... and what was that noise? He glanced up to see birds circling overhead, their grey and white feathers indistinct against the tones of the sky. They were like nothing he'd seen before.

His gaze moved to the large open space that spread out before him. There were people everywhere but his eyes were drawn to a majestic building to his right. It was magnificent in size but the end facing him had the same Roman pillars and gently sloping roof as the Town Hall in Birmingham. Would everything remind him of home?

Taking another deep breath, he moved away from the station and followed the crowds down the side of the hall. *St George's Hall* a sign said. *Concert Hall and Assizes Court.* He shrugged. *A strange combination.*

Within five minutes the steady stream of travellers became part of a larger crowd in the middle of a square. Shops surrounded him and William-Wetherby's mouth fell open as he turned a full circle.

His attention was caught by a number of trams passing along the far end of one of the streets. *Maybe they'll lead me to the docks.* Taking the road out of the square he reached the tramlines but stopped and scratched his head. There were tracks running everywhere.

"Get your paper 'ere," a voice shouted behind him. William-Wetherby turned to see a man selling newspapers. He waited until he was free before he approached him.

"Can you tell me the way to the docks?"

The street seller looked at him blankly. "D*u*cks?"

"No, the docks? With ships?"

The seller stared at him until a look of recognition crossed his face. "You mean the *docccks*?" The man pointed to his right. "Carry on down 'ere to Cherch Street, tern right an' keep goin' straight ahead 'til yer see de Mersey."

William-Wetherby's mouth dropped as his gaze followed the direction the man had indicated.

"Th-thank you." William-Wetherby offered him some money and accepted the newspaper the seller thrust at him before staring back down the road. *Don't they speak English around here?* Raising his hat he made his way to the crossroads and turned right. *I hope this is the way he said.* Encouraged that the crowds showed no signs of dispersing he continued to walk with them and ten minutes later, for the first time in his life, he caught a glimpse of the sea. Or at least that's what he thought he saw hidden behind the assortment of brick and wooden buildings that stretched in both directions as far as the eye could see. He stopped as a knot tightened in his stomach. There were so many ships and sailing boats berthed alongside them. *How on earth will I find Charles amongst all these? It's a good job I'm here a few weeks before he's due to arrive.*

After a moment's hesitation, he crossed the road and perched on a wall where he opened the newspaper and gave a sigh of relief. It was in English. Not that it helped. There were plenty of rooms to rent, but he had no idea where they were in relation to where he was now.

With his back to the water, he studied the buildings before him. Warehouses predominated, and were interspersed with offices, beerhouses and a bank, but where were the houses? It would be light for several hours yet, but he needed to find somewhere to stay before nightfall. He would have to ask someone. Pushing himself up, he crossed the road to the nearest beerhouse but as he leaned on the door, it hit a wall of bodies. Pressing harder with his shoulder, he tried again until he squeezed through the gap, pulling his bag behind him.

The place was tiny and he clutched his bag to his chest as he jostled through the crowd to the bar.

"A pint of ale, please." As he spoke the voices around him stopped.

"You're not from round 'ere den?" the barman said with an inflection he could barely understand.

"N-no. I'm from Birmingham. I-I need lodgings while I wait for my brother's ship to dock."

"You've come to the right place." A tall man to his left flashed a broad smile. "I kicked a couple out yesterday so I've got a spare room down on Tabley Street."

William-Wetherby gulped. "Is that near the docks?"

"As close as yer like."

"Don't you go sending him down there, Alfie Dixon." A woman appeared behind the bar. "Look at him. He wouldn't stand a chance with that lot you take in." She handed William-Wetherby a piece of paper. "Take this. It's details of a respectable establishment about five minutes' walk from here. You won't get no grief there. Tell Mrs McDougall I sent you."

WITH A PINT OF ale inside him and a set of directions etched in his mind, William-Wetherby found his way to the hotel he had been recommended. He climbed the front steps and was about to go in when he saw a sign on the door. Temperance hotel. What was the barmaid of a drinking establishment doing sending people to a place that didn't tolerate alcohol? After a moment's thought, he returned to the pavement and studied the properties around him. There was nothing except warehouses and beerhouses. Nowhere that could offer him an alternative room. *What do I do?* As he hesitated at the bottom of the steps his attention was drawn to a gang who appeared at the end of the street, their raucous voices echoing off the buildings. They staggered towards him causing the hairs on the back of his neck to stand on end. Instinctively he backed away up the hotel steps until he stumbled through the door at the top. As soon as it opened, a bell rang in the hallway and a middle-aged woman, with dark curly hair and wearing an apron, walked out to meet him.

"Can I help you?"

William-Wetherby coughed to clear his throat. "Mrs McDougall? The barmaid at the beerhouse down the road sent me; she said you might have a room."

"Have you been drinking?"

"No ... yes, well only a pint of ale. I needed to know where to find a room and it would have been rude to walk out without buying anything. I don't usually drink."

Mrs McDougall smiled as she walked towards him. "You don't sound like you're from around here."

"No ... no I'm not. I arrived this afternoon ... from Birmingham." William-Wetherby took a step back.

"Don't look so scared, I won't bite. I'm not from these parts either, moved down from Scotland a few years ago. I know what it's like to feel like you don't belong."

"So, do you have a room?"

Mrs McDougall laughed. "It depends how much money you've got. I may have for a well-spoken gent like you. You can have a room to yourself for three shillings a week."

"I ... erm ..."

"If you want to save your money, you can share for one shilling and sixpence."

William-Wetherby sighed with relief. "Yes, I'll share. I don't want to go through my money too quickly." He glanced around the hall as Mrs McDougall studied him.

"I don't suppose you've got a job, have you?"

"No ... not yet. I'll go out first thing in the morning and find one."

Mrs McDougall nodded. "In that case, I'll ask for five shillings in advance as well as this week's rent. Come with me and I'll show you the room."

He followed Mrs McDougall up two flights of stairs into a small room at the rear of the building. It was sparsely furnished with two single beds, one opposite the door, the other along the wall behind the door. Each had a small cabinet by the bed, and a single shared wardrobe stood in the far corner near the window.

"A sailor called Mr Robinson has this bed." She pointed to the bed behind the door. "And so this is yours if you want it."

William-Wetherby glanced around the room. It was no bigger than the servants' room they'd had in Handsworth and the window faced a brick wall, but what choice did he have? A shiver ran down his spine and he fought to push the memory of home from his mind before turning to answer Mrs McDougall. "Yes, thank you, I'll take it."

Chapter Two

The summer had dragged interminably and there had been times when William-Wetherby feared Charles would never arrive in Liverpool, but with autumn setting in, he finally received the letter he had been waiting for. He pulled his jacket tightly around him and held onto his hat as he headed into the stiff breeze blowing from the River Mersey. He needed to get to the Waterloo Dock and didn't want to be late. Not that he knew what time to be there. The letter from Charles had said he was due into Liverpool some-time this week. Today was the most likely day, but with the tides and weather as unpredictable as they were, it could just as easily be next week.

He reached the dock to find a selection of ships berthed. To his untrained eye, they were all pretty much the same, except some were larger than others. Charles had said he was on an iron ship, so William-Wetherby presumed that made it bigger, but he didn't know. He walked the length of the dock, peering at the names on each ship, but when he didn't find what he was looking for he found a sheltered alcove and sat on the floor to wait.

The morning wore on, and William-Wetherby became mesmerised by the activity around the ships. Once they had been emptied of their cargo they were ready to receive their next consignment. He had been a clerk in a shipping office for these last few months, writing out receipts and invoices for these sorts of transactions, but it was only now he was seeing it in real life. At least all he had to do was move paper around his desk, not these huge containers of materials.

He had become so engrossed with the loading and unloading that he failed to notice a ship gliding gently towards them. He sat up with a jolt as its enormous bulk filled his vision and there on the hull was the name he had been looking for. *The Argomene.* His heart rate increased as he surveyed the deck. There were men everywhere, some pulling down and tying back the sails while others let down the anchor. *Where is he? He must be somewhere.* William-Wetherby squinted into the weak midday sun but stopped when he heard his name being blown on the breeze.

"William-Wetherby. Up here."

William-Wetherby looked around until his eyes followed the line of a tall mast in the middle of the ship. Perched on the top was Charles, waving his arms.

William-Wetherby grinned and waved back, shouting into the wind.

It was over an hour later before a handful of men came ashore and William-Wetherby ran to the gangplank as Charles emerged.

"What kept you?" William-Wetherby threw his arms around his brother. "I thought you'd never get here."

"Never mind me, what are you doing here? You've got some explaining to do. And when did you grow that moustache?"

William-Wetherby ran his fingers across his upper lip. "I've had this a couple of years, but we've far more important

8

things to discuss than my moustache. How long do you have?"

"A full two days; I'm changing ship and the new one won't be here until Friday. Let's get a drink and I'll tell you all about it. I hope you don't mind me staying with you."

William-Wetherby put an arm around his brother's shoulders and steered him away from the dock. "I don't mind but my landlady might. I live in a temperance hotel and she won't let us in if we've been drinking."

Charles shot him a glance. "Tell me you're not serious."

"I am, but I don't mind. It's no fun at night when men who've been at sea for months are suddenly let loose on an already overcrowded city. The place was recommended to me and it suits me well enough."

"You'd better take us to a tavern then and we'll rent a room; you can go halves with me. I'm not having any landlady telling me what I can and can't drink."

With a room secured and a couple of pints of ale sitting on a small table in a corner of the bar, the two brothers huddled together with their backs to the room.

"How much do you know?" William-Wetherby asked. "Have you received many of Eleanor's letters?"

"A few have reached me, but I'm sure some have gone missing. I heard Father had been declared bankrupt and that he died earlier this year."

William-Wetherby nodded. "It was a terrible affair and I'll tell you about it later, but did you hear Mr Watkins died?"

Charles shook his head. "No, why's that more important than telling me about Father?"

"Because he left us some money in his will."

"Did he?" A sparkle brightened Charles eyes. "How much?"

"Well, that's the problem. He left one hundred pounds between the five of us, but we can't have the money until we decide how to divide it. I need a letter from you confirming you're happy to release the money in the agreed amounts."

Charles took a mouthful of ale. "Do we have to give the girls anything?"

"What do you think? Eleanor wasn't Mother's daughter for nothing."

Charles's shoulders slumped. "How much?"

"Eleanor and I suggest ten pounds each for the girls and thirty-five pounds for us. If you're happy with that, I've got a letter here for you to sign."

"I suppose so. Where's the money now?"

"Mr Diver's put it in a friendly society for us. Once he gets this he'll release the money and keep yours until you come back."

"When are you going home to Birmingham?"

William-Wetherby took a large gulp of ale. "I'm not."

Charles stared at him, his mouth open, before he spoke. "You're not? I thought you'd only come here to meet me."

William-Wetherby shook his head. "I've been here since April, right after the funeral. I had a bit of a disagreement with Mr Wetherby."

"What sort of a disagreement?" Charles's eyes narrowed as his eyebrows pulled together.

"It was all to do with the bankruptcy."

"That was going to be my next question. How did Father manage to go bankrupt? He had more money than he knew what to do with when I left."

William-Wetherby pursed his lips. "The official version was that when his partner Mr Ball left the business, the fellow who took over from him wasn't up to the job and lost them all their working capital."

Charles's eyes narrowed further. "And the unofficial version?"

"We have reason to believe that the new partner was deliberately put into Father's business to siphon off money ... by Mr Wetherby."

Charles choked on his ale as he took a mouthful. "What the hell happened? Why would Mr Wetherby do that to his own stepson?"

"I haven't told you the half of it yet. When Father was in hospital, he wrote down his memories of Mr Wetherby. They started off affectionately, remembering when Father was a boy and Mr Wetherby married Grandmother. In those early days Mr Wetherby would do anything for him, but something changed. Even before Grandmother died, Mr Wetherby was having a relationship with Aunt Sarah-Ann. Father reckons Grandmother knew about it too."

"With Aunt Sarah-Ann? So it was going on before they were married?"

William-Wetherby nodded. "That wasn't the worst of it though. Do you remember her husband, Mr Flemming? He wasn't so understanding and Father said he had a fight with Mr Wetherby outside our house. Mr Wetherby injured Mr Flemming so badly that he died about a week later."

Charles's eyes were wide. "Was Father sure?"

"I asked Mr Wetherby about it but unsurprisingly he denied it."

"You confronted him? What on earth did you do that for?"

"To be honest, I didn't have a lot of choice. He cornered me when we were at the funeral. I'd read Father's writing by then and so told him what I knew, which was more than the incident with Mr Flemming."

"So what else did you accuse him of?"

William-Wetherby took a deep breath. "We didn't tell you at the time, because ... well, Father and Aunt Mary-Ann told me not to, but when I found Mother's body in the canal, I saw

Mr Wetherby standing on the bridge at Tower Hill watching her."

Despite his weathered complexion, Charles's face paled. "He watched Mother drown? Why would he do that?"

"According to the letter, when Father started his own business he only got the money from Mr Wetherby because Mother blackmailed him. Apparently, years ago, Mr Watkins had given Father his business, but Mr Wetherby had taken it over under the pretence that Father was a partner. Mother was furious and when he refused to buy Father out, she threatened to tell the Liberals about the manslaughter of Mr Flemming."

Charles rubbed his hands over his face and shook his head. "How did we miss all this?"

"I've no idea what I was doing, but you would have been at school. Apparently they went around to Wetherby House one afternoon and got the money off him. That's why we think he was happy to watch her drown and why he wanted his money back from Father."

"Could he have pushed her?" Charles's eyes were wide.

William-Wetherby shrugged. "He could have done, but he denied being there, despite the fact I saw him."

The two of them were silent for a minute before Charles spoke. "What do we do about it? We can't let him get away with it."

"There's one final piece I haven't told you. I threatened to publicise Father's writing if Mr Wetherby didn't give us the money back. In the end, he promised to leave it to us in his will, on condition that I handed over the letter and left Birmingham for good."

Charles stared at his brother while he processed what he'd said. "So you handed over Father's writing and just walked away? How can you trust him to keep his word?"

"I didn't have any choice. Although I told him I wanted proof that he'd changed his will."

"But you gave him the letter before you got the confirmation?"

"Not exactly." William-Wetherby grinned. "I didn't give him the original writing. I copied it out and insisted he gave me one hundred pounds to leave."

"And did he?"

William-Wetherby's grin widened. "He had to. I told him I wasn't leaving without it."

"Do you have any left?" Charles's eyes sparkled as he spoke.

"Some. I needed money to get here and pay for lodgings while I found a job. I've got some for you too." William-Wetherby slid two gold sovereigns across the table.

"For me?" Charles's face lit up. "Thanks. Did you get the letter from Mr Wetherby?"

"No, I haven't. I wrote to him a couple of months ago, but haven't had anything back. I'll write again."

"Forget letters, you need to get on a train and go and see him."

"I told you, I can't. He said we'd only get the money if he never saw me again."

Charles's face was red. "He might have said that to you, but he didn't to me. When I finish my apprenticeship, I'll be straight round to Wetherby House."

Charles went to the bar again, coming back with two large shots of rum. He gestured to William-Wetherby's almost full ale glass. "I didn't think you'd want another one."

"Is this what being in the Merchants teaches you?" William-Wetherby said. "How to drink vast quantities of rum?"

"It's good for you." Charles took a large mouthful from one glass. "Besides, we need to think about what to do if Mr Wetherby refuses to confirm he'll leave us the money. We've no idea when he might die, so we have to do something before he does."

"I hope he doesn't wait too long, I want to go home."

"That's besides the point. You've had this information for six months and if you wait too long, people won't take any notice of it."

"You're right. I think the best thing to do is share Father's writing with the Conservative Association and the Liberals. He'd hate his friends to know what he's like and the Liberals would have a field day."

Charles nodded. "What about the police?"

"I don't think so. Father said he bought them off years ago. They wouldn't do anything to incriminate him."

Charles squinted at William-Wetherby as if deep in thought. "Do you think all police officers are crooked or only a few? He may only have influence with one or two of them, if you could get to the others ..."

"Knowing him he'll be on first-name terms with the chief constable."

"But you don't know that."

William-Wetherby stared at his brother. "And how do I find out?"

Charles banged an empty glass on the table. "You join the police, find out what goes on and how differently they treat those who have money compared with those who don't."

William-Wetherby shook his head. "What good would that do? In case it's escaped your attention, I'm in Liverpool and he's in Handsworth."

"But you'd learn the rules, get to know how the system works and find out if there's any way of getting him arrested. It's got to be worth a try."

William-Wetherby sighed. "I don't know."

"What have you got to lose? Do you want to stay a clerk for the rest of your life?"

"No, of course not."

"Well, there you go."

"All right, let me think about it. At least the police can work their way up to earning a reasonable wage, which is more than I can do now. They may get a pension when they finish work too."

"It would also mean you would have a job to move to in Birmingham when you go back. I don't know why you're hesitating."

Chapter Three

With Christmas over and Charles long gone, William-Wetherby read each Christmas card one last time as he prepared to put them away. It was past Twelfth Night and they needed to be taken down, but he couldn't bear to part with them. He'd had a card and letter from his sister Eleanor, and Mr Wetherby's wife, Aunt Sarah-Ann, had sent a card on behalf of his sisters Margaret and Florence, whom she now cared for. She'd even included a letter telling him that Florence was starting music school after Christmas. The third card he picked up was from Lydia and he gave a wry smile as he gazed at her handwriting. Why hadn't he asked her to come with him? He thought of her now working alone in the tobacconist's and shook his head. No, it was best that he hadn't. Her letter had said she was doing well and that his old friend Sid was keeping an eye on her. Dear Sid. He'd had a card from him and his mother, Mrs Storey, too. How he missed them. His final card was from his Aunt Mary-Ann and her husband Mr Diver. He didn't know what he would have done without them in his last few months in Birmingham.

His landlady, Mrs McDougall, had done her best to give

them a pleasant Christmas, but spending it with strangers wasn't the same as being with family. With a final glance, he knelt down and put the cards into the bag he kept under his bed before he retrieved his latest letter from Charles and put it in his pocket. As he straightened up, his roommate returned from the privy. Mr Robinson had the sea in his blood, but as he'd grown older, his voyages had become less frequent. He hadn't been to sea now for at least four months, and William-Wetherby doubted he would go again.

"What you hiding?" Mr Robinson said.

"Nothing … just putting my cards away. I can't keep them up all year."

Mr Robinson tutted. "You've already brought bad luck on yourself leaving them up so long. It'll be February soon."

"Nonsense, we're weeks off yet. I'm off out for a walk."

"What about church? You should be there on the Sabbath."

"With you, you mean?" William-Wetherby smiled as he reached for yesterday's newspaper. "I'll go when you do."

Once out onto the dock road, William-Wetherby turned left and walked past the Queens Dock, before turning left again towards the park where he hoped to find some privacy. He shivered as he walked, and increased his pace. Nobody else would be daft enough to go and sit on a park bench in this weather.

Sitting in a sheltered alcove, surrounded by bushes, he took the letter from his pocket. Since he had seen him, Charles had sailed to Cape Town and was now heading for Australia, if he wasn't there already. He must have had too much time to think while he'd been on board, and William-Wetherby reread Charles's thoughts on him joining the police. What his brother imagined William-Wetherby would be able to do, even in the obligatory blue uniform, he wasn't sure. He put the letter back in his pocket and picked up the newspaper. While he'd been reading it yesterday, he'd spotted an advertisement for the police. He hadn't had time to study it before Mrs McDougall had called everyone for tea, but he flicked through the pages again until he found it again.

'Job security for life' the advertisement said. *What good's job security if people hate you?* William-Wetherby crumpled the newspaper on his lap. *Do I want to be isolated from everyone around me?*

William-Wetherby shivered as a gust of wind nipped at the hairs on the back of his neck. *Why am I worried about being isolated? I haven't exactly made any friends working where I do.* Whenever he saw policemen on the streets, they were usually in pairs, sometimes groups. He studied the advertisement again. 'Single men – move into our section house and enjoy many comforts and conveniences.' *Living with a bunch of other constables would be an improvement on sitting with Mrs McDougall every night, as nice as she may be. Perhaps it wasn't such a bad idea.* 'Apply to Prescot Street station'. *How far's that from where I live now? I'll ask Mrs McDougall tonight.*

HAVING THOUGHT of nothing else all week, the following Sunday William-Wetherby finally made his way to the police station on Prescot Street. He took a deep breath as he gazed up at the miniature stone columns decorating the top of the building. There was no harm in going in. He took the newspaper advertisement from his pocket and pushed on the door where he was met by a half flight of stairs leading to a small hatch manned by a police constable. The officer looked up as William-Wetherby approached.

"Good afternoon, Officer," William-Wetherby said. "I've come about this." He straightened out the newspaper and pushed it through the hatch.

"Thinking of joining up, are you? You're the third this

week. The inspector's busy at the moment. Can you come back?"

William-Wetherby's shoulders slumped. "When?"

"Half an hour should do it. He's got someone in with him."

"Can I wait? It'll take me longer than half an hour to get home. I live near the Queens Dock."

The officer dragged air through his teeth. "You can't be living down there if you work for us."

William-Wetherby pointed to the advertisement. "It says single men can stay in the section house. I'd hoped to do that."

"If we've any rooms left, they get taken up pretty quickly when we advertise."

William-Wetherby's smile dropped.

"Don't look so worried, if you don't get in we have approved houses you can live in." The constable glanced over both shoulders before leaning forward to talk in a whisper. "Between you and me, if you can stretch to it you'd be better off outside. You'll never find a lady if you're in here all day and night." The constable winked before he pointed to the stairs. "Go up another flight and you'll find somewhere to sit. I'll tell the boss you're here."

William-Wetherby took the stairs and found a long landing with several wooden chairs. The brown and white tiled walls caused him to shudder. What was he doing here? It was like a bad dream. How he wished he could go home and once again wake up to the sound of the maid making up the fires. He hadn't realised at the time how happy he was.

He waited for twenty minutes before the inspector appeared at the top of the stairs and ushered him into an office.

"So you want to join the police force, do you? What makes you think you'd be right for the job? Have you done anything like this before?"

William-Wetherby shook his head. "No, although I suppose I did help with a police investigation a number of years ago."

The inspector raised an eyebrow. "Doing what? You don't sound like you're from round here; did you have some trouble in the countryside? It's different around here, you know."

"No, it wasn't like that. There was a missing person locally, and I helped the police to find her."

"What sort of help?"

"I suggested where she may have hidden and ended up tracking her down."

"So you were the one to find her? Did you receive any sort of commendation?"

William-Wetherby shook his head. "We were too late. We found her in the canal but she died before we could revive her."

The inspector eyed William-Wetherby from under his bushy eyebrows. "Did you attend the inquest?"

"I did. I gave evidence but as no one admitted seeing her enter the water, the verdict was left as found drowned in the canal."

"You don't sound happy with that verdict. Why didn't you pursue it?"

"I was only seventeen at the time. There was very little I could do, but if anything like that happened now, I'd want some answers."

The inspector sat back in his chair and made a pyramid with his fingers. "I get the impression you don't see yourself as a bobby on the beat. Do you have your sights set on being a detective?"

William-Wetherby shrugged. "Maybe one day, but I imagine everyone starts on the beat."

"They do, but some progress more rapidly than others. You sound like you've had an education."

"Yes, sir, I went to King Edward's Grammar School in Birmingham."

"But you want to work for us in Liverpool? Why here and not in Birmingham?"

William-Wetherby studied the wall behind the inspector's head. "My brother's in the merchant navy. I moved to Liverpool so I could see him when he comes ashore."

"Which is why you're by the docks?"

"Yes, sir."

"Well, I think we could make use of someone with your background and education. Come back next week and I'll see what we can do for you."

Chapter Four

With the first signs of spring in the air, William-Wetherby arrived home from work and glanced at the mail on the table in the hall. He was about to walk past it, when he spotted an envelope with an embossed letterhead addressed to him.

"There's a couple for you today." Mrs McDougall stood in the doorway to the kitchen, her hands on her hips. "You're popular all of a sudden. You only got one from your sister last week."

"So I did." William-Wetherby studied the envelopes.

"Aren't you going to open them?" Mrs McDougall asked.

"Yes, of course, I'll take them upstairs."

With his landlady watching him, he raced to his room, hoping Mr Robinson wasn't lying on his bed. As soon as he found the room empty, he closed the door, turned the key in the lock and sat on the bed. He tore open the first letter and studied the embossed letterhead; it was from his father's solicitors.

. . .

DEAR SIR

We are obliged to tell you that Mr William Jackson, formerly of Havelock Road Handsworth, has officially been discharged from his bankruptcy.

Yours faithfully

WILLIAM-WETHERBY THREW the letter onto the bed. What use was that to anyone? It was almost a year to the day since his father's death. Discharging him from his bankruptcy was hardly going to bring him back. He squeezed his eyes together to shut out the image of his father as he attended the public hearing. *They should have discharged him while he was still alive, then I wouldn't be here now.*

He took a deep breath and picked up the second envelope. It was from the police. He'd been back to the station twice since his first visit and now they were delighted to tell him that he had been accepted as a constable. He was to report for training on the twentieth of April but if he had any questions, he was to contact the duty sergeant.

William-Wetherby stared at the letter. *I'm going to be a policeman! Oh Lord, dare I tell anyone?* He shook his head. *No, they may turn on me. I'd better keep it to myself.* A shudder rippled through his body. *Where will I live?* Other than his visits to the police station, he had never been that far out of the city. He needed to pay the duty sergeant a visit.

WITH EASTER BEING EARLY, William-Wetherby took advantage of the extra day's holiday and walked back to Prescot Street. He reread the piece of paper the sergeant had given him, *Martensen Street* it said. The sergeant had told him to find Edge Lane and then take a left, right and another left. He must be nearly there. Checking up and down the road, he saw the sign he was looking for. The street was one of many rows of identical houses. They appeared grander than the small back-to-back houses of Birmingham, possibly because of the bay windows on the ground floor, but they were smaller than the terraced houses of Handsworth.

Glancing up at the house he had been looking for, William-Wetherby took a deep breath and knocked on the front door. On the third knock, the door was opened by a middle-aged woman with piercing blue eyes and fair hair arranged around the base of an elaborate hat. A floral apron mostly covered her dark, full-length dress.

"Mrs Booth? I'm Mr Jackson. I believe you're expecting me."

Mrs Booth looked him up and down and gave him a broad smile. "Yes, of course. Come on in. I've just put the kettle on, do you want a cup of tea?"

"Yes, thank you. That would be lovely." William-Wetherby stepped straight into a living room with a small dining table and chairs in the far corner and three armchairs set around the fireplace.

"Have a seat, I'll be with you in a mo. How many sugars?"

William-Wetherby grinned to himself as she headed for the scullery. After a year of being in Liverpool he had finally become used to the accent. "Two, please."

When she returned, Mrs Booth was carrying a tray with three cups and saucers, which she set on the table. "I've got some cake as well, I'll just fetch it." She disappeared back into the scullery to reappear with a large slab of fruit cake on a tray. "You'll have some, won't you? I made it this morning, specially."

William-Wetherby smiled as she passed him a plate.

"My daughter's joining us. She's taken the kiddies out for an hour but she'll be back any time."

"Children?"

"Oh, they're not hers. We mind them while their mams are at work; it's a bit of extra income. To be honest, I take what I can get. If I waited for someone to give me any money I'd be starving by now."

William-Wetherby noticed a plain band on the third finger of Mrs Booth's right hand. "Does Mr Booth work locally?"

"Mr Booth?" Mrs Booth paused. "Oh no, he's at sea. He's been gone so long I've forgotten what he looks like." She laughed to herself as she picked up her tea.

"It must be hard for you."

"We make our way. If you ever need any mending, I'm your woman. My daughter makes lovely hats, but only for ladies. She made this one." Mrs Booth put a hand to the side of her head.

"Very smart."

"She's a good girl. Thinks the world of those kiddies too. I couldn't manage them without her. She's here now." Mrs Booth jumped up and went to the door. "Come on in, luv. We've got a visitor."

William-Wetherby stood up as Miss Booth walked in pushing a baby carriage with one hand and holding the hand of a small boy with the other. She wasn't at all like her mother with her dark hair and brown eyes, although she too wore an elaborate hat that matched her navy blue dress.

"Mr Jackson, this is my daughter, Miss Booth; Bella, this is Mr Jackson."

William-Wetherby offered her his hand. "Pleased to meet you."

Miss Booth giggled as she shook it. "There's not many men around here with manners like that."

Feeling his face flush, William-Wetherby looked at the young boy clinging to her dress. "I see you have a friend."

Miss Booth ran her hand over the child's head. "This is Fred. We're best friends, aren't we?"

Fred nodded before he buried his face in her skirt.

"Come on, sit yourselves down. D'you want some cake?"

With the cake distributed, Mrs Booth turned to William-Wetherby. "So, Mr Jackson, what brings you to Liverpool? You don't sound like you're from round here."

"No, I'm from Birmingham. My brother's in the merchant navy and I came to Liverpool to meet up with him."

"If he's in the Merchants he won't be coming into port very often. Why haven't you gone home?"

William-Wetherby hesitated but relaxed when Miss Booth spoke for him.

"You've fallen in love with Liverpool, haven't you, and can't bear to leave?"

"Yes, that's it." He smiled. "Everyone's so friendly I decided to stay."

"So you're joining the police?"

"I am. I'm a clerk for one of the merchants at the Queens Dock at the moment, but the money's better with the police, and you get a pension."

Miss Booth turned to her mother. "Have you shown him the room yet?"

"Not yet. Come on, son, let me show you upstairs. You'll have the back room all to yourself. We decided you wouldn't want to share with Fred."

William-Wetherby hesitated. "Fred lives here? Doesn't his mother pick him up at night?"

"No ... no, she doesn't, but he's no trouble."

William-Wetherby stared at the child before following Mrs Booth. "So where does he sleep?"

"I share the front room with Bella and him and the baby come in with us." Mrs Booth led the way to the back bedroom, a compact square room with a single bed pushed along the wall behind the door. A small wardrobe stood in the opposite corner.

"It's clean and tidy," Mrs Booth said. "I'll change the bedding every week and there'll be a cooked breakfast every morning and a hot meal when you get home from work."

"And if you like, I'll do your washing for you." Bella spoke from the doorway where she now stood.

"Thank you, that sounds marvellous. How much do you charge?"

Mrs Booth looked him up and down. "Because I like you, I'll do it for two shillings a week."

Two shillings. That's more than I'm paying now.

Bella must have seen him hesitate and spoke to Mrs Booth. "Can't you do better than that, Mam?"

Mrs Booth rolled her eyes at her daughter. "I'll tell you what, seeing you're new around here, I'll drop the price to one shilling and sixpence for the first three months. You can't say fairer than that."

"No, I can't, thank you."

"You can move in when you're ready. I've cleaned the place from top to bottom."

"Oh ... I wouldn't need it for a couple of weeks. I have to tell my current landlady I'm leaving and I'm working a week's notice. I don't start my new job until the twentieth of April. If you want to fill the room sooner than that, I'd understand."

Mrs Booth studied him before she glanced at Bella. "I can't deny the extra money would come in handy, but I'll tell you what, I can wait."

BELLA SAT BY THE FIRE, feeding the baby, while her mam closed the door after William-Wetherby. Fred played with some wooden blocks by her feet.

"He seemed a bit reluctant," Bella said.

"I know, I wonder why. He won't find a better room for

that price. There's something about him that isn't quite right but I can't put my finger on it. I'd say he's too well-spoken to be worrying about two shillings a week. I wonder if he's on the run."

Bella laughed. "Who from? He's about to join the police. If he's on the run, he wouldn't be doing that."

"I don't mean he's a crook," Mrs Booth said. "But why would he stay here when his whole family is in Birmingham and his brother may not be back in Liverpool for another couple of years? It makes no sense."

Bella rested the baby over her shoulder. "Well, I thought he was charming so don't go driving him away."

Mrs Booth raised an eyebrow at her daughter. "You watch yourself, young lady. He isn't like us."

"Don't worry, I'm old enough to look after myself."

Chapter Five

As he prepared to leave the temperance hotel, William-Wetherby stared at the bag sitting on the bed beside him. He hadn't bought much in the year since his arrival but it was crammed full of the letters and cards he had received from home and he'd struggled to fasten it.

"You're about to go, are you?" Mrs McDougall leaned on his door frame, her arms folded across her chest.

William-Wetherby stood up. "Yes, thank you for everything. You know I'm not leaving on your account, I need to live closer to work."

"So you say. When do you start with the police?"

"Monday. I'm giving myself a day to settle into my new room." He threw his coat over his arm and put on his hat before picking up the bag. "Farewell, Mrs McDougall. I'll call in if I'm ever passing."

By the time he reached Martensen Street, the sun was warm and his shirt stuck to his back. He paused to catch his breath before knocking on the door. Mrs Booth opened it instantly.

"You're here." Her face broke into a smile as she held open the door. "We were beginning to wonder where you'd got to."

"It's quite a walk up that hill, I'd forgotten how long it would take."

"Well, come and take a seat." Bella patted the chair beside her. "I've made a pot of tea."

William-Wetherby hesitated as two pairs of eyes studied him. "Do you mind if I take my things upstairs? I'm rather warm after the walk and I'd like to rinse my face." Without waiting for permission, he hurried up the stairs. Dropping his bag on the floor he walked over to the window and slid open the bottom frame before poking his head through and taking a deep breath. *Why do they make me so nervous?*

It was a full five minutes before he arrived back downstairs and Mrs Booth and Bella were sitting on either side of the fireplace, leaving the central chair waiting for him.

"Come and tell us about yourself." Mrs Booth patted the chair.

William-Wetherby glanced between the two women and took a seat. "There's not much to tell. I moved up here from Birmingham about this time last year and I'll be working for the police from Monday."

"But what brought you to Liverpool?"

"I told you, my brother's in the Merchants."

"There must have been a reason you stayed, otherwise you'd have gone back," Mrs Booth said. "Was it a woman?"

"Yes ... yes, that's right."

"Are you still seeing her?" Bella's voice quivered as she spoke.

"Seeing her?" William-Wetherby's mouth dropped open. "Oh, no, you misunderstand. That's why I left Birmingham, to get away."

Mrs Booth gave her daughter a knowing look. "We knew there was more to it than visiting your brother, but now we know, we'll leave you in peace." Mrs Booth paused before she continued. "Does it still hurt to think of her?"

So much for leaving me in peace! "No, not at all ... In fact I haven't thought of her for months."

"Good for you." Mrs Booth took a sip of her tea. "Or is it? If you've forgotten about her, does it mean you'll go back to Birmingham?"

William-Wetherby stared into the fire. He'd go back to Birmingham tomorrow if he could. "No. I won't be going anywhere."

THE SUN WAS STILL SHINING as William-Wetherby left the police station and set off towards Martensen Street. He smiled at the thought of the week ahead. His three weeks of training were over and he was now a real policeman.

As he approached the house, he spotted Miss Booth walking towards him with the baby carriage and young Fred holding onto her skirt.

"Good afternoon, Miss Booth, you're out late."

She smiled when she saw him. "We've been to visit David's mam." She inclined her head towards the child in the baby carriage. "It's her half day on a Wednesday but I go to her so she can spend more time with David."

"What does she do?" William-Wetherby asked.

"She's a servant in one of the big houses in Toxteth."

William-Wetherby's brow furrowed. "Doesn't she have a husband to take care of them?"

Bella glanced in the direction of the sea. "He's away."

William-Wetherby nodded. "It's a noble profession for sure, but it's hard for those left behind. I know we miss my brother and we're not dependent on him. When's the father back?"

Bella pushed on the front door and turned around to pull the carriage in behind her. "I'm not sure."

"There you are." Mrs Booth took the baby carriage from her but stopped when William-Wetherby stepped into the room.

"Mr Jackson, you're early. I've only just got in from visiting me sister, tea's not ready yet."

William-Wetherby glanced at Bella before he turned back to Mrs Booth. "Not to worry, a couple of the lads were going to the beerhouse on Edge Lane to celebrate the end of our training. I may as well join them for a quick one."

∽

As THE FRONT door closed after William-Wetherby, Mrs Booth turned to her daughter.

"Are you all right?"

Bella sat Fred on one of the dining chairs and buttered him a piece of bread. "I bumped into him outside and he asked where I'd been. He was asking about David's dad and why his mam has to work."

"Did you tell him?"

Bella raised an eyebrow at her mam. "What do you think?"

"So what did you say?"

"The usual tale; that he was at sea."

Mrs Booth placed a hand on her daughter's shoulder. "Did he ask about Fred?"

"No, although I expect it's only a matter of time. What do we tell him?"

"More bread," a voice shouted from behind them.

Mrs Booth turned around to see Fred banging his hand on the table. "Here you go." She handed him another slice before sitting next to her daughter. "We tell him his mam died in childbirth and his old man pays for him to stay here."

"What if Jane comes back?"

Mrs Booth watched the young boy as he ran his finger through the butter on his bread and popped it into his mouth. "She won't be back, poor little mite. I think we can be sure of that."

Chapter Six

With the late summer sun shining through the open front door, Bella wiped a cloth over the top of the table before helping Fred down from his chair and ushering him to the bottom of the stairs.

"I want you in bed in two minutes, young man. I'll be up to tuck you in."

Fred clutched his toy train to his chest as he dawdled up the stairs. "Will you tell me a story?"

"Only if you're in bed when I come up." Bella turned back to the living room as the front door opened and William-Wetherby stepped in, the dark blue uniform on his tall frame dominating the room.

"Where is everyone?" he asked. "Has Mrs Booth taken David out in his carriage?"

Bella's eyes flicked to the space at the bottom of the stairs that housed the baby carriage. "No, me mam's next door. David's gone."

"Gone? Why?"

"His mam wanted him back."

William-Wetherby placed his helmet on the table, his brow furrowed. "Is his father home?"

"Yes ... yes, he is. He said he didn't want to go and leave them again."

"Will you take in another child to make up for the loss of income?"

Bella shrugged. "It's up to me mam. I can spend more time on me hats if I'm not minding babies, so maybe not."

"At least you still get money for Fred." William-Wetherby chuckled to himself as he sat at the table. "I worried when you first told me about David that his mam might not be married but I decided that a nice girl like you wouldn't mix with such women. I'm glad I was right."

Bella's face flushed scarlet as she walked to the kitchen before returning with her lodger's tea. "Where did you get such an idea?"

"Aunty Bella, where are you?" a small voice called from upstairs.

Bella put her hands to her face. "Oh my. I promised Fred I'd tell him a story and I've kept him waiting, I'd better go."

WILLIAM-WETHERBY SET his knife and fork at the side of his plate as he mopped the gravy up with some bread. As he reached for another piece, the front door opened and Mrs Booth walked in.

"It's still warm out," she said. "Are you only just finishing up? You're late tonight."

"Yes, a late shift, but I'm getting used to it."

"Did Bella give you the letter that came earlier?"

William-Wetherby's eyes darted up from his plate. "No, where is it?"

"Here it is." Mrs Booth picked it up from the sideboard.

"It's a thick envelope from Birmingham. Do you have much family left down there? You never talk about them."

"My sisters are still there. One works as a governess and the younger two are still at school."

Mrs Booth raised her eyebrows. "Does that mean your mam and dad are there too?"

William-Wetherby put his knife and fork onto the plate. "My younger sisters live with an elderly aunt. Will you excuse me, I'd like to read this upstairs."

As soon as he shut his bedroom door, William-Wetherby threw himself onto the bed and tore open the envelope. It was from Eleanor. He raced through the opening page describing Eleanor's now familiar routine with the children she was responsible for. She sounded happy enough although the tone changed as he turned the page. She had spent a week at Wetherby House, which explained the length of her letter. Aunt Sarah-Ann had summoned her because she was at her wits' end with Margaret and Florence. William-Wetherby paused while he thought of his sisters. He hadn't seen them for well over a year; he needed to write to them.

He returned to the letter and his stomach churned as he read that Florence was so unhappy at Wetherby House she wanted to leave and visit Liverpool. Margaret had made a temporary escape to stay with Aunt Sarah-Ann's daughter Elizabeth and her husband the Reverend Bloor, but that had only served to make Florence more miserable. *Why isn't she at school? Then she'd be away from Wetherby House. I need to find out what's happening.*

When he turned the page again, an elaborately written 'Private' notice piqued his curiosity. Eleanor suspected that Aunt Charlotte, Mr Wetherby's daughter, was finally carrying a baby. It obviously wasn't a subject she could broach with anyone, but she had watched her when she had been at Wetherby House and she had looked radiant. William-

Wetherby smiled. She must have been married for at least five years now and it wasn't her fault her father had forbidden her from adopting Lydia's baby, Arthur. *I hope she finally gets the child she wants.*

As he read on, his stomach sank again. Eleanor had overheard Mr Wetherby threatening to sack Sid because he was drinking heavily and often missed work. William-Wetherby shook his head. Other than an initial correspondence and a Christmas card last year he hadn't heard from him. He must have written three or four times, but had never received a reply. *Maybe the drink's getting in the way. I must write again and find out what's happening.*

Once he'd finished reading, William-Wetherby leaned back and scratched his head. He needed to write at least three letters, but he'd run out of writing paper. Dare he ask Mrs Booth for some? No, it would be best not to. It would only open him up to a further interrogation.

Chapter Seven

W ith his helmet in his hand, William-Wetherby stepped towards the front door and reached for the handle.

"Don't forget I'm on a late shift tonight. I don't finish until ten o'clock."

Mrs Booth straightened up from wiping the table. "Don't worry, I'll put a pan of scouse on. It'll heat up easy enough once you're home."

After he walked from the house, the postman waved two letters at him. "Both for you, sir."

William-Wetherby took the letters. Eleanor again. He'd only had a letter from her last week and he hadn't replied to that yet. The other was from Florence. How had she managed to send a letter without Aunt Sarah-Ann seeing it? He looked at his uniform and sighed. He'd have to wait until he got to work before he could read them.

As soon as he arrived at the station he found a chair in the corner of an interview room and opened Florence's letter. It made sense now; she was at school, which was why Aunt

Sarah-Ann hadn't seen the letter. He'd forgotten she'd been home for the holidays. His eyes widened as he read.

PLEASE CAN I come and live with you? I don't want to go back to Wetherby House, not after everything that happened in the last week of the school holidays. I've saved up some money for the train. Just tell me where to come.

WHAT HAD HE MISSED? Eleanor hadn't mentioned anything happening at the end of August. Perhaps that was why she had written again. He took out the letter and started to read. This time there were no pleasantries.

DEAR WILLIAM-WETHERBY

Something terrible has happened. Last week, Aunt Charlotte was confined to bed as she was feeling unwell. Aunt Sarah-Ann took Florence with her for a visit but while they were there Aunt Charlotte developed severe stomach pains and began delivering the baby. Without going into details, I believe it was a terrible situation and Aunt Sarah-Ann forgot that Florence was with them until Florence had an attack of hysteria.

Once he'd finished with Aunt Charlotte the doctor had to deal with Florence and gave her a dose of laudanum before sending her back to Wetherby House. The maids had to help her to her room.

Mr Wetherby was furious that Charlotte had received too many visitors and blamed Florence for causing Aunt Charlotte's misfortune.

I'm in Sutton Coldfield and don't know what to do. Aunt Sarah-Ann said Florence can't go back to Wetherby House with

Mr Wetherby being so angry but I won't be able to see her unless she comes back to Birmingham.

What shall I do? Please reply by return.

Yours affectionately.

Eleanor

WILLIAM-WETHERBY PUT his hand to his head and took a deep breath. What could he do? He could hardly turn up at Wetherby House and demand Mr Wetherby saw sense. *The man's a fool.* Footsteps approaching down the corridor forced William-Wetherby to his feet.

"What are you doing in here, Constable? You should have been downstairs ten minutes ago."

"Yes, sir. Sorry, sir." William-Wetherby stuffed the letters into his pocket and raced down the stairs. He'd have to think about it while he was walking the streets.

BELLA GLANCED at the clock before taking another sip of her hot milk.

"Mr Jackson's late tonight."

"His tea'll be dried up if he's not home soon." Mrs Booth stood up to go to the window, but as she pulled back the curtains the front door opened. "Here you are, let me go and fetch your tea. I've had it warming for the last half hour. I thought you said you'd be back by ten."

"No, I'm sorry, I finished at ten and then had to walk back. It smells good though."

He sat at the table and waited for Mrs Booth to place the stew in front of him. "Thank you. Don't let me keep you up, I'll be fine on my own."

"I'll take you up on that. I'm worn out after the day I've had. Are you coming, Bella?"

Bella watched William-Wetherby pick up his knife and fork. "You go and get settled and I'll follow you up. I won't be long."

Once Mrs Booth disappeared, Bella joined William-Wetherby at the dining table. "Is everything all right?"

"I'm fine." He put a forkful of food into his mouth and focussed on his plate.

"How are you liking work? I'll bet you know the streets around here better than I do by now."

"It's not just about walking the streets. We have the occasional mischief to sort out as well."

"So what have you done today? Did you have to take anyone to the station?"

William-Wetherby let out a small laugh. "No, not today. There were a couple of young boys who should have been at school and so we dragged them off and presented them to the headmaster."

"Do you like the men you work with?"

"They're nice enough. Still can't understand half of them, but I'm getting there."

Bella laughed but let the silence hang between them while William-Wetherby cleared his plate. "How's everyone in Birmingham? It was a thick letter you got last week."

"Yes, it was from my sister Eleanor. She's the letter writer in the family and keeps in touch with everyone. Her letters have to be long to fit everything in."

Bella smiled. "She's the governess, isn't she? She must be clever."

William-Wetherby returned her smile. "She is, but it was all Mother's doing. She was determined she should go to school."

"She's a lucky girl. I did what I had to but once I was ten

that was it. Not that I was sorry. The woman next door showed me how to make hats, and so that's what I do." When William-Wetherby didn't reply, Bella continued, "What about your other sisters? How old are they?"

"Margaret's seventeen; Florence is fourteen."

"Did they go to school?"

William-Wetherby nodded but said nothing.

"You come from a different world to me. None of the kids around here went after they reached ten."

William-Wetherby looked up, his eyes moist. "Having an education doesn't guarantee a happy life. Will you excuse me, I have a couple of letters to write."

Chapter Eight

With Christmas approaching, William-Wetherby arrived home from work and picked up another letter from Eleanor. He studied the bulging envelope and wondered when he had changed from looking forward to receiving her correspondence, to dreading it.

"Aren't you going to open it?" Mrs Booth said. "It came first thing this morning."

"Yes, of course. I'll take it upstairs."

With his bedroom door closed, he perched on the edge of the bed and pulled the letter from the envelope. At least there was no crisis on the first page. Eleanor was back to her usual self, telling him of the children she tutored before mentioning she had received a letter from Lydia earlier in the week. He let out a deep sigh; Lydia was walking out with a customer from the tobacconist's and they were to be married in the spring of next year. He let the letter fall to his lap. Why was he surprised? She wasn't going to wait for him to return to Birmingham. He should have brought her to Liverpool. It was too late now.

With his appetite for more news diminished, he turned to

the last page of the letter and skimmed the contents before he stopped and went back to the top.

WE NEED to decide what's happening to Florence at Christmas. We can't expect her to stay at school, but she can't come here. I know you said she couldn't come and stay with you, but could you change your mind? It would only be for a couple of weeks.

Please consider it and reply as soon as possible. Her letters sound so desperate that the sooner I can tell her the better.

DID HE HAVE A CHOICE? Where would she sleep? Mrs and Miss Booth already shared a room with Fred, and she couldn't come in with him. He took a deep breath and pushed himself up from the bed. He'd have to speak to Mrs Booth.

Mrs Booth had made a cup of tea when he returned downstairs and he took a seat at the dining table.

"Was it a letter from home?" Mrs Booth said.

"Yes, from Eleanor."

"She's the governess," Bella said to her mam. "All Mr Jackson's brothers and sisters went to school after they were ten."

"That doesn't surprise me, I can tell Mr Jackson's educated." Mrs Booth studied William-Wetherby. "Your dad must have had a good job if he could afford to send you all to school. You haven't told us anything about him. What did he do to make his money?"

William-Wetherby took a bite of bread, chewing it thoroughly before he turned to Mrs Booth. "Can I ask you a question? My youngest sister, Florence, has asked if she can visit over the Christmas holidays. Would that be possible? I'll pay you extra for the rent."

Mrs Booth glanced at Bella. "Of course she can come. We'd love to meet her."

"But where would she sleep?"

"I'm sure we can sort something out, even if we have to make up a bed for her down here."

"It would be for about two weeks and I'll be at work most of the time. Could you keep her occupied?"

"I think we can manage that, and Fred will love the company. When will she arrive?"

William-Wetherby shrugged. "She finishes school for Christmas at the end of next week. Could she come straight here?"

"I don't see why not."

William-Wetherby let out a long sigh. "Thank you. I'm sure she'll be delighted. I'll write and let her know."

TEN DAYS LATER, as he waited at the end of the platform, William-Wetherby pushed his hands into his pockets. It was the first time he'd been back to Lime Street since the day he had arrived in Liverpool and the wind blowing through the station was more severe than he remembered. He wished the train would hurry up.

Almost on cue, it came to a halt and a wave of people poured onto the platform, but as they headed to the exit, his heart fluttered. *Where's Florence?* He walked to the start of the platform as the last few stragglers climbed from the train. Was that her at the far end? He watched as the slight figure fumbled with her bag before walking towards him.

"Florence." William-Wetherby waved as he shouted at the top of his voice. "Florence."

About halfway down the platform she noticed him and increased her pace.

"Thank goodness you're here," William-Wetherby said as

she approached. "I was beginning to think you'd missed the train."

Florence flung her arms around her brother. "There were so many people. I couldn't move until they'd left me."

William-Wetherby returned her embrace. "It's all right, you're here now."

She rested her head on his shoulder. "Thank you for not making me go to Wetherby House. I couldn't bear it. I couldn't face Aunt Charlotte again after what happened. Did Eleanor tell you?"

"It's all right, try not to think about it. I live with two nice ladies, Mrs Booth and her daughter, and I'm sure they'll take care of you." William-Wetherby picked up Florence's bag and led her from the station. "How's school? I believe you're studying music."

Florence pouted. "That was Mr Wetherby's idea. I wanted to learn more about sums but he said that was no subject for a lady."

William-Wetherby closed his eyes as the image of his mother arguing with Mr Wetherby about the bookkeeping flashed through his mind. "Don't they teach you sums anyway?"

"Only easy stuff that we learned at primary school."

"Well, I'm sure you'll do fine. You have another year to go yet."

Florence clung to her brother's arm. "Do I have to go back? I'm never going to be able to play the piano."

"What would Mother say if she knew you'd turned down the chance to go to school? It was all she ever wanted for you. Let's enjoy the next couple of weeks and then we can plan your next trip."

By the time they reached Martensen Street, both were shivering and they hurried to the door.

"Before we go in, there's one more thing," William-

Wetherby said. "I haven't told Mrs Booth or her daughter anything about Mother and Father. Don't you go telling them; I'd like to keep it our secret."

"Are you embarrassed about them?"

William-Wetherby stopped and took Florence's hands. "No, I'm not, but it makes me angry when I talk about the things that happened to them ... and so I don't. Do you promise?"

Florence nodded.

"Good, now let's get in. I'm sure Mrs Booth will have a pot of tea waiting."

Mrs Booth jumped up as soon as William-Wetherby opened the front door. "Come in, come in. You must be freezin'."

"Mrs Booth, this is Florence; Florence this is Mrs Booth and her daughter, Miss Booth."

"It's lovely to meet you, Florence. Take your coat off and come and make yourself comfortable." Mrs Booth took Florence's coat and ushered her to a seat by the fire.

William-Wetherby grinned when he saw the look of confusion on Florence's face. "I forgot to tell you. They talk differently around here. Mrs Booth, you'll have to take it slowly." He turned back to Florence. "The next question will be, do you want a cup of tea?"

"None of your cheek, Mr Jackson. You should be thankful I don't have much of an accent."

William-Wetherby laughed and took the seat next to Florence. "It's my day off tomorrow and so I'll take you around Liverpool. It's different to Birmingham but I'm getting used to it."

"It's a shame you haven't come at the best time of the year," Bella said. "The wind off the Mersey can cut right through you."

"The Mersey is the river," William-Wetherby said. "Not that you can see much of it with all the docks."

"I hope you don't like it here too much." Florence reached for William-Wetherby's hand. "We want you home when Mr Wetherby dies."

Bella and Mrs Booth both stopped and stared at William-Wetherby.

"You haven't told them that either?" Florence's cheeks flushed.

"No ..."

"I'm sorry." Florence's voice was a whisper. "I'm no good at keeping secrets."

William-Wetherby stood up and glared at his sister. "I knew I shouldn't have let you come."

"Come on now," Mrs Booth said. "This should be a happy time, don't be angry with her. We won't pry, will we, Bella?"

"Of course not."

"You mean like you haven't been prying since the day I arrived? My past is past; I don't want to talk about it, now or ever. Florence, if you utter another word, you'll be on the next train back to Birmingham."

Florence said nothing, but pulled a handkerchief from her sleeve and wiped her eyes.

"Don't talk to her like that." Bella knelt beside Florence's chair. "She's travelled all the way from Birmingham to see you and wants you to be able to go home. You don't deserve her kindness if that's how you treat her."

William-Wetherby glared at Bella, his mouth open, but he was unable to speak. *Damn this woman. Why do I care so much about what she thinks?* He shifted his attention to his sister.

"Come with me, Florence. I'll show you upstairs. If you're going to be here for two weeks, you need to be comfortable."

WITH WILLIAM-WETHERBY PLACATED and back at work, Florence joined Mrs Booth and Bella on a trip into town to buy the Christmas groceries.

"Don't you ever take a carriage?" Florence asked as they walked up the hill, laden with bags. I'm amazed you can manage this hill at all."

"We don't usually have so much food, but it's only Christmas once a year. What would you normally do for Christmas in Birmingham?" Mrs Booth asked.

Florence smiled to herself as Fred pulled on her hand to help her up the hill. "When Mother was alive, it was lovely. We'd decorate the trees in the front and back rooms and my aunt and uncle and all my cousins would join us after church for dinner. We used to have goose. I've never tried turkey."

"How old were you when your mother died?" Bella asked.

The bounce disappeared from Florence's walk. "Eight. It was horrible. Lydia tried her best to take her place, but it wasn't the same."

"Was Lydia a friend?"

"She came to be our nanny and housekeeper, but then Father married her."

Mrs Booth and Bella exchanged glances.

"You had a nanny?" Bella struggled to keep her voice flat.

"Only Lydia, but once she married Father, we didn't need one. We still had the maids and they helped out ... until Father had his problems."

"So you don't have maids any more?"

Florence rolled her eyes. "We have more maids than we know what to do with at Wetherby House and in Bushwood. None of them stay for more than a few months though. Mr Wetherby scares them off and Aunt Sarah-Ann has to advertise for more."

Bella's heart was pounding as she spoke. "Is that the Mr Wetherby you wish was dead?"

Florence stopped in her tracks. "I can't tell you any more, William-Wetherby will be angry with me again."

Bella put her hand on the girl's shoulder. "Don't worry, we won't tell him. It can be our secret."

Florence nodded and carried on walking. "My sister Margaret says it's wrong to keep secrets. She hates it when nobody at Wetherby House will tell us what's happening. It's even worse when they tell us lies."

"So is that where you live, at Wetherby House? It sounds very grand."

Florence cocked her head to one side. "I suppose it is. It's bigger than our old house, but not as big as the house at Bushwood. We used to visit every Saturday and Sunday. We all had our own bedrooms and the servants had rooms on the top floor. There were two inside WCs and a bathroom. Wetherby House only has one."

"Don't you go any more?"

Florence shook her head. "The others do, but not me."

Bella raised an eyebrow at Mrs Booth. "That doesn't seem fair. Why would they go without you?"

Florence closed her eyes and pulled her hand from Fred's to cover her ears, causing him to fall forward. "I can't talk about that. Change the subject."

Bella bent down to pick the child up. "Fred, what have I told you about pulling like that?" Fred watched as Bella wiped her hands over his knees. "There, as good as new."

"Why don't we talk about what to do once we're home?" Mrs Booth said. "It's not long until Christmas and there's a lot to do."

Florence put her hand in the air. "Can I decorate the tree?"

"A tree?" Mrs Booth looked at Bella. "We've never had one before, there isn't a lot of room."

"You've never had a tree?" Florence stared at Mrs Booth. "But you have to. It's not Christmas without a tree. Let me ask William-Wetherby if we can have one. Please."

"Let's see what he says, shall we?" Bella said. "It would be lovely if we could find one that fits in the window."

"I can make some decorations for it. I'll start this afternoon. I'm sure he won't say no." Florence bounced on the spot, clapping her hands. "This is going to be the best Christmas since Mother died."

Chapter Nine

A s she took the last of the paper decorations from the Christmas tree, Bella handed them to Mrs Booth and carried the tree into the back yard. "I'm glad Florence enjoyed her stay. The place'll be quiet without her."

"Maybe to us, but I don't think Mr Jackson'll be sorry to see the back of her."

"Of course he will. You can tell he's protective of her, even if she is too talkative for his liking."

Mrs Booth laughed. "I noticed you took full advantage of that."

"I was only being polite." Bella joined her mother at the table as she folded the decorations. "Besides, I didn't notice you complaining."

"So what do you make of it all?"

"I've no idea, he's still hiding a lot from us. We need to ask the right questions and not be pushy." Bella glanced at the clock. "He'll be home soon, why don't you make yourself scarce and I'll see what I can find out."

Bella had no sooner sat herself by a partially made hat on a mannequin stand than the front door opened and William-Wetherby let himself in.

"Are you on your own?" He smiled as he hung up his coat and flopped into the chair opposite her.

"Me mam's next door with Fred. Did you get Florence safely on the train?"

"Eventually, but it wasn't easy. She didn't want to go back."

"Poor thing."

"It's for her own good. I've promised her that as soon as she gets her certificate, she can visit again. I hope you don't mind."

Bella smiled. "Of course I don't mind. I'm glad you think you'll still be here by then."

"Why wouldn't I be?" His eyes held hers. "I have everything I want here."

Bella's heart skipped a beat. "I just wondered ... Don't you think this Mr Wetherby will have died by then?"

William-Wetherby rested his head on the back of the chair and closed his eyes. "What's Florence been saying?"

"Nothing, but between the two of you it sounds like you don't have much time for him."

"No ... we don't."

"Is he the reason you've got Wetherby in your name? Is he a family friend?"

William-Wetherby sighed. "If only it was that simple. No, he's my father's stepfather, but he's a bully who thinks he can do what he likes to whoever he likes."

"There are plenty of men like that," Bella said. "That's why me and me mam have always been happy on our own." She smiled but he turned away. "Florence said he has a big house with servants and everything."

"He does. Two in fact, plus dozens of properties like this that he rents out. That's part of the problem. The more money he makes, the more power he gets and he makes sure he uses it."

"Is he the reason you came to Liverpool?"

William-Wetherby raised his eyes to the ceiling again. "You've no idea. And I'd like to leave it that way. Can we change the subject?"

"Of course we can, I don't want to intrude." Bella eyed William-Wetherby as he continued to rest his head on the back of the chair. "Are you working tomorrow?"

"I am, I'm on an early shift. I'm off on Saturday."

"That's unusual, will you go to the football?"

William-Wetherby shook his head. "I've never bothered with it. We used to live near the Aston Villa ground when I was in Handsworth, but I never went."

"Everton's football ground is about a half an hour's walk from here. You may end up doing some policing there so it might be an idea to go first and see what it's like. You never know, you might enjoy it."

William-Wetherby smiled. "Maybe I will. What about you? What do you do if you ever have any spare time?"

"I visit friends. In the summer we walk to Sefton Park; I like listening to the band when they're playing."

"I went there when I lived by the docks. I thought it would be too far to walk from here."

"No, only about twenty-five minutes. Straight down there." She swung her left arm to point towards the house next door.

"Perhaps you could show me the way one day."

Bella smiled. "I'd like that."

~

WITH THE FIRST signs of spring finally appearing, William-Wetherby sank into the chair by the fire and accepted the cup of tea Mrs Booth handed him.

"You look exhausted. Have you had a busy day?"

"You could say that. I had my first duty at the football ground. It was quite different to going as a spectator, and much busier than I expected. We didn't have crowds like that in Handsworth."

"The men around here like their football. Now they only work Saturday mornings, it's something for them to do in the afternoon. Who won?"

"Everton, three-nil against Accrington."

"Oh good." Mrs Booth smiled. "The mood of the whole city drops when they lose. That's when the police really earn their money."

"Thanks for the warning. I'm not sure how long it will last though. Some of the lads from the station heard that Everton might be leaving Anfield."

Mrs Booth laughed. "Don't be daft. Why would they do that?"

William-Wetherby shrugged. "How do I know? I only learned the name of the ground this afternoon."

Mrs Booth gave him a playful tap on the shoulder. "Get away with you. We'll have you liking football yet."

William-Wetherby leaned back in his chair. "Is Bella out?"

"She'll be back in a minute, she's gone looking for Fred."

"He's quite a handful, isn't he?"

"He is, but he's a love. He'll be starting school after Easter and so I'll have a bit of peace."

"Does he ever see his mother or father?"

"No, sadly he doesn't." Mrs Booth paused before heading for the scullery.

"It's lovely out there," Bella said as she walked in and took off Fred's coat. "Are you working tomorrow?"

"No, it's my day off. Why?"

"Now the weather's improving, I thought I could show

you the way to Sefton Park ... after church of course."

William-Wetherby smiled. "What a marvellous idea, although I'll let you and Mrs Booth go to church on your own. I'll be better engaged reading the newspaper."

∾

THE FOLLOWING DAY, once they left the tightly packed rows of houses around Martensen Street, Bella turned her face to the sky.

"It should be a lovely afternoon. Isn't it wonderful to feel the sun on your face after months of wind and rain?"

"It most certainly is. I'm sure it rains more here than it ever did in Birmingham, and it's windier too."

Bella laughed. "What's it like in Birmingham? Is it a nice place?"

"Like anywhere else it depends where you go. We lived in Handsworth, which was pleasant, but once you're in Birmingham, the overcrowding's intolerable. Mix that with the smoke from the factories and brass foundry and the smell of hops from the breweries and you'd wonder why I miss the place."

"I suppose it's your family and friends you miss rather than the place. Do you still have friends there?"

"Not really, only Sid. I'd like to see him again, but it's complicated."

"Why don't you invite him here?"

William-Wetherby shook his head. "He's had a tough time these last few years and I've heard he drinks heavily now. He's Mr Wetherby's nephew and the argument we had affected Sid as well. I've written to ask after him, but he never replies."

"What a shame." Bella waited until they'd passed through the park gates, before resuming her questioning. "If Mr Wetherby dies, will you go back?"

William-Wetherby put his hands into his pocket and kept

his eyes focussed on the footpath. "That depends."

"What on?"

It took a few seconds for William-Wetherby to reply. "You."

Bella's heart fluttered as she caught hold of his arm. "What do you mean?"

"I've grown very fond of you; if you gave me a reason to stay, I would."

Bella bit down on her bottom lip. "Are you asking me to walk out with you?"

William-Wetherby smiled. "In my own clumsy way I suppose I am. Would you?"

"Yes, of course." Bella's eyes sparkled in the sun. "Ever since Christmas I've worried that you'd go back to Birmingham and I'd never see you again."

"And there was me hoping you wouldn't start walking out with someone else." William-Wetherby offered Bella his arm as they continued walking.

"Since you've been with us, other men haven't interested me. There's something about you."

"It must be the accent." William-Wetherby's eyes twinkled as he smiled at her.

Bella laughed. "It's despite the accent."

"It must be my mysterious charm then."

The smile dropped from Bella's face. "No, it's not that. I hate it that I know nothing about your past. It's as if you don't want me to know the real you. If we walk out together, will you tell me what happened?"

William-Wetherby studied her face, running the back of his finger across her flawless cheek. "On one condition: that you won't think any worse of me."

"Why would I do that? I'm sure it can't be that bad."

"Wait until you know what happened before you make any judgements."

Chapter Ten

A smile crossed William-Wetherby's lips as he read the latest letter from Eleanor. Lydia was a married woman again. Eleanor and Margaret had attended the ceremony on Palm Sunday and the happy couple were now preparing for a new life in Yorkshire. *I hope she's finally happy.* He glanced up at Bella as she stitched a feather onto her latest creation, her tongue poking through her lips with concentration. What a difference a year had made. He wouldn't swap her for anyone.

He returned to the letter but gasped as he read.

"What's the matter?" Bella stopped what she was doing.

William-Wetherby finished reading before he replied. "Mr Wetherby's ill. The doctors don't know if they can treat him, but according to Margaret, he's in severe pain and hobbling around like an old man. He's spent the last week in bed, and even allowed Florence to stay at Wetherby House for Easter."

"He is an old man from what you've told me," Bella said.

"Mr Wetherby might be old in age, but not in energy levels. He must have been twenty years older than my father but he did twice as much as he did. I can tell you he won't be happy if he can't interfere in everyone's business."

"What will you do?" Bella gazed at him. "Will you go back?"

"Not yet. He's only got stomach ache; knowing my luck he'll be up and about again by next week."

"But I worry." Bella moved to kneel by his chair. "This last month has been the happiest of my life, I don't want you to leave."

William-Wetherby leaned forward and kissed her lips. "I'm not going anywhere, and if I do, I'll be back."

"Aunty Bella, why are you sitting on the floor?" Fred ran into the house and jumped on her knee.

"I'm talking to Mr Jackson." Bella tickled the boy's ribs until he squirmed from her grasp. "Where's Granny?"

"She's coming. Can we go to the park?"

"It'll be dinner time soon. You go and wash your hands and show her you're ready."

Fred lay spread-eagled on the floor. "I can't, I can't move."

Bella rolled her eyes at William-Wetherby and tickled Fred's tummy again. "Yes, you can, young man, into that scullery now."

"You're so good with him." William-Wetherby watched Fred disappear. "Now I've told you about my past, you need to tell me why he lives here and never see his mother or father."

"Not now." Bella pushed herself up. "Perhaps tomorrow if we go for a walk. You're on duty this afternoon and I need to get dinner ready."

William-Wetherby sank back into his chair. "Don't remind me. I'm up at Anfield for the last match of the season."

"It's more than that. It's the last time Everton'll play a league match there. It could be busy."

THE FOLLOWING DAY, they prepared to go out and Bella allowed William-Wetherby to help her on with her cape before she fastened the ribbon around her throat.

"Is that new?"

Bella rolled her eyes. "You've seen it before, it goes to show how observant you are. Me mam made it for me. You probably saw her making it."

"Well, it suits you." William-Wetherby held out his arm for her.

"See you later, Mam." Bella linked her arm through his as they stepped from the house. "Shall we go to the park?"

"Why not? It's a lovely day."

Bella snuggled into William-Wetherby's arm. "Have you got over yesterday yet?"

"Almost. The lads said it was one of the busiest matches they'd policed. I'm glad there was no trouble."

"At least there won't be so many people next season when the new team plays. They'll only be playing in the Lancashire League."

"Knowing my luck I'll be sent to the new Everton ground. It's miles away too."

"It's only the other side of the park, it'll be a pleasant walk."

William-Wetherby stroked her hand. "You're always so cheerful. I hope it rubs off on me one day."

"You've got to make the most of things. It wouldn't do us any good if we did nothing but worry."

"You're right, I'll try and remember that. How about telling me about Fred?"

Bella stared straight ahead and took a deep breath. "What do you want to know?"

"Well, why does he live with you and never sees his parents?"

Please let him understand. "Neither of them want him."

"His mother abandoned him?"

"It wasn't her fault. His mam was one of me best friends when we were growing up but her mam died when she was eighteen. With no one else to turn to, she came to live with us. She stayed for over a year but one morning we woke up to find a letter saying she'd gone and wouldn't be back. We've no idea where she went."

William-Wetherby's brow creased. "That still doesn't explain why you have Fred."

"He was born when she lived with us, but she didn't take him with her. He was only two months old."

"What about her husband?"

Bella paused. "She didn't have a husband."

William-Wetherby stopped and studied her. "She was an unmarried mother? What sort of friends do you keep?"

Bella felt the blood rushing to her cheeks but said nothing.

"So what happens to Fred? You can't keep him."

Bella stared at William-Wetherby, confusion clouding her thoughts. "Of course we can, what else would we do with him?"

"Find someone else who'll have him."

"We've had him for almost five years and we love him as if he was one of our own. He's not going anywhere."

"Who pays for his upkeep? You told me you took care of him to earn a bit of money?"

"We did. His dad gave us some money when we first took him in."

"After five years I would imagine that's long gone." William-Wetherby stared at her. "Are you telling me you're happy to ruin your own reputation for someone else's child without even being paid for it? The way you're talking I wonder if he isn't yours."

Bella's mouth fell open before she spoke. "Mine? Of course he's not mine. I can show you his baptism certificate if you don't believe me. For your information, his mam had every intention of marrying his dad."

"That sounds like the wishful thinking of a silly girl to me. She probably encouraged him."

"She did not. He was from a posh family with their own business and she was a servant girl, but he fell for her. They walked out together for months before she realised she was carrying Fred. Even then the father didn't leave her; it was only when he told his family he wanted to marry her that everything changed. His father threatened to disown him when he heard he'd fathered a child and sent him to one of their other factories on condition that he wouldn't see her again."

"Of course he did. Respectable men don't marry servant girls. She probably thought the only way to marry him was by having his child."

Bella glared at him. "What a terrible thing to say, especially from someone who's the son of a bankrupt."

William-Wetherby's face flushed red. "That wasn't Father's fault."

"Well, this wasn't her fault. Why don't you blame the father for abandoning her? He was the one who spotted her at work and couldn't control himself."

"She should have behaved more appropriately."

"She was a young girl who'd never known her dad, had lost her mam and was looking for love. She came to live with us because she was eighteen years old and had nowhere else to go. Imagine that, she wasn't much older than your Florence is now."

"Leave Florence out of this. She's had an education and knows how to present herself. She would never disgrace herself."

Bella's heart pounded as she pulled her arm from William-Wetherby's and turned on her heel. She hadn't gone more than a few paces before she turned back and glared at him.

"It's all right for you, you're never going to be left with an unwanted child and your reputation in tatters. Around here, women don't have much choice. Has it ever occurred to you that it's usually your lot who do the damage? The men in the big houses with lots of money and wives with faces like wet fish. When they don't get what they want at home, they take advantage of the servants. Those girls aren't there because they want to be, they're there because they're desperate. Desperate to eat or to have a roof over their heads, but suddenly one friendly smile and they're back on the streets with another mouth to feed. Even when you were at your lowest, I bet you never worried about keeping a roof over your head. There were always people who would help you. Well let me tell you, when people around here say they've got nothing, they mean it, and when you're desperate, you'll do anything."

Bella stormed back down the path towards home. Her chest rose and fell with each breath and she kept her eyes fixed on the gates ahead.

"Bella, wait, come back. I'm sorry. Please, don't go."

She kept walking. If she let him catch her up she feared she would say something she regretted ... if she hadn't already. *Me mam'll be furious if I've lost our lodger.* She let out a deep sigh as William-Wetherby caught her up and reached for her arm.

"Bella, stop, please."

She stopped abruptly, but refused to look at him.

"I don't know what to say." William-Wetherby stepped in front of her but she avoided his gaze. "I didn't mean to upset you, but ... I suppose I've never considered the woman's point of view. I'm sorry."

"And you think that makes everything all right?"

"What else can I say?" He kicked at the stones on the foot-path. "Mother always felt strongly about the way women were treated, but back then people didn't take much notice of her. I could imagine her getting angry like that."

"Well, she should have been more forceful. Me and me mam have had more abuse hurled at us than you can imagine because we bother to help other women. Oh, and just for the record, young David who used to live with us, he'll never know his dad either. We stepped in to help his mam after one of her master's friends forced himself on her. Whether you like it or not, we won't stand by while young girls suffer through no fault of their own. I suggest that if you can't deal with it, you'd better find yourself somewhere else to live."

Chapter Eleven

From her seat by the fireplace, Bella adjusted the base of the new hat she was fashioning. Mrs Booth put a cup of tea beside her and took the seat opposite.

"You're quiet again. Do you want to talk about it? I take it it's something to do with Mr Jackson."

Bella sat back in her chair. "When we went for a walk the other day, I told him about Fred's mam and dad."

"Ah. Let me guess. He didn't take it well."

Bella shook her head. "No, he didn't. He accused us of keeping bad company and said we should send Fred on his way."

Mrs Booth sipped her tea but said nothing.

"He thinks it's the woman's fault if she finds herself in the family way, with no blame attached to the man. I put him right of course, but what do I do now? What would you do, Mam? I like him so much, but when he gets all snooty I just don't know. He's not the same as us."

"He's lived the life of a gentleman before he came here and he's fallen on hard times. I imagine it's difficult for him to shake off everything that's been drilled into him over the years. I guess this Mr Wetherby's had a lot of influence on him too."

"But what do I do? He's apologised and still wants us to walk out together, but what if we're too different? So much of me wants to carry on as before, but what if I'm wrong and he really is a toff who'll never change his ways? I can't live like that."

Mrs Booth waited for her daughter to pause. "I've watched him these last few days, and I'd say he adores you. When you're around, he changes. He never takes his eyes off you and he's trying hard not to upset you. If I'm being honest, it's not easy being in the room with the two of you. I'd say you need to talk to him and clear the air."

"So you think I'm being unreasonable?"

"Not at all. You wouldn't be my daughter if you didn't feel strongly about it, but perhaps you should try to understand his point of view."

Bella sighed and leaned back in her chair. "Why couldn't he be a normal bloke from around here?"

"Because if he was, you wouldn't have fallen in love with him."

"Is it obvious?" Bella gave a shy smile.

"I'm your mam, of course it is. Now drink your tea and have a smile on your face for when he comes home tonight. If I don't see the two of you looking at each other like you used to, I'll bang your heads together."

BELLA WAS SITTING by the fire stitching a button onto the hat that was nearing completion when William-Wetherby arrived home.

"Are you on your own?" He peered into the scullery.

"Me mam's out searching for Fred again. Since he started school, he thinks he can do what he wants."

William-Wetherby smiled. "Well, I hope she finds him. I miss the little lad when he's not here."

"You mean you're glad we didn't get rid of him?" The tone of Bella's voice was soft.

"I am ... and I'm glad you shouted at me. I must have sounded like a right pompous fool. Will you forgive me?"

Bella took his hands. "I will. I'm sorry it's taken me so long to calm down."

William-Wetherby glanced at the window. "It's going to be light outside for another few hours yet. Shall we take a walk after tea? I've been so miserable knowing you're angry with me."

"I'd like that." Bella held her breath as William-Wetherby took her in an embrace and pressed his lips against hers.

"I told you months ago that the past is the past; I want to forget everything that's gone before and start again. Can we do that?"

Bella cupped her hands around his face. "I'd like nothing more."

Chapter Twelve

With the summer temperatures still too hot for comfort, William-Wetherby pushed his cup and saucer across the table and leaned back in his chair. His dinner felt as if it was stuck in his throat.

"Have you finished with that?" Mrs Booth pointed at the half full cup.

"Yes, thank you. It's too warm for hot drinks."

"You've not been yourself all through dinner. I hope you're not sickening for something," Bella said.

"I'll be fine with some fresh air. Do you have time for a walk?"

Bella turned to her mother. "Do you mind if I go? I can work on my hat when Mr Jackson's at work."

Mrs Booth glanced between the two of them. "Off you go. Don't let it be said I got in the way of a beautiful relationship."

Bella blushed. "Mam!"

William-Wetherby left the table and went for his hat. "Shall we go?"

"One moment." Bella hurried to the stairs. "I need a hat with a rim in this sun."

William-Wetherby smiled as he watched her disappear up the stairs.

"She's so happy," Mrs Booth said.

William-Wetherby hesitated before ushering Mrs Booth back towards the dining table. "Can I ask you a question? I-I don't know how to put this, but is Mr Booth likely to be back from sea at any time?"

Mrs Booth straightened up and glared at William-Wetherby. "Why?"

William-Wetherby glanced over his shoulder towards the stairs. "I need to speak to him."

"If it's about Bella you can speak to me. You've no need to involve him."

"B-but I have to speak to her father."

"If he was dead, you'd have no choice, so why don't you pretend he is, and speak to me." Mrs Booth crossed her arms over her chest.

"Yes, well ... I suppose you're right, it just feels ... strange." He glanced over his shoulder again. "I wanted to ask if he'd mind me having his daughter's hand in marriage."

Mrs Booth's features hardened. "What right would he have to give my Bella away? She's my daughter and for all that he's seen of her it's not his decision to make."

William-Wetherby held Mrs Booth's gaze with his deep brown eyes. "If I asked you, would you let her be my wife?"

Mrs Booth smiled. "Yes I would, I'd be delighted."

William-Wetherby breathed a sigh of relief and smiled as Bella returned to the foot of the stairs.

"What do you think?" She stood before the small mirror by the front door admiring the hat.

William-Wetherby winked at Mrs Booth. "I think it's

lovely, but if you don't stop admiring it, it'll be too late to go out. Are you ready now?"

The park was busy when they arrived and William-Wetherby steered Bella to a bench in a quiet corner. He waited for her to arrange her skirt before he sat beside her and took her hand.

"I've got something to tell you," he said. "Do you remember when we first met? I'd spent a miserable year in the temperance hotel with a group of people at least three times my age. All I wanted to do was go home. Well, that's changed. Since I've lived with you and your mam I've started smiling again. Even if Mr Wetherby died tomorrow, I wouldn't go back."

Bella smiled. "I'm glad."

William-Wetherby hesitated. "Do you know why?" When Bella shook her head, he gave a slight cough. "I want to spend the rest of my life with you. Will you do me the honour of being my wife?"

Bella's eyes sparkled as her smile filled her face. "Yes, of course I will. I couldn't imagine life without you."

"You will?" William-Wetherby grinned before he glanced around and placed a kiss on her lips. "Thank you. I promise you won't regret it."

William-Wetherby studied the perfectly oval face, his gaze hovering on the fullness of her lips as she smiled at him. "I'd like to buy you a ring to mark our betrothal. I've seen one decorated with diamonds and sapphires that I think you'll like. Will you come with me on my next day off and we can buy it?"

Bella's eyes widened. "Diamonds? Have you been saving up?"

William-Wetherby smirked. "I didn't tell you that when Mr Wetherby told me to leave Birmingham I insisted he gave me some money ... one hundred pounds."

"One hundred pounds? And you worried about paying us two shillings a week rent?"

"I'd no idea how long it would last, but I've been careful with it and have enough for a ring; I'd like to go to the photographers and have some pictures taken as well. That way we can remember this time forever."

Bella smiled. "I'd like that, as long as you don't think of Mr Wetherby every time you see either the ring or the photographs."

"Of course I won't." William-Wetherby gazed at her lips before leaning over to kiss them. "Besides, I'm expecting a legacy from him when he dies. Another reason I wish he'd hurry up and leave us all alone."

Chapter Thirteen

W illiam-Wetherby glanced around the church before he sat on the pew next to Bella. Mrs Booth was to her daughter's left with Fred.

"Don't look so scared," Bella whispered.

"The last time I was in a church it was for Father's funeral. In fact I've only been for marriages and funerals since Mother died. I hope they don't like long services here."

Bella rolled her eyes at him, but turned away to study her prayer book. William-Wetherby flicked through his but closed it again. He'd open it when the vicar told him which page to turn to. Why hadn't he insisted on getting a marriage licence rather than being forced to come here to discuss having the banns read? He glanced at Bella as she read the text. Because he wanted to make her happy, that was why.

To William-Wetherby the service appeared to go on forever and once they'd spoken to the vicar, he needed some air.

"So, two months to go," Mrs Booth said as they walked the short distance home. "We need to decide who to invite. We can have a bit of a do at the house after the service. Will you invite your sisters, Mr Jackson?"

William-Wetherby's posture stiffened. He hadn't considered the possibility. "No, I don't think so. It's a long way to come ... and where would they sleep?"

"I'm sure we could sort something out. Young Florence would love to visit again. She'll be finished school by November, won't she?"

"She will," Bella said. "She sounded excited about finishing in her last letter, although less so about going back to Wetherby House. I'm sure she'd be delighted to come."

"Things will be different this time. It was bad enough me sleeping in the living room last time, but I don't plan on doing that once we're married." He glanced at Bella as her cheeks turned pink.

"I can speak to the neighbours," Mrs Booth said. "A few of them have spare beds we can use."

"No, please don't put them to any trouble. The girls aren't used to ... well ..."

Mrs Booth glared at him. "Are you ashamed of us, Mr Jackson?"

"No, not at all. Please don't think that, but they've had a different upbringing and suddenly putting them in a stranger's house, well ... If it were Charles, I wouldn't worry. In fact I wish he were here so he could be my best man. As it is, I suppose I'll have to ask one of the lads from the station."

"There's a couple you go drinking with, why don't you ask one of them?" Bella said.

"I will, and once we're married and I'm allowed back in Birmingham, we'll visit my sisters. I want you to meet them."

As they reached the house, William-Wetherby opened the front door and stepped to one side to let the ladies in. When Fred didn't follow them, William-Wetherby gave him a shout.

"How did he manage to sneak off?" Mrs Booth said. "I bet

he saw some of the other lads with a football. He loves it at the moment."

Bella laughed as she looked at William-Wetherby. "You'll have to start taking him to the match. I'm sure you'll enjoy it."

"Only if we go to watch this new team at Anfield, I'm not going all the way over to Goodison to see Everton."

"I don't think he'll mind and it'll be better with the smaller crowds. Now sit yourself down, Mr Jackson. Bella can set the table and I'll get dinner."

Once Mrs Booth left them, William-Wetherby stood up and put his arms around Bella's waist. "These next two months are going to take so long to pass." He nuzzled into her neck and kissed it.

"Be off with you. If I've not done this table by the time me mam gets back, we're both in trouble."

William-Wetherby laughed before his smile dropped. "Before she does, can I ask you a question? Who'll give you away? I'm guessing it won't be your father."

Bella twisted her new sapphire and diamond engagement ring around her finger. "No, it won't. Mam's going to ask me brother."

"I didn't know you had a brother."

"No, well, we haven't seen him since he left, he went out towards Prescot way, and it's quite a distance. Me mam wants him to come and he won't mind sleeping at one of the neighbours'."

William-Wetherby went to sit by the fire. "Well, I'll look forward to meeting him."

THE FOLLOWING morning William-Wetherby was about to leave for work when he took Bella in his arms.

"I'll see you tonight. I'll be back as soon as I can." He gave her a lingering kiss before heading for the door. As he opened it the postman was about to push an envelope through the letter box.

"Here you are, sir, one for you," he said.

"Who's that from?" Bella asked.

"It's Aunt Mary-Ann's writing." William-Wetherby set down his helmet and tore open the top of the envelope. "Oh my." The colour drained from William-Wetherby's face. "It's my uncle, Mr Diver … he's dead." William-Wetherby stared at Bella, his mouth open.

"What happened?" Bella took the letter from him and read it aloud. "Bronchitis and asthma attack. Did he have a bad chest?"

William-Wetherby nodded but said nothing as Mr Diver's image flashed before him. Even now he remembered how angry Mr Diver had been about jumping in the canal after his father. His chest had never been the same since.

"What is it, luv?" Mrs Booth spoke to Bella as she walked down the stairs.

"William-Wetherby's uncle's died unexpectedly. Four days the letter says he was ill for."

"How old was he?"

William-Wetherby shrugged. "He was younger than my father so I'd say mid to late forties. Not old enough. My aunt will be devastated, but what can I do from here?"

"Will you go to the funeral?"

William-Wetherby shook his head. *How can I? Mr Wetherby's bound to be there.* "No, I'll write to Aunt Mary-Ann, she'll understand." He glanced at the clock on the mantelpiece. "I'd better go, I'll see you tonight."

Chapter Fourteen

William-Wetherby knocked on the front door of Martensen Street and waited for someone to answer. He smiled when Bella opened the door. "Can I come in yet?"

"No, me mam's still busy. She's doing the hem so it's going to be another half hour at least. Will you go to the beerhouse?"

He smirked. "How many men would love their wives to say that?"

Bella put her hands on her hips. "Don't get excited, we're not married yet. Here, why don't you take this?" She picked up a letter and thrust it into his hands. "It came this morning."

William-Wetherby studied the letter. It had come from New York. "I'll be back in half an hour then."

He found a corner seat in the beerhouse and put his ale on the table in front of him. The letter had to be from Charles. He opened it to find it had been written six weeks earlier and Charles expected to be in Cape Town by now. The good news was he hoped to be back in Liverpool early in the New Year.

William-Wetherby smiled and cursed at the same time. Two months too late for the wedding. How he'd missed having him around. He read on to find that Charles would write again from Cape Town to give him a better idea of timings. *It'll be good to see him and at least he won't mind sleeping on the living room floor.*

Bella stood in the bedroom while Mrs Booth pulled on the laces of her corset.

"Have you been losing weight?" Mrs Booth said. "I'm sure these laces weren't so long last time you tried the dress on."

"Not on purpose, but I'm so excited. I hope he doesn't change his mind."

"Of course he won't change his mind."

Bella admired the betrothal ring on her finger. "The house feels strange without him. It was kind of his best man to let him stay at his house overnight. I worried he might have to stay in a hotel on his own."

"Folks around here are nothing if they're not hospitable. You know that and hopefully he does too. I don't think his snooty friends in Birmingham are quite so generous."

"It's not his fault his old man had the stepfather he did."

"Well, you should be thankful he did. You wouldn't be marrying him if he hadn't."

Bella paused, her brow furrowed. "You're right. If his step-grandfather hadn't been so horrible, William-Wetherby would never have come to Liverpool. I suppose I should thank him if I ever meet him."

WILLIAM-WETHERBY STOOD at the front of St Mary's Church and looked around. He hadn't expected so many to attend. They certainly hadn't invited this number back to the house.

"Your wife-to-be's a popular lady." His best man nodded to the pews.

"Either that or everyone's come in for a warm."

The constable laughed. "We'll make a Scouser of you yet, you've already started picking up a bit of the lingo."

"Not too much I hope. Charles is arriving in a couple of months. I want him to be able to understand me."

His best man put a hand on his shoulder. "There's no danger that he won't. Blimey, stand up straight, she's here."

William-Wetherby watched as Bella walked down the aisle to meet him. The cream dress Mrs Booth had made clung to her slim figure before it fell into a flowing skirt. He fixed his eyes on her and smiled. Soon she would be his. She joined him at the front of the church and he lifted the veil from her face. No words were necessary as she gazed into his eyes.

The service was short with only two hymns and a Bible reading. Little over an hour later they walked back to Martensen Street with an entourage behind them.

"Do we have to bring all these people back with us?" William-Wetherby said. "I'd much rather be taking you home alone."

Bella smirked at him. "You be patient, William-Wetherby. We're going to celebrate and have a special day. You always said men and women should have restraint and so you'd better show yours now."

"So, Mr Jackson, you're one of Her Majesty's police officers, are you?" William-Wetherby turned to see Bella's brother John walking beside him.

"I am, yes, and pleased to meet you. Thank you for giving me your sister's hand."

John shrugged. "I do what me mam tells me. We'll have to go for an ale sometime before I go back to Prescot. It's such a trek that I can't say when I'll be back again."

"Can't you use the train?"

"I can, but it costs money and me mam can't afford to pay for it."

"Why don't you pay for it and visit her more often?" Bella said. "You know she misses you."

"It means taking time off work, and if I don't work I don't earn any money. We can go for an ale tomorrow, I'm going back on Saturday."

"Don't you go leading him astray, John Booth," Bella said.

"As if I would. He's my brother-in-law; it'd be rude not to have a drink together. Isn't that right, Willie?"

The hairs on the back of William-Wetherby's neck bristled. "Yes, I suppose so."

Chapter Fifteen

The wind that whipped off the Mersey hadn't become any more bearable since he had last walked up to the Waterloo Dock but as he pushed his hands further into his pockets, William-Wetherby didn't care. Charles's ship was due in today and he had so much to tell him. He knew he wasn't late but by the time he arrived, *The Laomene* sat proudly in the dock waiting for the crew to disembark. *Thank the Lord for that.*

"Over here," he shouted to Charles half an hour later when his brother walked down the gangplank.

Charles grinned and hurried towards him. "It's good to see you again."

William-Wetherby threw his arms around his brother. "Happy New Year. It seems a lifetime ago since you were last here."

Charles shivered. "It hasn't got any warmer though. Where's that tavern we went to last time? I need some warmth in my bones before I get back on board."

"You're not staying?"

"Not this time. I've got a commission as an able seaman so

I'm going to do one more voyage and see how it compares to being an apprentice. It's only a short trip before I do my final exam. At least they'll pay me more money now I'm qualified."

"We'd better hurry up then." William-Wetherby pulled his brother's arm. "I've a lot to tell you."

Once they were seated, William-Wetherby continued. "The first, and most important thing, is I'm now a married man."

Charles's eyes were wide. "When did that happen?"

"A couple of months ago. My wife's name is Bella and we live with her mam, not far from here."

"Her mam?" Charles laughed. "When did you learn to speak like that?"

"I'm nearly a native." William-Wetherby smirked. "They won't understand me if I ever go back to Birmingham."

"So what's happening in Birmingham? I've had the occasional letter from Eleanor, but I'm sure I've missed more than I've received."

"Did you hear about Mr Wetherby?"

"I heard he was ill. Has he died?"

William-Wetherby shook his head. "Not yet, but he's not well. According to Margaret, he spends some days in bed, but other days he's up and about. It depends how well the laudanum works. He must be ill though because he's letting Uncle William run the business."

Charles knocked back his measure of rum. "Well, let's hope he dies before Uncle William spends all the money and leaves nothing for our inheritance. Did he confirm that he's included us in his will?"

William-Wetherby nodded and pulled a letter from his pocket. "He did. I wrote to remind him that if I didn't hear from him, then I'd forward a copy of Father's writings to the local Conservative Association, the Liberals and the newspapers. He sent this back pretty quickly after that."

Charles picked up the letter and read it out loud. "I can confirm that I updated my last will and testament on the seventeenth of January, 1891 to leave you and your siblings one thousand pounds between you. My solicitor confirmed that this is an adequate amount to bequeath you and has countersigned this letter as confirmation of the change. If you challenge this amount, the legacy will be withdrawn by means of a codicil."

"Did you accept it?"

William-Wetherby shrugged. "What else could I do? I've no doubt he'd change his will if we challenged him. Besides, one thousand pounds is a lot of money."

"It is, I still think he's got off lightly though. Talking of money, what happened to Mr Diver?"

"That was a terrible shock. He got bronchitis and four days later an asthma attack killed him. Nobody could believe it. Aunt Mary-Ann's still in deep mourning but the probate was finalised a couple of weeks ago. He left almost seventeen thousand pounds. The majority went to Aunt Mary-Ann."

Charles took a deep intake of breath. "Did he leave anything to the young Miss Divers, Rose, Daisy or Lilly?"

William-Wetherby took a mouthful of his ale. "No, by all accounts, they weren't mentioned."

Charles whistled. "That's a shame."

"Everything about it was a shame. I wish I could have gone to the funeral but it was out of the question. Aunt Mary-Ann now has your money from Mr Watkins. I checked with her."

"At least that's something."

A pause settled between them before William-Wetherby spoke again. "Did you hear that Lydia had remarried?"

"I did." Charles raised an eyebrow at his brother. "How did you feel about that?"

William-Wetherby shrugged. "For months after I moved, I wondered if I should have brought her with me, but after everything that happened with Father I knew it wouldn't work. Not that I'm sorry. I wouldn't swap Bella for anyone."

"I wish I could meet her, but unless you live nearby it'll have to wait."

"No, we're about three quarters of an hour away. They'll be disappointed, they're expecting you."

"There'll be time later in the year, but for now, at least it means we can get another round in." He made his way to the bar before returning to set a selection of drinks on the table.

"So what will you do once you've done this trip?" William-Wetherby asked.

"Go back to Birmingham. Despite everything, I'm not sure I'm cut out for a life at sea. I need to post a few letters while I'm here to see if I can sort something out."

"It's a good job Mother took no notice of you and made you carry on at school."

Charles scowled at his brother. "Don't remind me of that. The worst days of my life."

"So, do you have any plans for work?"

Charles downed his rum. "I'm going to set up my own business."

William-Wetherby's forehead creased. "Doing what? You've no experience of anything."

Charles tapped his finger on the side of his nose. "You pick things up when you're on a ship ... and when you're in port. When we were in one of the ports in America I met a chap who imports India rubber from Brazil and makes a range of goods with it. He's planning to export them to England and I said I'd be interested in working with him."

William-Wetherby choked on his ale. "You can't just set up a business with someone you've met once in America. What will you do with the goods once they're here?"

"Stop worrying, I've met him a couple of times and got all his details. I'm hoping to meet him on this trip as well, which is another reason I'm going. We'll arrange for a solicitor to draw up a contract. What could go wrong?"

"Everything could go wrong, especially when he's so far away. Promise me you won't do anything foolish. I've enough to worry about with Florence."

"What about her?"

"I'm not sure, really. I had a letter from Eleanor this morning saying she's worried about her, but she didn't give much information. Florence finished school with a junior honours for her music theory exam but failed her practical on the piano. She didn't want to do music, but Mr Wetherby wouldn't let her do bookkeeping."

Charles shook his head. "What is it about the women in this family?"

"That's besides the point. She's back at Wetherby House now, as miserable as you like, and wants to come and live with us. We only have a small house and possibly can't squeeze her in."

"Why on earth didn't you marry someone with money? It would've made life a lot easier."

William-Wetherby shot his brother a glance. "You know jolly well why I didn't. Anyway, Florence is desperate to leave Wetherby House and we've no idea what to do with her. She can't come here and she can't go to Eleanor."

"Isn't Margaret at Wetherby House? Is she happy?"

"She's not as upset as Florence and she's friendly with Aunt Sarah-Ann's daughter Elizabeth. She spends a lot of time with her and the reverend in Birmingham."

"Can't Florence go with her?"

"Not a good idea at the moment. I believe Aunt Elizabeth's in the family way, and after what happened with Aunt Charlotte the last person she'll want to see is Florence."

"What happened with Aunt Charlotte?"

William-Wetherby shook his head. "I wasn't told the

details, but let's just say that having Florence around a woman who's expecting a baby isn't advisable."

Charles puffed out his cheeks. "Isn't there anyone else in the family? We've got enough aunts and cousins; there must be one who'd take her in? Do any have their own businesses? She could do the bookkeeping for them in lieu of rent."

The lines on William-Wetherby's brow deepened. "It's a thought. I'll tell Eleanor what we're thinking, and see if she can sort something out. She's much better at that sort of thing than us."

Chapter Sixteen

F rom her seat by the fire, Bella glanced at the front door as it swung open and Mrs Booth hurried in.

"My, it's cold out there." Without taking her coat off, Mrs Booth walked to the fire, rubbing her hands together. "Now he's six, it's about time Fred took himself to school. What's the matter with you? You look pale."

Bella sighed. "I don't feel well. I've been like this for the last few days but it's worse today. I couldn't face any bread this morning."

Mrs Booth crouched by the chair and took hold of her daughter's hand. "Is that the only thing that's changed?"

"No." Bella blushed, bringing a touch of pink to her pale cheeks.

Mrs Booth smiled. "I think you're expecting a baby."

"A baby?" Bella smiled. "Is this what it feels like?"

"It can, for a few weeks or months, but it won't last the whole time. When did you first notice a difference?" Mrs Booth nodded to her daughter's abdomen.

"Last month, why, what does that mean?"

Mrs Booth's brow creased as she counted on her fingers.

"I'm not an expert on these things, but I'd say the baby will be born around September or October."

"So what do I do?" Bella put her hand to her chest to calm her heartbeat.

Mrs Booth pushed herself up. "You carry on as normal. There's no reason why you can't sit and stitch your hats. I'll do the heavy cleaning, but for the next four or five months nothing need change."

"But then what?"

"Then you start to prepare yourself for your baby."

Bella turned her gaze to the fire. *I hope William-Wetherby's pleased.*

"William-Wetherby will be delighted, you mark my words." Mrs Booth smiled as if reading her mind. "I've never come across a married man who's not."

"But what about money? If I have a baby I won't be able to earn any money, and he doesn't earn much."

"We'll manage. There are many in a worse position than you."

THAT EVENING BELLA sat up in bed while she waited for William-Wetherby to join her. The room was smaller than the room she had shared with her mam and there was barely enough room for the double bed they now slept in, let alone a cot. Would it fit in the alcove between the chimney breast and window?

"You're deep in thought," William-Wetherby said as he climbed in beside her.

Bella turned to him, her eyes welling like pools of chocolate. "I'm going to have a baby."

William-Wetherby's mouth fell open. "A baby? How do you know? Have you seen a doctor?"

Bella shook her head. "No, me mam told me."

"You need to see a doctor not rely on your mam."

"Don't be silly, we can't waste money when all he'll do is tell me the same thing. Me mam's had children of her own so she knows."

The creases in William-Wetherby's brow faded as he broke into a smile. "So you're sure? When does she think it'll be born?"

"About September or October. Are you angry?"

"Angry? Of course not." He leaned over and kissed her. "Are you happy?"

Bella's nod was subdued. "How will we all fit in here? I can't throw me mam out of the big room, with her sharing with Fred, but where will we put a cot?"

William-Wetherby took her in his arms. "Don't worry, we'll work something out. Maybe we should look for a house of our own."

"And leave me mam?" Bella's eyes were wide.

"We won't go far, you'll still see her every day. If you're worried about where you'll put one cot, imagine what it'll be like when we have more than one. We'll have to leave one day."

"Perhaps, but I won't be able to work as much. Will we have enough money?"

"Let me worry about that. You need your rest. Now lie down and we'll talk about it in the morning."

WILLIAM-WETHERBY LAY awake listening to Bella's soft breaths as she slept next to him. How had she managed to find herself expecting a child so quickly? Not that he minded. He smiled to himself. *It's about time I had a family again.* But where would they live? Bella was right, this room was too small for three of them, but if they moved, he'd need to find more money. The hundred pounds he'd brought with him from Birmingham was going down faster than he liked.

With a sigh he rolled over and put his arm around her. Perhaps he could speak to the chief tomorrow about getting a promotion. Ever since he joined the police, he'd been told he wouldn't stay a constable for long, so there was no harm asking.

Chapter Seventeen

As he waited by the Pier Head for the overhead train to arrive William-Wetherby couldn't hide his grin. He had seen it running up and down the length of the docks for the last couple of months, but this would be his first time on board. As it came to a stop, he opened the door and took the nearest available seat. He was on the side overlooking the docks and would have a bird's-eye view of everything going on below.

The usual twenty-minute walk had been reduced to a five-minute ride and as he stepped off the train, *The Laomene* was in the dock. He hurried down the steps with a broad grin on his face; Charles shouldn't be long now.

It took half an hour for Charles to leave the ship and when he did, William-Wetherby walked over to meet him.

"I thought you were never coming. The ship's been empty for at least twenty minutes."

"I needed to get my final paperwork signed. I still have to do my exam, but I'm not going back."

William-Wetherby raised an eyebrow as he guided his

brother towards the alehouse. "You're sure? Didn't you like being an able seaman?"

"They don't pay enough money for everything they expect from you. Once you're a second mate, there are too many responsibilities and I can't see myself wanting to be a master mariner, so what's the point?"

Once at the alehouse, Charles pushed open the door and went to the bar while William-Wetherby searched for a couple of stools. The place was as full as he'd seen it but an advantage of wearing his uniform was that many men would move away from him. It would usually arouse his suspicions, but today he gave a curt thank you as a group of workers moved from a corner table.

"Here you go," Charles said. "I got us two each and a couple of rums to save having to break off the conversation."

William-Wetherby balanced the tankards on the available space while Charles pulled up a stool.

"Welcome back." William-Wetherby raised his tankard. "So what else is new?"

"I wrote to Aunt Mary-Ann before I left in January and asked if I could stay with her when I go back to Birmingham. I've just picked up a letter from her saying I can."

William-Wetherby sighed. "Eleanor says she's still suffering from melancholy after Mr Diver's death. Please don't upset her."

"As if I would. I'll be the tonic she needs." Charles flashed a smile at his brother.

"So what will you do once you're settled?"

"I'm going ahead with the India-rubber goods business. I met with my contact in America and we're having a contract drawn up. Aunt Mary-Ann's confirmed she has my money from Mr Watkins, although I could do with a bit more for the first consignment. You haven't got any, have you?"

"Me? Do I look as if I've got money to spare?"

"Only a thought; I'll go and ask Mr Wetherby instead."

William-Wetherby glared at his brother. "Don't even think of it, not after the way he was with me and Father."

"Don't be daft, he likes me. He paid for me to go through school and for the apprenticeship. He'll want me to succeed."

"He might think we're asking for more money and cancel the legacy."

"Don't worry so much, I can be charming when I need to be." Charles grinned. "I'll tell him it's a loan and hope he dies before I need to repay it."

"Well, I hope you're right there. What sort of things will you trade?"

"All sorts, but mainly bicycle tyres. They're in high demand at the moment."

William-Wetherby nodded. "I suppose they are. Isn't anyone making them in this country?"

"Not that I can tell. It'll mean me spending more time in Liverpool though; I hope you don't mind me staying with you. The goods will be shipped here and the train will transport them to Birmingham."

William-Wetherby grimaced. "It's going to be a squeeze in Martensen Street."

Charles shrugged. "No more than usual."

"I haven't told you, I'm going to be a father."

Charles patted his brother on the shoulder. "Congratulations. You should have said; I'd have bought another rum for a toast."

William-Wetherby studied the tankards squashed onto the table. "I think we've got enough for now. You know Bella doesn't like me drinking."

"She's got you well and truly under the thumb. You're a police constable, you should let her know who's boss."

"Police sergeant if you don't mind." William-Wetherby grinned at his brother.

"Good grief, I've only been gone four and a half months. That definitely calls for another drink." Charles stood up and flagged to the barman before sitting down with a wink at William-Wetherby. "I left a bit of money with him, he'll bring the drinks over."

William-Wetherby took a deep breath and downed his rum. *This could be a long afternoon.*

Chapter Eighteen

As he stepped out of the police station William-Wetherby stopped at the sight of Charles leaning on a tree outside the front door.

"What are you doing here? I thought you'd be at the alehouse by now."

Charles shook his head as they started walking. "Not today, I wanted to talk to you."

William-Wetherby raised an eyebrow. "You usually do that of an evening when I'm ready to go to bed. What's so urgent?"

"I'm leaving for Birmingham the day after tomorrow. I got a letter from Mr Wetherby this morning and he wants to talk to me."

William-Wetherby's stomach churned. "How did he know our address?"

Charles shrugged. "He'd had some correspondence from the examiner telling him I'd passed my exam; I expect he found out from there. He wants to know why I'm not going back to sea."

"How does he know you're not?"

"I wrote and told him when I first got here."

"He won't like that after paying for the apprenticeship. He'll expect you to make the most of it."

"He can expect what he likes. Five and a half years at sea is enough for me. Anyway, it could work in my favour. It'll give me a chance to talk to him about my plans for the business."

William-Wetherby shuddered. "Don't be surprised if you don't get anything from him. He said some nasty things to me and Father when we asked him for money to prevent the bankruptcy."

"I've told you before, he likes me. I'll tell him that trading rubber goods is a direct result of my time at sea ... which it is."

"Will you go straight to Aunt Mary-Ann's?"

"Yes and if you need me, send all correspondence there. I've written to Eleanor to tell her."

"At least you'll see Margaret and Florence; they should be at Wetherby House."

"How's Florence now? I thought Eleanor was going to find somewhere else for her to go."

William-Wetherby shook his head "She couldn't find anyone who would take her."

Charles rolled his eyes and nodded towards the local alehouse. "That's all I need. You'd better fill me in on what's been happening. If I'm going to walk into a drama when I arrive at Wetherby House, I need to be prepared."

Birmingham, Warwickshire.

THE DAY after he arrived in Birmingham, Charles stepped down from the carriage and smiled as he admired the imposing double-fronted façade of Wetherby House. Bella and Mrs Booth were nice enough, but this was what he wanted. A large house, lots of rooms, and servants. He knocked on the front door and stepped backwards until the maid opened the door and ushered him into the back room.

"Charles, how splendid to see you." Mr Wetherby spoke from his seat by the fireplace. "Forgive me for not standing up, the laudanum isn't working so well today."

Charles studied Mr Wetherby's sunken face as he extended his hand to him. "I'm glad to be back. Being at sea was all well and good, but there's no place like home."

As he spoke his Aunt Sarah-Ann walked into the room, accompanied by Margaret and Florence.

"Charles!" Florence threw her arms around him. "I thought you'd never come back. Why were you gone for so long?"

Charles pulled away and studied his sisters. "Well, you've certainly both grown since I went away."

"It's been nearly six years," Margaret said. "A lot's happened since you've been gone."

Sarah-Ann ushered them both to the settee. "Let Charles come in and sit down. We've plenty of time to talk."

"I've heard a lot of the news," Charles said. "I've been staying with William-Wetherby and his wife since June and he gets most of his information from Eleanor."

"Yes, I believe he's settled in Liverpool." Mr Wetherby steepled his fingers and touched them to his chin. "Living in squalor, I believe."

"Squalor?" Lines appeared in Charles's forehead. "No, not at all. It's only a small house, nothing like this." He glanced around the large living room with its deep red embossed wallpaper, chandeliers and expensive ornaments. "It's clean and tidy though. Mrs Booth sees to that."

"So he has a maid then?" Mr Wetherby raised an eyebrow. "Florence said the place only had two bedrooms."

"They do. Mrs Booth is Bella's mother; they live together. They're both very nice, would do anything for you."

Florence nodded her head. "They are and they said I could go back when I finished school, but William-Wetherby didn't invite me to the wedding and so now I wonder if they ever liked me at all."

Charles smiled at his sister. "Of course they like you, but if they'd invited you to the wedding, they would have had to invite Eleanor and Margaret as well, and there was nowhere for you all to sleep."

Margaret's forehead creased. "We could have stayed in a tavern."

Charles ignored his sister and turned his attention to Mr Wetherby. "I believe you're not well. How are you feeling?"

"I've been better. I'm in constant pain and some days the laudanum just doesn't touch it."

"Do you still work?"

"I do what I can, but I've passed the day-to-day running to William Junior."

Charles studied Mr Wetherby. "Has he left Bushwood?"

"No, he spends part of the week there and the rest in Handsworth. The doctor said the pain won't kill me, and so I try to go to the workshop when he's not around."

"And that's why you're in pain today, because you did too much yesterday." Aunt Sarah-Ann scowled at her husband before turning to Charles. "How's Mary-Ann doing? I haven't seen much of her since Mr Diver died."

"She's finding it difficult," Charles said. "She takes to her bed most afternoons and the girls do the chores the maids can't do."

"They're lovely girls," Sarah-Ann said.

Charles smiled as he thought of his cousins. *Rose certainly is.*

Mr Wetherby shifted in his seat to face Sarah-Ann. "Would you take the girls into the morning room. I'd like to speak to Charles alone." When Florence protested, he held up his hand. "I won't keep him long, you can see him when we've finished."

As Sarah-Ann closed the door behind her, Mr Wetherby fixed his green-flecked eyes on Charles. "I received a letter telling me you're now a second mate and considered an able seaman and then four days later I had a letter from you telling me you're not going back to sea."

Charles nodded. "I qualified in January and worked as an able seaman on my last voyage."

Mr Wetherby winced as he pushed himself up in his chair. "You've spent the last five years, and a considerable sum of my money, training to be a seaman and as soon as you qualify, you tell me you're not going back?"

"Being at sea wasn't what I expected, but it's not been wasted. I met a man in America and we've discussed working together."

Mr Wetherby's eyebrows came together. "What sort of work?"

"He has a company that manufactures goods from India rubber. He wants to import into the United Kingdom and I said I'd be interested. If I find a warehouse in Birmingham I can have the goods shipped into Liverpool and use the railway to transport them here."

"Wouldn't you be better working out of Liverpool?"

Charles shook his head. "I'll spend a fair amount of time there and I can stay with William-Wetherby whenever I want, but I want to expand and Birmingham is central to Liverpool and London."

Mr Wetherby studied Charles from under bushy eyebrows. "Have you thought about how you'll finance it?"

Charles shifted in his seat as Mr Wetherby's eyes bored through him. "I was wondering ... would you be able to help? It would be a good investment for you."

"How much do you want?"

"I'm not certain yet. Enough to rent some premises and buy the first consignment. I would say about a thousand pounds."

Mr Wetherby's glare didn't fade. "I need to think about it. That's a lot of money to put into an untested venture."

"I wouldn't let you down and I'll have a partner. Someone I went to school with ... he's done some buying and selling while I've been away. You could act as an advisor too, if you wanted to."

Mr Wetherby grimaced. "If I was rid of this pain I would, but I can't promise. Go and cost it all properly and come back to me."

Chapter Nineteen

Liverpool, Lancashire

S itting by the fireside Bella accepted the cup of tea her mother gave her.

"You're a godsend, exactly what I need. How can one baby make you feel so fat and tired?"

Mrs Booth smiled. "It's not for much longer and then you'll need all the energy you've got. I hope you've not been doing too much."

Bella shook her head. "Chance would be a fine thing. Other than helping with dinner for William-Wetherby and Fred before they went to the match I've done nothing."

"Fred was so excited about it."

Bella chuckled. "I'm not sure William-Wetherby was. Now Liverpool are in the Football League, he worries about the size of the crowd. I keep telling him he should be used to it by now."

"If you give him a son he'll have to get used to it. My grandson can't be the only boy in school who doesn't go to the game."

"Ouch." Bella squirmed in her chair and rubbed her free hand over her swollen belly. "I think he's playing football himself at the moment. I wish he'd hurry up and come out."

"It'll be out soon enough." Mrs Booth laughed as the front door opened and Fred burst into the room.

"We won, three-one." He took off his cap and kicked it into the air.

"That's enough, young man." Mrs Booth took him by the shoulders and pointed him in the direction of the scullery. "You're not in the street now. Go and wash your hands."

As Fred disappeared, William-Wetherby appeared at the door. "Did he come in?"

"He's out the back. I take it he enjoyed himself?"

William-Wetherby laughed. "He did; surprisingly I did too. I must prefer the better quality football of league division two."

"Well, sit yourself down," Mrs Booth said. "Tea's ready."

WILLIAM-WETHERBY PACED the floor of the living room before glancing at the clock for the fifth time in as many minutes. Half past ten. The baby had started yesterday afternoon and there was still no sign of it. *What's keeping them?*

A shriek from the bedroom caused him to jump to his feet. *What was that? Should I do anything?* He paced the living room, before going to the foot of the stairs.

"Is everything all right? Do you need a doctor?"

Mrs Booth appeared on the landing, her hair ruffled. "No, she's doing fine. Give her another half hour."

William-Wetherby sighed; he didn't have long before he was due at work.

By the time Mrs Booth came down to the living room, William-Wetherby was ready to leave for his shift. A smile spread across her exhausted face. "It's all over. We've got a little boy. The midwife's sorting everything out and then you can go up."

Tears stung William-Wetherby's eyes. "I've got a son? Is Bella all right?"

"She's fine, just a little tired. Why do babies always choose the middle of the night to announce their arrival?"

As soon as the midwife came downstairs, William-Wetherby raced up to the bedroom to find Bella sitting up in bed, her baby in her arms. William-Wetherby crept to the side of the bed and kissed her forehead.

"You're so clever." He took hold of the tiny fist extending from the blanket. "He's beautiful."

"He must take after you then." Bella's face shone as she gazed first at William-Wetherby and then at her son. "What will we call him? William?"

William-Wetherby didn't pause to think. "No. There are too many of us in the family and I don't want him tainted with a name connected to Mr Wetherby."

"What do you suggest then?"

"What was your father called?"

"Mine?" Bella flushed bright pink. "I'm not naming my beautiful boy after him. What about grandfathers, did you know any of yours?"

"No. My grandmother married Mr Wetherby when my father was a boy and an aunt and uncle brought Mother up. I don't even know the name of my father's father."

"Where did Charles's name come from? That could have been a grandfather?"

"It could, and I like the name, but there can only be one Charles. Perhaps it could be his middle name." William-Wetherby stroked his thumb over the back of the child's hand. "Just a thought, but by the time he's older, the Prince of Wales is likely to be king. Why don't we call him Edward?"

Bella gazed at her son. "Edward Charles Jackson. That sounds smart."

"And he will be. We'll make sure he wants for nothing."

Chapter Twenty

Keeping one hand on the bannister William-Wetherby walked down the stairs with his young son cradled in his other arm. Bella walked carefully behind him.

"I don't want you doing anything more strenuous than feeding Edward. Your mam'll be back from the shops soon and I'll be here this afternoon."

Bella took a seat by the fire. "Stop worrying. You'd think I was the first woman to have a baby. I'm going to ask me mam if we can go for a walk. It's two weeks since Edward was born and the weather's still decent for the time of year. I need some air."

"You'll do no such thing. I don't want you leaving this house without me, do you hear?"

Bella's bottom lip dropped. "I was looking forward to it."

William-Wetherby crouched beside her. "I'm sorry. I didn't mean to shout, but I don't want anything happening to you. I'll tell you what. I finish at three and we can go for a walk after that. Not far, but enough to give you some air."

Bella nodded. "All right, I'll wait, but hurry back."

. . .

AT PRECISELY QUARTER PAST THREE, William-Wetherby pushed open the front door and found Bella waiting for him with her hat and cape fastened.

William-Wetherby laughed. "I'd wondered if you might have changed your mind. As you clearly haven't, we'd better go."

With a final check on Edward, Bella pushed his carriage through the front door.

"Where do you want to go?" William-Wetherby asked.

"Can we go and see me granny? I'd like to show her Edward."

"Your granny? I thought she was dead."

Bella laughed. "She is, but I often go to the cemetery with me mam to visit the grave. She'll want to see the baby."

William-Wetherby opened his mouth to speak but closed it again. If she wanted to visit her granny's grave, what harm would it do?

It took twenty minutes to reach the gates of the cemetery and William-Wetherby paused before he went in. "Don't you think we've gone far enough for one day? We've still got to walk back."

"It's not far now. Just down here on the right. Please, I'm fine."

William-Wetherby nodded. "Another five minutes, no more."

They walked for the full five minutes and William-Wetherby was about to turn for home, when Bella pointed to the grave.

"There she is. I told you it wasn't far." She hurried on ahead and William-Wetherby watched as she took Edward from the pram and held him in front of the grave.

"Are you happy now?" He put his arm around her shoulders as he joined her.

Bella smiled. "I am ... and he's been good too."

William-Wetherby's eyes lingered on his son, before they wandered to the inscription on the gravestone.

In remembrance of
William Booth,
beloved husband of
Margaret,
who died on 2nd May 1860,
aged 49 years,
and of
Margaret Booth
who died on 5th December 1887,
aged 74 years.
May you always be remembered.

"BOOTH?" The word left William-Wetherby's lips without him realising.

Bella looked at him. "What did you say?"

William-Wetherby stared at her before rereading the inscription. "Were these your father's parents?"

"No, me mam's, but I never knew me grandad."

"But your mam, Mrs Booth ..." He turned to face her. "It should be Miss Booth, shouldn't it?"

Bella stared at the gravestone as if she was seeing it for the first time.

"Is she another one who had children without bothering to get married?"

"No ... I don't know." Bella put her hands on her cheeks. "She said me dad cleared off to sea and never bothered coming back. It won't have been her fault."

"Well whose fault was it ... twice? It's no wonder most of

your friends are fallen women."

Bella's cheeks were scarlet as tears filled her eyes.

"You've no idea what me mam went through bringing the two of us up on her own. The fact that I'm here with you now means she must have done something right." She clung to Edward. "Me granny never abandoned her and I won't either."

William-Wetherby watched as she turned away from him. *Why am I surprised? I should have guessed.* "I'm sorry, I shouldn't have said anything."

"You think we're little better than vermin, don't you?" Bella's voice squeaked as she spoke.

"Of course I don't." He pulled her into an embrace that squashed Edward between the two of them. "It doesn't change how I feel about you."

"You knew when you married me I came from a different world, it's not my fault."

He kissed the side of her head. "I didn't say it was, please don't cry. You made me the happiest man in Liverpool the day we got married and I don't regret a thing. Please, let's forget this happened and we won't speak of it again."

Chapter Twenty-One

As the New Year dawned, Charles stood on the steps of Lime Street Station and took a breath of the fresh air. That was his favourite thing about seaside ports, no smog. With a glance at St George's Hall, he turned left before heading up the hill towards William-Wetherby's home. *I hope they got my letter. I suppose I should have posted it before yesterday.*

From the corner of Martensen Street, he saw the postman ahead of him. If his letter had beaten him here, it wasn't by much. He waited at the top of the road for five minutes before sauntering towards the house. It took Bella a minute to open the door and when she did, she held Edward over her left shoulder, while a letter protruded from her right hand.

"You got my letter then." Charles smiled as he stepped into the living room.

"About three minutes ago," Bella said. "Did you stand at the end of the street and ask the postie to deliver it before you arrived?"

Charles laughed. "I didn't, but I wish I had. It would have saved me the price of a stamp."

"Get on with you." Bella flicked the letter at his arm. "D'you want a cup of tea?"

"Silly question for a man who's been travelling hours to see you." Charles hung his hat by the door and took a seat by the fire.

Bella shook her head. "I can tell you're in one of those moods today. I don't suppose you've eaten either. Well, you'll have to meet your new nephew while I go and find you something."

Bella placed Edward on Charles's knee and disappeared to the scullery. "I've just fed him, so he may need winding. Pat his back."

Charles held Edward away from his suit and stared at him. What did he know about babies? "Do you mind if I don't? I've only got one jacket." Charles leaned forward and put Edward on the floor before he crouched down beside him and tickled his tummy. The sound of Edward laughing brought Bella back into the room.

"What are you doing to him? He shouldn't be on the floor." She bent down to pick him up.

"He was enjoying that."

Bella rolled her eyes at Charles before putting Edward back in his carriage. "Go and sit at the table. Dinner'll be ready in a minute."

"What time will William-Wetherby be home?"

Bella came back carrying a plate of scouse. "He finishes at six tonight."

"Not to worry, I need to go to the docks and so I'll wait for him outside the police station."

Bella wagged her finger at him. "Don't go keeping him in the alehouse all night, he has a son now and he needs to see him."

WILLIAM-WETHERBY STOPPED dead when he opened the door of the police station to find Charles leaning on the tree outside.

"What are you doing here?" A smile spread across his face before he stepped out to shake his brother's hand.

"Just passing."

William-Wetherby slapped him on the back. "You seem in a good mood. What have you been up to?"

"It's my second week as company director of J.W. Hains & Co."

William-Wetherby's brow furrowed. "Why not Hains and Jackson, or Jackson & Co? Did Mr Hains put the money in?"

Charles indicated to his brother to start walking. "Not exactly. I borrowed the money we needed from Mr Wetherby but there were conditions."

"You do surprise me. What were they?"

"After everything that happened to Father he said he didn't want his money being associated with the Jackson name."

William-Wetherby's mouth dropped open. "He said that? How would anyone know the money had come from him?"

Charles shrugged. "I've no idea, but given it was the only thing standing between me and one thousand pounds, I wasn't going to argue."

"He gave you one thousand pounds? He wouldn't give Father one hundred when he needed it. What did you say to him?"

"I gave him a business case and he was all for it."

"So what are you doing here?"

"The first consignment of India-rubber goods arrives tomorrow and I want to check everything runs smoothly. You should see the premises we've got on Temple Street waiting for it."

William-Wetherby pushed open the door of the beerhouse and let Charles in. "I'd love to see them ... one day."

Charles went to the bar while William-Wetherby found a seat. He returned with two tankards of ale. "You've no need to worry, Bella knows you're here. As long as you're home before bedtime, she'll be fine. Trust me."

William-Wetherby shook his head and took a gulp of his drink. "We'll be home well before then. Did she tell you we had a letter from Eleanor yesterday? She's getting married in August."

Charles choked on his ale. "Eleanor is? Why didn't she write and tell me? Who's she marrying?"

"I didn't recognise the name of the chap. Joseph Keen."

Charles shook his head. "No, never heard of him. I wonder where they met."

"I think it was something to do with her employer. The son of one of his acquaintances or something like that."

"So what will she do? Presumably she'll stop work before the marriage."

William-Wetherby nodded. "She's moving into Wetherby House with Margaret and Florence. I'm not sure she's happy about it, but she doesn't have a lot of choice. How was Florence when you called there? Did you speak to her about working for you?"

Charles shook his head. "She seems to have settled down again and is even on speaking terms with Mr Wetherby. The trouble is, he's never far away and you know what he thinks about women doing bookkeeping. Eleanor's wedding may be the time to talk to her. I wonder if Eleanor would let Florence live with her once she's married. That way Mr Wetherby wouldn't know what she was doing."

"It depends on this Mr Keen, I suppose. Not that I'll meet him. I won't be going to the wedding."

Charles stared at his brother. "You should give her away."

"What can I do? A condition of leaving and getting the legacy was that I stay away from Birmingham. If his health's up to it, Mr Wetherby will be there ... and William Junior. I can't jeopardise everything. You'll have to do it."

"It's nonsense that you can't go to your own sister's wedding." Charles emptied his tankard and went to the bar. He returned with two more drinks and a smile on his face. "I haven't told you my news anyway. I'm walking out with someone."

William-Wetherby laughed. "You've been busy. You've only been back in Birmingham six months. Anyone I know?"

Charles nodded. "Rose."

William-Wetherby's eyes glazed over as he digested the name before sitting up straight. "Rose! Cousin Rose? Aunt Mary-Ann's daughter Rose?"

"The very same. I must say she's grown into a very desirable woman while I've been away. It's handy living in the same house as each other and even better that I don't need to impress her father."

"Is Aunt Mary-Ann happy about it?"

Charles shrugged. "Why shouldn't she be? She knows me and my background, and if we get married, it'll mean Mr Diver's money stays in the family."

"So will you ask her to marry you?"

Charles smirked and took a gulp of ale. "I'm biding my time, I can't appear too eager."

Chapter Twenty-Two

Birmingham, Warwickshire

Charles sat in the back living room of his Aunt Mary-Ann's house listening to the giggles that made their way down the stairs. *It may be Eleanor's wedding day, but why do women take so long to get ready?* He returned to the newspaper and tried to concentrate but before he could find his place, Rose flew through the door, a smile beaming across her face.

"What do you think?" She placed her hands on her narrow hips as she twirled around, dragging the short train of her lemon dress behind her.

"Very nice. Is it new?"

Rose tutted. "Of course it's new. You can't go to a wedding in something old."

"But you have a lot of dresses."

Rose walked towards him and took his hands to pull him up. "My dearest Charles. You've been living with a group of men for far too long, you've got such a lot to learn."

Charles put his arms around her waist. "Well you'd better start teaching me." He leaned forward to kiss her nose as Mary-Ann walked into the room.

"What's going on here? I'll have none of that in this house. Rose, go and put your hat on."

With her cheeks pink, Rose hurried past her mother to join her sisters in the hallway. Charles watched her leave.

"Did you buy the dress? She looks lovely ... as do you."

Mary-Ann ran her hands down her skirt. "I did, as it happens, but that's no reason to behave like that. Now, are you ready? The carriage is waiting for us."

Once at church, Charles escorted his aunt to their pew and watched helplessly as she positioned herself with her daughters on one side of her, while Charles was on the other. He looked around the old church. He hadn't been here since ... when? His mother's funeral? He paused to think and spotted his Aunt Charlotte sitting with Mr Mountford. No, it was at their wedding. It wasn't long after Mother's funeral though. Maybe eight years ago. He shook his head to clear the memory. That was a lifetime ago.

The congregation rose as the organist played the first notes of the processional music and the hairs on Charles's neck tingled as Mr Wetherby walked his sister down the aisle. Margaret and Florence followed close behind. *Why didn't it occur to me that he'd do it? That should be me.* He thumped one hand into the other. *In fact, it should be William-Wetherby and he's stopped that as well.* Charles glared at Mr Wetherby but a smile crept to his lips when he realised how grey his skin was alongside the white of Eleanor's dress. *It serves him right. I hope he's in pain and the laudanum isn't working.*

With the marriage ceremony over, the guests made their way to the waiting carriages to travel the two minutes back to Wetherby House.

"I notice Eleanor wasn't given the parade around

Handsworth that Elizabeth was," Mary-Ann said. "It appears Aunt Sarah-Ann has forgotten she started life in our family, not his."

"I couldn't have put it better myself."

Mary-Ann turned around to see Aunt Martha standing behind her, resting on a walking cane.

"How lovely to see you." Mary-Ann leaned forward to embrace her aunt. "Are you on your own?"

"No, I'm with your aunt Adelaide and cousin Hannah. They'll be over in a minute."

"I wasn't sure you'd be here today after your argument with Mr Wetherby."

Martha gave Mr Wetherby and Sarah-Ann a scornful glance. "I'm not being isolated from my family because of them. Why did he give Eleanor away though when Charles is here?"

Charles stepped forward. "My thoughts exactly. And Uncle William Junior was her chief witness."

Martha surveyed the congregation. "William-Wetherby didn't come?"

Mary-Ann shook her head. "Mr Wetherby is still stopping him from seeing the family."

"He doesn't look well though, does he?" Martha inclined her head towards Mr Wetherby. "Do you know what's up with him?"

Charles took a step closer to listen as Mary-Ann leaned towards her aunt. "Problems with his waterworks I believe."

Martha nodded as her sister Adelaide and niece Hannah, joined them.

"Are we going back to the house?" Adelaide asked.

"We are," Mary-Ann replied. "As the only male amongst us, Charles can escort us."

Mary-Ann linked her arm through Charles's and let him lead her from church.

"What are you doing now, Hannah?" Mary-Ann asked as they walked. "Did you travel all the way from Oxford for the wedding?"

Hannah laughed. "No, I'm visiting Mother at the moment and she asked if I could come along."

"Is that husband of yours treating you well? How are the children?"

"Yes, everyone's fine and my sister-in-law's watching the children while I'm here."

"You have your own business, don't you?" Charles asked.

"Yes, we run a laundry and washing service. We're thinking of expanding but the current landlord isn't being very understanding. We may end up moving."

"I'm hoping they'll move back to Birmingham," Adelaide said. "I don't see my grandchildren nearly enough when they're all the way down there."

WITH THE WEDDING breakfast in full swing, Charles stood in the corner of the dining room watching the guests. Half of them might be relations but he hadn't seen anyone since he was a child and he didn't remember them. He needed to find Rose. He walked towards the doorway as Eleanor came in.

"Here you are. What are you hiding in here for? I want you to meet Frank. Margaret and Florence are looking for you too."

"I don't recognise anyone any more."

"Of course you do. What's up with you?"

Charles gave his sister a sideways glance. "Why did Mr Wetherby give you away?"

"Are you sulking?"

"No, but it wasn't right. William-Wetherby should have been here, but with Mr Wetherby stopping him, I thought I'd do it."

"Don't be silly, he's only trying to help and he gave Frank enough money for our first three months' rent as a wedding present."

"He's trying to split us up." Charles unhooked his arm from Eleanor's. "Will you excuse me? I need to do something."

Charles walked into the front living room, where Rose was talking to her sisters Daisy and Lilly.

"You look deep in conversation," Charles said as he reached for Rose's hand.

"We're being rather gloomy, I'm afraid," Rose said.

"We were wondering who'll give us away now Father's gone," Lilly said. "Mr Wetherby may be dead by the time we're married and we have no brothers."

Charles turned to Rose. "Can I have a word with you? In private." He led her back to the dining room, into a quiet corner.

"What's the matter?"

"I want you." He gazed into her eyes as he took hold of her hands. "I hated it when your mother criticised us earlier and I don't want to live like this any more. Will you marry me?"

Rose's eyes filled with tears as a smile brightened her face. "Yes, of course I will. Thank you." She threw her arms around his neck and Charles glanced around the room before he snatched a kiss from her. "Have you asked Mother?"

"Not yet. I wanted to ask you first."

"I'm sure she'll say yes. Can we be married in the spring of next year?"

Charles shook his head as he held her chin. "I don't want to wait that long, I want you now. The sooner the better."

Rose hesitated. "But there'll be arrangements to make."

"So we can have another occasion like this?" Charles wafted his arm around the room. "I don't want a bunch of strangers at my wedding. As long as you're there, I don't care who else turns up."

"I'm sure Mother will want to give us a special day."

Charles stroked the side of her face. "It'll be special for us, and that's all that matters."

Chapter Twenty-Three

Liverpool, Lancashire

As soon as the front door opened and William-Wetherby and Fred walked in, Bella pushed herself up from the chair.

"Stay where you are and give me those coats, you'll have the place soaked if you come in like that."

"What a foul afternoon." William-Wetherby's coat dripped over the floor as he handed it over. "I've got so much rain down the back of my neck, my shirt's sticking to me."

"Was it a good match?"

"No, we didn't even win, two-two it was." Fred's shoulders slumped.

"Well, at least you didn't lose." Bella helped Fred off with his coat. "Run upstairs, both of you, and put some dry clothes on. I'll put more coal on the fire to dry these and I've a pan of scouse ready for you."

No sooner had Fred disappeared than the sound of Edward crying filtered down the stairs.

Bella let out a long sigh and turned to William-Wetherby.

"What's the matter now? I've only just got him to sleep. You'll have to serve your own tea, I could be a while." She trudged up the stairs to find Fred leaning over the side of the cot. "Did you wake him up?" she snapped.

"No, he was crying and I came to see him."

"Well, go and get changed." She picked Edward up out of his cot. "There, there, Mammy's here."

"Is he all right?" William-Wetherby followed her into the bedroom.

"He'll be fine, but he's teething. I need to give him something for it. Go and sit at the table and I'll be down in a minute."

With dinner served, Bella joined them.

"Where's your mam?" William-Wetherby asked.

"She's gone to me aunty's; she'll be back soon although she may wait for the rain to go off."

"I wish we could have done that, but you get as wet watching the game as you do walking home."

As Fred ate his last mouthful of food, Bella reached for his plate. "Up the stairs with you, and into bed. And don't you go anywhere near Edward."

Fred's mouth dropped. "It's still light outside."

"I don't care. It's not fit for playing out so you can have an early night. Off you go."

William-Wetherby followed her into the scullery as she took the dishes. "What's the matter? You're not your usual self," he said.

"I'm exhausted, that's what's the matter, and to make things worse I think I'm in the family way again."

William-Wetherby took hold of her hands to keep her still. "But that's wonderful. I thought that was what you wanted, a brother or sister for Edward."

"It is, but not if I feel like this. And tell me where we're going to put it? We've no space for another cot in our room and we can't put Edward in with me mam and Fred." Tears welled in her eyes. "How will we manage?"

William-Wetherby put his arms around her. "Don't worry, we'll find a way. We spoke about moving house when we had Edward, but perhaps now's the time."

"But we'll struggle to pay the rent on your wage when we have four mouths to feed." Bella was no longer able to stop her tears.

"Calm down, it's not that bad. I still have some money left from Mr Wetherby, which will help with the rent until I get my next promotion."

"That'll leave me mam on her own ... and what about Fred?"

"Have you told your mam about this?"

Bella shook her head. "Not yet."

"Well, that explains it. You've had no one to talk to and you're getting yourself all worked up. Get this tidied up and we'll talk to her when she gets in."

When William-Wetherby arrived downstairs for breakfast the next morning, Bella was feeding Edward while Mrs Booth busied herself in the scullery.

"Are you feeling better today?" he asked as he pushed his plate away.

"I couldn't eat anything, but I'm not so tired, if that's what you mean."

He reached for her free hand. "I don't want you doing anything other than looking after Edward today, do you promise?"

"Was that the postman?" Mrs Booth walked through the living room and went to the door. "For you," she said to William-Wetherby when she returned. "I'd say it's Charles's writing."

William-Wetherby put down his bread and opened the letter. "Good grief. He's getting married. He hasn't wasted any time."

"To your cousin?"

William-Wetherby nodded but his smile faded as he continued to read. "My aunt isn't best pleased about it and has said she'll oppose the banns."

"But he's family, why would she do that?"

William-Wetherby shrugged. "She clearly knows Charles too well. He's not put off though. They'll be married by special licence at Aston Register Office next month." He paused. "That'll upset my aunt even more. Her eldest daughter's getting married and there'll be no spectacle."

"Do you think she knows about the register office?"

William-Wetherby pushed himself up from the table. "Knowing Charles, probably not, but I'm staying out of it. We won't be going and so I'll send him a note of congratulations and wait for the dust to settle."

Chapter Twenty-Four

Birmingham, Warwickshire

Charles leaned back in his chair and pushed the cup and saucer across the table, away from him.

"Have you finished?" Rose stood up to collect the dishes but Charles caught hold of her waist.

"I've not finished with you." He pulled her onto his lap. "You've got no excuses now. No Mother snooping around the house checking up on us."

Rose giggled and kissed Charles's cheek before she wriggled free. "She did no such thing. You just never had your hands off me."

"That's besides the point. Who'd have thought, this time last year, that I'd have my own morning room and such a beautiful wife?"

Charles reached for her again and groaned when there was a knock on the door. "If that's your mother checking up on us again, I swear ..." He broke off as he walked to the door. "Mr Wetherby, Aunt Sarah-Ann, what are you doing here? Come in. If you'd sent word, I'd have come to you."

Mr Wetherby waved the hand holding his stick. "I wanted to see what you'd done with my money. Can I come in?"

"Yes, of course. Come into the back room. Rose will put the kettle on."

Mr Wetherby winced as he took a seat. "You don't have anything a bit stronger, do you? A drop of Scotch, perhaps."

Charles screwed his face up. "Not Scotch, I've some locally brewed whisky or some rum?"

Sarah-Ann smiled at Charles. "Take no notice of him. The local brew will be fine, but not too much. I'll go and help Rose with the tea."

Mr Wetherby glared at his wife as she left the room. "What does she know? She isn't in constant pain."

Charles retrieved the whisky from the sideboard and poured Mr Wetherby a generous measure. "How's that? If you're quick I'll top it up before she gets back." With a wink, Charles turned back to the sideboard and poured himself a glass. "Do you want a guided tour of the house?"

"I'll pop my head into the downstairs rooms as we leave, but I'm keen to hear how the business is going."

Charles sipped his drink. "We're doing very well. There isn't much competition and so we're moving the stock quickly. I'm thinking of expanding the premises so we can bring more goods in. Number nineteen, next door to the current storage, is vacant."

"And are you making a profit yet?"

"We've already recouped our initial outlay. The year end's approaching and so we should be able to let you have some of your money back, if that's what you're worried about."

"It's not urgent, but I like to keep an eye on my investments. I'd like to visit the storage next time I'm in Birmingham."

"Yes, of course. Tell me when you're well enough to travel and I'll arrange it."

Mr Wetherby held out his glass for another tot of whisky. "I'm moving William Junior and the family back from Bushwood at the moment and so it may not be for a while. We'll travel over there next week for Christmas, but I've found somebody to let it to."

"Is Uncle William running the businesses now?"

Mr Wetherby studied Charles with watery eyes. "I can't do much any more, not the running around I used to. I hate to leave everything to him when it's been my life, but there comes a time when you have little choice."

"What about Henry? Will he help?"

Mr Wetherby smiled at the mention of his grandson. "He's joining the business next year when he finishes school. He's a bright boy."

The conversation was cut short when Sarah-Ann came back into the room with Rose.

"I hope you've only had one of those." Sarah-Ann nodded at the glass.

"Of course he has," Charles said. "Why don't you take a seat and tell me what you're doing at the moment. I don't see nearly enough of you."

Sarah-Ann flushed as Charles helped her onto the settee. "Oh, you've no idea. I'm currently helping Olivia out with their new house. William Junior's bought one of those houses on Handsworth Wood Road. Why they need such a big place for the three of them, I don't know. I've advertised for a cook and a couple of maids, but they'll need more. They've got six reception rooms and ten bedrooms, not to mention the servants' quarters. You've no idea how difficult it is to find a good maid." Sarah-Ann shook her head.

"It must be a burden." Charles couldn't keep the sarcasm from his voice. "I'm so glad I don't have more money than I know what to do with."

"Patience," Mr Wetherby said. "You've a lot more than I

had when I was your age and with the help you're getting I fully expect you to make enough money to live comfortably. You'll have me to answer to if you don't."

Chapter Twenty-Five

C harles stepped from the carriage and glanced up at the clock on the front of Birmingham New Street railway station. Ten past eleven. *Florence should be here any time now.* He reached into his pockets and smiled as he pulled out two tickets to Liverpool. *First class. One of the benefits of having some of Mr Wetherby's money.* He put the tickets back in his pocket and picked up his bag as Florence's carriage arrived.

"Come on, we're going to miss the train at this rate."

"We've plenty of time." Florence linked her arm into his as he escorted her to their carriage. "Business must be going well."

"I can't complain. We've got a consignment of goods coming in most months now. I'll have to get used to making this journey."

"I'm so looking forward to seeing everyone," Florence said. "Edward's nearly eighteen months old and this will be the first time I've seen him. I wish William-Wetherby would come home."

"Maybe you can come with me more often," Charles said. "Have you ever thought about getting a job?"

"A job?" Florence stared at her brother. "Why on earth would I do that?"

Charles shrugged. "Someone told me you weren't happy at Wetherby House and so I thought you might want to leave."

Florence laughed. "That was years ago when Mr Wetherby was angry with me. If I'm going to be in Liverpool for the next three months I won't need to worry about him. Besides, the only job I'd want would be bookkeeping, and once I'm back in Handsworth Mr Wetherby won't hear of it."

"Would you like to learn though?"

Florence screwed up her forehead. "You mean go back to school?"

"No, I mean have someone show you what to do. You're good at arithmetic, aren't you?"

Florence nodded. "I suppose so, but there's no point learning any more. Mr Wetherby will take care of me until I'm married and then I'd have to stop working anyway."

As the train moved through the countryside, Charles watched the steam from the engine rush past the window. "I still think you'd enjoy it," he said eventually. "If you'd like to learn, you could work for me, my partner Mr Hains would teach you."

Florence studied her brother. "You want me to work for you?"

"Only for a couple of days a week, once you're back home, and you could do most of it at Wetherby House. I'd bring the books to you and you'd be paid. You'd be able to visit William-Wetherby more often if you had your own money."

"Money of my own?" Florence smiled but kept her eye on Charles. "And you're not teasing me?"

"Of course not. Talk to William-Wetherby about it and tell me your decision once you're back in Birmingham."

Liverpool, Lancashire.

BELLA RAISED the bedcovers and moved the bed-warmer further up the mattress. It would be the first time they had had visitors since they moved house and she had been airing the spare beds for the last couple of days. As she straightened up, she heard the front door open.

"It's only me, luv," Mrs Booth shouted up the stairs as she hung her coat up. "My, it's cold out today."

"Better put the kettle on then, Charles and Florence will be here soon." Bella joined her mam in the kitchen." I'm glad we've got the space to put them up properly."

"You've not been doing too much, have you?" Mrs Booth studied her daughter. "I know you want the place looking its best, but this is a bigger house than you're used to and it's not as important as that baby."

"Stop worrying, I'm fine. Let me put some more coal on the fire and then I'll sit down."

Bella hadn't picked up the coal scuttle when there was a knock on the door.

"I'll get it." Mrs Booth went to the door as Florence climbed from a carriage. "Oh my dear Florence, how lovely to see you again." She threw her arms around the young girl.

"It's lovely to be back." Florence's smile brightened her face as she moved to embrace Bella, who had followed her mam to the door. "I can't believe how much I've missed you."

"Come in." Mrs Booth ushered the two of them into the back room and took their coats.

"Welcome to our new house," Bella said. "I hope you like it. We've got three bedrooms now so Florence can have her own room, and Charles you're in with Edward. I hope you don't mind."

"Thank you for letting me stay so long," Florence said. "I'm so looking forward to it. Where is Edward? I've not seen him."

"He's having his afternoon nap. I'll fetch him when we've had a cup of tea."

"And where's Fred? Will I see him?"

Mrs Booth laughed. "I've no doubt you will, he's been asking after you, but he's still with me ... finally in his own bedroom."

"I'm sure he'll like that." Florence rested back into one of the armchairs. "I do like being here. It's about the only place I can be myself."

WITH HIS BUSINESS ATTENDED TO, Charles took up his usual position outside the police station while he waited for his brother to finish. At precisely six o'clock, William-Wetherby threw back the front door but failed to acknowledge Charles as he raced down the steps and headed towards home.

"You're in a hurry." Charles had to run to keep up with him.

"Yes, I am. I presume you've come to take me to the tavern, so we might as well go straight there."

ONCE THEY WERE at the bar, Charles caught his breath as William-Wetherby ordered the drinks. "This is a turn-up, you bringing me here. What's going on?"

"I've had it with the police." William-Wetherby took a mouthful of ale and walked to a corner table. "They've been promising all year that the next inspector's job was mine and I found out today they've gone and given it to someone else ... without a word."

"Ouch. Do you know the man they've given it to?"

"No. He's been brought in from outside when we have a strict policy of promoting from within our own ranks."

Charles studied his brother as his fingers banged on the table. "What will you do?"

"I've no idea, but I know what I'd like to do ... tell them they can find themselves another sergeant."

"What about your pension?"

"They can keep that as well. I've had enough of them."

Charles studied his brother. "Would you be interested in doing the paperwork for me when our consignments come in? It would save me coming up here every month and I'd pay you a decent wage."

"Where would I work?"

Charles shrugged. "You could do the paperwork at home, but you'd have to go to the docks to cross-check the stock, deal with the customs and excise, make sure the orders are ready for transportation, that sort of thing."

"I wouldn't be able to start for a few weeks and I'd need at least twenty-five shillings a week. Could you do that?"

"Start when you're ready." Charles smiled. "And seeing that it's Mr Wetherby's money, you can have thirty shillings."

Chapter Twenty-Six

With a new hat on the mannequin before her, Bella looked up as she sensed Florence's eyes on her.

"What's the matter?" Bella asked with a smile.

"Nothing. I'm just thinking how clever you are. I wish I could make beautiful hats like that."

"I only do it because I have to. With moving house and the new baby due soon, we need all the money we can get."

Florence studied her sister-in-law. "Doesn't William-Wetherby earn enough to look after you?"

Bella put down her needle. "Not as much as he would have done if he'd got the promotion to inspector."

"He's happy working for Charles though, isn't he?"

"He is, but happiness won't put food on the table. He lost his pension too, which I was furious about."

"Well, let's hope Charles's business is successful. You shouldn't have to do all this. Do you make much money on your hats?"

"I charge up to a crown for them."

"But that isn't all money for you, is it? Who does your bookkeeping?"

Bella stared at Florence. "Bookkeeping?"

"For your hats. Who keeps a record of the money you earn and the money you spend?"

"Nobody. Why?"

Florence's brow creased. "So how do you know if you're making money on them? If you don't keep records, you could be spending more on materials than you charge."

Bella continued to stare at Florence. "I don't think I am."

"You should keep a record of everything you buy. Do you do that?"

Bella picked up her needle again. "I'll have the receipts somewhere but I've never done anything with them. I was never good at sums."

"Can I help you? Charles has asked me if I'd like to do the bookkeeping for his business in Birmingham. I'd have said yes a few years ago when I wanted to leave Wetherby House, but now I'm not sure. Can I practise with you?"

Bella's nod was slow. "I suppose so, but why does Charles want you to help him? It's man's work, isn't it?"

"Not any more." Florence leaned forward in her seat. "It's becoming a respectable trade for women, although Mr Wetherby doesn't think so. I'm not sure it's worth upsetting him when I'll be married in a few years' time."

"William-Wetherby told me he wasn't happy about your mam doing his books."

"That's what worries me. Charles says everything will be fine, but I don't know ... he's always teasing me."

Bella laughed. "He's quite a character, isn't he? How does Rose put up with him?"

Florence sighed. "She adores him, it's as simple as that."

. . .

133

ONCE DINNER WAS OVER, Florence sat at the table copying the figures from a selection of receipts into a notebook. She looked up when Bella returned from putting Edward down for his afternoon nap.

"You're barely breaking even. You should be charging at least another five shillings to make it worth your while."

"Five shillings? That would put me out of business. Women around here can't afford money like that." Bella lowered herself up into a chair by the fireplace. "Maybe two shillings, on the extravagant hats."

Florence joined her by the fire. "With another baby to care for, you'll need the money. Try it and see."

Bella nodded. "And what about you? I know it wasn't much, but has it made your mind up about working for Charles?"

"Not really. I'd like some money of my own, but ..." Florence stopped and stared at Bella who had cried out in pain. "What's the matter?"

Bella took a deep breath and relaxed back into the chair. "I think the baby's coming."

"The baby? Now?" Florence's eyes were wide. "It can't be. I can't help. Let me go and fetch Mrs Booth."

Within seconds Florence had disappeared and Bella rested her hands on her belly praying her mother would be at home. *Why did we move so far away?*

It took twenty minutes for Mrs Booth to arrive and she burst into the back room.

"Is it coming?"

"I think so." Bella rocked herself back and forth in her chair. "Can you send Florence for the midwife? Where is she?"

Mrs Booth paused. "I left her at my house. I don't know what happened, but by the time she arrived she was having an attack of hysteria. I left her with a glass of brandy."

"You'd better be quick. The pains are coming too fast for my liking."

William-Wetherby had no sooner set foot inside the front door than Mrs Booth came down the stairs to meet him.

"Don't take your coat off. You're about to be a dad again, but I need you to go to my house. I left Florence there, quite hysterical, will you go and see how she is?"

William-Wetherby felt Mrs Booth's hand in the middle of his back as she pushed him through the door, but put up no resistance.

He arrived at the house to find his sister sitting upright in one of the chairs, staring into space. Fred was with her.

"She's been like this since I came home," Fred said. "She won't talk to me."

"Florence, what's the matter?" William-Wetherby knelt by the side of the chair and waved his hand in front of her face. Nothing.

"What shall we do?" Fred asked.

"Will you go into the scullery for a minute?"

As soon as Fred disappeared, William-Wetherby slapped his sister across the face. "Florence, speak to me."

A hint of recognition crossed Florence's face as tears welled in her eyes before streaming down her cheeks. "The baby's going to die. I can't watch it. Not again, don't make me." She wrapped her arms across her face.

"Florence, stop, you're scaring me. The baby's not going to die."

"Bella's in pain, it was exactly like the afternoon with Aunt Charlotte. I can't watch that again. Take me away, I can't bear it."

William-Wetherby pulled her arms from her face. "It's not the same. Aunt Charlotte's baby wasn't ready to be born, this one is."

Florence turned her face into the chair as her sobbing continued. "I can't bear it. Take me away from here."

She needs a doctor. "Fred, you can come back. Aunty Florence is upset. Can you sit with her while I get the doctor?"

Without waiting for a reply, William-Wetherby raced up the road. He returned five minutes later, the doctor following him.

As they entered the living room, Fred was sitting on his hands staring at his aunty.

"She hasn't moved," he said. "She's just cried."

William-Wetherby showed the doctor his sister, before escorting Fred to the front door. "You've been a good lad, I'm sorry you had to see this. Go and treat yourself to something from the shop."

Fred smiled as William-Wetherby dropped a penny into his hand. "Thank you, Mr Jackson."

William-Wetherby returned to the living room as the doctor helped Florence to her feet.

"I'll give her some laudanum to calm her down, but we must get her to bed. Is she staying here?"

"No, she's staying with us on Gannock Street, but we can't take her there." William-Wetherby scratched his head. "Put her in Fred's bed and he can come home with me. He's wanted to come and stay since we moved, so now's his chance."

It was late by the time Florence was settled and once he'd found Fred, all William-Wetherby wanted to do was go home. He was startled when Mrs Booth opened the door to him.

"There you are. You can tell me where you've been later, but first I suggest you get up those stairs and see your wife and son."

A smile filled William-Wetherby's face. "She's had the baby?"

"She has and he's a bonny little thing too."

William-Wetherby raced up the stairs but paused as he reached the bedroom door. "Are you awake?"

Bella smiled and opened her eyes. "Only for you. Did Mam tell you?"

William-Wetherby crept around the side of the bed as he gazed at his son. "He looks like Edward did. What time was he born?"

"About half past four. What kept you?"

William-Wetherby grimaced as he perched on the edge of the bed. "Don't ask ... but I think I understand why Mr Wetherby got so angry with Florence. Eleanor's baby's due sometime soon, isn't it? I must tell Charles to keep Florence well out of the way."

Chapter Twenty-Seven

Birmingham, Warwickshire

Despite being well into autumn, the weather was unseasonably warm and Charles opened the back door before taking his seat at the breakfast table. Once he had settled himself, Rose handed him the morning post.

"You've one from William-Wetherby."

Charles sliced open the top of the envelope and pulled out the letter.

"That's all I need." He slammed the letter on the table causing Rose to look up from her own correspondence. "I'm going to have to start travelling to Liverpool again. The police have finally realised they made a mistake not promoting William-Wetherby and so they've offered him his job back with an immediate promotion and no loss to his pension. He says he can't turn it down."

"That's good for him though," Rose said.

"It is, but not for us. I don't blame him and he's very

138

apologetic, but I'll have to go up next week and take all the paperwork from him."

"Can I come with you? I've never met Bella or seen the children."

Charles shrugged. "It's all right with me. Why don't you write and ask them?"

~

Liverpool, Lancashire.

CHARLES NOTICED the smile that had been on Rose's face since they'd left home several hours earlier disappeared as their carriage turned into Gannock Street.

"Is this it?" Rose stared at the row of terraced houses as Charles helped her out of the carriage.

"This is bigger than where they were, at least here we'll have a bedroom to ourselves."

Rose shuddered, pulling her coat more tightly around her.

"Stop worrying." Charles planted a kiss on her cheek before knocking on the door.

"Good afternoon, stranger." Bella put on her best voice as she opened the door. "You must be Rose. Come on in."

"Nice to meet you." Rose forced a smile as Charles squeezed her hand. "I've heard so much about you."

"All good I hope?" Bella let out a nervous giggle. "William-Wetherby will be home soon. I've done an afternoon tea and opened up the front room for you. We've hardly used it, but I wanted to make the most of it before we move out."

Charles handed Bella his coat and walked into the front room. "You're moving again?"

"We are, next week, a couple of days after you leave. We like this house, but it's too far from me mam's. I can't pop in when I need to."

"So, where are you going?"

"Back to Martensen Street. The house five doors down from me mam became available and we couldn't miss out on it."

"It's a good job we came this week then, you wouldn't have been able to put us up otherwise."

Bella laughed. "You don't need to worry about that, we can always send Edward to me mam's while you have his room."

"Is that where he is now ... at your mam's?" Rose asked.

"He is, but she'll bring him back in time for bed; Albert's asleep in the back room. Do you want to pop through and see him?"

With the room empty, Charles walked to the window and was relieved to see his brother approaching in his new inspector's uniform. He went to the front door to let him in.

"A new doorman, how civilised." William-Wetherby extended his hand to his brother.

"Inspector Jackson, do come in." Charles grinned. "The women are cooing over your new son so I thought I'd make myself useful."

William-Wetherby placed his cap on the coat stand before leading Charles back into the front room.

"So, how are you enjoying being back in the police?"

"It's like I've never been away ... other than the new uniform. There was a bit of embarrassment when I went back at the way things had been handled, but it's all forgotten now. There was even talk of me moving to the CID and doing some detective work." William-Wetherby rubbed his hands together. "All in all it's worked out rather well."

"I wish I could say the same."

William-Wetherby stared at his brother. "What do you mean? You've been getting bigger and bigger shipments in the short time I've been working for you. I'd have thought business was booming."

Charles sighed. "It was, which is why we increased the shipments, but we've overstocked our customers and the repeat orders aren't coming in at the speed we'd hoped. We've extended the premises into number nineteen but only because we can't fit all the stock into number twenty."

William-Wetherby's eyebrows came together. "You're using both buildings for storage?"

Charles nodded. "I'm not sure what we're going to do. With winter approaching there'll be less need for bicycles, which will hit us too."

"It'll be good for hot-water bottle sales though." William-Wetherby grimaced at his brother. "I'm sorry, this isn't the best time to practise my new-found sense of humour."

"You've got a point though. If we manage the goods more efficiently, we could have seasonal items. I'll have to go back to America and talk to my contact. We need to reduce the frequency of the shipments and tailor them for the seasons. Rose won't be pleased, but if I go next week, I can be back in time for Christmas."

"Are you sure? You know what the weather can be like at this time of year."

"Stop worrying. I crossed worse seas than the Atlantic when I was in the Merchants, there's nothing to it."

Chapter Twenty-Eight

Birmingham, Warwickshire

Charles yawned as he stood with his hands on his hips, surveying the stacks of boxes around him. He hadn't recovered from travelling to New York and back in less than three weeks. The weather had been some of the worst he'd encountered and when he was tired, he still felt himself swaying. How had he lost his sea legs so soon? It hadn't helped that he'd arrived home on Christmas Eve and without an ounce of sympathy, Rose had insisted he join her for an array of social events that had lasted until Twelfth Night.

Now, as he surveyed the stock, he wished he was still away. By all accounts, the winter had been hard and since Christmas the order book had been empty. *Damn the weather.* He might have been able to change future shipments, but the next one had been loaded by the time he'd arrived in America, and now he had no idea where he was going to put the new stock. He walked into the adjacent room; this was no better.

"This snow'll be the end of us." His business partner walked up behind him. "Nobody can ride a bicycle in this."

"The next shipment is due next week too. We need to find more storage space and hope we can shift this lot in the spring."

"Can we afford it?" Mr Hains asked. "We've got a lot of money tied up here at the moment."

Charles shook his head. "I spoke to Florence yesterday. The cash is running short and we don't have many invoices that still need paying. I'll have to pay Mr Wetherby a visit, tell him what's happened and hope he'll lend us a bit more. A couple of hundred should cover the rent and the next shipment, and that's nothing to him."

WHEN CHARLES ARRIVED at Wetherby House the following day, the snow was still fresh on the driveway. With a deep breath he knocked on the front door and waited for the maid.

"Mr Wetherby's only accepting visitors in his room," she said as she held the door open. "Can I show you upstairs?"

Charles nodded and followed the maid up to the bedroom.

"Come in, come in." Mr Wetherby beckoned Charles over to the side of the bed. "I'm afraid this room's as much an office as a bedroom nowadays. This confounded pain won't leave me alone. It doesn't matter how much laudanum I take ... but enough of me. What can I do for you? How's the business doing?"

Charles coughed to clear his throat. "Have you seen how much snow we've had lately?"

Mr Wetherby frowned. "Of course I have, I haven't been in bed for the last three weeks. What's that got to do with anything?"

"The biggest seller we have is rubber bicycle wheels along with other cycling accessories, but with the snow demand has dropped. The last shipment is still in the warehouses on Temple Street and we have another shipment due next week."

Mr Wetherby's frown deepened. "So you'll have to store that as well? You need to postpone the next delivery until the summer."

"I have, I went to New York before Christmas and changed the schedule for the rest of the year, but ..." Charles studied his hands "... the problem is, the next shipment was ready to sail and we don't have enough capacity to store it. By chance, the building next door on Temple Street is empty and if we could rent it for six months that should do us."

"But ...?" Mr Wetherby said.

"But with so much stock we're struggling with cash flow."

"So you need more money?" The lines on Mr Wetherby's face were rigid and he winced as he adjusted his position in bed. "You didn't have this problem last year, yet I remember we had snow then as well. Are you sure you're telling me everything?"

"Last year, the freezing temperatures didn't last for as long and we were getting fewer shipments. This has been a lesson for us and I've changed the orders so they're more suited to the seasons. Unfortunately, that won't take effect until the summer."

"I'm not happy about this." Mr Wetherby's chest wheezed as he coughed. "I thought you were different to your father and brother. They both thought I had a never-ending supply of money, always expecting me to give them what they wanted, but let me tell you, I won't waste money on projects that are doomed to fail."

"But I am different. Please, Mr Wetherby. This is no more than a seasonal glitch, as soon as the weather warms up ..."

Mr Wetherby sighed. "On this occasion, I'll loan you

another five hundred pounds. I don't want your business to fail but I will expect it to be repaid in the summer when the stock's moved. Let me tell you something I told your father years ago. This is all you'll get from me. I'm not a bottomless pit."

Charles allowed himself to breathe as he shook Mr Wetherby's hand. "Thank you. I won't let you down and you'll have your money back by the summer."

Chapter Twenty-Nine

With the worst of the weather behind them, Charles paced the main storeroom on Temple Street while Florence watched from a desk in the corner of the room.

"There are too many boxes in here to be able to tell how much stock we've moved over the last couple of months. Can you tell from the figures?" Charles walked behind Florence to look at the figures.

Florence shook her head. "Not yet but I have everything I need to work it out. Why don't you take me back to your house and I'll let you know by tonight. It's too dark to work in here with one gaslight."

Charles hesitated. "Rose is entertaining some of the women from church this afternoon. Can you do them at Wetherby House and I'll call round once Mr Wetherby's asleep?"

It was Florence's turn to hesitate. "I can't do that." Her hands fidgeted in front of her as she chose her words. "I've got something to tell you, please don't be cross with me."

Charles gave her his full attention.

"One day last week, Mr Wetherby found me doing your bookkeeping and was furious. He said it was his money financing the business and he didn't want me having anything to do with it. I haven't told him I'm here today, but I'm surprised he hasn't contacted you."

Charles slapped his hands on his thighs. "Damn man. How can I run a business when he keeps interfering? I hope you told him you'd do no such thing?"

Florence shook her head. "I couldn't, he made me cry. Aunt Sarah-Ann told me to go to Eleanor's for the night, which I did."

"What did you tell her for, why didn't you come to me?"

Florence continued to twist her fingers. "I thought you'd be cross with me for being careless ... but I didn't expect him to come downstairs when he did. He'd been in bed for weeks."

Charles put his hand to his head as he paced across the floor. "What did Eleanor say?"

"She was cross with him and said it wasn't my fault. She's arranged for me to go away for a few months while he calms down. I only found out I was going yesterday."

"Where are you going?"

"To Oxford to stay with Aunt Hannah and Mr Goodwood. Do you remember them? They have their own laundry business and Aunt Hannah thinks I'll be able to carry on with my bookkeeping. I leave next week."

Charles glared at her. "You can't leave, just like that."

"I'm sorry." Florence stared at her feet. "I don't have any choice. Mr Wetherby doesn't want me at Wetherby House any more."

"Damn that man, it's as if he's deliberately trying to sabotage me. It will cost me three times as much to hire a clerk to do the work you're doing. We haven't got that sort of money to spare. The sooner that man dies and stops interfering in everyone else's business the better."

. . .

CHARLES TOOK a deep breath as he climbed down from the carriage and stared up at Wetherby House. He'd been avoiding the place for weeks but since he'd received the letter instructing him to come for Sunday dinner, he hadn't slept. He held out a hand to help Rose climb down but before she had both feet on the ground, the sound of William Junior's carriage pulling onto the drive sent a shiver down his spine.

"Uncle William, Aunt Olivia. I wasn't expecting you to be here."

"Of course we're here, we come every Sunday. Charlotte and Mr Mountford will be here too."

Charles eyed his cousin Henry as he stood between his parents. *I bet he never has to explain himself like this.* "Lead the way then."

As the maid opened the door, Charles was relieved that Margaret was in the hallway. She clapped her hands together when she saw them.

"I'm so glad you could come. Aunt Sarah-Ann said I can sit with you over dinner."

Margaret showed them into the front room where Mr Wetherby and Aunt Sarah-Ann were seated on either side of the fireplace. Sarah-Ann looked elegant in a dark green dress, decorated at the neck with an elaborate brooch, but Charles flinched at the sight of Mr Wetherby. Slumped in his chair, he was a shell of his former self, and his spindly frame refused to hold him upright. His eyes had sunk into their sockets since the last time Charles had seen him and only the beard gave his face any fullness. Charles extended his hand to him.

"Mr Wetherby, thank you for the invite."

Mr Wetherby nodded. "Forgive me for not standing up. The pain is much more manageable if I stay seated."

"Of course." Charles looked around for a seat and positioned himself between Rose and Margaret on the settee.

William Junior stood behind his father's chair. "Father's seen some of the best doctors in the country and has tried the latest medicines, but alas, it is good old laudanum that serves him best. Are you due another dose?" His voice grew louder as he spoke to Mr Wetherby.

"I've had one. I'll be fine in a few minutes. Go and tell the maid to bring the sherry in."

"How's your mother?" Sarah-Ann said to Rose. "And Daisy and Lilly. I hardly ever see them."

"They're fine, thank you. She said you must call if you're ever in Kings Norton."

"I'd love to but I can't go far at the moment." She glanced at Mr Wetherby, who seemed not to notice.

"Do you get out much?" Charles asked Mr Wetherby.

"Not as much as I'd like. I've been to church this morning, but that will be it for a few days."

"I keep Father informed of everything he needs to know." William Junior accepted a glass of sherry from the maid. "I'm torn between Birmingham and Handsworth nowadays. It would have made life so much easier if your father was still with us."

Charles glared at his uncle as Margaret took hold of his clenched fist. "I'm sure he would rather be here than where he is." His voice was cold and steady.

"Enough," Mr Wetherby said. "We'll talk about the business after dinner, it's no conversation for the ladies. Now, tell me what your brother's up to."

"He's still with the police, he's an inspector now and doing very well."

Mr Wetherby grunted.

"And some news for you, Aunt Sarah-Ann. We received a

letter last week to say that his wife Bella is in the family way again."

Sarah-Ann clapped her hands under her chin. "How lovely, it will be their third, won't it? When's it due?"

Charles turned to Rose for an answer.

"In December. They're hoping it'll arrive before Christmas."

"It's such a shame I don't see William-Wetherby any more." She glanced again at Mr Wetherby. "Maybe one day."

BY THE TIME the ladies retired to the front room, Charles wished he hadn't eaten such a large portion of sponge pudding. His stomach churned as he watched William Junior pour the port and hand a glass to each of the men around the table.

"Another splendid dinner," Mr Mountford said as he stretched back in his chair to light his pipe. "If you ever let this cook go, you can send her to us. We're looking for another one. It'll be the third this year."

"I'm glad you didn't mention that while Olivia was here," William Junior said. "She's having so much trouble getting a full complement of maids, it's all she talks about. I bet she's at it now."

Mr Mountford laughed. "What about you, Charles? Do you have the same problems?"

Charles shook his head. "No we don't, we like to keep things simple."

"Enough of domestic issues, leave that for the women," Mr Wetherby said. "We need to talk about Charles's business."

Charles's heart skipped a beat and he wiped the palms of his hands on his trouser legs. "I'm sure Uncle William and Mr Mountford aren't interested in my business. Not to mention Henry."

"On the contrary. Both of them are picking up more and more of the day-to-day running of my affairs and as I'm a major stakeholder in your business, they need to understand the issues you face. I can't update them because I haven't spoken to you properly since I lent you the additional five hundred pounds. I had hoped you'd call to keep me informed, but instead I've had to summon you. Are you trying to hide something?"

Charles wiped his brow as beads of perspiration broke out around his hairline. "Not at all, we've been busy."

"I'm glad to hear it. As I recall, the last time we spoke, your sales had slumped owing to the bad weather and you were looking to increase your storage capacity. You promised to pay back the loan of five hundred pounds by the middle of the year, which will be upon us next month."

"Yes." Charles glanced around at the four sets of eyes staring at him. "Business has picked up, but not quite as we hoped."

Mr Wetherby's eyes narrowed. "Explain."

"We've moved quite a lot of stock since January, enough to pay you your five hundred pounds back, but we have another shipment due next month and I need the money to pay for that."

"You have another one coming and you haven't sold the stock you already have? I thought that was the reason for your trip to America last year, to reduce the number of shipments."

Charles gulped. "It was ... and I did, but it wasn't that simple. When I signed the contract I agreed to take thirty deliveries over three years. Unfortunately, my contact in America won't let me out of it. We've reduced their frequency and they'll now be spread over four years, but I have to take all thirty."

Mr Wetherby winced as he leaned forward in his seat. "How many have you had so far?"

"The one next month will be twenty-five."

Mr Wetherby's gaze was intense. "Then what?"

"The shipment after that is October with another one in February. It will give us more time to sell the stock and we'll be getting more seasonal items with each shipment so it should be easier to sell."

"Aren't you getting resales to previous customers?" Mr Mountford asked.

"We are, but slowly." Charles took a deep breath. "We sold a lot to them during the first year but they're not getting through the stock as fast as we'd like."

"You must have known that before you started," William Junior said. "Didn't you do any forward planning before you put your orders in?"

Charles turned to Mr Wetherby, his eyes wide. "Please, Mr Wetherby, can you give us more time? We know we've made mistakes, but we're learning."

"Have you replaced that fool of a sister of yours as bookkeeper? What were you thinking giving her a job like that? Don't you have any idea about the failure of your father's business? It was all your mother's fault."

"It was because he had a bad partner. Mother had been dead for three years by the time he filed for bankruptcy."

"Trust me when I tell you that if it hadn't been for your mother, he would never have needed that partner in the first place. Now, have you hired a clerk to do your accounts?"

"Not yet." Charles's voice was barely audible. "They cost about three times as much as I was paying Florence and I haven't got the money."

"You may find that when someone reputable goes through the figures, things aren't what they seem." Mr Wetherby's face was grey as he turned to William Junior. "Now, about this money he owes us, can we afford to be without it for another three months?"

William Junior and Mr Mountford exchanged glances. "It's putting us in a difficult situation," William Junior said. "We had planned to buy some new equipment with it. If it isn't repaid, we'll have to liquidate some assets."

"Mr Mountford?" Mr Wetherby eyed his son-in-law.

"The purchase of the two properties on Summer Lane is still to go through. We had planned on putting some of the money towards them."

Mr Wetherby turned back to Charles. "This can't go on. I hope you understand the inconvenience you're causing us."

Charles tried to speak but Mr Wetherby cut him off.

"I don't believe there's any intent in your underachievement, but rather I would say your problems are down to naivety." Mr Wetherby paused as Charles held his breath. "With that in mind, I'll extend the loan until September, on condition that William Junior takes over the running of the business. Henry, I want you to work with your father on this. It will be a lesson on how not to run a business."

"Take over?" Charles's eyes were wide.

"Yes, I'm sorry, but I can no longer trust you on your own. Three months should give you time to turn the business around. At that point you can either repay the money and continue unsupervised, or I call in the loan and you deal with the consequences."

Charles downed the glass of port in front of him and nodded. "Yes, Mr Wetherby. Thank you. I'll do everything I can to make it a success."

Chapter Thirty

Liverpool, Lancashire

As they approached midsummer, William-Wetherby waited on the concourse at Lime Street station as the Birmingham train pulled up alongside the platform. At least Charles had told them he was coming this time. He watched his brother plod down the platform as if he were carrying the weight of the world on his shoulders.

"What's the matter?" William-Wetherby held out his hand to his brother.

"Travelling third class for one thing. How do they get away with putting people in such terrible conditions?"

William-Wetherby raised an eyebrow. "Is the business still struggling?"

Charles sighed. "You could say that. We had cash flow problems, as you know, but Mr Wetherby lent us some money and we were managing until a month ago."

"Let me guess, he wants his money back."

Charles grimaced. "He does, but not yet. The problem is,

he's sent Uncle William in to 'help' us out and he's taken over the business. I'd swear he's trying to destroy us."

William-Wetherby put his hand on his brother's shoulder. "Come on, you sound as if you could do with a rum."

Once Charles was seated, William-Wetherby placed two large rums in front of his brother and sat down. The first lasted no more than five seconds before Charles slammed the glass back on the table.

"Did you ever deal with Uncle William when you worked for Mr Wetherby?"

William-Wetherby forced a laugh. "Fortunately, I managed to miss him. I was in Birmingham and he was in Handsworth. Father never had a good word to say about him though and Sid regularly told me how incompetent he was."

Charles took a deep breath. "If he's that bad, Mr Wetherby must be aware of it, he's not stupid."

"If he's as ill as you say, he may have no choice." William-Wetherby smiled. "It does give you a sense of justice though. After all those years of building up his empire, the only thing Mr Wetherby can do is pass it to William Junior. If there's a God in this world he'll see it all crash about his feet before he dies. That would make up for so much."

"I hope you're not including my business and our inheritance in that."

"Of course not, but they're nothing but a speck compared to everything else he's got going on. He could pay for both out of petty cash if he wanted to."

"Maybe, but the way he's shaping, it'll be my business Uncle William destroys first. I presume you heard that Florence has moved to Oxford to get away from him?"

William-Wetherby nodded. "She wrote and told me he found her doing your bookkeeping. She escaped lightly, he threatened to have Mother imprisoned when he found her doing his accounts. In fact, that was the reason she went into the asylum for the second time."

"I didn't know that." Charles shook his head. "What is his problem? He insisted we hire a qualified clerk. Have you any idea how much that's costing us?"

"A lot more than Florence, I imagine."

Charles downed his second rum. "Uncle William's come in and discounted everything to the point where we're making a loss. If he won't let us put the prices up again, we might as well give up now."

"Why don't you talk to him?"

"I've tried, but the problem is, since I signed my contract with the Americans, British manufacturers have started making similar goods for half the price it costs to import mine. I know we have to compete, but we're losing money with every sale. He's opened another warehouse in Old Square so we can buy British as well, but the profit on that isn't going to be enough to offset the loss on the American goods."

William-Wetherby put his hand on Charles's shoulder and signalled to the barman for another rum. "So, what are you doing here?"

"I'm expecting another shipment on Wednesday, which I need to sign for. Why did I think this whole venture was a good idea?"

"You did well for a couple of years, I'm sure things will pick up."

Charles stared at his empty glass as the barman handed him another rum.

William-Wetherby waited until they were alone again. "Would it be worth asking Mr Wetherby if you can offset the money he's lent you against the legacy he's leaving us? He needn't redo his will, just add a codicil to say that upon your inheritance, you would repay five hundred pounds to the estate?"

Charles sighed as he stared into his glass. "I don't know. It's difficult to talk about his death when he's looking so ill, but perhaps I'll try next time I visit him. I've got nothing to lose."

Chapter Thirty-One

As the darkness descended on Christmas Eve, William-Wetherby pushed open the front door before he stepped back onto the pavement to pick up the three-foot Christmas tree he had carried home.

"Look what I've got." He smiled at his sons as they raced towards him.

Edward's eyes were like saucers as he studied the tree. "What's that?"

"It's a Christmas tree," Fred squealed. "Is that right, Mr Jackson?"

"It is." William-Wetherby turned to his son. "If we put it up tonight, Father Christmas might come and leave a present for you while you're asleep."

"A present?" He turned to Albert who toddled up behind him. "We're getting a present."

Albert chuckled and grabbed hold of William-Wetherby's leg.

"Where's Granny?" William-Wetherby asked. "Isn't she here looking after you?"

"I'm here." Mrs Booth walked out of the scullery. "Tea's

almost ready and Bella's getting herself dressed so she can join us."

"Mammy's coming downstairs." Edward bounced around the living room. "Will she bring baby Stephen with her?"

"Only if you're good." Mrs Booth bent down to pick Albert up. "Now come and sit at the table."

"Is Bella up to dressing the tree?" William-Wetherby asked. "It's not two weeks since Stephen was born."

"She'll be fine. It's not as if he's her first." Mrs Booth walked over to the fireplace. "There's a card here for you from Birmingham."

"Eleanor." William-Wetherby smiled as he recognised the handwriting and tore at the top of the envelope. He took out a card with a picture of a robin on the front. "With love from Eleanor, Joseph and Dorothy." As he opened the card, a letter dropped from it. "Never one to miss an opportunity to write." William-Wetherby opened the letter and raised an eyebrow as he read. "She's expecting another baby ... in May next year."

"That's nice," Mrs Booth said. "Does she have anything else to say?"

"Nothing we don't know. Like everyone else, she's concerned about Charles. He's going to Aunt Mary-Ann's house for Christmas, but since he gave Mr Wetherby the money back, he's struggling."

"Well, I hope he gets himself sorted." Mrs Booth held out a bowl of soup to William-Wetherby. "Now, let me go and help Bella down the stairs."

As soon as Bella arrived at the bottom of the stairs, William-Wetherby stood up and held a chair out for her. "How are you feeling?"

"Fine. I've fed Stephen and put him down for a sleep so we should have a couple of hours to decorate the tree."

"Can I help?" Fred said.

"You can come home and help me," Mrs Booth said. "We have our own tree."

Fred jumped to his feet. "We do! Why didn't you tell me? Can we go now?"

"Sit and finish your soup. You can help me with the turkey as well. It still needs making ready for the oven."

Bella clapped her hands in front of her. "Did you save me some feathers when you plucked it? I'll be making hats again in the New Year so we can't waste them."

WITH JANUARY BEHIND THEM, William-Wetherby looked at the clock on the glass façade of the railway station and sighed. He needed to be in work for two o'clock and at this rate he was going to be late. Turning through ninety degrees, he began pacing the concourse. Charles should have arrived ten minutes earlier, but there was still no sign of him. Finally, as the clock struck one o'clock the train pulled into the platform and Charles was one of the first off. William-Wetherby watched as he hurried towards him.

"What time do you call this?" William Wetherby smiled as he spoke.

"Don't start," Charles said. "It's bad enough being in third class without being delayed as well. Come on, let's find a tavern."

"I can't, not now. I need to be in work in less than an hour."

Charles looked his brother up and down. "Hence the uniform?"

"Precisely. I need to be at the police station for two o'clock. You can tell me what's going on while we walk."

Charles's shoulders dropped as he followed William-Wetherby from the station. "Uncle William's basically ruined the business and refuses to give me any more capital."

"Which is why you needed money from me for the train fare?"

"Exactly. It was the only way I could agree to being Stephen's godfather."

"Won't Mr Wetherby help?"

Charles shook his head. "He's helped in so far as he's told Uncle William to look after the main business rather than overseeing mine, but that's only because his business is more important. To be honest, I think he's given up. Uncle William told me he rarely sleeps for more than an hour at a time and he's in constant pain."

"That's a shame."

"Quite." Charles sniggered. "But it means Uncle William and Mr Mountford are in charge of everything now."

"Has all your money gone?"

"If we manage to sell any stock, we'll have a bit, but I'm still contracted to take another three shipments after this one. I can't afford them but my 'friendly' American has threatened legal action if I don't."

"If you haven't got the money, you haven't got the money. Have you told him that?"

"He's not interested. I'm tempted to file for bankruptcy, just to get out of it."

William-Wetherby stopped and put his hand on Charles's arm. "Don't even think of it. You weren't around to see the effect it had on Father. I wouldn't wish it on anyone, especially not the public hearing. It was the one thing that affected Father more than anything else. That and Arthur."

"Arthur? Who's he?"

William-Wetherby sighed. "You didn't get that letter?" When Charles shook his head, William-Wetherby continued. "He was our brother, or at least our half-brother. He was born to Lydia while you were away. Poor little thing died of starvation because Father couldn't provide for them after the bankruptcy. Father tried to commit suicide when he found out."

Charles's eyes were wide. "Why didn't anyone tell me?"

William-Wetherby shrugged. "It was something we tried not to talk about. Now I think about it, only Aunt Mary-Ann, Mr Diver and Lydia knew about the suicide attempt. Father threw himself into the canal at the spot Mother drowned. Mr Diver jumped in to save him, which is quite possibly what killed him. His chest was never the same afterwards."

"Is that why he died? I always wondered how he'd developed a bad chest; he was as fit as a fiddle when I went away."

"I don't suppose we'll ever know for certain, but what I'm trying to say is, please don't make yourself bankrupt, unless you have absolutely no other choice. You've no idea what it's like."

"But what else can I do?"

"Why don't we talk about it tomorrow. I've got the day off for the baptism and as soon as the service is over and everyone's back at the house, we can slope off."

Charles nodded. "As long as the drinks are on you. I've only got two shillings to last me until I get home."

Chapter Thirty-Two

N o sooner had Charles become godfather to Stephen than he was required at his second baptism of the year, this time for Eleanor's newborn son. While he stood in the hall waiting for Rose, he examined his reflection in the mirror.

"You haven't got time for that, we're going to be late."

Charles stared at his wife as she hurried down the stairs, her hat and coat fastened.

"You're one to talk, I've been waiting half an hour. Eleanor's going to wonder where we are." Charles held the door open for her. "We'll have to go straight to the church at this rate."

"You know it's not easy for me going to these occasions. I'd rather not arrive an hour before the service to coo over someone else's baby."

Charles let his shoulders slump; she always put on a brave face, but he knew how much it hurt. "It'll be your turn soon enough."

"I just wish Mother wouldn't go on about it so much. I'd like her to be a grandmother as much as she would, but I'm sure she thinks I'm doing it deliberately."

As they took their seats in the carriage, Charles held his wife's hand. "This will be the last one for this year and we'll leave as soon as we can."

Rose gave a weak smile. "Thank you, I'll try and keep my smile in place."

With the late spring sun shining on the front of the church, Charles and Rose waited for Eleanor and Mr Keen's guests to arrive. They hadn't been there long when William Junior and Olivia arrived with Henry.

"Uncle William, Aunt Olivia." Charles nodded his head as they approached. "Didn't you go to the house either?"

"No, unfortunately not," William Junior said. "Father's in such pain we like to have someone with him around the clock, in case he needs anything."

"I'm sorry about that; it must be difficult."

"You've no idea. We have nurses attending to him, but the laudanum stopped working months ago. It's tragic to see such a proud and upstanding man reduced to a state of helplessness."

"I had hoped to speak to him; do you think that would be possible?"

William Junior shook his head. "No, it's out of the question. He has severe melancholy at the moment and he doesn't need you making him worse."

"Perhaps we can talk then. After the service." Charles nodded to a small procession of carriages arriving outside the church. "My soon-to-be godson has arrived."

ONCE THE FAMILY returned to Eleanor's house, Charles found his uncle alone by the fireplace.

"What did you want to talk about?" William Junior took a sip from a glass of sherry.

"I need your help. I have another shipment next month and if I can't raise two hundred pounds my only option is to file for bankruptcy. I've tried everything I can to avoid asking you, but without success. After everything that happened to Father, I hoped you might want to save me from that."

"What happened to all the stock you had when I left, did you sell that?"

"You know it's not that simple. With cheap British alternatives available, whenever I sell the American stock I make a loss. I want to hold on to it until the prices start to rise."

"Which means you want me to pay for stock that will sit in a warehouse and do nothing? Do I look stupid?"

Charles bit his tongue before he answered. "I don't want your money, I just want an advance from the money Mr Wetherby owes us. William-Wetherby's shown me the letter confirming we'll receive a legacy when your father dies, but I need it now. If you could loan me two hundred pounds, I'll be able to pay you back from the inheritance."

William Junior's face was stern. "My father owes you nothing and I'm not troubling him with this. To do what you ask would mean amending his will and he only rewrote it last year. He's in too much pain to trouble him with it."

"He rewrote his will?" Charles's eyes were wide. "Why?"

William Junior shrugged. "A lot had changed since the previous one and he wanted to make sure it was up to date. It's not unusual. Now, if you'll excuse me, I've finished with this conversation. My father has suffered enough over these last few years and God willing, the Lord will put him out of his misery before he gets any worse. That's when you'll get what's rightfully yours."

"You might have had enough of this conversation, but I need some money."

"Well, you have two warehouses full of stock. I suggest you get out there and start selling it."

Chapter Thirty-Three

Liverpool, Lancashire

Bella placed a plate of cold meat and cheese onto the table and walked back to the scullery to return with a pot of tea.

"I might be late home tonight," William-Wetherby said. "A few of the lads from the station are having a night out and they've asked me to join them. We're going into town."

"Well, don't make a noise when you come in." Bella walked to the door to collect the post that had just arrived. She handed the envelopes to William-Wetherby and buttered two slices of bread for Edward and Albert.

"Perhaps I won't go out tonight after all." William-Wetherby put his letter down and rubbed the fingers of one hand across his eyes.

Bella looked up. "What's the matter?"

"Charles and Mr Hains have filed for bankruptcy."

"Oh my. I didn't think it would come to that. Why?"

"The Americans wanted their money and they couldn't pay."

Bella's brow furrowed. "Can foreigners force someone into bankruptcy?"

"Not as such, but filing for bankruptcy was the only way for them to get out of paying their debts. Now all the assets of the business will be sold and the Americans will have to accept whatever money they make. It could be considerably less than they were owed, which serves them right. He told them often enough he wanted to cancel the contract."

"Poor Charles ... and Rose. She'll suffer as much as him."

William-Wetherby picked up the letter again. "He says Aunt Mary-Ann is going to pay the rent for them until he finds another job. I never got to the bottom of why she couldn't lend him the money, but at least he won't be homeless. He thought moving in with her would be the worst of it; he's no idea what's coming."

"It's not the same as it was for your father though, is it?"

"Things have improved, but he'll still have to go through the public humiliation. He'll hate that."

BY THE TIME William-Wetherby arrived home from work, there was a second letter waiting for him. Bella watched as he opened the envelope.

"Is it from Charles again?"

"It is, and judging by the handwriting I'd say he wrote it in a hurry." William-Wetherby's forehead creased as he studied the letter. "He went to Wetherby House to tell Mr Wetherby what he'd done, but Aunt Sarah-Ann wouldn't let him upstairs." William-Wetherby grinned at his wife. "He says the old man's developed blood poisoning and he's unlikely to recover. It's only a matter of days."

"You shouldn't be so happy to know that someone's dying."

"How else do you expect me to react? The man ruined my

life, and the lives of my brother and sisters, not to mention Mother and Father's. If you think I'll mourn his loss, you're mistaken. I like to think that this is God's way of punishing him."

"Don't mock," Bella said. "You should know God will judge us all before the end."

"Well, he'd better start now with Mr Wetherby, he's a lot to do."

"That's enough. Will you go to the funeral?"

William-Wetherby stared out of the window. "I'm not likely to be invited and it would be hypocritical if I did."

"What about the reading of the will? Is that likely to be after the funeral?"

"It could be and I should go for that. I've no reason to stay away from Birmingham any more and so it's about time I saw the rest of my family again."

THE LETTER WILLIAM-WETHERBY had waited seven years for arrived five days later. A cold chill ran down his spine as he read the words on the page. Mr Wetherby was dead.

"Has he gone?" Bella sat opposite him at the table.

"He has. Finally. The funeral's next week in Handsworth."

Bella reached across the table and took her husband's hand. "What are you thinking?"

"I don't know. I've wanted him dead for so long, but it's a strange feeling. It's the end of an era."

"I thought you'd be happy."

"I am, but it means he'll never be made to pay for the things he did. There's a part of me wishes I'd reported him to the police years ago, but I didn't because I wanted his money. Was that wrong?"

"Of course it wasn't. You knew the evidence would be difficult to prove. You did what you had to."

"Charles wants me to go to the funeral." He looked at Bella.

"I think you should. Laying him to rest may help you move on. He has no control over you now."

William-Wetherby nodded. "You're right. I'll write to Charles and tell him I'll take the train to Birmingham on Tuesday."

Chapter Thirty-Four

Handsworth, Staffordshire

As the front door of his sister's house opened, William-Wetherby stepped into the hallway and wrapped his arms around Eleanor, squeezing her as tightly as he dared. Within a minute, Margaret joined them and he gave her an equally affectionate hug.

"It's wonderful to see you both. I've been looking forward to this day for years."

"I can't believe you're here." Eleanor took hold of his arm and walked him into the front room.

As he was about to sit down, he heard someone racing down the stairs. Seconds later, Florence flew into the room and threw her arms around his neck.

William-Wetherby stared at her. "What are you doing here? I thought you were in Oxford."

"And miss everyone being together? When I knew you were coming for the funeral, I persuaded Mr Goodwood that I ought to go too. I can only stay until tomorrow evening though."

William-Wetherby smiled at her. "That's no worse than me. I struggled to get time off and I'm going to be working without a break for weeks after this."

"So we'd better make the most of it. How are the boys, and Bella and Mrs Booth and Fred? I'm so looking forward to seeing Stephen. He must be growing up already."

William-Wetherby laughed. "He is, they all are, but I haven't brought them with me this time."

Florence's shoulders slumped. "What a shame."

"This is supposed to be a solemn occasion," Margaret said.

"You're right, but you have to make allowances for the fact that Mr Wetherby caused us so much pain," William-Wetherby said. "I for one will not shed a tear."

WITH THE SUN high in the sky, William-Wetherby leaned forward in the seat of the carriage to open the door. He jumped down and held out a hand for Margaret before glancing up at the house in front of him. Wetherby House.

Charles joined him. "Have they got enough horses and carriages?"

"What did you expect? This was never going to be your average funeral." William-Wetherby studied the funeral cortège lining the street. "A family could live for weeks on the money they'll spend on this, and for what?"

Charles put his hand on his brother's shoulder. "Don't upset yourself."

"I won't." William-Wetherby sighed. "I'll see you in church, I'm not coming into the house." As he made to leave, a small carriage pulled up beside him causing a grin to break out on his face. "Sid! How marvellous to see you, and you, Mrs Storey."

"Mr Jackson, my brother has just died. This is no time for

joviality." Mrs Storey straightened her back as she stepped from the carriage.

"No, I'm sorry." The smile slipped from William-Wetherby's face. "May I offer my condolences."

Mrs Storey nodded, the thickness of her veil shielding her face. "Thank you. We're in deep shock as you can imagine."

William-Wetherby watched her walk towards the house before turning back to Sid. "She's taken it badly?"

Sid kicked at some loose stones on the pavement. "I suppose so."

William-Wetherby glanced at the ruddy face of his friend before noticing him scratching at the red skin on the palms of his hands. "They look sore, have you been working too hard?"

Sid let out a sarcastic laugh. "Chance would be a fine thing. Are you coming in? I need a couple of sherries before we have to leave."

William-Wetherby patted Sid on the back. "No, you go in. I'll see you after the service."

WILLIAM-WETHERBY POSITIONED himself alongside Charles in the middle of the mourners as they filed out of church to follow the coffin to its final resting place. He tried not to stare at his uncle, but he barely recognised him with his heavily receding hairline and significantly expanded waistline. He clearly still liked entertaining customers. Maybe now Mr Wetherby had gone, he would actually do some work.

As the group left the church, William-Wetherby glanced to his left, to the site of his parents' graves. He must try to find them before he left, but it wouldn't be easy with no headstone to mark them. As soon as he got some money, getting a headstone would be the first thing he did.

With a sigh, he followed the group as they turned to the right and headed up the incline towards the upper graveyard.

At the top, the magnificent headstone, which had been erected in memory of his grandmother and her sister, had been moved to one side and would no doubt be engraved with Mr Wetherby's name in the days to come.

He didn't hear the words of the rector but glanced up when he heard the first thud of earth landing on the light oak of the coffin. William Junior handed the spade to Mr Mountford, who in turn passed it to Mr Wetherby's brother Thomas. *I'd forgotten he'd be here. They must have made up while I was away.*

"Come on, let's go back to the church before William Junior accosts us." Charles tugged on his jacket. "The will's going to be read before we go back to the house."

William-Wetherby and Charles walked back into the church and took their seats on the aisle next to their sisters.

"I didn't see Sid by the grave, did you?" William-Wetherby asked.

Charles cocked his head to one side. "I didn't notice, but now you mention it, he's probably nipped off for a quick drink."

William-Wetherby shook his head. "Such a shame."

Aunts Charlotte and Olivia were seated on the front pew as the mourners returned, and William Junior and Mr Mountford joined them before Mr Wetherby's solicitor took his position at the front of the church. After welcoming everyone, he withdrew a scroll from his bag and slowly unfolded it.

"This is the Last Will and Testament of Mr William Wetherby of Wetherby House, Handsworth, in the County of Staffordshire. It was signed on the twenty-first day of July, in the year eighteen hundred and ninety-six."

William-Wetherby glared at Charles. "Eighteen ninety-six, that was only last year."

Charles nodded as the solicitor read slowly, pausing after each sentence. "I bequeath to my son, William Wetherby

Junior, all my household effects. I bequeath to my executors and trustees, the aforesaid William Wetherby Junior, my daughter Charlotte Mountford and my friend James Green, control of my fifty freehold houses on Summer Lane and my thirteen leasehold houses on Frankfort Street until such time as they see fit to convert them into money."

"Who knew he had so many houses," Charles said. "He must have owned most of Summer Lane."

"Until sold, the houses and all the monies and investments will be placed in trust for my daughter Charlotte Mountford. From this trust she will receive the net proceeds as an annual income for the rest of her life."

"Aunt Charlotte's getting the lot?" Charles's eyes were wide. "What about everyone else?"

William-Wetherby continued listening. "They haven't given up on having a child. Any future baby will inherit the lot when she dies. Uncle William only gets it if she has no children."

"He won't like that."

"To the children of my late wife by her former husband ..." The solicitor paused and Charles nudged William-Wetherby. "To the children of my late wife by her former husband ... I leave nothing as they have been sufficiently provided for by me in my lifetime."

The words reverberated around William-Wetherby's head as the blood drained from his face. *Nothing. I gave up everything for nothing?* The solicitor's voice faded in his ears and he swayed in his chair and spots flickered before his eyes. His attention was brought back to the church when Charles jumped to his feet.

"Nothing?" Charles shouted. "That's a lie. We have a letter from Mr Wetherby promising us the money he stole from our father. If this will is allowed to stand, it makes him nothing more than a common thief."

Charlotte gasped as William Junior got to his feet. "Get out of this church."

"You knew about this, didn't you?" Charles strode down the church, his nostrils flaring as he approached his uncle. "You've known all along. Well, let me tell you, you've not heard the last of this. We have detailed records of how Mr Wetherby stole money from our father and we won't hesitate to use them. William-Wetherby, tell him."

William-Wetherby nodded as he swallowed the bile that had risen to the back of his throat. "We have. All the documentation's ready for the police."

"Gentlemen, please." The solicitor held up his hands. "These were Mr Wetherby's wishes and cannot be challenged."

"I think you'll find they can be if he made his money through illicit means." Charles glared at those on the front pew before turning back to William-Wetherby. "We'll see, shall we? Let's get out of here, we've got things to do."

Chapter Thirty-Five

Birmingham, Warwickshire

When William-Wetherby and Charles arrived at
Mary-Ann's house, Rose was waiting to greet
them.

"You're here early."

Charles ran his hand down his wife's back. "Would you
mind taking Daisy and Lilly into the other room. William-
Wetherby and I need to talk."

Rose glanced at her brother-in-law before turning back to
Charles. "I'll ask the maid to bring you some tea."

Once they were alone, Charles handed William-Wetherby
a glass of brandy.

"Drink this. It might help."

"How could he do it? After everything I did to keep out of
his way. Not once did I break the terms of our agreement and
yet this is how he repays me."

Charles drained his glass. "Uncle William knew about this,
but we're not going to leave it unchallenged. If he thinks we're
going to roll over and accept it he can think again."

"He might be as unhappy as us, given that most of the estate went to Aunt Charlotte. He won't get much unless she dies and leaves no children."

"Is that all he left though?" Charles said. "I didn't hear any mention of Wetherby House or Bushwood Farm. They'll be worth a bob or two."

William-Wetherby sipped his brandy. "I'm sure Aunt Mary-Ann will tell us. Although I wonder how she stayed so calm."

"She doesn't need the money like we do."

"I suppose not." William-Wetherby stopped when he heard the front door open. "That'll be her now."

Mary-Ann walked into the back room accompanied by Eleanor, Margaret and Florence. She stared at her nephews before taking a seat.

"That was quite a scene," she said. "Was it absolutely necessary?"

"Of course it was," Charles said. "Mr Wetherby promised us Father's money and William-Wetherby's been stuck in Liverpool for seven years because of it. What did you expect us to do, sit back and say nothing?"

"Like I did?" Mary-Ann raised an eyebrow at Charles.

"With respect," William-Wetherby said. "He didn't ruin your life in quite the way he ruined ours."

Mary-Ann took a deep breath. "And with respect to you, can I remind you that your father was my brother, and he was the only remaining member of my original family. Not only that, the devastation caused by Mr Wetherby led indirectly to the death of my husband. His chest never recovered after he saved William's life."

William-Wetherby stared at the floor. "You're right. I'm sorry, I wasn't thinking."

"I also know about his relationship with Aunt Sarah-Ann and what happened to Mr Flemming. My mother, your grandmother, knew too. Do you think I've found that easy to live with?"

William-Wetherby shook his head.

As the silence grew, Charles spoke. "Did he leave everything to Aunt Charlotte or did we miss anything?"

"She'll get the proceeds from the bulk of the estate, although it's all in trust. I'm not sure William Junior's happy, but he'll receive a sizable amount as well. Mr Wetherby had more houses besides those he left to Charlotte and he put them into a separate trust. Half the money from that will go to Henry and the other half will be split between Charlotte and William Junior. They'll also get annuities of six hundred pounds each."

Charles let out a long whistle. "I knew he was well off, but I'd no idea he had that much. What about everyone else? Did he leave Aunt Sarah-Ann anything?"

Mary-Ann smiled. "She got a paltry two hundred pounds per year."

"I wouldn't say no to two hundred pounds," William-Wetherby said.

"Not many of us would, but Aunt Sarah-Ann looked rather put out. Not as much as his sisters and Thomas though. I think they got a pound a week for life, or something like that. I could be wrong, I'd stopped listening by then."

"So Sid didn't get anything?"

Mary-Ann shook her head as Charles walked to the sideboard and poured her a brandy. She accepted it from him and took a sip. "Despite what you may think, Charlotte isn't happy."

"She's not happy?" Charles stared at his aunt.

"A lot of people misunderstand her, but I spoke to her as we were leaving church and she believes the legacy is nothing more than guilt money for the damage Mr Wetherby did to her."

"What damage?" Charles and Eleanor said in unison.

William-Wetherby glanced at Mary-Ann. "They don't know."

Mary-Ann took another sip of brandy as her cheeks flushed. "No, it's as well they don't."

Charles stood with his mouth open as his aunt refused to say any more. "You can't leave it at that. I thought Aunt Charlotte could do no wrong in Mr Wetherby's eyes. How did he upset her so much?"

Mary-Ann glanced at her nieces who sat silently on the settee. "Eleanor, can the three of you go into the front room. You should spend some time with your cousins."

William-Wetherby noticed his sisters glare at their aunt, before Eleanor led them from the room. Mary-Ann waited for the door to close before she spoke to William-Wetherby. "Have you told him about Arthur?"

"Only that he lived and died and that Father threw himself into the canal."

"You mean there's more?" Charles's mouth dropped open.

"Arthur was born on the day Father was declared bankrupt," William-Wetherby said. "When it was clear that they'd lost everything, I had the idea to let Aunt Charlotte and Mr Mountford have Arthur, for a fee, to raise as their own."

"Mr Wetherby refused to let Charlotte have him, despite her pleading with him," Mary-Ann continued. "Ultimately the child died and she never forgave him. To add to the upset, Mr Mountford refused to consider a child from the workhouse, which is why they never adopted."

"And so she blames Mr Wetherby for the fact she's childless?"

William-Wetherby stared at the floor. "Is there a person in this family whose life Mr Wetherby hasn't destroyed?" He glanced up at Mary-Ann.

"I'd say William Junior's the only one."

"Even he must be upset about the will though. It might mean he has to do some work for a change."

"Unless he gets his hands on Henry's share of the money," Charles added.

William-Wetherby's mouth dropped open. "I hadn't thought of that. If Wetherby House is in trust for Henry, Uncle William will take control of it until he comes of age. That's another four years off. What'll happen to Margaret?"

Mary-Ann considered her nephew. "As long as Aunt Sarah-Ann's there, she'll be fine; even William Junior wouldn't force her out."

"From what I could tell under all the mourning clothes, she's very frail," William-Wetherby said. "She might not last much longer. We need to challenge the will before she dies and leaves Uncle William in charge."

"What will you do?" Mary-Ann asked.

William-Wetherby shrugged. "I've no idea, but I imagine the first thing is to pay the solicitor a visit and find out what he has to say."

Chapter Thirty-Six

William-Wetherby stood on the footpath and stared up at the ornate, four-storey building towering above him. Standing to his left, Charles let out a long whistle.

"Solicitors around here don't come cheap. Can we afford the legal fees if he agrees to the challenge?"

"If he thinks we can win, then I would say so, but not otherwise. Thank goodness he's agreed to give us fifteen minutes for nothing."

Charles stepped forward and pushed on the front door before entering an elegant waiting area.

"Can I help you?" A clerk looked up from behind a desk.

William-Wetherby cleared his throat. "We're here to see Mr Berry. He's expecting us."

The clerk disappeared into another room and came back seconds later. "He's ready for you. Follow me, please."

"What can I do for you?" Mr Berry asked once they were seated.

William-Wetherby spoke. "We've come about Mr Wetherby's last will and testament. We were in church when you read it out."

"Ah yes, an unfortunate incident. How can I help you?"

William-Wetherby pulled a letter from his pocket. "Seven years ago, when our father died, Mr Wetherby promised he would leave one thousand pounds to ourselves and our three sisters as repayment for money he took from our father. I have the letter here to prove it. The will you read out in church is in direct contravention of that undertaking and we want to challenge it."

Mr Berry sat back in his chair without picking up the letter and eyed the two men before him. "You're the sons of his stepson, Mr William Jackson, is that correct?"

"Yes, sir."

"Yes, I remember the conversation well. When he redrafted his will, last year, he was adamant that none of the Jacksons should receive any inheritance due to the amount he had given them over the years. If I remember correctly, he said to me that he had given the family more than they ever deserved and rather than being grateful, they kept coming back for more. As I remember, he commented that he had given Mr Charles Jackson five hundred pounds to support his ailing business."

"That was a loan and I repaid the money earlier this year." Charles's face turned crimson.

"Well, Mr Wetherby said his priority was to his own children, and if they so desired, they could provide any support their stepfamily may need."

"But what about the letter? He promised the money would come to us."

Mr Berry finally picked up the paper before him. "Yes, I remember drafting this. It states that 'based on my Last Will and Testament, dated the fourth of April, 1890, the sum of one thousand pounds will go to the children of my late wife by her first marriage'. The will I read out yesterday superseded all previous versions of the document including the one drafted in eighteen ninety."

William-Wetherby stared at his brother before turning back to the solicitor. "So this letter isn't worth the paper it's written on?"

"I'm afraid not."

William-Wetherby sank back into his chair.

"What about the money Mr Wetherby embezzled from our father?" Charles said. "He caused the bankruptcy, which ultimately led to his death."

"That's a very serious charge. Have the police been informed?"

"Not officially, although I am an inspector with the Liverpool Constabulary." William-Wetherby straightened himself up. "I've a written statement from my father containing a number of accusations that Mr Wetherby wanted destroying. That's why he promised to leave us a legacy and why he had you draft this letter. It's the only reason I didn't report him sooner. I could make the complaint official if it would help."

Mr Berry's frown creased. "In your professional capacity, how robust would you say the evidence against Mr Wetherby is? Would it stand up in court?"

"It's difficult to say for certain, but I do have information to show that payments from my father's business were made to Mr Wetherby even though my father had no knowledge of it. My father testified that the monies paid were the exact amounts that should have gone to his business partner."

"But you don't have the original documents?"

William-Wetherby shifted in his seat as Mr Berry studied him. "I don't, but Uncle William, that is Mr William Wetherby Junior, will have. They were in Mr Wetherby's accounts."

"When did you last see them?"

William-Wetherby's face coloured. "It was a few years ago now, before Father died."

"And do you think Mr Wetherby would leave incriminating evidence lying around for so long, if he knew you were aware of it?"

"Destroying evidence is a criminal offence."

"It's only an offence if an investigation is ongoing. If you were so concerned about it, you should have reported him at the time."

William-Wetherby jumped from his seat and leaned over the desk. "I couldn't because Mr Wetherby promised he would leave us the money in a legacy."

"So you were complicit in the crime? You let him get away with everything because he was going to pay you? You do realise that as a police inspector, you could find yourself in a great deal of trouble over such a matter."

"He was blackmailing me; can't you see that?"

The solicitor shook his head. "I'm sorry, Mr Jackson, but I would suggest that the best course of action is to forget we had this conversation. With it being a free consultation, it hasn't been logged in our records and as long as you make no further allegations, I'll forget everything you've said."

"So you're blackmailing us now?" Charles was on his feet next to William-Wetherby. "After all the sacrifices William-Wetherby's made, isn't there anything we can do?"

Mr Berry shook his head. "You misunderstand me, I'm only trying to help you make the right decision. The only other course of action I can suggest is to wait until we give notice asking for any persons who have claims or demands against the estate to send particulars of said claims to ourselves. We'll pass the details to the executors for consideration."

"When will that happen?"

The solicitor glanced at his calendar. "The will has to be proved first. This could take up to six months from the date of death, and only then can the notice be served. Due to the complex nature of Mr Wetherby's estate, I would anticipate the notice to be served in January."

"But the claims will still go to Uncle William for consideration?" William-Wetherby asked. "Even before we submit anything, you know what his response will be."

"I'm sorry, that's all I can suggest. They are the executors and beneficiaries of the will and I can do little to influence their decisions."

Chapter Thirty-Seven

Neither Charles nor William-Wetherby spoke as they walked down Colmore Row towards the Town Hall. On reaching Christ Church, Charles nudged his brother and pointed towards a public house.

"We need a drink after that."

William-Wetherby nodded and followed him into the bar. "Don't forget we've got no money. A pint of ale and that's it."

Once seated, Charles took a long gulp of his drink. "So, what do we do now?"

William-Wetherby shook his head. "What can we do other than appeal to Uncle William? Although I doubt he'll change his mind."

"You never know, Aunt Charlotte might talk him around. We don't have any argument with her."

William-Wetherby forced a laugh. "Maybe we don't, but you've seen the way Uncle William treats her. She'll have no say in the matter."

"We have to try though. I'm sure Mr Wetherby will have left more than enough money for everyone."

"I hope so." William-Wetherby hooked his thumb into the pocket on his waistcoat. "When's your bankruptcy hearing?"

"Not for another couple of weeks, on the nineteenth of August, but that's only the preliminary hearing. The public hearing is two weeks later."

"At least you have Aunt Mary-Ann. You won't starve or go homeless as long as you have her and Rose."

Charles nodded.

"What do we do about Margaret? I know Aunt Mary-Ann said not to worry, but we have to think of her. Uncle William's going to want to sell Wetherby House, or at least rent it out."

Charles downed his pint. "When do you need to go home?"

"I should have gone today, I'm going to be in enough trouble as it is."

"We must talk to the girls and tell them what's happening. If we go to Aunt Mary-Ann's now we can travel to Eleanor's this afternoon. Florence will have gone, but Margaret should still be there. Come on; drink that ale, we need to go."

AS THE MAID showed them in to Eleanor's house, Margaret stood up and embraced William-Wetherby.

"I thought you'd gone without seeing me."

"As if I would; although I expect I've missed Florence?"

"Yes, she left this morning. Come and tell us how you got on with the solicitor."

William-Wetherby told his sisters what Mr Berry had said before he explained that they would put in a claim when the time came. "We may have a more immediate problem though. As you know, Wetherby House was left in trust to Henry, but we're worried that until he comes of age, Uncle William effectively has control of it." He turned to Margaret. "Have you heard him talking to Aunt Sarah-Ann about what will happen to it?"

Margaret shook her head. "Not as such, but Aunt Sarah-Ann was talking to Elizabeth about moving to Coventry to live with her and Reverend Bloor. Mr Wetherby's death has affected her heart and she doesn't want to live at Wetherby House without him."

William-Wetherby's brow creased. "If Aunt Sarah-Ann's moving out, you'll have to move as well. Uncle William won't keep the house running for you."

"I don't mind." Margaret's cheeks flushed. "It's not been the same since Florence left and now everyone's in mourning, it's even worse."

"I can imagine." William-Wetherby rolled his eyes at Charles. "Aunt Mary-Ann has said you can stay with her when you're not visiting elsewhere. Would you like that?"

Margaret's cheeks changed from pink to scarlet. "I hope you don't mind but Florence has asked if I'd like to go and stay with her at the Goodwoods'. She misses me ... and so I've said yes."

"What do you want to go there for?" Charles said.

"Because I do."

"Leave her alone." Eleanor took her sister's hand. "If that's what she wants to do, then let her."

Charles turned to Eleanor. "When we saw Aunt Hannah at your wedding, she said they might be moving."

Eleanor nodded. "They were thinking about it, but it didn't happen."

Margaret smiled. "Mr Goodwood wanted to grow the business but when the property next door to the laundry became free, he rented that as well. I stayed with them when Florence moved and had a lovely time. They said I could go back whenever I wanted to."

Charles eyed his sister. "Are you sure Florence is the only reason you want to go? You appear a bit too keen to move when you could stay here."

Margaret twisted her fingers together. "Of course it is. Why else would I want to go?"

Chapter Thirty-Eight

Liverpool, Lancashire

I t had been a difficult day at work and the evening sun felt good on William-Wetherby's back as he strolled down Martensen Street. After three weeks with no time off, all he wanted to do was sit down. The front door was open when he arrived home but the sound of crying caused him to pause.

"Aren't you going in, Mr Jackson?" William-Wetherby turned to see Fred standing in the middle of the road, a football under his arm. "Will you come and play football with me? All the lads have gone in."

"Isn't it about time you were in bed?"

"Not yet! I'm ten now."

William-Wetherby glanced up the stairs before turning back to Fred. "Two minutes, before Mrs Jackson comes down."

It took fifteen minutes for Bella to appear at the door. "And how long do you plan on staying out here, William-Wetherby? Your sons are waiting for you upstairs."

William-Wetherby shrugged at Fred. "You heard her, I've got to go. It's time you were in bed too."

Ruffling Fred's hair, William-Wetherby picked up his helmet from the makeshift goal and followed Bella inside.

"That's a turn-up."

"I felt sorry for him," William-Wetherby said. "He's never going to have a dad to play with him, is he?"

Bella put her hands on her hips and smiled. "Are you going soft on me all of a sudden?"

William-Wetherby grinned. "Not at all."

"That's a shame, I like it when you do." She stood on her toes to kiss his cheek. "Stephen's asleep, but go and say good-night to the other two and I'll put your tea on the table."

By the time he came back, a letter rested beside the plate of minced meat and mashed potatoes that waited for him. He opened it immediately.

"Charles?" Bella asked.

William-Wetherby nodded as he read. "He had the first hearing of the bankruptcy earlier this week. He's now officially bankrupt and not allowed to start up any other business until he gets discharged."

"How long does that take?"

William-Wetherby thought back to his father's case. "It should be about a year, but sometimes it's longer." *Sometimes they wait until the shame kills you.*

"At least he has somewhere to live. Can he work in the meantime?"

"He can if anyone will have him." William-Wetherby put the letter on the table and picked up his knife and fork as he continued to read. "He's been to Wetherby House to say farewell to Margaret. She's about to leave for Oxford."

"Well, I hope she finds happiness ... and perhaps an eligible young man."

William-Wetherby ignored Bella and slammed his knife

and fork onto the table before leaping to his feet, the letter grasped in his shaking hand.

"What's the matter?"

"Margaret overheard Uncle William saying he's going to approach the local Conservative party about putting up a memorial for Mr Wetherby. Nothing as simple as a plaque in the local church, apparently he wants something to rival the monument erected in the middle of Birmingham for Mr Chamberlain, the local Member of Parliament. Well, he can think again. I may not be able to get my hands on Father's money but that crook will have a memorial over my dead body." William-Wetherby turned full circle in the middle of the room before glaring at Bella. "Where's the damned writing paper? We've got to stop this. I've used up all my holiday, but if I need to, I'll jolly well go straight back to Birmingham myself."

Bella took hold of her husband's hands. "Calm down. Charles has got time on his hands, surely he can sort it out ... whatever it is you're planning on doing."

"We need to make sure the police, the Conservative Association, the Liberals, the council, the ... the newspapers and anyone else I can think of, know what sort of a man he was. He should not be honoured and I'll make sure no one remembers him if it's the last thing I do ... or if they do, it'll be because he should have hanged."

Bella squeezed his hands. "Take a deep breath. They're not going to do anything immediately, so you have time to think about it. Let me find the writing paper and you can reply to Charles and work out between you what you're going to do."

Chapter Thirty-Nine

After a day at work, William-Wetherby turned into Martensen Street relieved to see that the boys weren't in the road playing.

He arrived at his own front door but walked straight past and into Mrs Booth's living room. She put down her sewing when she saw him.

"I don't often see you here on your own; is everything all right?"

William-Wetherby sighed. "If you mean are Bella and the boys all right, then yes, they're fine, but there's a problem in Birmingham. I'm going to have to go and sort it out and I'd like to take Bella with me. Would you take care of the boys for a few days next week? Maybe move into our house?"

"You've never taken her before."

"No, but she's been saying she wants to meet Eleanor and Aunt Mary-Ann, and so I thought she'd like to go. Besides, I'd like her to travel with me, to take my mind of this memorial they're planning for Mr Wetherby."

"What's happened now?"

"I'd hoped Charles would be able to do most of the work,

but I got a letter today saying he won't be any help. He had the public hearing about the bankruptcy earlier this week and he's in shock. We may need to visit the political associations, church, police, the newspapers, but after everything he's gone through, he says he can't do it. I tried to warn him about it, but he wouldn't listen."

"What will you do?"

"I'll write a number of letters before we leave, but I'm going to hand-deliver them and make sure everyone reads them. I might visit the Conservative Association first and if they drop the memorial plans, there'll be no need to follow up with the others. It would make life easier ... I need to think about it."

"How long will you be away?"

"As long as it takes. I can't take any more time off work so I'm going to have to tell them I'm ill and hope no one comes looking for me."

"Are you sure you know what you're doing? Is this memorial important enough to jeopardise your job?"

William-Wetherby's vision dimmed as the image of Mr Wetherby watching his mother fight for her life leapt to the front of his mind. "Oh yes, it's worth it."

A WEEK LATER, William-Wetherby stood behind Bella as she climbed into the third-class carriage of the train.

"How exciting." She took a seat by the window and glanced around.

William-Wetherby grinned as he placed his hat and their small bag on the overhead storage shelf. "Tell me you feel the same in a couple of hours. These seats will dig into your back long before we arrive in Birmingham, although I wouldn't swap with the passengers who'll stand up all the way."

"I don't care. I've never even been on the overhead railway

VL MCBEATH

around the docks, let alone left Liverpool. I can't wait to see Birmingham and your sister's house. It sounds so grand."

"I'll tell you what, if we have time, and I can borrow Eleanor's carriage, I'll show you our old house on Havelock Road. I might even take you to Wetherby House and show you where we ended up on Summer Lane."

"I'd like that." Bella studied her husband. "As much as I love you, I know you're not one of us, and I'd like to understand where you came from."

William-Wetherby sat up indignantly. "I am not, I'm almost a native Scouser now."

Bella laughed. "And I wouldn't have you any other way."

≈

Birmingham, Warwickshire.

BY THE TIME they arrived in Kings Norton, Eleanor was waiting for them with a pot of tea and a tray laden with cakes.

"Come in," she said as the maid showed them into the back room. "It's lovely to meet you, Bella. William-Wetherby's told me so much about you."

"And he's told me about you too, and about your house, but he didn't say it was this grand." Bella's eyes were like saucers. "What a wonderful room. Lovely, heavy curtains that match the chairs." She ran her hands over the back of the deep red velvet settee. "And a chandelier too."

"Oh, it's not much, but we're comfortable." Eleanor took out a fan and waved it gently in front of her face.

"I'm sure you are. Where are the children?"

Eleanor smiled. "Since I had the baby, I've had a mother's help. She's with them in the nursery."

Bella's mouth fell open. "How marvellous to have so

much help around the house, and not just your mam." She put her hand to her mouth. "I'm sorry."

"Nobody in our area has servants." William-Wetherby explained to his sister.

"They do in Toxteth, which isn't far from us, but once you reach our streets, there's not enough room for the family, let alone maids as well."

"Still, I'm sure it's pleasant," Eleanor said. "Now, come and sit down and tell me all about yourself."

Eleanor was pouring the tea when Charles walked in.

"Here you are." William-Wetherby shook his brother's hand. "How are you doing?"

Charles shook his head. "I know you tried to warn me about the public hearing, but nothing can prepare you for such humiliation. I understand exactly why Father took it so badly."

William-Wetherby's eyes glazed over. "It was hard for everyone. Why they need to humiliate people to such an extent I don't understand. They should be lenient with those who try their best to stay solvent."

"At least it's over now and if I keep a low profile, folks will forget about it."

"So you're not coming with me tomorrow? I'd hoped you might accompany me."

Charles stared at his brother. "I can't do that, not at the moment. Where are you going to start?"

"The Conservative Association. I decided that if we can persuade them to drop their plans for the memorial, we won't need to bother anyone else."

Charles shook his head. "You can't just walk in. Uncle William will be there. I think you'd do better speaking to Mr Barton. He worked closely with Mr Wetherby and I think he's chairman at the moment. He works at the Town Hall, I'd suggest trying there first to see if you can catch him on his own."

Chapter Forty

W illiam-Wetherby stepped down from the carriage as it stopped in Chamberlain Square, directly outside the Town Hall. He paused to study the familiar Roman columns and smiled. It appeared small compared to St George's Hall in Liverpool. He turned slowly to take in his surroundings; Christ Church was still there, even though it was due to be pulled down, and so was the memorial to Mr Chamberlain. It stood like a half-sized church spire with a pool to one side to catch water from a fountain. *Uncle William can think again if he believes Mr Wetherby deserves something like that.*

He pushed on the door into the Town Hall and approached a clerk sitting nearby.

"I'd like to see Mr Barton, please. Is he available?"

"Do you have an appointment?" The man spoke without looking up.

"No, but could you tell him Inspector Jackson would like to speak to him."

The clerk jerked his head up. "I beg your pardon, Inspector. Please, take a seat, I'll tell him you're here."

William-Wetherby smiled as he watched the man scuttle into an office before returning to hold the door open for him. "Please, Inspector, follow me. Mr Barton's between meetings."

"Mr Barton." William-Wetherby held out his hand as the clerk ushered him into the office. "Thank you for seeing me so promptly. I hope I won't take up too much of your time."

Mr Barton wiped his brow with a handkerchief. "Not at all, Inspector. What can I do for you?"

"I've been made aware that you're considering a memorial in honour of the recently departed Mr Wetherby. Is that correct?"

"W-well, yes. But that's Conservative Association business. Not part of my role here."

"Quite, but I wanted to catch you alone. Did you know Mr Wetherby well?"

Mr Barton studied William-Wetherby. "Yes indeed. We were both with the Conservative Association for many years. It was such a shame when he became ill, he was unable to carry out his usual duties."

"Were you aware that during his lifetime he was the cause of a number of crimes, several of them serious?"

Mr Barton paused and stared at William-Wetherby. "Absolutely not. As far as I'm aware, Mr Wetherby was a respectable and generous man. I'd have difficulty believing he was capable of any crime."

"I'm afraid details of his activities have been passed to the police and I'm here to advise you that in light of this information, which may soon become public, it would be wise to abandon any plans for a memorial."

Mr Barton retrieved his handkerchief and wiped his face again. "What sort of crimes are we talking about?"

"I'm afraid to say that the most serious is murder."

Mr Barton gasped and William-Wetherby waited for him to regain his composure before continuing. "I have reason to believe that Mr Wetherby had quite a temper, which on at least one occasion led to him fatally striking a man with whom he had a disagreement."

Mr Barton shook his head. "I don't believe you. It's true he could get angry, but to kill someone? Were there any witnesses?"

"There were, two in fact, and we have the written testimony of the events from one of them. The second witness was unable to testify as we believe Mr Wetherby wilfully left them to drown when he could, in fact, have saved them."

Mr Barton stared at William-Wetherby. "Why are you telling me this?"

"As I'm sure you'll appreciate, while he was alive, Mr Wetherby was an influential man with many powerful friends."

"Well, yes."

"We now believe it was this power that helped him suppress details of these and other offences for years, but with his passing people may be less inclined to keep such information to themselves. It would be most unfortunate if word of his misdemeanours found its way into the press at a time you're planning a memorial in his honour. As someone who was born and raised in and around Birmingham myself, I'd suggest that the idea be quietly dropped to avoid any unnecessary embarrassment."

"Well ... I don't know. I'd need to speak to his son, Mr Wetherby Junior."

"Yes, of course. But before you do, can I leave you a copy of the witness statement concerning the life of Mr Wetherby. I'd particularly like to point out the sections on pages eight and nine." William-Wetherby found the relevant pages and gave Mr Barton time to start reading them. "I'm sure that once you've read the whole document, you'll understand why I would suggest you drop the memorial."

Mr Barton stared at the document, his eyes wide.

"One final thing," William-Wetherby continued. "I have it on authority that the press have received a similar copy of the document. They've agreed to delay publication pending your consideration, but if the memorial goes ahead I've been told they'll have a public duty to publish the information. I've also persuaded them to resist the urge to pass the letter to the Liberals for the time being. I'm sure you wouldn't want them using a letter like this to tarnish the Conservative Party further."

Mr Barton turned the letter over in his hands. "I think I can speak for the whole of the Conservative Association when I say we won't be proceeding with the memorial. It would be better to remember Mr Wetherby as he was."

William-Wetherby stood up and extended his hand to Mr Barton. "A wise decision."

Mr Barton shook William-Wetherby's hand and escorted him into the outer office but they both stopped as the door opposite opened.

"Mr Wetherby Junior." Mr Barton's voice squeaked as he spoke. "I wasn't expecting you today."

William Junior glared at his nephew. "What's this trouble-maker doing here?"

William-Wetherby stood tall, causing his six-foot frame to tower over his uncle. "I came to discuss the memorial you're planning for your father; I don't want you embarrassing the Conservative Association by moving forward with it."

"My father was a loyal servant of this city for nearly forty years and chairman of the Conservative Association for over ten of them. He deserves a memorial."

"I've just given Mr Barton a copy of a testimony relating to some of your father's shadier dealings. It would be unfortunate if the Liberals and the press also received copies."

"You don't have that work of fiction, it was destroyed years ago."

William-Wetherby smirked. "Do you think I was stupid enough to give you the original? Mr Wetherby never could work out whose handwriting was whose. All I did was copy it out for Sid to give you."

William Junior grabbed the lapels of William-Wetherby's jacket. "You blackguard. You'll pay for this."

William-Wetherby pushed his uncle away. "I already have, in more ways than one. If we don't get our rightful share of your father's estate then that letter will be all over the town and his memory will be disgraced."

"My father specifically excluded you from his will."

"Your father cheated us. I have a second letter saying we'd receive one thousand pounds, but Mr Wetherby deliberately changed his will prior to his death. I've spoken to our solicitor and we'll be putting in a claim when the call for creditors is issued."

"You won't get a penny."

William-Wetherby's eyes narrowed. "That would be most unfortunate, but the decision shouldn't all be down to you. I'll be writing to Aunt Charlotte as well. At least Mr Wetherby left more of his money to her than he did you. He wasn't as daft as all that."

"He left my sister that money because she can't work for herself."

William-Wetherby laughed. "She has a husband who's worth more than you; she had no more need of that money than you did."

William Junior lunged forward, but William-Wetherby neatly sidestepped him and opened the door. With an eye on his uncle he turned back to Mr Barton. "If you've ever wondered where Mr Wetherby Junior gets his temper from, wonder no more. As the saying goes, like father like son."

William-Wetherby smiled as he left the Town Hall. That had gone better than he could have hoped for. They just needed to wait for the probate to be finalised, and they should get their money.

~

Liverpool, Lancashire.

SINCE THE TRIP TO BIRMINGHAM, William-Wetherby had worked every day for a month, but as his shift came to an end, he arrived home and threw his helmet across the living room before flopping into a chair. Bella raced into the living room, but stopped when she saw him.

"What's going on?"

"Look at this." He pointed to the three stripes adorning the arm of his tunic. "I've been demoted back to a sergeant."

Bella's mouth opened and closed several times before she spoke. "Why? What happened?"

William-Wetherby sighed. "They found out I wasn't ill when we went to Birmingham. Some kind soul reported me to the Birmingham Constabulary for acting as a local officer when my authority's restricted to Liverpool. They wrote to Liverpool asking why I was working there without permission. The chief was furious."

Bella's eyes were wide. "Who'd do such a thing?"

William-Wetherby laughed. "Isn't it obvious? It's that damned uncle of mine. After I threatened to expose his father, he must have gone to the police."

"But you don't know that."

"They didn't tell me, but it must have been him. Who else would it be? I only kept my job because of what happened over my promotion and they didn't want to lose me again."

William-Wetherby squeezed the arms of the chair until his knuckles were white.

Bella knelt beside him. "You need to forget about them. Once you get your money, you never need to see him again."

William-Wetherby glared at his wife. "You've no idea what I've had to deal with because of them. Even now Mr Wetherby's dead, they're still in my dreams, night after night. If I can do anything in my power to make Uncle William's life difficult, then by God I will."

Chapter Forty-One

With the New Year barely two weeks old, Bella waited by the window for William-Wetherby to walk down the street. As soon as she saw him, she hurried to the door.

"What's the matter?" he asked.

"I think something's happened, but I don't know what." Bella waited while he took off his cape and put his helmet on the table by the door. "You've got three letters from Birmingham, one from Eleanor, one from Charles and one whose handwriting I don't recognise."

William-Wetherby raised an eyebrow and took the letters from her, opening the one with the unknown handwriting.

"It's from Aunt Mary-Ann. Why's she writing to me?" He scanned the text before staring at Bella.

"What's the matter?"

"One of the reasons she wrote was to tell me Aunt Sarah-Ann died last Tuesday. I don't suppose we should be surprised, she looked terrible at Mr Wetherby's funeral."

"But there's something else?"

William-Wetherby stared back at the letter. "Oh yes,

there's something else. I bet that's why Charles has written too." He took a deep breath. "The probate's finally been granted on Mr Wetherby's will. Are you ready? Seventy-three *thousand*, eight hundred and thirty-nine pounds, nineteen shillings and tuppence."

Bella's eyes grew larger. "Seventy-three thousand?" She picked up one of the envelopes and fanned her face.

"I always knew he had a lot of money, but nothing like that. Aunt Charlotte must be getting about fifty thousand pounds. She doesn't need that; it's not as if Mr Mountford's short of a bob or two."

"Open Charles's letter. What does he have to say?"

William-Wetherby tore open the envelope and as he did, a newspaper cutting fell from the folds of the letter. He examined the article before unfolding the piece of paper.

"It's a summary of the will and details of the probate. That's what Charles thinks." He handed Bella the letter, which had nothing but '*£73,839 19s 2d!!!*' scrawled on one side. William-Wetherby stared at Bella. "Nearly seventy-four thousand pounds and he couldn't leave us anything. You know, I didn't think I could hate that man any more than I do, but I was wrong. He didn't make that much money in the last ten years of his life and yet he let Father and then Charles go bankrupt. If I could bring him back to life, I'd kill him."

Bella put the letter onto the table and put her arms around her husband. "We don't need his money. We're happy enough as we are."

"Whether we need his money or not, we're going to get what we were promised. I must reply to Charles about putting in a claim against the estate. The question is, how much do we go for?"

As he spoke, the sound of crying from upstairs caused Bella to rest her forehead on his shoulder. "I'd better go, but you know what, that aunt of yours may have all the money in the world, but I wouldn't swap it for our boys."

William-Wetherby watched Bella head towards the stairs, before he picked up Eleanor's letter and moved to a seat by the fireside. It was the same news, but typical of Eleanor, she was more concerned about Aunt Sarah-Ann. The death of Mr Wetherby had been too much for her, and despite moving to live with Elizabeth her heart had failed. The funeral was being held at Reverend Bloor's church.

"Any more news?" Bella said as she came back downstairs.

"Only that we're too late to go to Aunt Sarah-Ann's funeral. It's tomorrow in a small village near Coventry. It's as well I don't want to go."

"Well, I'm glad. With no more family ties to the Wetherbys I want you to forget about them."

William-Wetherby rested his head on the back of the chair. *I won't ever forget them and if we don't get anything from this estate, the whole of Birmingham will find out what sort of a man he was.*

Chapter Forty-Two

Birmingham, Warwickshire

Charles stared at the letter in his hand before tossing it onto the table and putting his head in his hands. He supposed he should be happy, but it was impossible when his only thought was that they'd been cheated again.

"What's the matter?" Rose asked.

"It's about our claim to Mr Wetherby's estate. When my father was made bankrupt, Mr Wetherby had siphoned about three thousand pounds from his business and so that's what we asked for. We also enclosed a copy of our father's testimony and made it clear we would make it public if the executors refused our claim."

"Did they turn you down?"

"Not exactly. We have another letter from Mr Wetherby promising to leave us the sum of one thousand pounds in his will and that's all they're prepared to give us … between the five of us."

"One thousand pounds is still a lot of money."

"I know and I should be happy but they said that unless we accept the one thousand pounds offered and hand over the original documents, they'll report us to the police for attempted blackmail."

"They can't do that; the money should belong to you."

"They can and I've no doubt they will. They've got enough money to hire the best solicitors in the country; we wouldn't stand a chance."

Rose sighed and took hold of her husband's hand. "It's not the end of the world, on a normal day you'd be delighted to be given two hundred pounds."

Charles glared at her. "We're not splitting it equally. When we got Mr Watkins's money, William-Wetherby and I got thirty-five pounds and the girls got ten. At the very least, I expect we'll simply add a zero to those figures."

"Well, you should be happier. You've been given three hundred and fifty pounds and you'll be discharged from your bankruptcy soon."

"Not soon enough."

"Stop this, I've had enough of you feeling sorry for yourself."

Charles slumped back in his chair. "You've no idea what it's like."

"Of course I do, I've been living with you for long enough, and don't think people don't stop and stare at me too because I'm a bankrupt's wife." Rose paused for breath. "We may have a solution though. Mother came around yesterday and suggested we all go to Oxford to visit Margaret and Florence for a few weeks. I think it could be what we need."

"What do we want to do that for?"

"I've missed having them around and it would take your mind off the bankruptcy."

"Your mother's missed Florence?"

Rose giggled. "She's more interested in this new man

Margaret's walking out with. She thinks we should meet him in case he proposes marriage."

A crease formed on Charles's forehead as he thought of his sister. "That should be for me to decide, not her. Besides, Margaret's not known this fellow five minutes, there's plenty of time."

"You may be surprised. She seems very fond of him."

Charles groaned. "You've already arranged this, haven't you? When do we leave?"

~

Littlemore, Oxfordshire.

ON THE EVENING of their arrival, Charles led Rose, her sisters and his aunt into his cousin's dining room. Mr Goodwood welcomed them as Hannah placed a large pot of beef broth in the centre of the table.

"Welcome to Oxford. I hope you enjoy your stay with us. Now, please help yourself to the food on the table and make yourselves at home."

Charles positioned himself between his sisters and waited while Margaret served him some broth. "So, what have you both been up to?" He turned to Florence. "How's the book-keeping going? Are you doing a good job?"

Florence smiled. "Mr Goodwood says I am. I don't work all the time, because I have to help around the house, but it's such fun having our cousins here." She nodded across the table to her younger cousins. "We don't see so much of the boys though, they help with the deliveries."

"I hope you don't see much of any boys." Charles's face was stern. "You're much too young."

"Have you forgotten?" Florence put her hands on her

hips. "I come of age next month. I thought that was why you'd come."

"Yes, of course, but you're still too young. I don't want to hear of you walking out with anyone for a while yet." As he spoke, Charles sensed Margaret tense on his other side. "Don't tell me you're still walking out with your farmer."

Margaret nodded as she fidgeted with a spoon on the table. "His name's Mr Earl."

"She sees him about three times a week," Florence said. "He's always making excuses to call."

"Well, perhaps I should meet him while I'm here," Charles said. "I can't have you walking out with anyone."

"He's not just anyone. Mr Goodwood says he's from a reputable family, I'm sure you'll like him."

Mr Goodwood glanced down the table when he heard his name being mentioned. "Did someone mention me?"

"Nothing that won't keep until tomorrow," Charles said.

"It's a good job." Mr Goodwood stood up and walked towards them. "We all need to be up for work by five o'clock in the morning and so if you've all finished, I'll bid you goodnight."

Charles glanced at the clock on the mantelpiece. *Half past eight.*

Aunt Mary-Ann must have seen the look on his face and leaned across the table to speak to Hannah. "My dear, do you think we could have a pot of tea before we go upstairs? I presume you don't expect us to rise at the same time as yourselves."

Hannah sighed. "Of course you can. I don't know why we have to start quite so early, but that's the way Mr Goodwood prefers to work. The maid finishes at nine o'clock. Leave the cups and she'll do them in the morning."

"Poor Hannah looks exhausted," Rose said once the five of them were alone. "Mr Goodwood must be a hard taskmaster."

"We must make sure we don't marry laundrymen," Daisy said to Lilly, who fanned her face as she laughed.

"I have no intention of making such a marriage," Lilly said. "I want to marry a gentleman."

"That's enough, you two." Mary-Ann's voice was stern. "I don't want to hear talk of either of you getting married for several years yet."

"Just because you have your own business doesn't mean you have to start so early," Charles said. "I don't remember Mr Wetherby keeping these hours."

"Talking of Mr Wetherby," Mary-Ann said. "Did you hear Hannah telling me about Aunt Sarah-Ann's will?"

Charles shook his head. "No, I was talking to Florence and Margaret."

"Well, according to your aunt Adelaide, Sarah-Ann had a decent amount of money of her own, which explains why Mr Wetherby didn't leave her much in his will. Over four thousand pounds she left, mainly to Elizabeth. The only other person who got a mention was Aunt Martha, who'll receive a small annuity. Aunt Adelaide got nothing and wasn't happy, as you can imagine."

"I wonder why she did that."

Mary-Ann took a sip of her tea. "I've no idea but I'd guess that Aunt Sarah-Ann finally wanted to make peace with her sister."

Chapter Forty-Three

As the new week began and Sunday morning turned into afternoon, Charles and Rose returned from their walk to find the table ready for dinner and most of the family gathered in the living room.

"Here you are." Mr Goodwood offered Rose a seat. "Have you been to church?"

Charles laughed. "No, we're not regulars. It's a lovely day for a walk though. Do you get out much?"

"Never have time," Mr Goodwood said. "I'm either working, eating or sleeping. We keep Sundays as a day of rest, naturally, but not for walking. It's always seemed rather pointless to me."

Mr Goodwood paused when there was a knock on the door and Margaret joined them on the arm of a well-built young man with dark hair and a thickset neck sitting on muscular shoulders.

"Can I introduce Mr Earl? Mr Earl, this is my brother, Mr Charles Jackson."

Charles inclined his head in greeting and offered Mr Earl his hand. "Mr Earl, I'm glad you could join us."

"Thank you," Mr Earl said. "Margaret's missed seeing her family. Are you here for long?"

"Another couple of weeks. As long as Mr Goodwood's agreeable, we'll stay for Florence's birthday at the beginning of May and then leave."

"No objections from me," Mr Goodwood said. "Now come and sit down and let's get this food served."

WITH DINNER EATEN, and the plates cleared away, the ladies disappeared into the living room, leaving Charles with Mr Goodwood and Mr Earl around the table. Mr Goodwood handed around a tub of pipe tobacco, which Charles declined.

"So you're a farmer I believe, Mr Earl," Charles said.

"Actually, I'm a farm bailiff. My father has a cottage on the land but we oversee all the tenant farmers to make sure they're doing what they're supposed to."

"And is your father in the same line of work?"

"He is, and I have two younger brothers who are learning the trade as well. It helps to be on good terms with the landowner."

Charles nodded. "Indeed. So how did you meet my sister?"

Mr Earl smiled. "Through church initially, although I would only admire her from afar, of course. We never spoke at the time, but several months ago, we were both fortunate enough to be invited to a social event at the village hall. I plucked up the courage to speak to her and discovered what a wonderful woman she is."

"You've been walking out ever since, haven't you?" Mr Goodwood said.

"We have, and we've become very fond of each other." Mr Earl coughed to clear his throat. "Mr Jackson, I know we've only just met, but I wonder, would you permit me to ask for Margaret's hand in marriage?"

Charles stared at Mr Earl. "I must say, this is all rather sudden." He turned to face Mr Goodwood. "You know Mr Earl better than I do. Can you offer me any words of advice?"

Mr Goodwood took a long drag on his pipe and stared at Mr Earl. "I would say that he's from a reputable family and Margaret's always happy when he's around. She could do worse."

Charles studied Mr Earl before holding out his hand. "Very well then, as long as Margaret's in agreement, I'll give you my consent. Will you ask her tonight?"

"Thank you, but no, not today. There are too many distractions. I'll wait until one day in the week when we take a walk."

THE EVENING before they were due to leave, Charles stood at the head of the dining table flanked on one side by Florence and on the other by Margaret and Mr Earl. Mr Goodwood called for silence, before motioning to Charles to address the family.

"When we arrived, several weeks ago, I thought we would only be here for one celebration and that was Florence's coming of age. It now appears we have two reasons to raise our glasses." He turned to Florence. "Firstly, Florence. Many happy returns of the day, may you have a long and prosperous life." He clinked his glass of sherry against hers as the rest of the family repeated his toast.

"Thank you, everyone." Florence bounced on the spot. "I've had a lovely day."

"Thank you, Florence." Charles held onto her arm to keep her still. "Now we come to Margaret. I'm delighted to announce that she has accepted a proposal of marriage from

Mr Earl. They'll be married in Birmingham at the end of July before moving back to Oxfordshire to live with Mr Earl's parents." He raised his glass. "To Margaret and Mr Earl."

"Why are they getting married in Birmingham?" The smile fell from Florence's lips as the rest of the family repeated the toast.

"Because it's usual for the bride to marry in her own parish," Charles said. "I've spoken to Margaret and Mr Earl and they've agreed that in order to have the banns read in Small Heath, they'll accompany us home. Margaret will stay with us, while Mr Earl returns here to attend to his farm."

"Will I be able to go to the wedding?" Tears formed in Florence's eyes.

"Of course you will," Margaret said. "I was going to ask you to be my bridesmaid. I'm only having one, and I want it to be you."

The smile returned to Florence's face. "Of course I will … but won't Eleanor be cross?"

Margaret embraced her sister. "She'll understand."

"This is the best birthday present ever." Florence beamed. "Will I get another new dress?"

Charles retook his seat. "We need to discuss that."

THE FOLLOWING MORNING, with their last breakfast in Oxfordshire over, Charles and Mr Goodwood stood at the side of the road watching the coachman load their bags onto the carriage.

"Do you go back to Birmingham much?" Charles asked him.

"Not been for years. Hannah's mother's still there and so she visits occasionally, but I can't be taking days off. We want to expand."

"Hannah mentioned something about that years ago, but I thought you'd changed your minds."

"Now the children are growing up and helping out we need somewhere bigger, but we can't do it around here."

"Where will you go?"

"We've thought about moving to the north Kent coastline to help Hannah's breathing. It's popular with the well-to-do from London and they'll always want their laundry done."

Charles whistled through his teeth. "That's a long way to go. What will you do with Florence? Are you happy to take her with you or will you be sending her back to Birmingham?"

A glint flashed across Mr Goodwood's eyes. "Of course she can come with us. She's a lovely girl and if I'm being honest, she's very handy with the bookkeeping."

"Have you mentioned it to her?"

"Nothing's finalised yet. I suggest we wait until Margaret's married before we say anything and don't tell her how far away Kent is. She'll be none the wiser."

Chapter Forty-Four

Birmingham, Warwickshire

T he sun was high in the summer sky when William-Wetherby and the family climbed down from the train in Birmingham and headed towards the exit. They were only halfway down the platform when he spotted Charles and he pointed him out to the boys.

"Why don't you run and see him." William-Wetherby let go of the boys' hands and smiled. "I hope he recognises them," he said to Bella. "He's not seen them for eighteen months."

When they arrived at the end of the platform, Charles was crouched down beside Edward while Albert told him of the delights of rail travel.

"You had a good journey then?" Charles extended his hand to William-Wetherby.

"I'm glad Margaret delayed getting married until after we'd got our money. First class is definitely better than travelling third." William-Wetherby grinned. "I could do with a cup of tea though. You'd think they'd serve it given the price of the tickets."

"I can do better than that." Charles winked at his brother and flashed a sterling silver hip flask in his direction. "For when we're in the carriage."

"Where did that come from?"

Charles grinned. "It was Mr Diver's, but since we went to Oxfordshire, I've been getting on better with Aunt Mary-Ann and she gave it to me ... and a bottle of brandy to pour into it."

Bella sighed. "Isn't that either supposed to be for special occasions or for cold weather, neither of which apply on a lovely July day like this."

"You may scoff, but we do have something to celebrate," Charles said. "On top of Margaret's marriage and getting our money, a week ago today I was discharged from my bankruptcy. I've already got my eye on some business opportunities."

William-Wetherby slapped Charles on the back. "Congratulations. Perhaps I will share a tipple with you then."

IT WAS with some trepidation that Bella stepped into Mary-Ann's formal living room but within seconds Margaret had hold of her arm.

"I'm so glad you're here." Margaret smiled at Bella before turning her attention to the boys. "I've been so looking forward to meeting you all, you've been William-Wetherby's secret for too long."

"Hardly a secret, just a little distant," William-Wetherby said. "But we're here now."

"Let me see this little fellow." Aunt Mary-Ann took Stephen from Bella. "He's adorable. How old is he?"

"Just turned eighteen months," Bella said.

Mary-Ann retook her seat on the settee and sat Stephen on her lap. She indicated for Bella to join her. "My baby boy didn't make it to eighteen months." She closed her eyes as she held Stephen to her chest. "He was my pride and joy, but he was taken before he was two months old. I found him one morning in his cradle. Cold as ice."

"I'm sorry, I didn't know. I can't imagine how you must have felt."

Mary-Ann played with Stephen's fingers and her voice dropped to a whisper. "It was a long time ago and I don't ever talk about it. I can't tell you how I felt other than I thought my world had ended. You're so fortunate to have three healthy boys."

"I said that to William-Wetherby. When he was upset about the family money, I told him I wouldn't swap places with Aunt Charlotte if it meant giving her my babies."

"You're very wise."

Bella smiled at the affection in Mary-Ann's eyes.

"We've made afternoon tea." Margaret interrupted them. "I've asked the maid to bring it in."

"When does Florence arrive?" Bella asked. "I thought she'd have been here by now."

Margaret rolled her eyes. "She's coming with Mr Earl and Aunt Hannah, but they won't be here until tomorrow."

"That's not like her," William-Wetherby said. "I thought she'd have been waiting for us; she's been saying for months that she hasn't seen the boys."

"I'm afraid it was Mr Earl's fault. With the whole family coming to the wedding, they couldn't take much time off work."

"What's the plan for the marriage ceremony?" William-Wetherby said. "Where's Mr Earl staying?"

Margaret smiled. "Aunt Adelaide has arranged their accommodation. They'll all travel to church together and pick up Aunt Martha on the way."

"There is another thing." Charles gave a slight cough.

"When we went to church for the banns to be read, the vicar asked who'd be giving Margaret away."

"William-Wetherby will, won't he?" Bella asked.

Margaret's face flushed red. "I'm sorry, because I've been staying with Charles for the last couple of months, I told the vicar he would. I hope you don't mind."

William-Wetherby looked from one to the other. "No, I don't suppose I do. As long as it's one of us and there's no sign of Uncle William. I don't ever want to see him again."

Chapter Forty-Five

The organist struck up the first notes of the processional hymn and William-Wetherby stood between Bella and Eleanor as Charles led Margaret down the aisle. He smiled at Florence as she followed them in her new dress.

"Mr Earl's a good-looking man," Bella whispered. "They make a handsome couple."

William-Wetherby nodded. "If you say so, but I'm not too bothered as long as she's happy. She's not had a good life up until now, so let's hope Mr Earl takes care of her."

"We just need Florence settled now."

William-Wetherby glanced at her. "Don't be in too much of a hurry, she's still only twenty-one."

"Which means she's an adult. Don't discourage her if she finds a nice young man. She deserves happiness too."

William-Wetherby struggled to concentrate as the service proceeded but once the register was signed, he escorted the small wedding party back to Mary-Ann's house, where a selection of food had been laid out on the morning room table.

"Can we bring the boys down from the nursery yet?" Florence said to Bella once they had finished eating. "If you're going back tomorrow, I'll hardly see them. Why couldn't you stay longer?"

William-Wetherby overheard his sister and rolled his eyes. "I'm only allowed seven days a year off work with pay; I'm already in trouble for having so much time away. Once I'm home, I'll be working every day of the week until I make the hours up."

"At least it's a steady job," Charles said. "You're not likely to be made bankrupt."

"That's true, I'm not complaining really. Shall we go into the front room and make space for the children?"

"Not so quickly, I've a surprise for you," Mary-Ann said. "I've an acquaintance who has one of those new cameras and he'll be here shortly to take some photographs."

"Photographs! How exciting." Florence clapped her hands together. "Even more reason to fetch the boys downstairs."

"It's a good job I brought their best clothes then," Bella said. "I'll have to go and get them changed."

Charles watched Bella and Florence leave the room before he spoke. "Let me go and unlock the back door, I suppose we'll be out in the garden." He led the way to the morning room and opened the door before William-Wetherby, Mr Earl and his brother-in-law Mr Keen filed through it.

"I've never been out here before." William-Wetherby inspected the flower beds. "It's not a bad size. Better than our cobbled yard. I'll wager it's nothing to you though, Mr Earl. Do you have much of a garden?"

"Not much more than this, to be honest, but enough to grow our own vegetables."

"I believe you and Margaret are moving in with your mother and father."

A smile lit up Mr Earl's face. "We were, but the cottage

next door became available last month and we signed for it immediately. It'll be nice to have a place to ourselves."

"Until you fill it with children," Mr Keen said.

"You've got a big enough house," William-Wetherby said. "I wish we had the space you do. How's the business going?"

"Couldn't be better," Mr Keen said. "Metal-framed structures are popular at the moment, so much so, I'd like to expand if the bank manager'll lend me more money."

Charles's brow furrowed. "Have you considered taking on a partner? I've got money to invest, if you're interested. Maybe we can help each other out."

Mr Keen studied his brother-in-law as Mary-Ann appeared with the photographer. "Maybe we can. Let's talk once we've got this out the way."

THE FOLLOW MORNING, William-Wetherby was reluctant to hurry the family breakfast, but as the clock approached eight o'clock he had no choice.

"Is the carriage ready?" he asked Mary-Ann.

"It is, but stop worrying, it only takes half an hour to get to the station; you've plenty of time."

William-Wetherby checked the time against his pocket watch. "We might have plenty of time if we leave now, but it's going to take at least half an hour to get out the house. Come on, boys, finish that bread and go and put your shoes on."

"I'll help them." Florence took Albert's hand in hers and disappeared with him into the hallway.

"Would you take Stephen for me for a moment?" Bella handed her son to Mary-Ann.

"It will be my pleasure. You come to Aunt Mary-Ann, my little man." Stephen nestled on Mary-Ann's knee and chuckled as Mary-Ann tickled his tummy.

"I do wonder how long I'll have to wait to be a grandmother. Rose and Charles have been married for almost four years now and not a sign."

"Talking of Rose and Charles, where are they? I thought they said they'd be here by eight."

"They'll be here but they're never early. I'm going to miss you all when you've gone. I enjoy having a house full of people."

Rose and Charles arrived five minutes later and joined Florence, Margaret and Mr Earl as they said farewell to their young nephews.

"I'm going to miss you all so much." Florence picked Stephen up and held him to her. "I wish I could come to the railway station with you."

"It would have made sense to all go at the same time, but we wouldn't have fit in the carriage," William-Wetherby said. "When Mr Goodwood doesn't need you for a few weeks, you must come to Liverpool again."

"If only it wasn't such a long way away." Florence pouted. "Why can't they make faster trains?"

"If they go any faster, they'll have no passengers because no one will be able to breathe on them." William-Wetherby laughed as he took his son from Florence.

Florence ignored him and crouched on the floor between Edward and Albert. "Don't you grow up too quickly, are you listening?"

"I'm big already," Edward said.

"And I am. I'm bigger than Stephen," Albert said.

"And you're both adorable." Florence gave them a squeeze.

"Right, come on." William-Wetherby passed Stephen to Bella and picked up Albert as they headed for the door. He stopped beside Margaret. "You take care of yourself, and if you ever need me, you know where I am."

Margaret flushed. "Thank you for coming. Please say we'll see each other again."

William-Wetherby put his arm around his sister. "I'm sorry I ended up so far away, but I was given no choice. Keep in touch."

Chapter Forty-Six

With the daylight fading and the leaves falling from the trees, there was no denying that winter was approaching, but it couldn't wipe the smile from Charles's face. He'd been waiting for today for far too long, but finally he was once again a company director. By the time he arrived home, Rose was in the living room reading the evening paper.

"You're here." She stood up and kissed his cheek. "I presume you're now a partner with Mr Keen?"

Charles allowed his smile to break into a grin. "I am; Keen, Jackson & Co. makers of metal frames. It's got a nice ring to it, don't you think? He'll start teaching me everything I need to know first thing in the morning."

"Congratulations." Rose retook her seat by the fireplace. "It'll be nice to be able to hold my head up again when I go out."

Charles took a seat opposite her. "What are you doing with the newspaper? It's not like you to read it before me."

"I wouldn't normally, but Mother called earlier and

showed me a short piece in the news section." She held the paper out for Charles to read.

"September 1898: The will of Mr William Wetherby from Handsworth, Staffordshire, which was proved on the first of January, 1898, by Mr William Wetherby Junior (son) and Mrs Charlotte Mountford (daughter, and wife of Mr C. Mountford) was resworn in London. Total effects are now confirmed as seventy-five thousand, four hundred and fifty-five pounds, ten shillings and four pence." Charles stared at Rose. "They found another one thousand six hundred pounds? Just like that? How on earth do you miss that amount of money?"

"That's what Mother wants to know."

"Did she have any answers?"

Rose shook her head. "No. She thought perhaps it could have been something to do with the Artisans Dwelling Company."

Charles threw the paper back onto the table. "Uncle William would have known about that. It sounds like he had a stash hidden away somewhere. Mr Wetherby's been dead for over a year, which suggests they got an annual payout they weren't expecting."

"Come and sit down. There's some tea in the pot if you want it."

"I could do with more than a cup of tea." He hunted in the sideboard for his bottle of rum. "He made me repay that five hundred pounds and yet he had three times that amount hidden away. If I hadn't had to give it him back, I might have been able to keep going." With a swift movement of the wrist, Charles downed the first tot of rum and reached for the bottle to pour another. "As if that lot need any more money. I need to tell William-Wetherby, he'll understand."

"It's over now, don't upset yourself again. You need to focus on the new business and make sure that makes money."

"Don't worry, I will and I won't be letting Uncle William anywhere near it."

CHARLES HAD BEEN WORKING for a month and was still amazed at how much there was to learn about metal frames. It wasn't like him to work late, but he had his first important client meeting tomorrow and had to make sure he knew what he was talking about. It was turned eight o'clock when he arrived home and Rose had placed an envelope for him on the table.

"From Florence." Charles raised an eyebrow before ripping open the envelope. "Ah, Mr Goodwood's told her of his plans to move to Margate."

"Will she go?"

Charles shrugged and glanced back at the letter. "She doesn't say, but she doesn't sound happy."

Rose didn't look up from her embroidery as she spoke. "Why? Because he wants her to go with them and she doesn't want to or because she wants to go and he won't let her?"

"That's the strange thing. He told me when we visited that he wanted her to go with them, but he's given her the choice."

"What will she do?"

"She doesn't know. On the one hand she loves working for them and being part of the family, but on the other, she realises Margate is such a long way away. She fears she won't see us again."

"Of course she'll see us again, why wouldn't she?"

Charles took a seat. "It's a big decision and she wants to know what I think."

Rose cocked her head to one side. "Why don't you tell her to give the move a try to see if she likes it? It doesn't have to be permanent."

"I could, but I wonder if it would make life simpler if she

moved back to Birmingham. I could speak to Mr Keen about offering her a job."

Rose sighed. "Where would she live? We don't have room and I'm sure Eleanor has enough to cope with."

"You're right." Charles nodded, and read the letter for a third time. *What am I missing?* His sister sounded distraught at the idea of moving, but if that was the case, why was she considering it? Was the job so special?

"I don't know why she has to work at all," Rose continued. "She needs to find herself a husband and settle down."

"I'm sure she will one day, but for now she needs money of her own. She doesn't have a wealthy mother to go to."

Rose glared at her husband.

"Don't look at me like that. We're fortunate, but at the moment the closest person Florence has to a father is Mr Goodwood. Maybe that's why she's so keen to stay with them."

"Well perhaps it would be for the best if she went. I'm sure there must be eligible gentlemen in Margate."

Chapter Forty-Seven

Liverpool, Lancashire

Although spring was approaching and the nights were getting brighter, it was still dark when William-Wetherby arrived home from work. He sank back into the chair and watched Bella pour a cup of tea.

"You look exhausted, I'll pop you an extra sugar in," Bella said. "Have you had a busy day?"

"Not so much the day itself, it's the constant work. I've not had a day off for six weeks and I've got another three weeks to go before I have a Sunday off. The boys will be growing up not knowing who I am."

Bella kissed the top of his head as she handed him his tea. "Edward was asking about you earlier, wondering when you'd be able to take them to the match."

William-Wetherby closed his eyes. "I can't see it being this season. On top of everything else, the chief wants me to move to the Main Bridewell on Cheapside. I don't know if I've got the energy for it."

"Will they give you more money?" Bella asked.

William-Wetherby sighed. "If only. The problem is, it'll take me twice as long to walk there and back each day. Not to mention there's more trouble down there than around here."

"Can't you say no?"

"After what happened last year, I'm not in much of a position to argue, besides, it might be the only way I get my job as an inspector back. Let me sleep on it, things may not seem as bad in the morning."

AFTER AN EARLY BREAKFAST, William-Wetherby walked the fifteen minutes to the station where the chief inspector was waiting for him.

"Sergeant Jackson, just the man. Can you spare me a minute?"

William-Wetherby followed the chief into his office and stood before the desk. "Yes, sir. How can I help?"

"Have you had any thoughts about the move to Cheapside? They're desperate for new men and your name is mentioned regularly."

William-Wetherby's stomach flipped. "Not yet, sir, although I'm honoured to be considered. I'm only halfway through a sixty-day rota and so I didn't expect any move to be imminent."

"Oh, don't worry about rotas, we can change them easily enough. Cheapside has too many staff shortages to wait. I imagine the move would be more desirable if you had a few extra shillings a week and several more days off a year."

William-Wetherby raised an eyebrow. "Do the men get paid more?"

"Not for the same job, but if you prove yourself and keep out of trouble, you stand a chance of promotion. I'm sure you wouldn't turn that down."

"No, sir."

"Excellent. Right, I'm on my way there now. Why don't you join me and I can show you around."

IT WASN'T the first time William-Wetherby had been to the city's main lockup, but as he climbed from the chief inspector's carriage, it was the first time he had considered working there. He shuddered as he looked up at the red brick building, four storeys high with bars set across the small windows. The chief led the way through the gate in the thick outer wall, before pausing by the door to the reception.

"Here we are, the Main Bridewell. It's quite different to Prescot Street, although obviously you have cells there as well. We have about sixty here and you'll be moving prisoners in and out as they go to the magistrates' courts. A lot of work is done in the early hours of the morning and so you'll be expected to do night shifts. Let me show you around."

William-Wetherby followed the chief up several flights of stairs to what he presumed was the top floor. The corridors were dimly lit, with low ceilings, and walls of solid brick that were broken only by heavy wooden doors.

"How many men do you have in a cell?" William-Wetherby asked.

"Only one, unless we're especially busy. Each cell is only about seven foot square, so not a lot of room. The doors are solid too." He hammered his fist on the outside of one. "We've not had anyone escape in the thirty years the building's been open and we're not going to start now."

William-Wetherby nodded. "There must be a risk of escape when the men are transferred."

"Our predecessors thought of that and built an underground access to the courts, I'll show you. Nobody gets out of here unless two officers accompany them or they're found not guilty."

With his tour completed, William-Wetherby found himself back in the reception area facing a stern-looking police inspector.

"Sergeant Jackson, this is the duty inspector. He'll be your immediate supervisor and will fill you in on all the procedures."

With a nod of the head, the chief inspector left.

"So, you've been at Prescot Street, I believe," said the duty inspector. "Did you do much in the way of checking in the prisoners and locking them in their cells?"

"Y-yes of course, although we also had a lot of men on the beat as well."

"Good, so you'll know the drill. Let's have you around this side of the desk and we'll get some work out of you."

WILLIAM-WETHERBY HAD NEVER KNOWN a job that encouraged recreational activities during work hours, and he'd initially been delighted to be invited to award the prizes at the annual police sports festival, but as he and several colleagues stepped onto the Mersey Ferry at the end of a blisteringly hot afternoon he wished he was back inside the cool walls of the lockup.

He ran his finger around his collar as he took a seat towards the back of the boat. *Why do they have these events at the height of summer?* He'd spent the afternoon standing in a field and now all he wanted to do was take off his helmet and shoes.

"That went well, Sergeant. A pleasant afternoon all round." The chief took a seat beside him on top of the ferry.

I'm sure it was, if it was spent sitting in a pavilion sipping lemonade. "Yes, sir. I'm hoping to catch a breeze up here as we head for home."

"A sensible idea, I'm here to do the same. If I'm not

mistaken, you have an early start in the morning."

"Yes, sir. I'm on at five o'clock. It's going to be a busy shift."

"They're all busy at the moment, unfortunately the summer weather brings more crooks onto the streets."

The chief glanced around to check the rest of his men were otherwise occupied. "Now I have you, I wanted to tell you that they're looking for new inspectors at Cheapside. I know you've only been with us for a couple of months, but your name's been mentioned. Would you be interested?"

William-Wetherby glanced at his superior. "Yes of course, sir, thank you for telling me. What do I need to do?"

"Nothing for the time being, but leave it with me. I'll make sure you have the information you need."

WILLIAM-WETHERBY WALKED HOME with a spring in his step and as he rounded the corner into Martensen Street, he spotted Edward sitting on the doorstep. His son noticed him immediately and ran towards him.

"You're home. Mam's putting Albert and Stephen to bed and said I could wait up for another ten minutes."

William-Wetherby ruffled his son's hair. "It's as well I hurried then. Let me go in and you can sit with me."

With his helmet and shoes stored next to the front door, William-Wetherby took his seat by the fireplace and pulled a chair up for his son.

"Have you been to school today?"

Edward nodded. "It was too hot though. I wish we didn't have to go."

"Of course you need to go. You want to be clever when you grow up, don't you?"

"Did you go to school?" Edward asked.

"Of course I did. I wouldn't be a police officer if I hadn't."

"I don't want to be in the police." Edward's face was stern. "People are scared of you and say you spy on them."

"Well, they're wrong. They only need to be scared of us if they're naughty. If you're good, then we'll like you a lot."

Edward smiled. "I'm a good boy, aren't I?"

"You will be if you're up those stairs in two minutes." Bella stood with her hands on her hips at the bottom of the stairs. "Will you take him up and say goodnight to the other two?"

William-Wetherby groaned and was about to object when Edward reached for his hand. "Please come with me, you'll make Albert happy. He says he hasn't seen you for weeks."

By the time he came back downstairs, Bella had a plate of scouse on the table and sat beside him with a cup of tea.

"I'm glad you're home early for a change. I had a letter from Eleanor earlier. She had her baby last Wednesday, a boy. Cyril they're calling him."

"Is she all right?"

"Seems to be, although now Charles and Mr Keen are expanding the business she never sees him. Not that he'd be any help, but I do feel for her with no mam to help her. At least Mr Keen's hired a mother's help again for a couple of months. Do you think we could visit them?"

William-Wetherby shook his head. "Not the way things are at the moment. The chief mentioned they're looking for more inspectors so I can't do anything to jeopardise my chances. I'm on a new rota tomorrow too. For the next two weeks I'll have to be up at four o'clock to be in work for five."

Bella sighed. "Can't they make you an inspector sooner so you don't have to do such early mornings?"

"Inspectors still have to do the early shift, but it should mean I'll be home by about four o'clock in the afternoon."

Bella smiled. "That makes it worth it then and it should keep the boys happy for a few days at least."

Chapter Forty-Eight

Bella straightened herself up and rubbed the small of her back before she leaned forward once more and pulled the sheets from the washing tub. Starting with one end she fed them into the mangle, turning the handle to squeeze out the water. After putting both sheets through twice, she wiped away a bead of perspiration that rolled down her temple before shaking out the sheets and throwing them over her shoulder.

She glanced up at the clear blue sky as the sun bathed the back yard but it was the last thing she wanted to see. *I need it to go cloudy.*

"What are you doing out here?" William-Wetherby leaned forward to kiss the side of her cheek.

Bella sighed. "Pegging washing out. Stephen's not well. He's been sleepy all day and has a fever. Every time he's woken up, he's been sick in his bed." She pointed to the sheets now on the washing line.

The smile on William-Wetherby face disappeared. "Have you called a doctor?"

"Not yet. I think this weather's too much for him, as soon as it breaks, he'll be back to normal."

Bella followed her husband as he walked up the stairs to his son's bedroom. The curtains were closed, but they failed to keep the heat from the room.

"He's wringing wet." William-Wetherby ran the back of his finger across his son's forehead.

"I've been wiping his face with a wet cloth all day and I've got the window and front door open to give him a breeze. I hope it starts cooling down soon."

William-Wetherby studied the figure of his youngest son stretched out across his mattress. "Is he in pain?"

"I don't think so, he's not been crying, he's just limp and lifeless."

"If he's no better tomorrow, I want you to call a doctor, do you hear me? We have the money."

Bella nodded. "What will we do about Florence? Have you remembered she's coming to stay tomorrow?"

William-Wetherby groaned. "I'd completely forgotten. I said I'd meet her off the train too, but I'll be at work. What time did she say she was arriving?"

"It won't be until about three o'clock. Could you finish work an hour early?"

"I doubt it. The chief wants to speak to me about the new inspector roles. I'll have to make myself scarce and find some business to attend to around Lime Street." He shook his head. "This is all we need but at least she's staying with your mam. We'll have to keep her out of the way until he gets better."

AFTER A SLEEPLESS NIGHT, and an anxious morning when Stephen complained of a sore head and stiff neck, Bella begged her mam to fetch the doctor. As she watched the doctor examine her son, she thought her heart would explode from her chest.

"Do you know what's wrong, Doctor?"

The doctor shook his head. "This heat isn't helping, but I'm concerned by his brain fever. I'll call again tomorrow, but for now carry on wiping him with cold water and give him as much clean drinking water as you can. He's losing a lot of fluids with the sickness and high temperature."

"How long do you think it will last? Will a change in the weather help?"

"He's a healthy young lad and so there's a chance he'll recover if you keep him hydrated. Just keep your eye on him."

Bella showed the doctor out and as she did, she paused in the doorway, watching Edward and Albert play football with Fred. *Stephen should be out here with them. He loves kicking the ball.*

"Is Dad coming home early again?" Edward ran towards her, gasping for breath.

"He is and he's bringing Aunty Florence with him too."

Edward's eyes lit up. "Is she the one who plays with us and makes us laugh?"

"She is." Bella licked her thumb and wiped a smudge of dirt from her son's cheek.

"Do you think she'll play with us tonight?"

Bella thought of Stephen. "Perhaps, but Stephen's still not well so you can't make a noise."

"Stephen needs to get better soon." Edward stood with his hands on his hips. "We've got the wrong number of people playing without him. It's only Fred against me *and* Albert."

"Fred's a bit bigger than you two." Bella glanced up the street and caught sight of William-Wetherby and Florence walking towards them. "Here they are now."

As Edward and Albert ran to meet them, Fred burst past

and reached Florence first. "Aunty Florence, we didn't know you were coming."

She gave the boys a hug before she spoke to William-Wetherby. "Why didn't you tell them? Where's Stephen?"

William-Wetherby sighed. "He's not well. I have to go home and see how he is."

"Will you play football with us, Dad?" Edward said. "We need to practise if we're going to play for Liverpool one day."

William-Wetherby stared down at the expectant face of his son. "You can't make a living playing football, you need a proper job."

Edward's shoulders dropped. "Do we have to?"

"Yes, you do, and besides, ladies don't play football so don't bother Aunty Florence. Now be off with you. I need to talk to Mam."

Florence took hold of Edward's hand. "I don't mind kicking a ball with them. They're still only little."

"Well, don't let them have you doing things you shouldn't."

As they reached the front door, Florence embraced Bella. "How lovely to see you again. It's been too long."

Bella glanced at William-Wetherby. "It has, but would you excuse us, I need to speak to William-Wetherby. Edward, why don't you and Albert take Aunty Florence to Granny's house."

"Can't I see Stephen? He is going to be all right, isn't he?" Florence asked.

William-Wetherby patted his sister's hand. "We don't know. Let me go and see him, and I'll talk to you later. Please."

Florence let Edward lead her away as William-Wetherby took Bella's arm and ushered her into the living room.

"How is he?"

Bella gazed up at her husband trying hard to contain the

tears that were forming. "I called the doctor, he's got brain fever."

William-Wetherby put his arms around her. "What did the doctor say?"

"He doesn't think it's the heat. I have to keep him cool and give him plenty of clean drinking water. The problem is, he just sleeps. How do I get water into him if he doesn't wake up?" A tear overflowed and ran down Bella's cheek.

"Let's go and see him. Bring some water and I'll help you."

Once in the bedroom, Bella dipped a cloth into the luke-warm water on the dresser and wiped her son's face. "He looks like an angel when he's so peaceful, but I don't want him like this. I want him playing outside with the others."

William-Wetherby stroked her hand. "Let's sit him up and see if he'll take a drink. We'll make him better."

THE NEXT MORNING Bella was out of bed before William-Wetherby, but there was no breakfast on the table. She stood up from Stephen's bed when William-Wetherby appeared at the door of the boy's bedroom.

"How is he?" he asked.

"He's been restless all night. Did he keep you awake?"

"Only a little." He kissed her forehead. "Try not to worry, I'm sure he'll be fine. I'll grab myself a piece of bread and come home as soon as I can."

"Is that Dad going to work again?" Edward couldn't suppress a yawn as he spoke.

Bella stroked his head. "He'll be back in time for tea, you just try and get back to sleep."

With Edward settled, Bella cradled Stephen in her arms but as she stood up to take him to the other bedroom his screams pierced the air.

"What's the matter?" Albert asked.

Bella stared at the child writhing in her arms. "Stay where you are, I need to get Stephen settled."

"We can't go to sleep with that noise." Edward and Albert followed her into the other room.

"It's not his fault, his head hurts. Go back to your room. He needs to be quiet."

Bella wiped Stephen's face with the cool water and wafted a newspaper over his face. "There, there. Mammy's here." As Stephen's body once again relaxed, Bella dropped to her knees at the side of the bed and closed her eyes.

"Dear God. Please don't let him suffer. He's done nothing to deserve this and he's so helpless. Please speed him back to health and don't abandon us. Please. Amen."

Bella held onto Stephen's hand as she rested her head on the mattress, her tears dropping onto the bedcovers beneath her. *I want him better again.*

Chapter Forty-Nine

I t had been another hot day and Bella clung to William-Wetherby's arm as the doctor rested his hand on Stephen's forehead.

"He's been like this all day, Doctor," Bella said. "He won't settle and all he says is that his head hurts."

The doctor lifted his vest to listen to his chest, but paused when he saw a rash covering his body. "How long has this been here?"

"I-I've not noticed it before. It wasn't there this morning," Bella whispered.

The doctor ran the back of his finger across the red spots. "Has he been eating?"

"No, not a thing for over a week now. If he has anything, even water, it either makes him sick or comes out the other end."

"What about laudanum, Doctor. Will that help?" William-Wetherby said.

The doctor shook his head. "It may reduce his discomfort, but it won't help in the long run. My fear is that he's contracted a condition called meningitis, an infection that affects the lining of the brain. That would account for the brain fever. We know as well that it's often accompanied by a rash that doesn't fade when pressed, such as this."

"Will he get better?" Tears fell down Bella's cheeks.

The doctor took a deep breath. "It's impossible to say. If we keep him comfortable and shower him with prayers, he has a chance."

Bella fell to the floor and put her head alongside her son's. "Pray for him, Doctor, please. We need the vicar here too." Her voice squeaked as she sobbed. "He has to get better ... he has to."

BELLA'S KNEES ached from kneeling by the bed, but she couldn't stand up. That would mean giving up hope, and she couldn't do that. As she kissed Stephen's hand she heard footsteps on the stairs moments before Florence appeared in the bedroom.

"There you are." Florence said. "How is he?"

Bella wiped her eyes before her mam also appeared. "He's getting worse," Bella said, her voice cracking with every word. "The rash seems darker and he screams if I open the curtains. It's as if the sun's too bright for him."

"Has the doctor been today?" Mrs Booth asked.

Bella nodded. "This morning. He didn't say much, other than to pray for him."

Florence fell to her knees. "We have to help him."

Mrs Booth leaned over the bed and stroked Stephen's hand. "Is the vicar coming again?"

"Tomorrow." Bella grabbed Mrs Booth's free hand. "What am I going to do, Mam? What's going to happen?"

"Sshhh, nothing's going to happen. We'll all pray for him until he gets better."

"But what if he doesn't?"

Mrs Booth stroked her daughter's head. "You have to have faith. We'll take Edward and Albert back to our house so you can keep this one quiet."

"We can't leave Bella on her own," Florence said. "I'll stay and pray with her."

When Bella didn't object, Mrs Booth nodded. "All right, but do it quietly. Stephen has a headache."

With her mam gone and Florence reciting the Lord's Prayer, Bella reached for her son's hand, but as she did, his body went rigid. For an instant she froze before she darted around the bed and rushed to the top of the stairs.

"Mam, come back, something's wrong." She hurried back to the bedroom and took her son's hand again.

"What's the matter?" Mrs Booth rushed into the room.

"He was as stiff as a board, from his head to his feet. It's passed for the minute, but he's never done it before. Florence, did you notice?"

Florence shook her head. "I had my eyes closed."

"He looks all right now–"

Mrs Booth's words were cut short as Stephen's body jerked on the bed, his arms and legs flailing about him.

"Noooo ..." Bella's cry cut through the room as she reached over to restrain him. "Mam, make him stop. What's happening?"

Florence reached across the bed to grab Stephen's legs, but he kicked her arms away as his small frame twitched and jerked.

"Get the doctor," Bella screamed. "He has to stop this."

Mrs Booth couldn't move.

"Mam, now," Bella cried.

"Yes, I'm going." Mrs Booth ran down the stairs as Bella lay across her son, trying to calm him.

"Stop," she sobbed. "Don't do this."

Suddenly, as soon as it had started, the jerking stopped and

Stephen arched his back before crying out in pain. Bella picked him up to cradle him, but his screams filled the room, forcing her to release him. As his cries subsided she heard footsteps pounding up the stairs.

"What on earth's going on?" William-Wetherby appeared in the doorway. "I could hear you in the street."

Bella threw herself into his arms. "He went all stiff ... his arms and legs were moving all over the bed ... it was like he was possessed."

William-Wetherby extricated himself from her embrace and knelt by his son. "I'll go and fetch the doctor, he's in pain."

"Me mam's gone ... didn't you see her? He's got to give us something for him. We can't leave him like this." As Bella turned back to Stephen she noticed Florence standing in the corner, her eyes squeezed tight shut.

William-Wetherby followed Bella's gaze and took hold of his sister's arms. "Florence, stop this."

"The devil's possessed him. We must cleanse him ... get him out of here." Florence rushed forward, but before she reached the bed, William-Wetherby caught her around her waist and dragged her onto the landing. "Florence, stop it. He isn't possessed."

He struggled with his sister on the landing, and over their shouting Bella heard Mrs Booth arrive with the doctor.

"He's possessed ... we need the vicar ... don't go in there." Florence tried to stop them entering the room, but the doctor pushed past her.

By the time the doctor reached the bedside, Stephen's cries had faded to a whimper, but perspiration covered his body.

"Doctor, you have to do something." Bella grabbed hold of him. "It wasn't normal, he scared the life out of me."

The doctor patted her hand. "Calm down, Mrs Jackson, and tell me what happened." He bent down and put his hand on Stephen's forehead as Bella's voice competed with Florence's to describe Stephen's movements.

"Get her away from here." William-Wetherby glared at Mrs Booth who was still on the landing holding onto his sister's arm. Mrs Booth hesitated before she coaxed a sobbing Florence down the stairs.

"The fever's getting worse," the doctor said. "We need to cool him down; fill a bath with cold water."

Bella stared at William-Wetherby as he hesitated in the doorway. "Go and get it, it's in the yard."

William-Wetherby carried the metal bath upstairs followed by several buckets of cold water before the doctor gently lifted Stephen from the bed. His screams pierced the room and his back arched as he was lowered into the water.

"Calm down, Mam's here." Bella held his hand as tears flowed down her face. "Be brave."

The doctor fought the struggling child until gradually his body stilled and only his subdued cries filled the room.

"He's clearly in pain," the doctor said. "It won't make him better, but I'll give him a dose of laudanum to make him more comfortable. I'm afraid it's all I can do."

Bella laid a towel on the bed and wrapped her son in it as the doctor reached in his bag for the medicine. "Hold him still while I get it into him."

With her arms shaking, Bella propped Stephen up but he fought with her causing more of the medicine to go down the front of him than in his mouth.

"That's all we can do for now." The doctor wiped his hands once he had administered as much of the medicine as he dared. "I'll call back in the morning."

As the doctor left the room, William-Wetherby pulled him to one side. "Can you call at Mrs Booth's and see my sister, I suspect she needs a sedative as well."

. . .

ONCE SHE WAS ALONE, Bella lay on the bed with her son, finding sleep when she could, but at half past four the next morning when William-Wetherby looked in on them, she was awake.

"Is he any better?" he asked.

"No." Bella sobbed as she stood up and allowed her husband to wrap his arms around her. "He's been restless all night, and he's so hot. We need to put him in the bath again. I'm frightened ... will you stay with me?"

William-Wetherby kissed the top of her head. "Let me walk into work and tell them what's happening. Fridays are usually quiet and so I'll come straight home. Will that do?"

Bella nodded as she wiped her eyes on the back of her hands. "Please be quick." She lay back on the bed and dozed until she heard the front door open.

"How is he?" Mrs Booth said as she stepped into the bedroom.

Unable to speak, Bella threw her arms around her mam.

"Don't cry. Is the doctor coming this morning?"

"He is, but why can't he make him better?"

Mrs Booth stroked her daughter's hair. "I don't know, but I'll stay until he comes. Edward and Albert have gone to school and Florence is sedated."

By the time the doctor arrived, Bella and Mrs Booth had recited every prayer they could remember and more besides.

"Did the laudanum settle him?" the doctor asked as he bent over Stephen.

"For a while, but he was crying and writhing around the bed again in the middle of the night. I feel so helpless."

"Let me give him another dose so you can both rest. At the moment, sleeping might be the best thing for both of you."

"I can't go to sleep with him like this ..."

"You must do what the doctor says." William-Wetherby

walked into the room and took hold of his wife's hand. "You'll be no use if you're exhausted."

"Now that Mr Jackson's here, why don't you have a lie-down?" the doctor said.

"I will once you've gone. Please make him better."

With the medicine administered, the doctor packed up his bag and was about to leave when Stephen's body once again tensed before his arms and legs began jerking uncontrollably.

"Noooo, this is what happened before." Bella threw herself onto the bed and held his arms, but with his legs kicking, she struggled to hold him still.

The doctor moved back to the bed and put his hand on her shoulder. "Don't try and hold him, you may hurt him." The doctor took her place on the bed and rolled Stephen onto his side. "We need to stop him choking."

Bella flinched when William-Wetherby put his arm around her shoulders but didn't take her eyes off her son. The doctor worked to keep him on his side until finally his body stilled. When he didn't move, Bella reached out for his hand.

"Doctor, he's not responding ... is he all right?"

The doctor leaned forward and took Stephen's limp wrist in his hand. He immediately reached into his bag for a stethoscope and after positioning the ends in his ears, he placed the cold, flat metal on Stephen's chest. The child didn't move. After what felt like an eternity, he folded up the stethoscope.

"I'm afraid he's left us. I'm so sorry ... there was nothing I could do."

Bella stared at the doctor before she turned to William-Wetherby. "He's gone? He can't have." She noticed the glance from the doctor to William-Wetherby. "Doctor, he can't have, you must do something."

Bella flopped onto the bed and took Stephen in her arms as stars danced before her eyes. *My baby's gone ... he can't have, he's not three yet.* She closed her eyes, conscious she was swaying. *This can't be happening. Someone tell me it isn't happening.* With the taste of bile in the back of her mouth she lay down, careful not to disturb her beautiful son.

For the first time in their lives they'd had the money to pay for a doctor, but what good had it done them? She'd swap all the money they had if it would bring him back.

Chapter Fifty

William-Wetherby's shoulders drooped as he walked to Mrs Booth's house. The door was open and he slipped in and took a seat at the table without saying a word.

"How is she?" Mrs Booth put some dinner in front of him.

"She's sleeping now." William-Wetherby stared at the plate of food before him, but didn't reach for his knife and fork. "Years ago, when I lived in Birmingham and when Father was going through his problems, his wife Lydia gave him a baby. Arthur his name was. The poor child was doomed from the day he was born. He wasn't four months old when he died and my father tried to kill himself."

Mrs Booth put her hand on William-Wetherby's shoulders, but said nothing.

"Fortunately, my uncle saved him, but for months afterwards, my father and Lydia lived in a daze. He became addicted to laudanum. I didn't understand at the time."

"Unless you've lost a child, you can never fully understand."

William-Wetherby gazed at Mrs Booth. "I'd rather not. We'd give anything to bring Stephen back. I want Bella back too, but she's ..." He bowed his head and let his forehead rest on his hand.

"She's tougher than you give her credit for," Mrs Booth said. "She'll never forget Stephen, but she'll recover. I know my daughter."

William-Wetherby took out his handkerchief and blew his nose. "Where are the boys?"

"Don't worry about them. Fred took them off somewhere; they'll be back for tea. I haven't told them yet."

William-Wetherby picked up his knife and fork. "Good, don't tell them yet."

Mrs Booth made two cups of tea and sat down alongside her son-in-law. "What are we going to do with Florence?"

"I've no idea. Why was she even here? She could have come any time in the last year, but she chose this week. Has the doctor seen her again?"

"He has. He tries to call when the laudanum's about to wear off, but as soon as he sees her, he gives her another dose."

"Why?"

"The only image she has in her head is of Stephen flailing about on the bed and she can talk of nothing other than the devil having possessed him."

"So she doesn't know he died?"

Mrs Booth shook her head.

William-Wetherby sighed. "I have to speak to the doctor; I'll write to Eleanor as well. I don't know whether it will help, but I need more details of what happened when Aunt Charlotte lost her baby. I'm wondering if Florence's reaction stems from that."

. . .

WITH THE NEW week beginning and the hearse waiting for them, William-Wetherby held open the front door for Mrs Booth. They watched silently while the pallbearers placed the coffin inside ready for its short journey to the church. With Bella too weak to attend, William-Wetherby helped his mother-in-law into the carriage that would follow.

The two of them stood alone at the front of the church, while the vicar read through the funeral service. It seemed like no time at all since they were here for his baptism, and now ... William-Wetherby rubbed his fingers across his eyes.

A little over ten minutes later, the trio travelled to the graveyard where the vicar committed Stephen's body to the ground. Mrs Booth sobbed into her handkerchief and once William-Wetherby had thrown the first lump of earth onto the coffin he put his arm around her shoulders to escort her home. When they arrived, he was surprised to find several letters behind the front door.

"One's from Eleanor. She didn't waste any time." He hung up his coat and took the letter to his chair. He read in silence, before he put it on his knee and gazed out of the window.

"Is everything all right?" Mrs Booth returned from the scullery with a cup of tea.

William-Wetherby glanced back at the letter. "She sends her condolences, naturally, but she's explained more about Florence's behaviour when Aunt Charlotte lost her baby."

Mrs Booth sat herself in the chair opposite. "Go on."

"By the sound of it, it was similar to the situation with Stephen. She happened to be in the room when Aunt Charlotte started delivering the baby. They believe she was traumatised by what she saw, but because she was like a mute in the corner, nobody noticed her, until it was too late. By the time they brought her back to reality she was screaming, much as she did here."

"It sounds like there's something else."

William-Wetherby glanced back at the letter. "When they took her to Wetherby House, Mr Wetherby was so angry with her that he had her admitted to Winson Green Lunatic Asylum for hysteria."

"And they didn't tell you?"

William-Wetherby sighed. "It would appear not. Apparently she was only there for a few days before Aunt Sarah-Ann persuaded him to have her released. That must have been why she wasn't at school and why she didn't want to see Mr Wetherby ever again."

Mrs Booth stared into her cup of tea. "We can't send her to the asylum."

"Of course we can't, it's barbaric. I remember when Mother was admitted ..." William-Wetherby shook his head. "It was because she thought she might be sent back that she left home and ... had her accident."

"I'm sorry," Mrs Booth said. "I can't begin to imagine the sort of man Mr Wetherby must have been. Leave Florence with me, I'll try and soothe her, perhaps tell her Stephen's in heaven watching us ..."

William-Wetherby closed his eyes. "Do whatever you have to. She's not going to the asylum and that's the end of it."

Chapter Fifty-One

William-Wetherby's shoulders drooped as he made his way to Cheapside. Was it really only four days since he had last walked along the cobbled alleys around the Main Bridewell? It felt like a lifetime ago and yet he hadn't been ready to leave Bella this morning. It was too soon. Thank goodness for Mrs Booth.

He walked into the reception to find the chief inspector waiting for him.

"Good afternoon, Sergeant. I was hoping to catch you. Do you have a minute?"

William-Wetherby followed his superior into an office and stood before the desk as the chief inspector took his seat.

"You seem to have settled in here," the chief said.

"Yes, sir."

"I'm pleased to say that your calmness and efficiency haven't gone unnoticed."

"Sir?"

"I mentioned a few months ago that we require more inspectors and that your name had been raised, despite your

256

previous misdemeanours. Tell me, have your problems in Birmingham resolved themselves?"

William-Wetherby nodded. "Yes, sir. I'm pleased to say they have."

"I'm glad to hear it, it was a terrible nuisance." The chief glanced up from a letter in his hand. "The chief superintendent has suggested you retake the exams for the position of inspector."

William-Wetherby's eyes flicked towards his boss. "Thank you, sir. I'd be delighted."

"They'll be held next month and you'll be given three days' leave to prepare for them. I remember you excelled in them last time and so I don't expect any problems."

"No, sir, I'll try my best. Will that be all?"

"One final thing. Condolences on losing your son. That's not gone unnoticed either."

WILLIAM-WETHERBY WAS SITTING with Bella eating breakfast when Mrs Booth let herself in.

"Oh good, you're both here."

"I'm on another late shift, but I'm hoping they'll soon be a thing of the past. I've just told Bella that they want me to take my exams again."

"That is good news, but I've called to speak to you about Florence. What are we going to do with her?"

William-Wetherby leaned back in his seat. "Don't think I haven't thought of it, but with things as they've been ..."

"I know she's not been your top priority, but do you think we should send her back to Margate?"

"Has she been out of bed yet?" Bella asked.

"She got up for a couple of hours yesterday afternoon and I'm going to take her for a walk later. She's a lot more stable than she was, but still tearful."

William-Wetherby held Bella's hand. "Anyone would think it was her who'd lost the child. Let me write to Eleanor and ask if she'll have her for a couple of weeks, it might be better than sending her straight to Margate. They're giving me three days off work to study, so I could take her as far as Birmingham."

"What about your exams? You can't put them at risk," Bella said.

"At the moment they're the least of my worries; I passed them without too much trouble last time and if I need to I'll sit up at night and do the work."

THREE DAYS LATER, William-Wetherby walked to Mrs Booth's and pushed open the front door to find Florence fixing her bonnet.

"Are you ready?" William-Wetherby asked his sister.

Florence scanned the room. "I think so. I said goodbye to Fred and your boys this morning and my bag's packed." She put her arms around Mrs Booth. "Thank you for being so kind to me. I'm sorry I became hysterical, but ..."

Mrs Booth took her hand. "You've no need to apologise, we just want you better. I believe Eleanor's looking forward to seeing you."

Florence smiled. "She is, she wrote and told me. I'm going to stay with Charles and Rose in their new house too, although I'm not sure why they've only moved a short way down the road."

William-Wetherby took her arm. "Do we ever understand why Charles does what he does? If you find out, you must tell me."

Florence smiled. "I will. Farewell, Mrs Booth. I hope I see you again one day."

Florence linked her brother's arm as they walked to the

railway station. "You're fortunate having such a lovely family. I hope I meet a nice young man one day."

"I'm sure you will. Have you written to Mr Goodwood about returning to Margate or will you stay in Birmingham?"

Florence sighed. "I haven't decided. Margate is such a long way away, but I don't want to be a burden to anyone in Birmingham. Mr Goodwood said he's missing me and that they need their bookkeeper back and so maybe that's where I should be."

"At least you aren't desperate for money, so you needn't factor that into your decision."

"But if I don't work, the money from Mr Wetherby won't last long. I've used some of it to buy a couple of dresses and I have to pay all my own expenses. Travelling up here isn't cheap either."

"Mother would be so proud of you, looking after yourself as you do."

"Would she?" Florence's eyes sparkled. "I hope she would. I hardly remember her, but I like to think she's watching over us."

"If you tell yourself she is, she'll be there for you."

Chapter Fifty-Two

12 months later

William-Wetherby checked his pocket watch and collected his cap from the table near the front door.

"Right, I'll be off," he said to Bella. "Don't forget I've got a day off tomorrow. You need to decide what you'd like to do."

"As if I'm likely to forget something like that." Bella walked towards him. "A simple walk to the park is enough for me, but can we go to the cemetery on the way?"

William-Wetherby put his arms around his wife. "Of course we can. I can hardly believe it's a year since we lost Stephen."

"No." Bella sighed. "I still think he'll toddle through the front door with Edward and Albert when they've been playing football."

William-Wetherby gave her a squeeze. "At least the other two are growing up well enough. They've got you to thank for that."

"You know the one thing I regret?" Bella said. "That he

wasn't on the photograph with Edward and Albert that was taken at Margaret's wedding." Bella picked up the photograph from the mantelpiece. "I can't even remember why he wasn't. Even to see his little face would be such a comfort."

William-Wetherby pulled a handkerchief from her apron. "Come on, wipe your eyes, no more tears."

Bella put down the photograph and blew her nose into the square of material. "I'm sorry. I couldn't bear losing another one."

William-Wetherby gave her a final embrace as a letter was pushed through the letter box. "It's for you, it looks like Eleanor's handwriting." He handed it to Bella. "Why does she write to you all the time nowadays and not me?"

Bella's eyes regained their sparkle. "Because she knows I'll write back the same day. She can't wait until you have a day off to remember you haven't written."

William-Wetherby laughed. "So what's she got to say?"

"I'll read it properly when you've gone but let me see." Bella pulled the letter from its envelope and hesitated.

"What's the matter?"

"Nothing. She's having another baby, that's all."

"She shouldn't be telling you that at a time like this."

"She won't have remembered the date, I'll be fine. Come on, off you go, you'll be late."

BELLA REREAD ELEANOR'S letter for the umpteenth time before glancing at the clock. Twenty past ten, five minutes later than when she last checked. *Do I go to bed or wait up?* The same question had tormented her all day, but with only ten minutes left she was running out of time. She put the letter back in the pocket of her apron; it could wait until tomorrow ... although would it ruin William-Wetherby's day off? Perhaps it could wait until the day after. She couldn't face it now. She switched off the gaslight and was halfway up the stairs when the front door opened.

"You're up late." William-Wetherby closed the front door and peered up the stairs. "Why aren't you in bed?"

"I was just going ... y-you're early."

William-Wetherby's eyes narrowed as he studied her. "Not by much; what's the matter?"

After a moment's hesitation, Bella walked back down the stairs and set her candle on the table. "Do you want a cup of tea?"

"I want to know what's wrong. Come and sit down."

Bella took a deep breath and lifted the letter from her pocket before sitting in the seat William-Wetherby held out for her. "It's the letter I got this morning."

"You're not upset that Eleanor's having another baby, are you? We can have one too if you want."

Bella shook her head. "It's not that ... it's Florence."

William-Wetherby closed his eyes as he took the seat next to her. "What's she done now?"

"Don't be cross with her, but she was found in an intimate embrace with one of the local lads in Margate. Someone reported her to the police and she was hauled back to Mr Goodwood's house in disgrace. She's been kept under lock and key ever since."

"Don't be cross with her?" William-Wetherby was on his feet. "She brings shame on the family and you tell me not to be cross with her."

"Keep your voice down." Bella pulled her husband back to his seat. "Why is it her fault? She was with a young delivery boy from one of the shops and yet nobody's said a word about him."

"Because she's obviously encouraged him. Decent girls don't behave like that."

"She didn't encourage him. Eleanor's written to her and Florence has said he forced his way onto her."

"And Eleanor believes her?" William-Wetherby was back on his feet. "She should know better. Did he ruin her?"

"No, I don't think so; the police got to them before anything like that happened."

"I can imagine Mr Goodwood's shame. I'm not surprised he's locked her in her room. She's lucky he doesn't have her put in an asylum."

Bella took out a handkerchief to wipe her eyes. "I knew I shouldn't have told you tonight. It wasn't her fault and yet she's getting the blame ... like every other innocent woman before her."

"Men wouldn't behave like that if they weren't tempted."

Bella glared at her husband. "That statement is not even worthy of a response. I'm going to bed. Goodnight."

It had been a week since Bella had learned of Florence's attack and now as she picked up the letters from behind the front door she said a prayer of thanks. Mr Goodwood must have passed on her letter because Florence had replied. With the boys playing outside and William-Wetherby not due home for hours, she had time to read and reply to it.

Florence's story hadn't changed from the version she had given Eleanor. She'd walked into town one Wednesday afternoon, only to be kept talking by a local delivery boy. When he offered to walk her home, she had no reason to refuse but as they walked through the park, he had pulled her into the bushes. Even now, a month later, the poor girl was still distraught, while the young man had gone back to work as if nothing had happened.

Bella only realised she had been holding her breath when she turned the page and gave a sigh of relief. Mr Goodwood had ended her imprisonment and allowed her to return to work. Whether it was out of kindness or because he needed his bookkeeper back, Bella couldn't be sure, but it was something. She stood up to pour herself another cup of tea as Mrs Booth let herself in.

Bella smiled. "You're just in time."

"I could do with one too. It's warm outside and that hill doesn't get any easier." Mrs Booth accepted the cup Bella pushed across the table. "Any news?"

"Read it." Bella handed her mam the letter. "I can't decide whether to show William-Wetherby or not. He's still furious with her for bringing shame on the family; he's no idea how upset she is."

"Poor girl."

"I feel so sorry for her that I want to invite her to stay for a couple of weeks, to give her a break, but I don't know how I can. I still feel guilty about the way we had to send her back down south after Stephen died. It wasn't her fault."

Mrs Booth patted her daughter's hand. "It wasn't your fault either. I'll tell you what. You've no room for her here, but I have. If I invite her, it would be up to William-Wetherby whether he chose to visit her or not."

Bella pulled her lips together. "Do you think he'll be mad at me?"

"Why should he be? I can invite whoever I want to stay at my house."

"But he'd know it was me who'd written to her."

Mrs Booth put the letter back on the table. "You only wrote to find out how she was. I'll write and ask her to visit. It'll be nothing to do with you ... or him."

Chapter Fifty-Three

Birmingham, Warwickshire

Charles straightened his necktie before he knocked on his sister's front door and stepped back. A maid greeted him.

"Good evening, is Mr Keen home yet?"

"No, sir, but your sister's in the back room if you'd care to come in."

Charles stepped into the hall and handed the maid his hat before walking to the back room.

"What time do you expect …?" Charles stopped in his tracks as Florence's frightened eyes gazed up at him. "What's she doing here?" He glared at Eleanor.

"Come and sit down and I'll pour you a whisky." Eleanor stood up and plumped up the cushion on her brother's favourite chair.

He glared at Florence. "I'll need more than a whisky. Has Mr Goodwood kicked her out?"

"No, he hasn't," Eleanor said. "She needs time away from Margate, so she's visiting."

"Please don't be angry with me." Florence fell to her knees and clung to Charles's leg. "It wasn't my fault, I didn't know what was happening."

Charles glared at Eleanor. "And I'm supposed to believe that?"

Eleanor pulled Florence to her feet and back to the settee. "Why would you doubt her? The poor girl's never had any male attention before and she'd no idea what was happening. It's as well the policeman caught them when he did or it could have been a lot worse."

Charles stared at Florence as she sobbed into Eleanor's shoulder. "Did she let him ruin her?"

"She didn't let him do anything ... He forced himself onto her. Why is it so difficult to understand?"

"What's she doing here then?"

"She's travelling to Liverpool and wanted to call here on the way. Is it so wrong to want to come home?"

"William-Wetherby's letting her stay with him?" Charles emptied his glass. "Are you sure? I thought he'd be furious."

Eleanor held her sobbing sister. "Perhaps he's more forgiving than you. Look at her. If she could do anything to change things, she would."

Charles helped himself to another drink and sat down. "We should be thankful it happened down there; at least nobody around here knows anything about it."

"You are unbelievable. Assuming you didn't come to give Florence any sympathy, what did you want?"

"I want to speak to your husband. He is my business part-ner, in case you'd forgotten. What time are you expecting him?"

Eleanor glanced at the clock. "Any time now. Why didn't you talk to him at work?"

"I've been in Birmingham all day and didn't have time to

go into the office." Charles gave a quick nod of the head towards Florence. "How long's she staying?"

"Not long enough for you to need to come here again. She's getting the train to Liverpool the day after tomorrow."

"I'm going to write to William-Wetherby and find out what on earth he's playing at."

~

Liverpool, Lancashire

WILLIAM-WETHERBY SMILED at Bella as he walked through the front door and put his cap on the stand. "I'm ready for this, it's turning cold again." He took his place at the dining table as Bella put a plate of stewed kidneys and mashed potatoes in front of him.

"There's a letter for you from Charles."

William-Wetherby took a bite of his bread and butter before he tore open the envelope. His eyes grew wider as he read, and he swallowed his bread in a lump to clear his mouth. "Have you invited Florence to come and stay?"

Bella picked up the teapot and gave it a swirl. "No."

"So, why is Charles under the impression she's coming to visit us?"

Bella's face reddened as she poured the tea.

"Well ... I'm waiting."

"Please don't be angry." Bella's voice sounded breathless. "She's been treated so badly by everyone that me mam thought she'd like to see some friendly faces."

"Your mam invited her?"

Bella nodded.

"You knew full well what I thought of her behaviour and yet you deliberately went behind my back?"

"She needs support. It's horrible for these women when they're attacked; we wanted to help."

"But you didn't think to ask me first?"

Bella gazed at her husband with doe-like eyes. "I thought that if she was here, you'd be able to talk to her, perhaps even take pity on her."

"Pity? When she's throwing herself at men?"

Bella's eyes narrowed and she moved to a chair by the fire. "Suit yourself, you don't have to see her if you don't want to. She's staying at me mam's and I'll tell her you're stuck in work, just like you're stuck in your self-righteous middle-class ways."

"What did you say to me?"

Bella swung round and glared at him. "You heard. I'm sick to death of you and your condescending attitude. Why does everyone always assume it's women who tempt men? It's about time you realised that men have a duty to treat women as human beings. We may not be as strong as you, but that doesn't mean we can be forced into doing things we don't want to."

William-Wetherby stared at his wife, his mouth open, but Bella continued.

"You once told me how angry your mother used to be when she couldn't do the things she wanted to do; well, this is no different. How do you think she'd react knowing her daughter had been attacked and you'd turned your back on her?"

William-Wetherby glanced at his food and put his knife and fork back on the table. "I'm going to the tavern. Don't wait up."

Chapter Fifty-Four

William-Wetherby stepped down from the carriage and waited for the driver to leave. He wasn't sure whether to be pleased that being an inspector allowed him to use one of the police carriages, or annoyed that he was home so early. After last night's outburst, what did he say to Bella?

With the sun hidden behind the houses, he shivered before pushing the front door open. As he went inside Bella glanced up from her sewing but said nothing.

"I managed to get the carriage tonight."

"Good."

"Yes, it was. Are the boys not in yet?"

"Not yet, they've another half an hour."

"Right, good. Is there any tea?"

Bella sighed and put down her mending before disappearing into the scullery. Seconds later she slammed down the kidneys and mash he had left the night before. "It's been warming in the oven."

William-Wetherby hesitated. "About last night ..."

"Unless you're going to apologise, I suggest you sit and eat

your tea before it goes cold. I'm not going to argue with you."
Bella focussed all her attention on her sewing.

William-Wetherby took his seat at the table but turned to
face her. "I'm sorry we argued."

"Eat your tea."

William-Wetherby turned back to the table in silence until
his plate was empty.

"I'm sorry I said those things about Florence."

He finally had Bella's attention. "You are?"

"I've been thinking about what you said and you're right.
Mother wouldn't be happy if I turned my back on her
youngest daughter. When I went to bed last night, I could
almost hear her talking about how unfair life is for women."

"Well, I'm glad someone managed to talk some sense into
you."

William-Wetherby joined Bella by the fire. "Is she here
yet?"

"She is, but don't worry, you won't see her around here.
I've told her you're busy."

Why's Father always too busy to see us? The words of his
younger sisters raced through his mind as he thought back to
the time of his father's bankruptcy and illness. *We've got so
much to tell him ...*

"You shouldn't tell her that. I'm not too busy. Why don't
you invite her for tea tomorrow night? I should be home
about the same time ... and I promise I won't shout."

TWENTY-FOUR HOURS LATER, William-Wetherby took a
deep breath before pushing open the front door. Bella was
setting the table.

"You're early," Bella said. "Florence has just gone back to
me mam's."

William-Wetherby took his seat by the fireplace. "What's she been up to today?"

"Not much, she walked the boys to school and back and looked over my books. I've made a few shillings on me hats."

"That's good. Is Florence all right?"

"Outwardly she's fine, but she's quieter than usual. If she so much as sees a man in the street, you can see her hesitate as they walk towards her. It's knocked her confidence."

"At least she has you to talk to ..." William-Wetherby trailed off mid-sentence as the front door opened and Florence walked in.

"You're home." Florence hovered by the door. "Are you angry with me?"

William-Wetherby studied his sister, subdued in a way he'd never seen her before.

"Not any more." He stood up and put his arm around her shoulders. "Bella told me what happened. How are you feeling?"

Florence's blue eyes welled with tears as she stared at her brother. "It was horrible. I didn't know what he was doing and ... his hands ..."

"It's all right ... you don't have to tell me. You need to forget about it."

"I can't ... it's in my dreams ... if I close my eyes ..."

"That's enough, you need to be strong. Bella and Mrs Booth will help you." He smiled at Bella. "Won't you?"

"Of course we will, that's why you're here. Let me go and fetch the tea. The boys will be here in a minute and they'll help take your mind off everything."

ON THE EVENING before Florence was due to return to Birmingham, William-Wetherby hadn't had time to take his coat off before Florence jumped from her chair and threw her arms around him.

"What's that in aid of?" William-Wetherby shrugged Florence off as gently as he could.

"For being so kind to me. It's hard to believe it's my last night here, I wish I didn't have to go."

"I'm sure you'll be fine once you're on your way."

Florence took her seat again. "I thought you'd be mad at me when I arrived, like Charles was, but you weren't. You're my favourite brother."

William-Wetherby smiled. "Are you ready to see Charles again? I've written to tell him to be nice to you."

Florence beamed at her brother. "I should give you an extra hug for that. Can you write to Uncle William as well?"

William-Wetherby stared at her. "Why, what's he done?"

"He's been horrid. When I was in Birmingham, Aunt Charlotte visited Aunt Mary-Ann and she invited me, Rose, Daisy and Lilly for afternoon tea at her new house."

William-Wetherby raised an eyebrow. "Did you go?"

Florence's eyes sparkled. "I did. She sent her carriage for us and it took us all the way to Edgbaston. Oh, she has the most splendid house you've ever seen, although why she needs one so big with only her and Mr Mountford living there I can't say. I'm sure they've got more servants than they need, just to fill the place up."

"How was Aunt Charlotte? I presume there's no sign of a child."

Florence's face grew stern. "No, but it was all she could talk about. She asked about you and wanted to hear all about Edward and Albert."

"She did?" William-Wetherby's brow furrowed.

"I'd told her about Stephen and she was very sorry. I hope you don't mind."

William-Wetherby cracked his knuckles. "No, I don't

mind you telling her as long as you don't talk to Uncle William about me."

"As if I would, but that's what I was coming to. When we were there, Uncle William arrived with Mr Mountford and he was the rudest man you've ever met. Since Mr Wetherby died, he thinks he can tell everyone what to do. He asked if we'd visited so we could beg for money, and before we could say a word he ordered Aunt Charlotte to send us away."

Bella perked up. "And did she?"

Florence chuckled. "No, it was marvellous. She told him she would invite who she wanted into her house and if he didn't like it he could go. Thankfully, he went."

William-Wetherby didn't laugh. "Where does he live now? Is he still in Bushwood?"

"No, they left years ago. They moved back to a huge house on Handsworth Wood Road before Mr Wetherby died. The trouble is …" Florence laughed again "… it isn't as impressive as Aunt Charlotte's and he hates the fact she has more money than him."

"Serves him right," William-Wetherby said. "Do they still have Wetherby House?"

Florence shuddered as she nodded her head. "They do, but Aunt Sarah-Ann had barely moved out before they had someone renting it."

"They'll get a pretty penny for that." William-Wetherby gave a low whistle. "What about the business? Does he still run that?"

Florence cocked her head to one side. "I don't think they've sold it. I heard Charles talking to Aunt Mary-Ann and I got the impression that now Henry's back from Cambridge, he does the work."

"He went to Cambridge? The university?" William-Wetherby shook his head. "I thought he was working in the family business?"

"He was, but then he got the chance to go up to Cambridge and so he went."

Bella's forehead creased. "Who's Henry?"

"He's Uncle William's son and I don't know why I'm so surprised he went to one of the best universities in the country. You can do anything with money."

Bella stroked her husband's hand. "Don't upset yourself. You've not spoken about them for months."

William-Wetherby grunted. "At least Henry doesn't sound as work-shy as his father."

"He's not," Florence said. "He's really quite nice."

William-Wetherby stared at his sister. "He's a Wetherby, how can he be?" He picked up one of the boys' wooden blocks and threw it at the wall. "God, I hate that family."

Chapter Fifty-Five

Birmingham, Warwickshire

William-Wetherby stood on the concourse of Birmingham New Street Station, his hands stuffed deep into his pockets. With Christmas approaching, the weather had taken a turn for the worse and now a biting wind swirled about him. He hadn't been waiting long when Charles ambled up the causeway towards him.

"You're early, I wasn't expecting you yet."

"I managed to catch an earlier train, but I didn't mind waiting."

Charles gave his brother a sideways glance. "So what are you doing here? You didn't give much away in your letter."

William-Wetherby pulled his overcoat more tightly around him. "I'm here on official business. We have reason to believe a group of scoundrels who've been reported thieving and causing trouble down by the docks in Liverpool are from Birmingham. Given I know the area, they asked me to come and speak to my colleagues down here."

"More likely because they knew it wouldn't cost them any money to put you up." Charles smirked at his brother.

William-Wetherby returned his grin. "Well, whatever it was, I wasn't going to say no. Are we going to Eleanor's?"

"Yes, she's doing tea for us before we go back to Small Heath. If you've anything to tell me in private, you'd better say it now."

William-Wetherby laughed. "No, I think my news is suitable for both of you."

ELEANOR WAS WAITING for them in the living room when they arrived.

"Here you are. Why did you take such a late train?" She pushed herself up from the chair as soon as William-Wetherby entered the room.

"And it's lovely to see you, too." William-Wetherby grinned. "I'm going to be here for a few days yet, you'll be fed up with me by the time I go home."

"Come and sit yourself down and tell me what you're up to. How are those lovely boys?"

"They're fine, but you're not the only one eating for two." William-Wetherby nodded at Eleanor's swollen belly. "Bella told me this morning that she's in the family way again. It's due around July next year I believe."

Eleanor brought her hands to her mouth. "I'm so pleased for her. After everything she went through with Stephen, she must be delighted."

"She is. Despite what she might say, she's not over him. Hopefully this new baby will give her something to occupy her time while the other two are at school."

Eleanor smiled. "I hope so. Did Bella tell you about Margaret too? She's expecting her first baby the month after mine's due."

"No, she didn't! I'll have to have a word with her."

Eleanor laughed. "Don't be too hard on her, Margaret only told me a few weeks ago. She probably didn't realise what was happening; it's a shock first time around if you're not close to someone who's gone through it. That was when I missed Mother the most."

"I'm fortunate Bella has Mrs Booth, but less of that." William-Wetherby paused as he became aware of his brother's silence. "Is there any chance of getting a drink around here? I've not had one for hours."

"Oh my, where are my manners? Take a seat both of you." Eleanor went to the door and asked the maid to fetch the tea. "Mr Keen will be home shortly, you'll have to wait for him if you want anything stronger."

William-Wetherby glanced at Charles. "I wasn't strictly honest with you when you met me at the railway station."

Charles raised an eyebrow but said nothing.

"I did catch an earlier train, but it was so I could make a few visits."

"Where to?"

"Up to Handsworth and then over to Edgbaston."

Charles sat up straight. "You went to visit Uncle William and Aunt Charlotte? What on earth did you do that for?"

"I didn't go to see them, or at least that wasn't the intention, but I had to see the houses they live in. Florence told me how grand Aunt Charlotte's was and I had to see for myself."

"Did they see you?"

"If Uncle William saw me, he's probably still walking to the front door. Have you seen the size of the house? It's obscene."

"The man's obscene, what did you expect?"

William-Wetherby shook his head. "I don't know, but not that. He doesn't need anything like that with only the three of them living there. Florence told me the house has over twenty

277

rooms. Twenty! At least half of them must be empty or closed up with dust covers over everything."

"What did you think of Aunt Charlotte's house?" Eleanor asked.

William-Wetherby flushed before glancing at Charles. "She saw me and invited me in."

"No! Did you go?"

"I had no choice, she'd sent 'one of her men' to fetch me."

"What did you think?" Eleanor asked. "I called with Aunt Mary-Ann a couple of months ago. The place is stunning."

"I don't know about stunning … frightening I would say. She gave me a cup of tea, but with china cups and a cream-coloured settee I was too frightened to pick it up."

"Never mind the furniture," Charles said. "What did she say? I'm surprised she could look you in the eye after only giving us a fraction of our claim."

"She said she knew nothing of it; it was Uncle William and Mr Mountford who sorted everything out."

"And you believe her?" Charles stared at his brother.

"Actually, I do. What husband wouldn't take control of his wife's money when it was such a substantial amount? He wouldn't have trusted her with it. Or more to the point, Uncle William wouldn't."

"She's an educated woman," Eleanor said. "She'd be perfectly capable of sorting out her own affairs."

William-Wetherby feigned a laugh. "You sounded like Mother then, but you said the magic word. She might be educated, but she's a woman and in Uncle William's world that makes her incapable of doing anything with money. I imagine it was him who insisted on working with Mr Mountford."

"I expect he thought Aunt Charlotte would be more sympathetic to us," Charles added. "Did she offer you any money?"

"It's all tied up in investments or the bank and she'd need Mr Mountford's permission to withdraw it."

"She's probably not lying about that either," Eleanor said.

"Maybe not, but it's her money. She should tell him what she wants to do with it," Charles said. "It's 1900 now, for better or worse, women are demanding more rights."

William-Wetherby choked back a laugh. "I'd say she can find money when she wants to. I didn't see anything in her drawing room that didn't cost less than a week's wages for one of the lads at the station. She had some dining chairs that were so elaborate, with curved backs inset with pointed arches, they looked as if they'd been designed to match the windows. They must have cost a fortune. The only reason she can't draw money out is to give it to us."

"You might be right, but moaning about it won't change anything," Eleanor said. "We're all happy and healthy and unlike them our family's growing. Let's be thankful for what we have and stop worrying about them."

Chapter Fifty-Six

The midwinter sun lightened the sky over Birmingham as William-Wetherby and Charles climbed into Mary-Ann's carriage and took seats opposite each other.

"One of the benefits of being married to Rose," Charles said. "I can usually have the carriage whenever I want it."

"It's all right for some." William-Wetherby settled into his seat. "Are you still getting along with Aunt Mary-Ann?"

"She's got used to me and she knows she can't get rid of me even if she wants to."

William-Wetherby laughed. "And how are things between you and Florence? Did you make your peace when she came back here from Liverpool?"

Charles grunted. "I did, thanks to you, but what got into you? I thought you'd be mad at her for bringing shame on the family, then the next thing I knew you'd invited her to stay with you."

William-Wetherby sighed. "It's a long story, but let's just say I have a wife who has strong feelings about this. It was her and Mrs Booth who invited Florence to Liverpool, I knew nothing about it until I got your letter."

"Really?"

"Really. Do you remember Mother used to get angry at the way women were treated? Well, Bella has a similar streak in her, especially when she believes they've been wronged. The whole situation caused a furious row and I had no choice but to back down. Once I saw Florence, I came around. I don't think she did it on purpose."

"She still brought shame on the family."

"Maybe she did but I wondered what Mother would have said if she knew we'd abandoned her. When I thought of it like that, I wasn't proud of myself for being so hard on her."

"Perhaps you're right. Do you know how she's getting on now she's back in Margate?"

"Bella had a letter from her the day before I left. She said she's settled again and that Mr Goodwood is being especially kind and chaperones her whenever she goes out."

"He's probably more bothered about saving his own reputation. Although why he agreed to have her back I don't know. Everyone in the area must know about the incident."

William-Wetherby shrugged. "She says everyone's been friendly, although whether she's deluding herself I don't know. I'm just relieved she's happy again. Hopefully it won't be long before she finds herself a husband."

By the time Charles dropped him off, it was almost eight o'clock and William-Wetherby stopped to study the three-storey building he was about to enter. Birmingham police station was a lockup, like the Main Bridewell in Liverpool, but was more ornate and less prison-like than Cheapside. Straightening out his jacket, he pushed on the front door before presenting himself at the front desk.

"Inspector Jackson here to see Inspector Cooper." William-Wetherby saluted the duty officer.

The officer returned his salute. "Yes, sir. He's expecting you. Follow me, please."

William-Wetherby followed the officer down a short, tiled corridor into a room at the far end. Inspector Cooper was waiting for him.

"Inspector Jackson, come in and take a seat. Thank you for making the journey. I can't imagine travelling as far as Liverpool, especially not in this weather."

William-Wetherby removed his cap and took the seat that was offered. "It's no trouble at all. I'm glad to be of assistance. This gang of scoundrels are causing mayhem around Liverpool and so anything we can do to apprehend them will be appreciated. What can you tell me about them?"

Inspector Cooper opened a large manila file on his desk. "We've been after them for several years, but they've been quiet since the middle of the year. We thought they'd changed their ways until your chief superintendent contacted us."

"If only that was the case. We first caught sight of them over the summer. They were at the docks stealing items as they were unloaded from the ships and starting fights with anyone who tried to stop them. As soon as our men got anywhere near, they'd clear off."

"That sounds like them. We believe they have a lookout who tips them off." Inspector Cooper passed William-Wetherby several papers from the files. "We think these men are the ringleaders and if we can capture them, the network will break down. This is the main man here, Thomas Hudson."

William-Wetherby read Hudson's details. *An overly tall man, at least six feet, two inches with receding, greying hair and a gash on his right cheek.* "Did these descriptions come from eyewitnesses?"

"They did, in fact we have several accounts for each man which are remarkably similar. I've spoken to my chief here and we believe the best way to apprehend them is to get close, befriend them and learn of their plans in advance."

"They're never going to talk to a police officer."

"No, that's the point. We believe someone with enough authority needs to act as a civilian to gain their trust. You're a natural choice given your rank and the fact that your accent will tell them you're from Birmingham. They're more likely to trust you."

"Me? You want me to trick them?"

"My chief has written to yours, Chief Inspector Lucas, and it will be up to him to decide. I imagine it would only be for a few weeks."

William-Wetherby's stomach churned as he reread the descriptions. He was a desk-bound inspector, not a plain-clothes detective. Birmingham accent or not, he didn't have the training for it.

AN HOUR after he entered the police station, William-Wetherby left and headed for Charles's workshop. It wasn't yet nine o'clock and he'd need to catch the next train back to Liverpool.

"You're leaving already?" Charles said. "I thought you'd be here for another couple of days yet."

"So did I." William-Wetherby's shoulders sagged. "I was expecting some desk work down here but they want me to go straight back to Liverpool and get my instructions. They want me to find the gang and befriend them."

Charles sucked air through his teeth. "Are they dangerous?"

"They could be, which is why we're so keen to catch them. Bella'll be furious if I have to work on Christmas Day. I told her I had the day off."

"She'll be even less happy if you clear off for weeks at a time."

William-Wetherby sighed. "I hadn't thought of that. I'll try to arrange a week's worth of desk research and suggest I don't start until the New Year. The city often gets an influx of newcomers in January, that could be my cover."

"You will be careful, won't you?"

William-Wetherby smiled at his brother's concerned face. "Are you giving me practice for what I say when Bella finds out? Telling her is going to be the hardest part of this whole assignment."

Chapter Fifty-Seven

Liverpool, Lancashire

An icy wind blew from the River Mersey as William Wetherby trudged headlong into it, towards the Albert Dock. He stopped in the shelter of a wall and scanned the crowds of workers unloading the ships berthed at the quayside. Since he'd started his assignment on New Year's Day, he'd got used to walking the beat in his civilian clothes and pausing to watch others at work. What he hadn't got used to was not going home each evening. It was three weeks since he had last slept in his own bed and he cursed the gang from Birmingham. *Where the hell are you? All I need to do is find you and tip off one of the uniformed officers and then I can go home. How can you have disappeared off the face of the earth?*

For the first couple of days of the assignment he'd come down to the docks looking for work. Being tall and healthy he'd never been turned away, but within hours his hands were in shreds and his back refused to move without pains shooting down his legs. But that wasn't the worst of it. Men were chosen at eight o'clock every morning and so by quarter past eight every day, he knew that the gang from Birmingham wouldn't be joining him, yet he had to put in a full day's work.

By the third day, he'd changed tack and stopped looking for work. He'd recognise a Birmingham accent anywhere and so he'd walk the length of the docks listening for telltale signs ... but they hadn't come. Neither had there been any trouble. Instead, the only times he encountered any disturbances were when the men spilled from the docks to the public houses at the end of each day and consumed far too much ale. That was always when he knew it was time to go back to the room in the hostel the police had arranged for him.

With the dark grey clouds threatening snow, William-Wetherby pulled his overcoat tightly around him. How he longed to be by the fire, a cup of tea in hand, talking to Bella. It was the longest they'd been apart since they'd met and with another baby due in the summer, he hoped she was coping better than he was.

When he was sure there were no Birmingham accents within earshot, he turned away from the water and made his way to a public house opposite. If he was to blend in as one of the lads, he had to play the part to the full.

"A pint of best," he called when he caught the barman's attention.

"Are you from Burmingham?" a voice beside him asked. William-Wetherby turned to see a young man, no more than twenty-five years old, addressing him. He smiled when he saw him.

"I am, and I presume you are too?"

The man offered William-Wetherby his hand. "I am. Stan's the name. It's unusual to hear a friendly voice, there aren't many of us around these parts."

William-Wetherby shook Stan's hand. "Billy."

"So, Billy, what brings you to Liverpool?"

William-Wetherby had rehearsed his lines. "The same as most men I shouldn't wonder. Here for the work. Split up with a woman back home ... you know how it is."

His new acquaintance laughed. "You and everyone else here."

"Are you on your own?" William-Wetherby asked.

"I am for the minute, but a few of us work around the docks when we can. I wasn't picked for work today, but the rest of the lads were."

William-Wetherby studied the short stature and slim frame of the man beside him. He wasn't surprised. "It's heavy going; I'm having a few days off; my hands were ripped to shreds with rope burns the other day. I'll be back at it tomorrow though; I don't want to be kicked out of my room because I can't pay the rent. Where do you usually work?"

"All over, but we've had most success around the Kings Dock. That's where the lads are now. Come and sit with me and wait for them to arrive."

William-Wetherby hesitated. Should he go and tell the chief where the gang were? They could have them arrested within the hour. He stared down at the pint of ale he had just paid for. One drink wouldn't hurt.

Two hours later, when the rest of the lads arrived, William-Wetherby spoke slowly as Stan introduced them, determined not to slur his words.

"Pleased to meet you, Tommy." The scar on Tommy's cheek reminded William-Wetherby of the type of man he was dealing with. "Where will you be tomorrow?"

"We don't decide until we leave the lodging house. We don't like to be predictable."

Don't I know it. "That's a shame. I thought I might join you. It makes a change to be with people I can understand ..."

William-Wetherby paused to smile but continued when he got no response. "Where are your digs?"

"That'd be telling." The older man leaned forward across the table and stared at William-Wetherby. "Nobody needs to know that."

"N-no ... no. I'm sorry ... didn't mean to pry, but it would make a change to have some friends."

The man continued to stare at him before he nodded. "You're right. It's no fun being on your own. I'll tell you what; I'll make an exception. Meet us by Mann Island at half seven in the morning and we'll decide what we're doing."

AT SEVEN O'CLOCK THE following day, William-Wetherby splashed his face with the icy water from the washstand and shivered. How many pints of ale had he drunk last night? Far more than he should have, that was for sure, and now he was too late to go to Cheapside to arrange for the gang to be arrested. He pulled his shirt over the two woollen vests he had slept in and reached for his jacket. What had he been thinking? If only he'd been to see the chief yesterday afternoon, he'd be going home now, but instead, he could be signed up for a full day's hard labour with some of the most wanted men in Liverpool. *Thank the Lord Bella has no idea what I'm doing.*

He arrived at Mann Island at twenty past seven and pulled his coat tightly around himself. There was no sign of the lads from Birmingham. At least it would be easier to find them now he knew what they looked like. *I suppose I'd better act as if I want a day's work in case I'm being watched.* After waiting for fifteen minutes, he glanced around one last time, before setting off for the Albert Dock. He hadn't gone far when he heard footsteps running up behind him.

"Billy, wait."

"Stan, there you are. Are you on your own?"

"The lads are on their way. Tommy had a spot of bother he needed to deal with."

"Bother?"

Stan laughed. "Oh, nothing to worry about and it's all sorted out now. Here they come."

"That's a relief. If we're not quick, we're going to miss our chance of work. I was just heading for the Albert Dock."

When no one objected, William-Wetherby led the way to the dock gates allowing the men behind to push in front of him. He had no desire to put in a full day's work, and besides, his best chance of going home tonight was if they got work and he didn't. If that happened he'd be able to nip off and raise the alarm.

"Another five." A foreman stood by the gate with his hand in the air displaying five fingers. "Don't all push at once. You … you … in you get."

That's two of the Birmingham lads in, another three to go.

"Nobody under five foot eight." The foreman stared down at Stan as he pushed through another one of the Birmingham group.

"I'm five foot eight and a half."

"And I'm ten foot," the foreman said. "You behind him, you'll do."

William-Wetherby glanced over his shoulder.

"Not the fella behind you, you. Get in here." The foreman pulled William-Wetherby's arm. "Can't waste a tall lad like you."

"Only if you take me mate." William-Wetherby grabbed hold of Stan's arm. "We're together."

With the crowds pushing at William-Wetherby's back, the foreman stared at him. "He gets one day and if I see him slacking he needn't bother coming back."

With the entrance gate closed behind him, William-Wetherby took a deep breath. What did he do now? Although he had Tommy trapped along with a couple of other hooligans, he couldn't do anything about it while he was in here with them. The only option was to stay close to them. He also had Stan to think about. The poor fellow hadn't worked in over a week and he'd only brought him in so he could earn a day's wage. He didn't deserve locking up. Not everyone in this gang was equal.

At the end of a ten-hour shift, William-Wetherby excused himself from the gang and made his way back to the hostel. His back was aching and he thanked the Lord tomorrow was Sunday. With a few slices of bread inside him, he lay on the bed thinking about the day ahead. He was going to meet Bella, and more than anything in the world that would make up for the hard labour he'd put in today. He smiled when he thought of her; he hadn't seen her since last Sunday and his body ached for her. The only thing stopping him going home was getting these men behind bars. That was something for tomorrow too, to get a message to the chief telling him where they'd be on Monday. He'd do it once he'd seen Bella.

As soon as dinner was over the following day, William-Wetherby wrapped himself in his overcoat and left the house. As expected, the weather was bitterly cold, but he didn't care. He was heading for the park and once he was with Bella, all this would be forgotten. He took the most direct route, but at every street corner, he stopped to check he wasn't being followed. When he finally reached his destination, he headed for the Palm House and, without stopping to admire the plants, he walked straight to a secluded seat in the back corner. *At least the icy temperatures have kept people away.*

It was another five minutes before he heard footsteps approaching and he stood up to see a new creation of velvet and feathers sitting proudly on top of his wife's head.

"I like the hat." He smiled as he bent forward to kiss her.

Bella let her hand rest on the side of his face and gazed into his eyes. "I've got to find something to occupy me time. I thought a fancy new hat might encourage you to come home again."

William-Wetherby wrapped his arms around her and as his lips found hers, he held her tight. "Not long now, I promise." They parted and he stroked his finger down her cheek, never moving his gaze from her dark eyes. "I thought I had them yesterday, but I couldn't raise the alarm. I'm hoping they'll be arrested tomorrow and all this will be over."

Bella took his hand as they sat down. "The boys are missing you. They ask after you first thing every morning and again last thing at night. They think they've upset you."

"I'm not doing this again. If I get a promotion out of it I'll make sure someone else does the dirty work."

Bella nestled into his shoulder and William-Wetherby breathed in the scent from her newly washed hair. Neither of them moved until they heard footsteps approaching.

"Did you hear about the Queen?" Bella asked.

"No, what?"

"She's not well. It said in the paper that they think she may not recover."

William-Wetherby's brow creased. "How old must she be? I'd say at least eighty, although with the doctors she's got, they'll be able to do something for her."

Bella snuggled back into William-Wetherby's embrace as a couple walked past. "I hope so, it won't be the same without her."

"What about you? Is the baby moving yet?" He let his hand rest over the subtle swelling of her belly.

"Not yet, another month or so and it should. Me mam's looking after me so you needn't worry."

"I should be there for you." He wrapped his arms around her again. "I wish we could stay here and forget about everything outside these glass walls. It's as if we're in another world."

"Just come home in one piece, that's all I ask."

With the light starting to fade, William-Wetherby wiped the palms of his hands on his trousers as he watched Bella disappear behind the broad leaves of the palms. She shouldn't have to walk home alone, but he daren't be seen with her. He clenched his fists; this was the last time she would make that journey alone. *If I go to Cheapside now I can make sure the letter is waiting for the chief when he arrives in the morning.*

Once outside he walked across the park, heading for the city centre. He couldn't risk being seen and stayed well away from the docks, but by half past four all daylight had disappeared and he walked in the shadows cast by the newly electrified streetlights. Finally, an hour after he left the park he reached the Main Bridewell, but he couldn't go in. No one except the chief knew what he was doing and his colleagues had been told he'd been posted out of town for a few weeks. He fumbled in his coat pocket for the letter he had written earlier and glanced down at it.

PRIVATE AND CONFIDENTIAL
For the Attention of Chief Inspector Lucas Only

HE NEEDED to get it to the chief before he met the gang again tomorrow morning. He waited on the street corner for over ten minutes before he saw a constable returning from his beat.

"Excuse me, Constable. Are you going into the Bridewell? Would you pass this to Chief Inspector Lucas for me? He's expecting it."

The constable studied him. "It's Inspector Jackson, isn't it? Why don't you come in and give it to him yourself?"

"I can't right now, could you do it for me? It's rather urgent and I need to be somewhere else. If everything goes according to plan, I'll be back by the end of the week."

Chapter Fifty-Eight

I
t was with a feeling of déjà vu that William-Wetherby waited at Mann Island with his coat pulled tightly around him. He closed his eyes and clenched his teeth. He could do this. All he needed to do was hang back and point out the gang to the chief, and then he could go home.

"What's up with you?" Stan arrived at the side of William-Wetherby.

"Stomach cramps, nothing to worry about I hope. Where are we going?"

"You tell us."

"What? M-me?" William-Wetherby gazed at the six pairs of eyes staring at him. "I-I don't mind." His voice was an octave higher than it should have been.

"Why not?" Tommy stepped towards him. "We were arguing amongst ourselves on the way here and you must have a preference for where to go. We'll let you decide."

William-Wetherby allowed himself to breathe. "Why don't we go to the Albert Dock again? We got work there on Friday."

William-Wetherby's smile froze on his lips as Tommy glared at him.

"I didn't like it there. I think we'll go to the Prince's Dock. They take more men there ... but we'll have to get a move on."

William-Wetherby nodded before falling in line with the rest of the gang, his eyes scanning the area for the chief. *Where is he? I hope he's got someone following me. They'll never find us otherwise.* As they approached the entrance to the dock, the crowds grew and William-Wetherby struggled to keep up with the men. Where were the police when you needed them?

The men pushed through the crowd, fighting for each step as they approached the entrance. William-Wetherby noticed Tommy go through, but his stomach churned when he yanked Stan in after him. For some reason, he didn't want him involved. He watched as three others followed. Where was the last of them? He flinched as a voice whispered in his ear.

"Aren't you going in, Billy?" It was Tommy's right-hand man and although he was the same height as William-Wetherby he was twice as wide. William-Wetherby shrank back from him.

"Yes, of course ... but I'm not feeling too well. You go first ... make a path for me."

The man grabbed William-Wetherby's arm and pulled him towards the entrance. "We can't go in without you."

At the sight of the burly labourer, the dock foreman opened up the gate and allowed the two of them through before he closed it to the rest of the crowd. "Right, follow me," the man said. "We've got a large windjammer in today that needs unloading by tonight."

William-Wetherby stopped and ran his hand across his face. He wasn't lying about his stomach ... he felt as if he could be sick at any moment. Could he make his excuses and leave? He turned back to the gate and his discomfort lifted momentarily. The chief was here with half a dozen constables. *Don't look too eager. They can't suspect me.* He turned back to face the men seconds before a hand landed on his shoulder. "You're coming with us, sonny."

"No, Officer, stop. Tommy, Stan ..."

The sound of their names was enough to grab their attention and William-Wetherby thought his heart had stopped as they stared at him before eyeing the constables behind him. William-Wetherby watched everything in slow motion as police officers charged towards them, scattering men all around him. The gang turned to run, but came face to face with the dock policemen. Tommy and his mate swung at the nearest men, leaving two officers on their backs, blood oozing from their faces.

"Tommy, no ..." William-Wetherby broke free from his captor but stopped when Stan froze and stared at him. "Stan, run. There's a gate at the other end."

"Oh no you don't." A police officer was upon Stan before he could move and strapped a pair of handcuffs on him, fastening his arms around a nearby lamppost. As the lock clicked into place, the officer jumped on a second suspect who had wrestled his colleague to the ground. William-Wetherby watched helplessly as his colleagues chased and caught the remaining four men. When they were all cuffed and back at the lamppost, Tommy glared at him. "Where're your cuffs?"

William-Wetherby stared at his bare wrists before looking back at the men.

"How should I know? Maybe because I didn't run."

Without a word, the chief, who'd been behind him, grabbed him by the arm and fastened his hands behind his back. "That's it, lads. Let's get them back to the Main Bridewell."

"Why didn't you run?" Stan said as they route marched from the dock.

"Why would I?" William-Wetherby said. "I had no idea what was going on until one of the officers had my arm up my back. What have you been up to?"

"We ain't been up to nothing," Tommy said.

"Well, they clearly think you have."

"Tommy stepped on William-Wetherby's foot as they waited to be let through the gate. "If I find out you had anything to do with this, I'll be back for you."

"Me?" William-Wetherby's voice squeaked. "Why would it be anything to do with me? I only met you last week."

"And less than a week later, this happens. I'm telling you, I'll be looking out for you."

WITH THE MEN in the cells, William-Wetherby was released and shown into the chief's office.

"Well done, Inspector." He indicated to William-Wetherby to be seated.

"Thank you, sir. What happens now?"

"We've confirmed the names of each of them. Thomas Hudson's the ringleader. He looks like a nasty piece of work and so if we can pin anything else on him, we will."

"When will you move them?"

"They'll have to stay here until the trial and then we'll make a case to have them sent to the prison at Walton."

"That could take weeks; they can't see me here."

"Don't worry, Inspector. Your bravery hasn't gone unnoticed and we've an opening for a subdivisional inspector back at Prescot Street. If you'd like to accept, you'll be in charge of the whole station."

"Thank you, sir. I would like to accept, but I do have one concern. If the men don't see me standing trial with them, they'll be suspicious ... Not that I want to stand trial, you understand, but I don't want them knowing I had anything to do with their arrest."

The chief leaned back in his seat, his index fingers set in a triangle, pointing at his chin. "On what grounds would we charge you? You weren't present at any of their burglaries or disturbances, and we have no witnesses to testify against you. We have several who'll identify them. Don't worry, Inspector. If it comes to it, we can always say you were released without charge. They'll know we don't have anything on you."

William-Wetherby let out a long sigh. "Yes, sir, you're right. I'm sorry. It's been a long three weeks. Do you think I may be allowed to take the rest of the day off?"

The chief smiled. "As you're not on the rota this week, I'd say we can manage without you for a few days. The only thing that might change is if Her Majesty dies. I take it you've heard the news."

William-Wetherby shook his head. "Only that she's been ill."

"We have it on good authority that the doctors can't revive her and family members have started gathering at Osborne House. If she dies, there'll be a time of national mourning and we'll need you back."

"Yes, sir. " William-Wetherby stood up to leave. "I'll report for duty if anything happens."

WILLIAM-WETHERBY DIDN'T NOTICE the walk home from Cheapside and without pausing he opened the front door and went straight in. Bella was by the door, fixing her hat ready to go out but as soon as she saw him, she threw her arms around his neck.

"You're back."

He returned her embrace. "I am, and that's the last time

I'm doing anything like that ... even if it means missing out on further promotions."

Bella pulled away and studied him. "Further promotions? Does that mean you've been given one already?"

William-Wetherby couldn't contain his smile. "I have. I'm going to be a subdivisional inspector in charge of the station on Prescot Street."

Bella's smile widened as she took in his words. "You're going to be back at Prescot Street? That's wonderful ... and with more money too?"

William-Wetherby paused. "We didn't actually talk about money, but I would imagine so."

"At least some good's come out of it. The boys'll be pleased too. I'm about to go and pick them up from school, why don't you come with me."

William-Wetherby shook his head. "It's been a busy day. I'd rather sit here with a cup of tea and wait for you. Is there one in the pot?"

"Oh my dear, why didn't I think of that?" Bella hurried to the table and peered into the teapot. "You should be able to squeeze one out and I'll make a fresh pot when I get home." She paused to kiss him. "I won't be long."

With his legs stretched out in front of the fire, William-Wetherby rested his head on the back of the chair and closed his eyes. He could still see the confusion in Stan's eyes as he was handcuffed to the lamppost while William-Wetherby stood free beside him. Why would the police not have arrested him if they were chasing everyone from Birmingham? Until they'd questioned them, they wouldn't have known he hadn't been involved. He knew he had a valid excuse for not being locked in the cells, but that one small detail had been wrong. *I hope it doesn't come back to haunt me.*

The sound of the front door closing made William-Wetherby jump.

"Didn't you want to pick up the post?" Bella asked as she took her coat off.

"I must have dozed off, I didn't hear the postman. Where are the boys?"

"Outside. I haven't told them you're here yet. I thought I'd keep you to myself for a few minutes before they come in." Bella's eyes sparkled as she spoke.

"I won't argue with that. Did the postman bring anything interesting?"

Bella opened a letter from Eleanor. "You have two new nieces. Eleanor and Margaret have both had baby girls in the last few weeks."

William-Wetherby smiled. "Are they all well?"

"Yes, I think so. I picked a newspaper up for you as well while I was out." Bella handed the paper to her husband. "Does it say anything about the Queen?"

William-Wetherby glanced at the headlines. "No, only that the family are gathering by her bedside, which we knew. I didn't tell you, but I have to go into work if anything happens to her. Everyone's bound to turn up at St George's Hall."

"Let's pray for her then. You need more than one day at home after being away for so long."

William-Wetherby smiled. "We should want her to get better for reasons other than my work schedule."

"You're right, I'm sorry. I'll go and make you that cup of tea." Bella wandered into the scullery, but returned a moment later. "Can you hear church bells?"

William-Wetherby stopped reading and stared at her. "I can."

Bella went to the front door and opened it. Outside, the sound of the bell tolling was more distinct.

Bella shuddered. "She's gone."

William-Wetherby joined her at the door. "I would say so."

He stood to attention. "May Her Majesty rest in peace. God save the King."

"The King." Bella's voice was a whisper. "I hadn't thought of that; we've never known a king before."

William-Wetherby laughed. "Don't look so worried. If a little old lady can do the job, I'm sure he'll be fine."

Chapter Fifty-Nine

With summer upon them, William-Wetherby smiled and raised his face to the sun as he approached the police station. It was so nice being in charge at Prescot Street.

"Good morning, sir." The duty officer stood to attention as he walked in.

"Good morning, Sergeant, and a lovely day it is too. Do you have anything to report?"

The sergeant reached behind the desk and pulled out a manila envelope. "This came for you earlier. The delivery boy said it was urgent."

William-Wetherby took the letter from the sergeant and walked into his office. Within a minute, he walked back out into the reception.

"I've been called to a meeting at Cheapside. If anyone needs me I should be back this afternoon."

By the time he reached the Main Bridewell, perspiration was running down his temples. The sun that had been so pleasant an hour earlier was no help on such a walk and he gratefully stepped into the cool air of the building.

"I'm here to see Chief Inspector Lucas," he said to the duty officer.

"He's expecting you, sir, go straight through to his office."

William-Wetherby walked down the tiled corridor to a room near the end. The door was open.

"Inspector Jackson, come in. Thank you for being so prompt."

"You're welcome. What's the problem?"

The chief inspector picked up a pile of papers from his desk and coughed to clear his throat. "It's about the Birmingham case."

The hairs on the back of William-Wetherby's neck stood on end. "What about it? They're all behind bars, aren't they?"

"They are, but one of them's got himself a defence lawyer and hopes to overturn his sentence."

William-Wetherby's eyes bulged. "Which one?"

"The young one, Stanley Jones."

"Stan? Where on earth has he got the money from for a lawyer? I had to help him get day work because they wouldn't take him at the docks."

The chief raised an eyebrow. "It seems he didn't tell you everything about himself. Apparently he has family in Birmingham with money and his letters have appealed to their better nature. He claims he had no involvement with the trouble."

William-Wetherby gave an involuntary shudder. He'd always suspected Stan was different to the rest.

"When's his hearing?"

"The preliminary's this morning and they'll set a date. He could be out before the autumn."

William-Wetherby ran his finger around the collar of his tunic. "Will I be needed?"

"No, I shouldn't think so. I wanted to warn you as a matter of formality."

"Thank you, sir. Will that be all?"

"Yes, I think so. Is everything running smoothly at Prescot Street?"

"Yes, sir, no problems at all."

William-Wetherby stepped from the chief's office and paused for breath. If Stan was found not guilty he had to make sure he went back to Birmingham; he couldn't risk him staying in Liverpool. They'd have to petition the magistrate to make sure it was a condition of his release ... if it came to that.

After a moment, William-Wetherby headed for the reception but when the door leading to the courts opened behind him he glanced over his shoulder.

"Billy?" Stan's voice was confused as William-Wetherby froze and stared into the young man's eyes. After a second's hesitation, he turned away and hurried towards the front door. *I've got to get out of here.* As soon as he stepped outside, the warm air hit his face and he leaned against the wall of the building. *He saw me ... He'll know I'm a police officer ... He'll know it was me who set him up.* Despite the heat of the day, William-Wetherby shivered. *I have to make sure he goes back to Birmingham.*

By the time William-Wetherby walked back to Prescot Street he couldn't go into the station. They could manage without him for another couple of hours; he needed to go home.

"You're early." Bella was sitting on a dining chair outside the front door and let her knitting fall to her lap. "Is everything all right?"

William-Wetherby glanced up at her. "Yes, of course. I may need to stay late tonight and so I thought I'd take an hour back now. How are you? Why are you sitting out here?"

Bella stroked her heavily swollen belly. "Because it's too hot. You try carrying this weight around with you all day. I wish it would hurry up."

William-Wetherby bent forward and kissed her forehead. "I'm sorry. I'm sure you've not long to go now. I don't remember you being this big with the others."

Bella shifted in her chair. "Will you help me up? I've been here for too long. Standing up might remind the baby that it has to come out."

William-Wetherby smiled and moved the chair from the doorway as Bella shuffled to the scullery.

"I'll put the kettle on."

William-Wetherby nodded. It was too hot for a cup of tea, but if she wanted to make him one, he wasn't going to argue.

WHETHER IT WAS the temperature of the room or the image of Stan looking straight at him, William-Wetherby wasn't sure, but as he lay in bed that night he knew sleep wouldn't come easily. After the arrests, he'd been so relieved to get home he'd forgotten that Stan wasn't like the rest. *What if he was innocent? What would happen then? He'd be well within his rights to be angry with me.*

"Will you lie still." Bella lay on her back, her arms splayed out by her side. 'It's bad enough trying to sleep without you tossing and turning."

"I'm sorry, it's this heat. I can't settle. I'll go and sit downstairs for half an hour. Let you doze off."

William-Wetherby rolled onto his side but as he pushed himself up, Bella gasped.

"What's the matter?"

"It was only a twinge but I think the baby might be ready to come out."

William-Wetherby reached over for her hand. "Do you want me to fetch the midwife?"

"Not yet, it's too early. I should last until the morning."

"As long as you're sure, I'll go downstairs. Shout if you need me."

William-Wetherby had barely settled in the chair when he heard Bella calling. He raced back upstairs to find her perched on the edge of the bed.

"Will you go and fetch me mam and the midwife, I've a feeling it's closer than I thought."

At seven o'clock the next morning, as William-Wetherby sliced himself a piece of bread, he heard a shout from Bella followed by the crying of a child. He ran upstairs to find Edward and Albert on the landing outside the bedroom door.

"What's happening?" Edward's eyes were wide. "What's up with Mam?"

William-Wetherby put his finger to his lips. "Let me ask Granny." He knocked on the bedroom door. "Mrs Booth, is everything all right?"

As soon as the bedroom door opened, his mother-in-law slipped out. "Everything's fine." She bent down to her grandsons. "You have another brother."

"Another one," Edward said.

"Is he here because Stephen went to heaven?" Albert asked.

"He's here because God wants your mam to be happy again. Now, are you two ready for breakfast? Let's go and see what's in the pantry." Mrs Booth straightened up and spoke to William-Wetherby. "Don't look so worried. They're both fine. Give the midwife a few minutes and you can go in and see them."

Chapter Sixty

Birmingham, Warwickshire

As the shorter days heralded the end of summer, Charles pulled his jacket around him as he headed for work. By the time he arrived, Mr Keen was waiting for him.

"What time do you call this? I was expecting you half an hour ago."

"I'm sorry. Rose was out all night and didn't come home until I was leaving for work. They think Lilly's got typhoid fever and so she was with Aunt Mary-Ann and Daisy. You'd better tell Eleanor when you get home."

"How is Lilly?"

"Rose thinks she's a little better than she was yesterday. The doctor's calling again this morning and they're hoping the vicar can come and pray for her. I've been told to go straight there after work."

"I hope she's all right, send her my regards. Now, I wanted to show you this." Mr Keen picked up a piece of paper from his desk and thrust it into Charles's hand.

"What's this?" Charles scanned the order form. "An order for a steel frame to be added to the back of a workshop. What's so special about that?"

"Have you seen who's signed it?"

Charles looked back at the paper and shrugged. "Mr Wood?"

"What is it with you this morning? Keep reading." He leaned over the piece of paper and pointed to the bottom line. "Mr Wood, foreman Wetherby Hooks & Eyes Manufacturers. Proprietor Mr H. Wetherby."

Charles's eyes stared at his partner. "No!"

"That's what it says. I'm wondering if Henry or Uncle William know about it."

"I doubt it. Uncle William would be furious." Charles laughed to himself. "When did you last see Henry?"

Mr Keen shrugged. "Probably not since our wedding, so eight years ago."

"He's more likely to remember me from a few interactions I had with Mr Wetherby. I'd still like to do the site visit though, see what they're doing to the place. I don't think there's any danger Uncle William will be there. Why don't you arrange it for next week. I'm going to have to leave for a meeting shortly."

As he strolled towards his aunt's house that evening, Charles checked his pocket watch. *Only five o'clock, Rose'll be pleased.* He paused at the bottom of the drive, but as he did, he noticed the front curtains. They were closed. With bile rising to the back of his throat, he hurried to the front door. The maid let him in before he had time to knock and he went straight into the back room.

"What's happen–" He stopped where he was and stared at

Mary-Ann in her mourning clothes. Rose jumped up and threw her arms around him.

"Charles."

"She's gone?"

Daisy's eyes were swollen as she turned to him. "She passed away this afternoon ... It was quick in the end."

Charles clung to Rose, afraid to let go in case she saw the tears in his eyes. "I'm so sorry. Where ... where is she?"

"In the front room." Rose buried her head in her husband's chest as Charles noticed Mary-Ann wipe a tear from her cheek.

"I don't know what to say."

"What good are words at a time like this?" Mary-Ann's back was rigid as she spoke. "My beautiful daughter ... now with her father and the young brother she never knew. What have I done to deserve such wrath from God?"

"Nothing." Daisy's voice croaked as she clung to her mother. "You've done everything a mother should and more. Why would God do this to us when we worship Him every week?"

Charles was about to answer but thought better of it. "Let me pour everyone a brandy, we could all do with one. Has the doctor been?"

"He left seconds before you arrived," Mary-Ann said. "He left some laudanum, but from experience, I won't allow it to be taken until we're ready for bed. I won't ever become dependent on the stuff again."

Charles shot a glance at his aunt but neither Rose nor Daisy appeared to have heard her. *When on earth was she dependent on laudanum?*

FIVE DAYS LATER, with the wind whipping around the gravestones, the mud squelched under Charles's feet as he and

Mr Keen led the mourners from the church to the open grave. Standing to the right of the vicar, he watched as the male members of the funeral party joined them. He hadn't expected to see Uncle William and Henry quite so soon, let alone Mr Mountford. So much for calling on Henry unexpectedly.

The vicar read the burial service at pace and as the only male from the immediate family, Charles threw the first piece of earth onto the coffin before turning to lead the mourners back to church. As he approached the door he spotted his Aunt Charlotte talking to Mary-Ann, Rose and Daisy.

"Good afternoon, Aunt Charlotte." Charles kept his tone formal. "I wasn't sure whether we'd see you today."

"Why wouldn't you?" Charlotte straightened her back as she raised herself to her full height. "She was my niece."

Charles nodded. "Yes, of course she was. It's a terrible shame we've all been brought together under such circumstances."

Mary-Ann shivered. "Shall we go back to the house? I need to sit down."

Charles watched as Charlotte escorted Mary-Ann to the waiting carriages and once he was sure they were out of earshot, he turned to Mr Keen.

"What do we do about the order? Do we mention it to Henry while he's here or just turn up next week?"

"We'll have to say something. It would look strange if we didn't."

"All right, but wait until we're away from Rose and Eleanor. They won't be happy if we're talking about work at such an event."

The two of them had no sooner arrived at the house and helped themselves to a glass of sherry when a smartly groomed young man with a slim figure and pencil moustache approached them.

"Good afternoon, gentlemen." Henry smiled as he spoke.

"I hoped I might catch you. I take it you've seen the order we've placed with you for a new metal structure to be added to the back of the workshop?"

"We were going to pay you a visit next week," Charles said. "We didn't know if you were aware it was our company your foreman placed the order with."

Henry checked over his shoulder before he spoke. "I didn't when he first sent the order, and I must confess I was tempted to cancel it when I noticed your names on the form, but ... well, events like this remind me of how fickle life can be. We've no need to argue."

Charles cocked his head to one side as he studied Henry. "You know, you're right. We haven't seen you for years but it's only because of your father and grandfather. Talking of which ..."

William Junior sidled up to his son. "So this is the company you keep when I disappear for five minutes. You ought to know better."

Henry glared at his father. "Would it be too hard for you to be civil on a day like today? I think we've had enough upset without you adding to it."

"There you go again, sounding like your mother. She's been far too soft with you."

"It makes a change for one of the Wetherbys to be civil," Charles said. "Perhaps you can take a leaf out of Henry's book."

William Junior glared at Charles and then his son before he turned on his heel and left them.

"Is he always like that with you?" Charles asked.

Henry shrugged. "He hates the fact that Mother takes more notice of me than she does of him. I ignore him and carry on."

Charles's laugh sounded out of place and he put his hand to his mouth. "Let's see if we can upset him a little bit more, shall we? Shall we come to the workshop while he's there?"

Henry grimaced. "You'll be lucky, I never know when he's going to turn up and when he does, he doesn't stay more than half an hour."

"Maybe I can leave my bill in a prominent place then, show him he owes me some money."

Henry laughed. "I can do better than that. I'll leave the paid invoices on his desk to let him know how much money we've sent your way. He'll be furious."

Chapter Sixty-One

Liverpool, Lancashire

Bella put the stop on the baby carriage and smiled as she glanced at her young son George lying fast asleep on his back. She tucked the blankets around him and was turning to go into the house when Mrs Booth walked towards her.

"I was beginning to wonder where you were. The other two will be home from school in five minutes."

"I know. I went to the botanical gardens and lost track of time."

"I'm surprised you weren't cold in this weather."

"It's not that bad and I wanted time to think. William-Wetherby's not been himself lately but I don't know why."

"Have you asked him?"

"Of course, but he says everything's fine. I'm not sure if the death of his cousin's upsetting him, whether it's the fact he couldn't go to the funeral, or something at work."

Mrs Booth cocked her head to one side. "George hasn't been waking him up at night, has he?"

"No; he's been as good as gold this last couple of weeks."

"Maybe it's the goings-on in Birmingham then."

Bella sighed. "Perhaps, but I wish he'd talk to me. We shouldn't keep secrets from each other and it's as if he's deliberately blocking me out. I'll have another go tonight."

WITH GEORGE IN BED, Bella sat with Edward and Albert as they waited for William-Wetherby with their glasses of bedtime milk. As soon as he opened the front door, Edward jumped up.

"You're here."

"Why aren't you in bed?" William-Wetherby picked up the newspaper and sat by the unlit fire.

"We ... we wanted to see you." Edward glanced at Bella as she put her hand on his shoulder. Albert said nothing but stared at his father.

Bella tried to keep her voice level. "Have you had a busy day?"

"No more than usual."

"Well, why don't you come and sit at the table. Your tea's ready."

William-Wetherby groaned as he pushed himself up from his chair. "Can't a man have some peace while he eats? I don't need an audience."

"I'd hardly call us an audience." Bella stormed into the scullery and returned with a plate of stew.

"What else would you call it; you sit and watch me, don't you?"

"Come along you two, it's time you were in bed. Dad's tired."

Without another word Bella led them upstairs and by the time she returned, William-Wetherby's plate was empty and he had taken his usual seat by the hearth.

"What was all that about?" Bella's voice was shrill.

"All what?"

Bella ripped the newspaper from her husband's hands and threw it to the floor. "You know jolly well what. Those boys have waited three days to see you and when they do you act as if they're nothing more than a pair of orphans begging for food. You're going to tell me what's upsetting you, whether you like it or not."

"Nothing's upsetting me."

"Stop lying." Bella took a deep breath and lowered her voice. "We've been married for ten years and I know when you've got something on your mind. Whatever it is, I don't like what I'm seeing at the moment."

"All I want is some time to myself when I come home after a twelve-hour shift. Is that too much to ask?"

"All they want is two minutes of your time and a smile when you come in. Is that too much to ask?"

William-Wetherby leaned over to pick up the newspaper but Bella put her foot over it.

"Oh no, you're not getting away with it that easily. I want you up those stairs to say goodnight to two little boys who think their dad no longer cares about them. And then I want you back down here with an explanation. This has been getting worse for weeks and I'm not putting up with it any longer."

William-Wetherby glared at her as he pushed himself up from his chair. By the time he came back downstairs Bella was waiting for him with a cup of tea.

"Did you see them?"

William-Wetherby nodded.

"And did you manage to put a smile on your face?"

"Will you stop going on? I've had enough of it."

Bella choked on her cup of tea. "You've had enough? How

do you think we feel putting up with your moods every night?"

"I'm not in a mood."

"Well, heaven help us if you ever are. Now tell me what's upsetting you. How can I help if you won't talk to me?"

"It's not anything you can help with."

"Tell me what it is and I'll decide."

William-Wetherby exhaled as he rested his head on the back of his chair. "It's only a case at work."

"If that's all it is, why's it upsetting you so much? You've been with the force for over ten years and I've never seen a case affect you like this."

William-Wetherby opened his eyes and held her gaze. "It's to do with the work I did at the start of the year. One of the men I had arrested has been released."

"What's wrong with that? You've had convicts released before."

William-Wetherby stood up and walked to the window. "The Birmingham gang were different. Other criminals I've arrested knew I was a police officer and they knew they'd been nicked ... but this lot ... they thought I was their mate ... and I betrayed them."

"They don't know it was you who turned them in. You said they didn't know you were in the police."

"They didn't, not to start with, but a couple of months ago one of them saw me at the station in uniform. His conviction's just been overturned."

"That doesn't mean anything. Just because he's back on the streets doesn't mean you'll see him."

"I told the chief he'd seen me and he tried to get the magistrate to send him back to Birmingham, but because his conviction was quashed, there were no grounds to place any restrictions on him."

A knot formed in Bella's stomach. "Are any of the others likely to get out early?"

William-Wetherby shook his head. "No, fortunately we had eyewitness accounts for all the others. They'll be behind bars for a few more years yet."

"Well, there you go. I expect he'll go back to Birmingham of his own accord, he won't want to be here on his own, not with Christmas coming up."

William-Wetherby let out a deep sigh. "I hope you're right."

Chapter Sixty-Two

With the arrival of mid-summer Bella sensed renewed hope in her husband. His sleepless nights had become a thing of the past and she watched as he stood on a stepladder waiting for Edward to pass him the bunting to tie around the drainpipe. Albert waited beside his brother and watched the Union Jacks and coloured triangles being raised into the air.

"I'll pass you the other end," Edward said as his father descended the ladder.

"Come on then, run across the road. I've still got Granny's to do yet."

Bella stayed by her front door and smiled as her mam walked towards her.

"I'm feeling left out," Mrs Booth said. "Mine's the only house not decorated."

"Yours'll be done soon enough and the coronation isn't for another couple of days."

"I know but I want to feel part of the celebrations." Mrs Booth's shoulders slumped. "Even I'm not old enough to remember a coronation before."

"Why didn't you ask Fred to do it?"

Mrs Booth laughed. "There was no chance of that. He's baking again. It's become an obsession with him since I showed him my recipe book. As soon as he gets home of an evening, he's in the scullery. I suppose I shouldn't moan, it saves me doing it."

"And it's better than him being in the tavern every night."

William-Wetherby walked back across the road and winked at Bella. "Right, Mrs Booth, it's your turn. Come and tell me where you want these flags."

With the street decorated and half the neighbours taking advantage of the evening sun, Bella pushed George's carriage while she and Mrs Booth walked the length of the street. The older boys raced underneath the flags, jumping as they tried to reach them.

"William-Wetherby's cheerful tonight."

"He is, it's the best I've seen him for a long time."

"I'm glad, I don't like either of you being upset." They stopped at the end of the street to head for home. "Who's that he's talking to?"

Bella put her hand above her eyes as she squinted towards their house. "I can't tell from this distance. I hope it's not anyone from work telling him his shifts have changed again."

"He's already working all day Thursday for the coronation, isn't he?"

Bella sighed. "He is, but I don't trust them not to pile more hours on him."

They hadn't walked much further when William-Wetherby came striding towards them.

"I've had a message from work. The coronation's been postponed. The King's ill and has been admitted to hospital."

Bella glanced at the decorations. "And we've just put all these up too. Typical."

William-Wetherby grinned. "You could be a little more sympathetic."

"I'm sorry, honest, but it's such a shame to have all this ready and then not to need it."

"Will he be all right?" Mrs Booth asked. "It sounds serious if he's in hospital."

"I didn't get the details, other than I'm not needed on Thursday. They hope the coronation will still go ahead, but they don't know when."

"That's even worse. Do we leave the decorations up and hope it's not for long, or take them down and put them back up again?"

William-Wetherby laughed. "I've no idea, but what I do know is that I'm not taking them down tonight. Let's wait and see what it says in the paper tomorrow."

BELLA STOOD on her front step with Mrs Booth, looking at the decorations as they danced in the summer breeze.

"Six weeks they've been up, but I suppose they'll have to do," Bella said. "We haven't got time to take them down and wash them all before Saturday."

Mrs Booth followed her daughter's gaze. "It doesn't feel special having them up now though, does it? Everyone's used to them."

Bella shrugged. "At least we tried and whether we leave them up or take them down, the coronation will go ahead on Saturday and the King will be none the wiser."

Mrs Booth laughed. "You're right."

Saying farewell to her mam, Bella was about to go back inside when the postman shouted over to her.

"A letter for you, Mrs Jackson. Another one from Birmingham by the looks of it."

Bella glanced at the handwriting before she went in. *Rose. I wonder what she wants. She's not written since she's been in mourning.*

With a freshly brewed cup of tea, Bella sat at the table and scanned the letter. Charles's business was doing well; they were all looking forward to the end of their mourning period and Aunt Mary-Ann was thinking of moving house. Bella paused. *Imagine a whole year of seeing no one but close family. That must be hard. With the folks around here, I couldn't go that long without seeing anyone if I tried.* She smiled as she turned over the page, but within seconds her stomach somersaulted.

You won't believe that Charles and I, along with Mother, Daisy, Eleanor and Mr Keen have been invited to the marriage of Henry and his betrothed, Edith, at the end of September. It's less than a week after we finish our time of full mourning and with our minds as they are, we can't possibly think of gowns for such an event. Charles of course thinks we're being silly and insists we travel all the way to Leicester for the event.

Charles wanted to go to a Wetherby wedding! Bella dropped the letter and put her head in her hands. *Please God, don't let us get an invite; that's the last thing we need.* Bella glanced again at the letter and paused. She needed to get rid of it before William-Wetherby got home. *What he doesn't know, he can't worry about.*

Chapter Sixty-Three

Birmingham, Warwickshire

Charles paced the back room of Mary-Ann's house while Mr Keen sat on the settee drinking the tea he'd been handed.

"Why do they always have to take so long? I told Rose last night that we'd need to leave here no later than eight o'clock and it's already five past. We're going to miss the train."

"We shouldn't have let them get ready together," Mr Keen said.

"You don't need to tell me, but Aunt Mary-Ann insisted on keeping their new dresses here." Charles walked to the bottom of the stairs. "What are you doing up there? We're going to miss the train."

"We're coming." Rose held her husband's gaze as she descended the stairs. "Do you like it?"

A grin appeared on Charles's lips as he stared at the elegant, slimline dress hugging his wife's curves. "I do and even though it's purple, it's such an improvement on black."

"They had a similar dress in a beautiful deep blue, but

Mother said it would be inappropriate, perhaps you'll buy it for me one day." Rose flashed her eyes at her husband as she took his arm.

"Perhaps I will." He leaned forward to kiss her lips as Mary-Ann appeared at the top of the stairs.

"I thought we were in a hurry," Mary-Ann said. "Is the carriage ready?"

"Yes, of course. As soon as you're all downstairs, we can go."

BY THE TIME the carriage transporting them from the train station to the church pulled up outside the venue, most of the guests had gone inside.

"I hope we've made it before the bride," Charles said. "Why trains can't run on time, I don't know."

"Don't be too critical," Mr Keen said. "If it had left Birmingham when it should have done, we'd have missed it."

Charles shook his head. "Don't remind me. Come on, let's go inside."

With the family seated, Charles watched his aunt Olivia fuss around Henry, while Uncle William did everything he could to get her to sit down. *Can't they leave him alone? He's a grown man. I'd been around the world by the time I was his age.*

Mr Keen leaned into Charles's right shoulder. "Henry may be the favoured one, but would you swap places with parents like that?"

Charles stifled a laugh. "I would if I could inherit the money and disappear. I think that's what he'll do. He won't hang around to be treated like that."

"I don't think he has a choice. Henry told me they're moving in with his parents when they come back from their honeymoon."

"Poor Henry ..." Charles stopped and turned around as

the organ music sounded. "Time to stand up, the bride's here." *Nice-looking girl ... although with his money he could have his pick ...*

"Stop staring." Rose pulled on his arm. "You'll see her soon enough."

Paying little attention to the service, Charles studied the guests in front of him. *Is that Sid?* It was certainly Mrs Storey, Mr Wetherby's sister, and probably her daughter and her family, but Sid looked different. He didn't know him well, but he had done a lot for William-Wetherby ... and Father, by the sound of it. He'd speak to him later.

With so many faces to study, Charles was surprised when they reached the end of the service.

"What are you smiling at?" Rose asked as they followed the bride and groom out of church.

Charles shrugged. "I wasn't aware I was. I was just looking at everyone, trying to remember when I last saw them. I haven't seen many of them since before I went to sea; it's like turning the clock back."

"That must be fifteen years ago."

Charles banged his hand to his head. "That's why I can't remember them all. Come on, let's go, there's a few folk I'd like to catch up with at the wedding breakfast."

After escorting Rose to a table with her mother and sister, Charles glanced around the room before heading over to a ginger-haired man standing slightly apart from the rest of his group.

"Sid? Is that you?"

The man stared at Charles, his eyebrows drawn together. "No, I'm Sam. Sid's my brother. Have we met?"

"If we have, you probably won't remember me, but you may have known my father, William Jackson."

The frown on Sam's face deepened. "Of course I

remember Mr Jackson, but don't tell me you're William-Wetherby."

Charles laughed. "No, I'm his brother. When your uncle forced William-Wetherby out of Birmingham he went to Liverpool and never came back."

Sam took Charles's arm and guided him away from his mother's table. "With good reason as I understand. Mother says all Sid's problems are down to your brother."

Charles flinched at Sam's words. "All his problems? What's the matter?"

"Were you the one who was away at sea?"

Charles nodded.

"So you may or may not know that before your father died, your brother got Sid into a lot of trouble with Mr Wetherby. Because of that, he lost his job and ended up working in the pub your father managed. He was with your father when he died, too. Before he passed, your father gave Sid a letter with a lot of accusations about Mr Wetherby. Sid handed it to William-Wetherby, but the whole situation was too much for him. He started drinking more than ever and although Mr Wetherby gave him his job back, it was short-lived. He started spending more time in the pub than in work and as you may expect, Mr Wetherby sacked him for the second time."

"I'd no idea."

"As Sid sees it, everyone came out of the whole situation with Mr Wetherby better than he did. He told me William-Wetherby has a fancy house in Liverpool, while he's living in the dosshouse."

Charles raised an eyebrow at Sam. "William-Wetherby's doing nothing of the sort. When he left here, he went with nothing and now lives in a small house, similar to those in Frankfort Street, with his wife and three sons."

"What about the hundred pounds Mr Wetherby gave him?"

Charles opened and closed his mouth several times. "I'd forgotten about that; I'd say it's long gone."

"That should have set him up for life. Sid said it was hush money in return for keeping quiet about the letter."

"It was, but one hundred pounds doesn't last long when you're starting from nothing. Don't forget, he had nowhere to live and no job when he arrived in Liverpool." Charles glanced around the room. "Where's Sid now? Is he here?"

"Don't you understand what I'm saying?" Charles sensed the frustration in Sam's voice. "When he's not sleeping in the poorhouse, he's in the pub. Mother kicked him out because she couldn't cope with him coming home drunk every night. His life's ruined, and both he and Mother blame Mr Jackson and William-Wetherby."

Charles walked to the nearest table and sat down; Sam followed him. "I know about the letter and was told Father wrote it to set the record straight about Mr Wetherby. He believed Mr Wetherby had destroyed our family and wanted us to be able to prove it. I'd no idea Sid was caught up in it all."

"So you've seen the letter?"

Charles nodded.

"Was it that bad?" Sam asked.

"It was if you were Mr Wetherby. Father believed Mr Wetherby had a relationship with Aunt Sarah-Ann before they were both widowed and that he was responsible for the death of Aunt Sarah-Ann's first husband. On top of that, William-Wetherby saw Mr Wetherby stand by and do nothing while our mother drowned. He also found out that Mr Wetherby was responsible for Father's bankruptcy."

Sam let out a low whistle. "So if Mr Wetherby gave your brother one hundred pounds to keep quiet, it suggests there's some truth in it ... otherwise he'd have sued him for slander."

"William-Wetherby's convinced it's true."

Sam looked across to his mother, Mrs Storey. "She's no idea. Mother thinks Sid made it all up when he was drunk, and won't hear a word against Mr Wetherby ... not since he died anyway."

Charles followed Sam's gaze. "Does she see much of Uncle William or Aunt Charlotte?"

"Uncle William calls every week to collect the rent."

"Of course he does." Charles paused as he caught sight of William Junior speaking to the bride's father. "She's not going to upset him and risk being thrown out of her home. Look, I'm sorry about Sid, really I am, but we'd no idea. I was going to have a word with your mother, but perhaps I'll just slip away. I don't think she's recognised me."

"I'd be grateful if you did, I don't want her upset any further."

Chapter Sixty-Four

Liverpool, Lancashire

B ella sat at the table with an extravagantly written envelope in her hand. It was addressed to Mr and Mrs W-W. Jackson, but she had no idea who it was from. Prising open the envelope she slipped out a card and read it slowly. Aunt Mary-Ann had moved house and to mark the occasion was inviting them to spend Christmas with her. Not only that, according to the writing on the back, Charles, Eleanor, Margaret, Florence and their families had been invited as well.

Bella felt the blood drain from her face. *What about me mam? I can't leave her on her own all over Christmas with only Fred for company.*

"What's the glum face for?" Mrs Booth said as she walked in several minutes later.

Bella studied her mother before she passed her the invite.

"But you must go. You can't deprive William-Wetherby of the chance of seeing his brother and sisters again."

"But what about you? I can't leave you on your own over Christmas."

Mrs Booth patted her daughter's hand. "I've got enough sisters. I can always ask one of them to have us. You have to tell William-Wetherby about this, he'll find out one way or another."

Bella got up from the table. "I don't know. It's not only you I worry about. Every time he goes to Birmingham, something happens. I wish he could be allowed to forget the place. This is his home now."

"And he'll always come back, but you can't make him forget his family. They went through a lot together."

Bella walked to the baby carriage and lifted out her young son. "I suppose they've not seen George either."

"All the more reason to go. Now, keep that smile on your face and tell him you're happy to go if he wants to. And don't worry about me and Fred, we'll be fine."

~

Birmingham, Warwickshire.

WITH CHRISTMAS EVE almost upon them, Bella watched Edward and Albert as they sat on either side of Mary-Ann's carriage, peering through the holes they had wiped in the condensation on the windows.

"Why don't we have a carriage like this?" Edward asked. "Everyone at school would be amazed."

"Why do we need a carriage when we can walk everywhere?" William-Wetherby said. "This is for Aunt Mary-Ann. Ladies can't walk the streets on their own and the driver looks after her."

"What about Mam? Why doesn't she have a carriage and driver to watch out for her?"

William-Wetherby squirmed in his seat. "Mam's perfectly capable of looking after herself. Besides, where would we keep the horses? They wouldn't fit in our back yard."

Edward's brow creased as he thought. "Why don't we get a bigger house?"

Sensing her husband's discomfort, Bella interrupted. "What do we want to do that for? It's hard enough for me to keep the one we've got clean, besides, who'd look after Granny if we moved?"

"She could come with us."

"And Fred," Albert added.

"We'd need a big house for that many people. Now that's enough. We're perfectly happy where we are."

As William-Wetherby helped the boys from the carriage, Bella saw their eyes widen as they took in the house before them.

"Are we going in here?" Edward asked.

"I would hope so, it's too cold to stay out here for long."

William-Wetherby knocked on the front door and waited for the maid to answer before he ushered the family inside. Daisy and Mary-Ann were standing in the hallway.

"Oh my word, look at this bundle of joy." Daisy took George from Bella and showed him to her mother.

"Thank you for joining us," Aunt Mary-Ann said. "After everything that's happened, I didn't want to spend Christmas on my own and what better way to spend it than with all the family."

"Are the others here yet?" William-Wetherby asked.

"Not everyone. Eleanor and Mr Keen are in the living room and Florence should be here shortly but goodness knows when Charles and Rose will arrive. Did you hear Margaret and Mr Earl won't be joining us?"

"No ... why not?"

"She wrote to tell me that she's expecting another baby

and has been ordered to take bed rest."

"What a shame." William-Wetherby's shoulders drooped. "Not about the baby of course, but I haven't seen her for so long."

"I know, maybe next year. Come and take a seat."

It was almost five o'clock before Florence arrived and William-Wetherby watched as Edward and Albert raced into the hall to meet her.

"We've been waiting for you." Edward's voice carried into the back room.

"I'm sorry, but the train wouldn't go any quicker. Let me take my cloak off and you can take me into the living room. I believe you've got a new brother to show me."

"His name's George," Albert said as he slipped his hand into Florence's. "He's only little though."

William-Wetherby smiled as the boys guided Florence to the back room and took her to George. *What a marvellous Christmas it promises to be.*

After a minute, Florence sank into the chair beside Bella. "How lovely to be here. Mr Goodwood is so busy at the moment, it's a wonder he let me have any time off. Poor Aunt Hannah and the girls will be fortunate if they have a few hours off on Christmas afternoon. At least they have a maid who can cook, so they won't need to do that as well."

"And will he carry on working?" Bella asked.

"He'll keep his eye on them, but the customers all wanted their laundry delivered before Christmas and so he and the boys can have the day off."

Bella raised an eyebrow. "She needs to tell him. Why should he have the day off when they don't?"

"He wouldn't like that." Florence's expression was serious. "Everything has to run according to plan; he's a stickler for doing things right."

"Enough." Mary-Ann raised a bell to summon the maid.

"I'm tired of hearing about Mr Goodwood. Let's have some mulled wine while we wait for Rose and Charles. We have an announcement."

"You have an announcement and we have to wait!" Florence huffed at those around her. "Why is Charles always late for everything?"

Seconds later, she jumped to her feet at the sound of the front door opening. "You've arrived! How can you live the closest and still be last here?"

"What's the rush? You'll see enough of us over the next few days."

"But Aunt Mary-Ann has an announcement ... and we've had to wait."

"You've waited for all of a minute," Mary-Ann said. "Why do you have to be so dramatic, but yes, I do have an announcement ... or rather we do. Don't we, Daisy?"

Daisy smiled and turned her face to the floor. "You tell them."

"As you wish. You may be aware that for the last few months, Daisy has been walking out with a charming young man by the name of Mr Wilks. They asked me yesterday if I would give my blessing to them becoming husband and wife, and I said yes."

Rose was the first on her feet and hugged her sister. "Why didn't you tell me before everyone else came? I was with you yesterday."

"I'm sorry, somehow the time wasn't right."

"Well, it's perfect now." Bella paused as the maid carried in nine cups of mulled wine and passed them around. "Congratulations. When do we meet this Mr Wilks?"

"He's joining us for dinner on Christmas Day." She turned to Charles. "You will be nice to him, won't you?"

"I'm always nice. What line of business is he in?"

"He's a surveyor for an insurance company."

Charles raised his eyebrows at Mr Keen. "That could come in handy if we're looking for premises. We need to have a chat with him."

Edward had been standing alongside William-Wetherby and was unable to remain silent any longer. "Uncle Charles, do you remember me?"

Charles glanced down at him. "How could I forget? And Albert as well. Shouldn't there be another one of you?"

"There is." Edward laughed and pointed to his brother. "George is over there."

Charles smiled. "So he is. Isn't this going to be marvellous? Our first Christmas as a proper family in almost twenty years."

Once William-Wetherby finished his mulled wine he watched Bella and Mary-Ann round up the boys to take them up to bed.

"Say goodnight to everyone," Bella said.

Edward's shoulders drooped. "Do I have to? It's still early."

"I want you with Albert and George, they need their big brother when they're in a strange bed."

"I'll come with you," Florence said. "We've hardly seen each other yet."

Rose took hold of Albert's hand and gestured for Daisy to follow her. "Why don't we all come."

"Before you disappear, it's time we were leaving." Mr Keen stood up, causing Eleanor to follow suit. "We'll see you tomorrow ... and the day after. We'll bring your cousins to play with you as well."

Edward's face lit up. "Can we play in the garden?"

Eleanor smiled. "You can, but they're not as big as you."

As the room emptied, Charles turned to his brother. "That was a stroke of luck; a quick whisky while they're all gone? Aunt Mary-Ann said nothing about that."

"I don't suppose it would do any harm ... as long as Aunt Mary-Ann doesn't mind you helping yourself."

"Of course she doesn't." Charles set two glasses down on the table. "I wanted a word with you while everyone's gone."

William-Wetherby raised an eyebrow at his brother. "What about?"

"I met Sam Storey at Henry's wedding the other month and he told me something rather interesting."

William-Wetherby took a seat. "What was he saying?"

"You know you're not popular in Birmingham? Well, apparently it's not only the Wetherbys ... Mrs Storey's furious with you too."

William-Wetherby's brow furrowed. "Why?"

"It sounds like Sid's in a bad way ... too much ale ... and she blames you for it."

William-Wetherby took a sip of his whisky. "Perhaps that explains why she was so curt with me when I last saw her, but why blame me? When I left Birmingham, Mr Wetherby had given Sid his job back and he wasn't drinking that much."

"Maybe, but somewhere along the line, he became fixated on the money Mr Wetherby gave you. They're under the impression that you're living a life of luxury in Liverpool."

"A life of luxury? Have they any idea? One hundred pounds doesn't last long when you have no job, no home and you're in a strange city. Even when I joined the police, I wasn't earning much ... certainly not compared to the money the Wetherbys have. I've been in Liverpool over ten years; do they think I've still got it?"

Charles shrugged. "I suspect they did, but I told Sam it was long gone and you were only in a small terraced house. He seemed convinced, but I didn't go near Mrs Storey; I didn't want to upset her." Charles topped up their glasses. "I'd forgotten you had the hundred pounds from Mr Wetherby; did you spend some of it on Bella's ring?"

William-Wetherby scowled. "I hope nobody begrudges her that. She deserved something nice and at least she appreciates it. If Mrs Storey or Sid are short of money, it's Mr Wetherby they should be angry with. They've no idea how fortunate they are."

Chapter Sixty-Five

Liverpool, Lancashire

With Christmas over and the day barely light, William-Wetherby fastened his cape around his shoulders and pulled his cap down over his forehead before leaving the house. Rain bounced off the pavement and by the time he reached the police station, his undershirt was sticking to him where the rain had run down his collar and onto his back. After greeting the duty sergeant he walked straight to his office and shook out his coat.

He hadn't been at his desk long when he was disturbed by a knock on the door. "Chief Inspector, come in. What can I do for you?"

Chief Inspector Adams came in and placed his cap on the desk. "Good morning, Inspector Jackson. I was hoping you'd be on the early shift. Something's come up and we need you at Cheapside for the foreseeable future. Would you mind travelling there with me now?"

William-Wetherby stared at the man in front of him. "You mean a permanent move? Who'll take care of things here?"

"We need your skills on a case in the city centre. We have a new inspector we're going to place here."

It looks like I won't have a say in the matter. William-Wetherby sighed before fixing a smile on his face. "Yes, of course. Shall we go?"

Once in the meeting room at Cheapside, William-Wetherby watched as several colleagues joined them.

"Now, I won't beat about the bush," the chief said. "You'll no doubt have heard about the foreigners who've been brought into the port accused of murdering the captain of their ship along with six other sailors."

"They've been charged, haven't they?" one of the sergeants said as William-Wetherby listened.

"They were, but only so we could remand them in custody. At the moment we need to gather evidence, take statements and make a case. If the allegations are true, they'll be going to the assizes court."

William-Wetherby noticed he was the only inspector on the team. "What about the CID lads, shouldn't they be dealing with it?"

"They're already involved. Detective Inspector Duck-worth's leading the investigation, but they need support to plough through all the evidence." The chief looked at William-Wetherby. "It will be good experience for anyone thinking of moving to the CID."

William-Wetherby raised an eyebrow. "So, what do we know?"

"So far, the only evidence we have comes from the ship's cook, Moses Thomas. He claims that the other four men systematically killed their shipmates before setting fire to the ship. They subsequently jumped into the lifeboats and with what seems like good fortune, they were rescued by a nearby steamship. It was only when Thomas refused to share accom-modation with his fellow shipmates, the captain of this rescue ship became suspicious and pushed him for an explanation. Eventually, he confessed to the role of the other men in the killing spree and the captain of the steamship set sail for Liverpool."

"If you have a confession, what do you need us for?" It was the sergeant who had spoken before.

"Well, for one, we need to substantiate the claims. We only have the word of the cook to say the other four did the killing, but what of his role? We can't be certain it wasn't all down to him. At the moment, there are too many questions and we'll need answers if these men are to get the death penalty they clearly deserve."

"Where are they now?" William-Wetherby asked.

"All upstairs." The chief pointed towards the ceiling, indicating the cells on the higher floors of the building.

"We'll need them brought down to the interrogation room to hear what they have to say for themselves. How's their English?"

"I haven't spoken to them, but I believe it's passable. We have two Germans and two Dutch."

"Do you have an office we can use for the case? We'll need to prepare ourselves."

The chief nodded. "I'll take you now, but a word of warning, the press are all over the story, and not only in Liverpool, nationally as well. I want these men hanging before the daily newspapers lose patience with us."

William-Wetherby walked out with the chief. *So much for them being innocent until proven guilty.*

DESPITE HIS EARLY start that morning it was turned seven o'clock before William-Wetherby arrived home.

"Where on earth have you been?" Bella took his soggy coat from him.

William-Wetherby grinned. "I've only been asked to work on the biggest case in Liverpool."

Bella's face paled. "You're not becoming a detective again, are you?"

"No, but I'll be working on the case of the foreigners who've been brought to Liverpool accused with murdering the captain and crew of their ship."

Bella hesitated as she put her husband's tea on the table in front of him.

"Don't look so worried, they've asked me to lead a team to pull together the case for the prosecution."

"They want you to work with murderers?"

William-Wetherby laughed. "I am a police inspector, it's part of the job."

"But you're used to dealing with robberies or assault, not murder. How did they kill the crew?"

"That's what we need to find out, but initial thoughts are that they were shot."

"Shot!" Bella's eyes were wide. "You can't get involved with them."

William-Wetherby swallowed his food. "They haven't got their guns with them. They're all locked in the cells and when they're brought out they wear handcuffs and leg irons, and are escorted by two constables. They can't do anyone any harm."

"Well, see that they don't, besides, we received an invitation to the marriage of Daisy to Mr Wilks this morning. I hope you're not going to be too busy to go."

"When is it?"

"The beginning of March."

"I'm sorry, but this case will keep me occupied for months. I think I can say now that we won't be going. We won't be able to go to the baptism of Margaret's son either. I know you're disappointed, but this case could change everything. I may get another promotion out of it and with the boys growing the

339

way they are, the extra money'll come in handy. It'll be worth it, I promise."

Chapter Sixty-Six

With the hours he'd been working, William-Wetherby knew he should be tired but as he marched down the hill into the city centre, sleep was the last thing on his mind. Today was the day they'd been working for and with the evidence complete they expected the men to be formally committed for trial. It was fortunate that one of them had turned King's evidence and had supported the cook's story. They wouldn't have built such a strong case otherwise. It was still only five minutes to seven when he arrived at Cheapside but his sergeant was waiting for him.

"The prisoners are ready to be transferred to court. Do you want us to take them yet?"

"Yes, I think so. Let them stew in the cells over there. I expect the magistrate will call them first and we don't want to keep him waiting."

William-Wetherby walked to his office where he picked up the case files and flicked through them. They should have done enough. *Gustav Rau is pure evil and this evidence should send him and his accomplices to the gallows without any questions.* It may have been early, but knowing he wouldn't do anything else before the trial started, he tucked the papers under his arm and made his way to court.

He stood at the back of the court to listen to the proceedings and with all the evidence presented and the magistrate summing up, he studied the men in the dock. Rau was an arrogant-looking man with a hooked nose, fair hair and an untidy moustache. Definitely a ringleader but none of them had shown an ounce of remorse. Rau had even had the nerve to accuse the cook of being the ringleader. He wasn't going to get away with that.

The magistrate was coming to a close. "Having listened to the evidence presented by both sides, it has been decided that the prisoners should be charged with the wilful murder of Captain Shaw and six members of his crew. They should also be charged with arson and conspiracy to murder." The magistrate paused to study the accused before collecting up his papers and standing up. "Court dismissed."

"An excellent verdict, Detective Inspector." William-Wetherby shook his colleague's hand as the door closed behind the magistrate.

"Indeed it is. We need to make sure we get the same points across to the judge and jury when it goes to trial. We can't rest yet."

"Let me know if you need anything else," William-Wetherby said. "I'm always happy to help."

THE SUN WAS SHINING as William-Wetherby left work that evening, and he hadn't gone far when he heard his name being called from behind him.

"Good evening, Fred. What brings you down here at this hour? Mrs Booth will have your tea on the table."

"I know you've been busy lately, but have you forgotten I work here now?"

William-Wetherby laughed. "I had forgotten. I've been so wrapped up with my own business I've stopped noticing what's going on around me. You're working as a clerk, aren't you?"

"I am, but it's not what I want to do forever. One day, I'm going to start selling some of the pies and cakes I make; try and make a living out of it."

William-Wetherby studied the young man walking beside him. "Are you still doing that? I thought it was a phase you were going through."

Fred shook his head. "That might have been how it started, but I sell some of the best pies in Liverpool now. If ever I make a batch, I sell them almost before they're out of the oven. I need more time and a bigger oven."

"Well, I wish you luck. If you can find a job you enjoy, make the most of it. For the first time in years, I've been enjoying my policing and it makes the days pass so much quicker."

"Is that with this murder case?" Fred's eyes sparkled. "It must be very exciting."

"It has been, but we heard the charge today and the men will be at the assizes court in St George's Hall in the next couple of weeks charged with murder, arson and conspiracy to murder."

"Do you think they're guilty?"

William-Wetherby smiled at Fred's enthusiasm. "Without any doubt. They claim to be innocent and are even blaming the cook who accused them, but they've made up the most fanciful stories you've ever heard. I hope the jury will see them for the callous murderers they are."

Fred shuddered. "I hope so too. I don't want them being released to walk around Liverpool. What will you do when the case is over? Will you go back to your normal police work?"

"That's a good question." William-Wetherby stared into

the distance. "If I'm fortunate, I may be offered a promotion to detective inspector."

"Really! That sounds exciting."

"I don't think it's as exciting as you might imagine, but it beats sitting at a desk all day."

IT HAD TAKEN the best part of a month for the judge to listen to all the evidence against the men in the dock and as Mr Justice Lawrence read out the sentences of death for each of the accused, William-Wetherby stood at the back of the court. It was the first time he'd heard a death sentence being passed and despite the heat of the room he shuddered.

The jury had reached their decision in little more than a quarter of an hour and he watched as the men were led from the dock, their faces pale. For a moment he pitied them before remembering the number of lives they had taken. No, they had brought about their own fate; they couldn't blame anyone else.

"Well done, Inspector Jackson." The chief held out his hand as he approached him. "We got the verdict we wanted."

"Yes, sir, although the youngster may yet be let off lightly because of his age."

"The decision will be taken by the proper authorities, but he'll likely have his sentence cut to a life of penal servitude. Not much less of a punishment in my opinion."

"Perhaps not." William-Wetherby walked out of the court with the chief. "Can I ask if you have any plans for me from now on, sir?"

"I'm glad you asked. I do as it happens." He looked at his pocket watch. "I don't have time now, but you've not done yourself any harm with this investigation. If you'd like a move to CID I'll speak to the chief superintendent about it."

William-Wetherby smiled. "Thank you, sir. I'd like that."

. . .

EDWARD AND ALBERT were still out in the street as William-Wetherby arrived home and they ran down the street to meet him.

"You're early," Edward shouted.

"I was out of the house before you were out of bed this morning and so it's no surprise. Don't I deserve an hour off?"

"Will you play football with us?" Albert asked. "You haven't played for ages."

"Let me go and see Mam first. Is George in bed?"

Edward shrugged. "He didn't come out again after tea, so maybe he is."

William-Wetherby went into the house as Bella was setting a place for him at the table. "You're early." She walked to him and kissed his cheek.

"We got the verdict we wanted so most of the lads went to the police club to celebrate. I thought I'd come and see you instead."

"Well, I'm glad you did. Since the start of this year I feel as if I've hardly seen you."

William-Wetherby wrapped his arms around her. "Now the case is over we should get back to normal, although Chief Inspector Adams suggested there may be a job in the CID if I want it."

Bella pulled away. "You don't want to do that, do you?"

"Of course I do. The work's much more interesting."

"But it's longer hours and more dangerous. You often read about police officers being injured."

"The lads in the CID are no more likely to be injured than we are, and I promise I'll be careful. I've enjoyed working on this case and so if they offer me a detective inspector role, I'll take it."

Bella glared at him. "Well, don't expect me to be happy about it."

WILLIAM-WETHERBY SAT in silence in the chief inspector's office, but as he listened to the proposals for his new role his smile grew wider.

"So I could move to CID immediately?"

"It would save making changes to the men who've been covering for you. Detective Inspector Duckworth is happy to show you the ropes and so I suggest you team up with him this afternoon and see what he has for you."

"Is he at Walton Gaol this morning?"

"He is. He wanted to make sure the noose was tied securely around the necks of those villains." The chief checked his watch. "It should all be over by now."

"And good riddance to them. They didn't once show any remorse for what they did."

"That's common with murderers of their type. They can't understand why it upsets other people."

William-Wetherby was about to leave when there was a knock on the door and Detective Inspector Duckworth sauntered in.

"You've made good time," the chief said. "Did everything go according to plan?"

"It did. The men were brought from the condemned cell at eight o'clock this morning, and the two of them were hanged simultaneously. You wouldn't believe it though, even once he had the black cap over his face, Gustav Rau turned towards those of us in the room and declared his innocence."

William-Wetherby shook his head. "The man's been lying since the day he was arrested. He was as guilty as they come; their statements even contradicted each other. It was no surprise the jury only took quarter of an hour to reach their verdict."

"Well, whatever he said, it didn't change anyone's mind."

"I'm pleased to hear it," the chief said. "Now, before you go, it's been agreed with Inspector Jackson that he's going to be working with you from now on. Can I leave him in your capable hands?"

Detective Inspector Duckworth extended his hand to William-Wetherby. "Welcome to the team, although I can't promise anything as exciting as the case we've just finished."

"I'm sure I don't mind. I'd rather be out and about again than sitting at a desk."

Chapter Sixty-Seven

For the first time in weeks, the sun was fierce on William-Wetherby's back as he walked beside Detective Inspector Duckworth to Walton Gaol.

"What are you expecting when we get there?" William-Wetherby asked.

Duckworth groaned. "Nothing but trouble. It's someone I had convicted last year for robbery and he's managed to find himself a fancy solicitor and appeal his conviction. This morning is about being quizzed by the solicitor so he can make his case."

"I was nearly involved in something similar a couple of years ago. I went undercover for several weeks to infiltrate a gang suspected of a series of thefts and disturbances. They were convicted and locked away, but one of them had wealthy parents and they put in a successful appeal. Fortunately, because I'd been undercover, I wasn't the one who had to answer the defence's questions."

"Was that the gang from Birmingham?"

William-Wetherby glanced at his colleague. "That's right. Do you remember it?"

"I was only a detective sergeant at the time but I remember hearing about it. Who was the ringleader again?"

William-Wetherby gazed at the sky as he thought. "Tommy something ... Tommy Hudson, I think it was."

"That sounds right. He's coming up for release soon, isn't he?"

William-Wetherby shuddered. "I hope not. I thought he'd got more than two years."

"They got five, if I remember correctly, but they may be eligible for parole."

William-Wetherby raised an eyebrow. "So soon? How's he managed that? He must be up to something. Good behaviour wasn't part of his nature."

The two of them walked in silence before the detective spoke. "Why don't we have a word with the gaol governor before we leave and find out what's going on. I never like it when they let them out early."

WITH DUCKWORTH'S cross-examination over they waited in silence while the defence solicitor was shown out of the room.

"What do you think?" Duckworth asked when they were alone. "Did I do enough to convince him his client's guilty?"

"You convinced me." William-Wetherby grinned. "Although I'm biased. It won't be easy for them if they decide to proceed though."

"I hope not. I know that solicitor of old and the only reason he'll push for a retrial is if his client's come into money. The problem for both of them is that if the client has found a stash of money, it's almost certainly come from somewhere it shouldn't and so we'll arrest him for that as well."

"It sounds like you can't lose." William-Wetherby reached for his cap. "Shall we pay the governor a visit?"

The door to the governor's office was open when they arrived and Duckworth knocked before going in.

"Good morning, Governor."

"Detective Inspector." The governor stood up as the two men shook hands.

"Can I introduce Inspector Jackson. He's recently moved to CID."

The governor offered William-Wetherby his hand. "So, what can I do for you?"

"We've been talking about a case Inspector Jackson was involved with. A Birmingham gang with a leader by the name of Thomas Hudson."

"I don't remember you being involved in that case, Inspector." The governor peered at William-Wetherby.

"No, I was undercover at the time, so took no part in the prosecution."

"Ah ... and you're no doubt here because you've heard there could be an early release?"

"Is it true?" William-Wetherby perched on the edge of his chair.

"I'm afraid it is."

"But how have they managed that? Parole should be given for good behaviour, but the Tommy Hudson I knew wasn't capable of it."

The governor shifted in his chair. "No ... this is an unfortunate incident. We've been ordered by a judge to prepare the whole gang for release."

William-Wetherby and the detective exchanged glances before William-Wetherby spoke. "You've been told to release him? It's not even parole? On what grounds?"

"I'm afraid that information is so confidential even I haven't been told. It appears that Mr Hudson has friends in high places who are prepared to pull a few strings for him."

William-Wetherby shook his head. "Who?"

"I've no idea."

"But that doesn't make sense. If his friends were that important, why did they wait two and a half years? A young man called Stan was arrested with them, but thanks to his parents' money, Stan's been out almost two years."

The governor raised his hands. "I'm only telling you what I've been told, I'm sorry I can't be any more help."

"So there's no chance of keeping them in?" Duckworth asked.

"I'm afraid not. We're preparing for a release date of the last week in July and hoping they go straight back to Birmingham."

"Is there any way to make sure they do?" William-Wetherby wiped the palms of his hands on his trouser legs.

"Not that I'm aware. As far as I can tell, they'll be free to go wherever they want."

Chapter Sixty-Eight

William-Wetherby hadn't been in work for more than an hour when Detective Inspector Duckworth barged into his office.

"There's been a shooting by the Albert Dock. We need to get there now."

William-Wetherby dropped his pen and reached for his hat before following his colleague from the office. "Do we have any details? Any witnesses? A body?"

"I've not got much, but fortunately it doesn't sound like we have a body, just an injured man who was on his way to work."

William-Wetherby gave a sigh of relief. "At least that's something. Is there someone at the scene?"

"A couple of beat constables were in the area. One stayed with the injured man, the other chased the shooter, but whether he caught him, I don't know."

Ten minutes later as they reached the constable standing where the man had lain, William-Wetherby put his hands on his hips, gasping for breath. *That walk would normally take at least fifteen minutes ... thank goodness the weather's cool again today.*

"Has the ambulance been?" Duckworth asked the constable.

"Yes, sir."

"And will he live?"

"He was shot in the leg, sir, and so as long as he doesn't get an infection, he should."

"Good." William-Wetherby glanced around them. "Do we know why he was shot? Was it a robbery?"

"We don't know, sir. My partner gave chase, but he lost them once they reached the city centre."

William-Wetherby's eyes widened. "There was more than one of them?"

"Three we think, sir, but the victim only noticed one gun."

"Can you give us a description of the men we're looking for?" Duckworth asked.

The constable shook his head. "Not really. The victim was in too much pain. He was being taken to the Royal Infirmary and so he may have been given laudanum by the time you get there."

Duckworth nodded as he examined the pavement, still smattered with blood. "Has the bullet been found?"

"No, sir. I've searched for it, but it doesn't appear to be here. It could still be in the victim's leg."

"Very well. We're not going to find much here, why don't you tidy this up, Constable, and Inspector Jackson and I will head to the hospital."

As they arrived at the entrance to the hospital, William-Wetherby took out a handkerchief to wipe his forehead.

"I swear that hill's got steeper," Duckworth said.

William-Wetherby nodded in agreement and opened the door for them to go in. A nurse in a clean white pinafore greeted them and William-Wetherby showed her his police badge. "We believe you've had a gunshot victim admitted within the last hour. We need to speak to him."

"One moment." The nurse disappeared and came back several minutes later. "He's been taken to surgery. The bullet was lodged in his knee and the doctors believed the only way to save him was to take his leg off."

William-Wetherby's stomach churned. "That seems harsh."

"They'd have done a lot of damage to the knee trying to remove the bullet, which would have increased the risk of infection compared with a standard amputation." She smiled. "Don't worry, they know what they're doing."

"When can we talk to him?" Duckworth asked.

"The doctor will be free in about an hour if you'd like to come back. He'll be able to help with the patient's outlook then."

They bid her good day, let themselves out and walked across the street.

"Unless the fellow's six foot tall with several distinguishing features, we don't stand a chance of catching him now." Duckworth leaned back against a wall.

William-Wetherby nodded before he stared at his colleague. "What date is it?"

"The fourth of August. Why?"

"The Birmingham gang were due for release last week. Do you think they could be involved?"

Duckworth shrugged. "It's a possibility. We might find out from the victim if we can talk to him."

"Tommy Hudson was over six feet tall, with a long gash running down his right cheek. He'd be easy to identify."

"I suggest we take a walk and come back here in an hour then. Let's hope that fortune's on our side."

IT WAS a full twenty-four hours before the doctor escorted William-Wetherby and Duckworth onto the ward to question the patient. He was a young, slim man with a head of blond hair that made the grey of his skin appear more pallid than it otherwise might have. William-Wetherby made the introductions.

"Can you tell us anything about the man who did this to you?"

The man visibly shrank into the pillows supporting him as his eyes glazed over. "He was big ... much bigger than me ... with a gun ... he pointed at me ..." The man stared at William-Wetherby. "It wasn't an accident ... but I didn't know him ... why pick on me?"

William-Wetherby stood up. "Would you say he was as tall as me?"

The man nodded. "But wider ... and with a long scar on his cheek."

William-Wetherby sat down again and turned to Duckworth. "It's him."

"Can you tell us anything about the men who were with him?" Duckworth asked. "How many were there?"

"Three ... but they were smaller than him."

"Three?" William-Wetherby's brow creased. "Three including the tall man you mean?"

"No, three plus him. Two who looked similar with grey hair and beards, but one shorter, with fair hair."

"Stan. What was he doing there?" William-Wetherby stared at his colleague before turning back to the patient. "Did you hear any names, like Stan or Tommy?"

The patient shook his head and closed his eyes.

"The patient needs to sleep now, gentlemen." The doctor motioned them towards the door. "If he continues to recover, I can let you have a further five minutes with him tomorrow."

William-Wetherby sighed as he stood up. "If he remembers anything, could you write it down for us until we can call again?" With a final glance at the patient he was about to move away when the patient's eyes opened again.

"There was a name ..." The man paused for breath before he spoke. "Billy. They said they were looking for Billy."

Chapter Sixty-Nine

As soon as they got outside, William-Wetherby braced himself against the wall of the hospital, his head hung low and perspiration covering his face.

"Are you all right? You look as if you've seen a ghost."

William-Wetherby shook his head but said nothing as he attempted to keep the contents of his stomach where they belonged.

"Do you know who Billy is?" Duckworth asked.

Swallowing the bile that had reached the back of his mouth, William-Wetherby raised his head.

"It's me. When I went undercover, I told them my name was Billy."

Duckworth put his hand on William-Wetherby's shoulder. "Good God ... but why would they be looking for you?"

William-Wetherby wiped the perspiration from his brow. "They found out I was in the force and that I set them up?"

"Ah. That puts a new complexion on the case." Duckworth stood up straight and glanced around. "At least you're in plain clothes now, so if they're looking for a uniform, you won't be so easy to spot."

"Except for the fact that, like Tommy, I'm six foot tall." William-Wetherby rested his head on his forearm. "That bullet was meant for me."

"We don't know that. Why would they shoot an innocent man they'd never met before? I'd suggest it was a robbery that went wrong."

"Why would they mention Billy then?"

Detective Inspector Duckworth paused. "Let's go back to Cheapside. You'll be safe there."

"What about Bella and the boys?" William-Wetherby's eyes were wide. "I need to go home."

Duckworth stared at him. "The gang know where you live?"

William-Wetherby shook his head. "N-no, of course they don't. I was in a bedsit while I worked on the case." He straightened up and wiped his face again. "How am I going to tell Bella?"

Duckworth paused as he studied his colleague. "I'd suggest you don't go home for a few days ... certainly not until we've found Tommy Hudson. We don't want them following you."

William-Wetherby's stomach churned again and he reached for the wall. After taking several deep breaths, he glanced at Duckworth. "I can't do this."

"You can. Come on, once we're at the station we'll work out a plan of action."

WITH GEORGE SETTLED IN BED, Bella kissed his forehead before standing up.

"Dada home?" George said.

"He'll be home soon and he'll come up and say goodnight. Sweet dreams." She blew him another kiss and left the bedroom door ajar as she went downstairs to prepare her husband's tea. As she walked into the scullery, there was a knock on the front door.

What now, don't people use clocks in the summer? As she approached the open door she hesitated at the sight of a man in a dark suit wearing a bowler hat.

"Can I help you?"

"Mrs Jackson? Detective Inspector Duckworth. May I come in?"

Bella's heart sank. "What's happened? Is it my husband?"

Duckworth walked past her into the living room. "Don't be alarmed, he's fine but he won't be home for a couple of days." Duckworth handed Bella a letter and explained about the shooting. "He's sent you a note, but he doesn't want to risk leading the villains here and putting you or the boys in danger. As soon as we have them back in custody, he'll be home."

"I told him that working for the CID would bring trouble." Bella's hands shook as she read the letter. "He should never have done that undercover work."

"That was done before he joined the CID, it was nothing to do with us, he's just been unfortunate."

As one week in police accommodation turned to two, William-Wetherby stared at the walls before him. Other than standing in the courtyard of the Main Bridewell, he hadn't seen daylight since he had arrived and it looked increasingly like the Birmingham gang had disappeared again. Every policeman in Liverpool was searching for them, but there was no sign of them. Dare he risk going home? Maybe they'd gone back to Birmingham after all.

He lay on the mattress and closed his eyes. He knew sleep wouldn't come, but in his mind he saw Bella and the boys smiling and happy. Not that they would be happy with him stuck in here. Bella would be furious. *I need to see her.*

With his mind made up, nothing Duckworth said the next day could persuade William-Wetherby to stay where he was.

"I've been here for two weeks and the lads are no closer to finding Tommy Hudson. I could be here for months."

"Give us another few days. You don't want to put yourself at risk."

"If they've gone back to Birmingham you'll never find them and I'm not staying here indefinitely." He reached for his bag. "I'll report for duty the day after tomorrow."

His heart thumped as he left the Main Bridewell, but as he turned into Martensen Street, a smile crossed his lips. The older boys would be at school at this time of day and George should be having a nap. He should have Bella to himself for an hour.

As he approached the house, the sun was in his eyes and he didn't immediately notice the man walking towards him from the other end of the street. As soon as he saw him, he stopped.

"Stan? What are you doing here?"

Stan gave him a crooked smile. "Looking for you. You've not been easy to find but we knew if we were patient, you'd turn up." Stan momentarily swung his head over his left shoulder. "TOMMY."

"Listen, I'm sorry about what happened. You were never meant to get caught up in it, I knew you were different, but ..."

"Save your stories." There was an edge to Stan that William-Wetherby hadn't heard before. "You were after us from day one and don't think Tommy forgets things like that."

"But you ... why do you stick with them? You could do better for yourself."

"Didn't you work it out? He's my stepfather. Teaching me the trade he is."

William-Wetherby's mouth opened and closed several times. "But you've got wealthy parents ... they got you released ... I tried to get you released ..."

"What makes you think Tommy hasn't got money? I was just easier to release than the rest of them."

William-Wetherby gasped as the frame of Tommy Hudson temporarily shielded him from the sun, the larger man's steely blue eyes pinning him to the spot. "Well, well, what do we have here? You cost me two and a half years of my life and a lot of money." Without pausing, Tommy whipped a revolver from his inside pocket and pointed it at William-Wetherby. "Let's see how long it takes you to recover from this."

As a shot rang out, William-Wetherby's leg crumpled beneath him and he staggered back towards the railing in front of the house. He slipped to the ground and became aware of a warm liquid on his leg. "What have you done?" He glanced down to see blood seeping into his trousers. In that instant, a burning sensation grew above his knee, contorting his face and forcing him to grab his leg. Blood coated his fingers. "You won't get away with this," he managed.

Tommy took several steps towards him. "I'd better, otherwise I'll be back. I've a long memory."

William-Wetherby's heart thumped as he tried to stand, but an excruciating pain forced him back to the ground. As his vision blurred he watched Tommy put the revolver back in his jacket before he and Stan turned and headed out of the street.

"What's happened?" Bella's voice pierced the air. "I was in the back and it sounded like ... oh my ... you're bleeding." Bella glanced up and down the road in time to see Tommy and Stan disappear around the corner. "Help! Someone help!"

Bella knelt down beside William-Wetherby and within seconds her next-door neighbour was at her side. "Did you see what happened?"

Her neighbour shook his head. "We heard a gunshot and

shut the door. He was a big fella though, I wouldn't have liked to mess with him."

William-Wetherby groaned and Bella noticed the growing puddle of blood seeping around the cobbles of the pavement.

"Go and fetch Doctor Peters for me. I haven't got enough bandages for this."

~

BY THE TIME the doctor arrived, Bella was on the pavement surrounded by a group of neighbours, cradling William-Wetherby's head in her lap. The doctor pushed his way through the gathering.

"Thank goodness you're here." Bella wiped the tears from her eyes as she spoke. "I'm struggling to keep him awake."

The doctor studied the bandage wrapped loosely around William-Wetherby's leg. "This needs to be tighter if it's to stop the blood."

William-Wetherby screamed as the doctor cut away his trouser leg and secured the bandage. "That's better. Now we can move him inside."

With William-Wetherby lying flat on the living room floor, the doctor raised his head to give him some laudanum before turning his attention to the wound.

"I'd say he's been fortunate." The doctor spoke without looking up. "The shot went straight through his thigh and hasn't damaged the main blood vessel. You'll probably find the bullet outside; it might help the police."

"Will he be all right?" Bella wiped William-Wetherby's grey face.

"It's difficult to say. Without operating, I can't tell whether the bone's been damaged although I'd suggest some of the tendons have been. I need to get him to hospital."

William-Wetherby's eyes flickered open. "No hospital."

"But you must. I can't deal with you here if the bone is damaged."

"No hospital ... I ... need ... my leg."

With her husband's eyes once again closed, Bella stared at the doctor. "Can you do anything until he comes around?"

The doctor shook his head. "He's lost a lot of blood. He needs fluids, and I'll need to drench the wound with carbolic acid, dress it and splint the leg in case the bone's broken. He ought to be in hospital."

"Please, Doctor, for whatever reason, he doesn't want to go. Can someone come here and treat him? We can pay him."

The doctor sighed. "Let me do what I can and we'll see how he is tomorrow."

Bella wiped the back of her hand across her eyes as she left the doctor with William-Wetherby and let herself into her mam's house.

"How is he?" Mrs Booth was sitting at the table where her grandsons were eating their tea.

Bella sat next to Edward and put an extra spoon of sugar into the tea her mam handed to her. "The doctor says he's been fortunate, but he can't tell whether there's been any damage to the bone."

"Will you go to the hospital with him?"

Bella shook her head. "He won't go. He's said nothing since it happened, except that he won't go to hospital. The doctor's going to do the best he can for him."

Mrs Booth reached for her daughter's hand. "Have you got the money?"

Bella glanced at the boys before nodding. "We'll be fine."

"Well, the boys are going to stay with me and Fred for a few days, aren't you?"

"What's the matter with Dad?" Edward asked. "Why has he been away for so long, but we still can't see him?"

Bella's eyes watered as she glanced at her son.

"I've told you," Mrs Booth said. "He had to go away with the police for a couple of weeks but as he was coming home, he hurt his leg."

"But how did he hurt his leg?"

Bella stared into her cup of tea. "He was getting down from a carriage and one of the horses kicked him."

"Ouch, that must have hurt," Albert said. "I'm glad it wasn't me."

"I want to go and see him." Edward made to leave the table but Bella reached for the hands of both her sons.

"Not tonight. The doctor's with him now and he's given him something to make him sleep. Perhaps tomorrow."

FOR THE SEVENTH day in a row Bella opened the door to Dr Peters, but this morning her smile faded when she saw the man next to him.

"Good morning, Mrs Jackson. This is my colleague from the hospital, a surgeon. I've brought him to examine Mr Jackson's wound."

Bella's eyes flicked between the two of them. "Is there a problem?"

"I want a second opinion on the injury."

Bella nodded and showed both men to the makeshift bed under the front window. William-Wetherby didn't open his eyes, but lay on his back, his skin grey in the morning sunlight. Dr Peters knelt down beside him and drew back William-Wetherby's eyelids.

"I've been keeping him sedated but I believe he needs hospitalising." Dr Peters spoke to his colleague in a hushed voice. "I suspect the bone's been broken but he refuses to go into hospital. From the snippets I've picked up, I think he fears losing his leg if he does."

The surgeon removed the bandages from William-Wetherby's leg and examined the entry and exit wounds. "He's more likely to lose it if he doesn't," the surgeon said. "Looking at the damage to the muscles and tendons, I'm amazed the blood vessels remained intact." The surgeon covered the wound again and glanced around the room. "I can't do anything here, it's bound to become infected if I do, besides I haven't got the right instruments."

Dr Peters sighed. "What do you think about taking him to hospital and bringing him back while he's still sedated? I can watch over him once he's back."

"You can't take his leg." The words were out of Bella's mouth before she could stop herself.

The surgeon nodded and turned to Bella. "It's most irregular, but I'll go back to the hospital and send an ambulance for him. It's the only chance he has of keeping his leg."

Chapter Seventy

C harles jumped from the train onto the platform below before he turned and extended his hand to his sister.

"Not far to go now."

"I'd no idea it would take so long to get here," Eleanor said. "I'm glad we waited until the weather turned. I should have hated to make that journey at the height of summer. Will we go straight to the hotel?"

"We will. It's only a five-minute walk."

"We need to walk?"

Charles scowled. "Don't look so horrified. Since when were you above walking? I've told you, William-Wetherby doesn't live an extravagant life and we don't want to embarrass them. I hope you haven't told them we're staying at the Adelphi Hotel."

"But you said yourself, we couldn't stay with them."

"We couldn't, but we didn't need to stay in the best hotel in Liverpool either."

"We've got nothing to be ashamed of. I'd thought of

inviting Bella to the hotel for afternoon tea. I'm sure she'd appreciate it."

Charles studied his sister. "Let's leave that for now. She's got enough to worry about other than dressing herself up to come here."

Eleanor stared back at him. "You're right, I hadn't even thought of that."

As the carriage carrying Charles and his sister arrived in Martensen Street, Eleanor glanced at the rows of terraced houses lining both sides of the road. "You weren't wrong when you said he was struggling. Surely police inspectors earn enough money to move away from houses like this."

"You'd think so, but this is where Bella's from and so perhaps he has other reasons to stay."

They climbed from the carriage, and before they reached the front door Bella had opened it. "You're here. Thank you for coming, you should have come straight here rather than wasting money on a hotel."

"My dear, you have enough to worry about without putting up with us for a week." Eleanor stepped inside. "It sounds like we have a lot to catch up on."

Charles followed his sister in and went straight to William-Wetherby, who lay on a newly acquired settee. A smile flickered across William-Wetherby's lips, but Charles noticed the pain in his eyes and reached over to shake his brother's hand. "How are you getting on? Bella's told us how ill you've been."

William-Wetherby shook his head. "You've no idea."

"Have they caught the scoundrel who did it?" Eleanor asked.

William-Wetherby sighed. "We know who it was, but the lads at the station can't find him anywhere. He's the villain from

Birmingham I helped lock up a couple of years ago; we're hoping he's gone back where he came from, but we don't know for sure." William-Wetherby glanced towards the scullery where Bella had disappeared to make afternoon tea. "He came looking for me."

"No!" Eleanor said. "Why?"

"He said it was because of me that he'd lost two and a half years of his life in prison and he wanted me to suffer. Fortunately, the bullet missed the main blood vessels, but it broke the bone and damaged the muscle and some tendons."

"You'll make a full recovery though?" Eleanor sat by her brother, taking hold of his hand.

"I don't know. It's still too painful to stand on and I'm going to have to learn to walk again."

Eleanor looked from one brother to the other. "Bella didn't tell us that."

"No, I hoped I wouldn't need to. I was determined not to go into hospital but the doctor sedated me and took me anyway. When I woke up they told me I'd have lost my leg if they hadn't." He gave a sigh. "That was the reason I hadn't wanted to go in the first place. Anyway, it's done now and I still have two legs." He gestured to a set of crutches in the corner of the room. "The hospital gave me them to get about on, but it's going to take time."

"So you won't be able to work?" Charles said.

William-Wetherby shook his head. "Certainly not for the rest of the year; we'll have to see after that."

The lines on Charles's forehead deepened. "Are you still getting paid?"

William-Wetherby glanced again at the scullery to see Bella arranging a selection of food on a tray. "I am at the moment but there's an issue about it."

"They're trying to wriggle out of paying you?"

William-Wetherby nodded. "Before I was shot we knew the gang were looking for me and so for my own protection, the police had given me a free room in their accommodation. It was only supposed to be for a couple of days but I'd been there for two weeks and they were no closer to finding the men. I decided I'd had enough and told the detective who'd arranged it that I was coming home. He was furious with me and now they're blaming me for the shooting, saying it wouldn't have happened if I'd stayed where I was." William-Wetherby turned his head again. "Don't tell Bella, I don't want to worry her any further."

"Have you still got money from Mr Wetherby's inheritance?"

William-Wetherby grimaced. "I have, thank goodness. I'll need it until I'm back on my feet."

"Here we are, a pot of tea, and Fred, me mam's lodger, has made us a selection of pies and cakes. You won't find better in Liverpool." Bella put a large tray on the table.

"I'm sure we won't." Eleanor raised a discreet eyebrow at Charles.

"She's right," Charles said. "That lad's got talent. Try one and tell me I'm right."

"You may see him later; me mam's bringing the boys around once they've had their tea. I told her to bring Fred as well if she can tear him away from the oven."

William-Wetherby accepted the sausage roll Bella offered him but put it on the table. "Have you mentioned anything about the shooting to Florence or Margaret?"

Eleanor wiped her fingers on a napkin. "I have to Margaret. She sends her regards and hopes to see you in the not too distant future."

"Yes, it's been too long," William-Wetherby said. "How's the latest baby?"

"He's doing fine by all accounts and so is she. Life on a farm must suit her."

"What about Florence, did you tell her?"

369

Eleanor shook her head. "No, I didn't. You know she reacts badly to medical problems and so we didn't want to tell her until we knew you were all right."

"It's as well I didn't write to her," Bella said. "I was close to sending her a letter, but something held me back. I presume Margaret won't say anything?"

"No, I told her not to. No one's got time for another bout of hysteria at the moment."

Chapter Seventy-One

With Charles and Eleanor leaving Liverpool on the ten o'clock train, William-Wetherby hadn't bothered to move from the settee. He wasn't expecting any other visitors and despite the laudanum, his leg still throbbed. He dumped his blankets onto the floor and reached for the newspaper.

"I'll be glad when you're back upstairs." Bella collected up the blankets and folded them onto one of the chairs. "The place is never tidy nowadays."

"Not as glad as me," William-Wetherby said.

Bella stopped what she was doing. "I'm sorry, I know you're suffering. How is it today?"

"I'm ready for some laudanum although the pain never goes away. I wonder if I'll ever get better."

"Of course you will, but you need to give it time. Let me fetch the medicine and then I'll help you to the sink, having a quick wash always makes you feel better."

Bella hadn't made it to the scullery when there was a knock on the front door. "Who on earth's this?" She opened it cautiously to a man of medium build wearing an overcoat and bowler hat.

"Chief Inspector Adams here to see Inspector Jackson."

William-Wetherby let out a deep sigh. *Couldn't he give me a couple more weeks?* He forced himself to smile as Bella showed him in. "Chief Inspector. Excuse me for not getting up. What can I do for you?"

"Inspector Jackson, I had expected you to be on your feet by now."

"No, sir. The bone and muscle will take time to mend." William-Wetherby took a deep breath as Bella left them to go to the scullery. "Please take a seat."

With both men seated, the chief gave a small cough. "I called to talk about your return to work. As you know, I'm under pressure from the head constable to stop your pay. He believes you got yourself into this situation and that you weren't acting on police business."

"With respect, sir, I was working on police business when I first encountered the men. Had it not been for that, they wouldn't have come looking for me."

The chief held up his hands. "I know and let me tell you I'm sympathetic to your plight. We still haven't caught any of the gang who shot you, and so had this not happened you'd have been away from home for a lot longer. That, however, does not solve my problem. If I want to keep paying you, I need to find you a job."

"I just need more time, sir. I'd hoped to be able to convalesce until the New Year."

The chief drew a sharp intake of breath. "I'll try my best, but I'm not sure I'll be able to stretch it for that long. Let me be frank with you. You're a bright man and we don't want to lose you, but you can't go chasing around the city as you are. If I'm not mistaken, you've previously worked as a clerk, haven't you?"

"Yes, sir, although it was a long time ago."

"I'm sure you could pick it up again. If you're interested, leave it with me and I'll get back to you on a return date and position. I'll try and delay it for as long as I can."

William-Wetherby nodded. "There's one other thing, sir. The gang still haven't been captured. Will it be safe for me to go back to work?"

"We're fairly certain they've left Liverpool. Our men haven't been able to find them and there've been no reports of trouble involving them. We've sent word to Birmingham to keep an eye out for them. I'm sure you'll be fine."

Bella showed the chief out, before rounding on William-Wetherby.

"You can't go back to work. Look at you, you can't even stand up."

"He's going to try and delay it for as long as he can."

"I don't want him to delay it, I want you to leave. I told you months ago there'd be trouble if you worked in the CID and look how right I was."

"That's not true, this had nothing to do with the CID. Besides, I'm hardly going to get into trouble if I'm a clerk."

"I don't care. If you hadn't been in the police, this wouldn't have happened. I don't want you going back to it."

"What about my pension? If I leave after they offer me a job, I'll walk away with nothing."

"We've got the money from Mr Wetherby, I'm sure that's more than a pension would be worth and you can find a job somewhere else."

"Doing what?" William-Wetherby ran his hand across his encased leg.

"Being a clerk somewhere else. I've had it with the police. All this is their fault and they want to stop paying you. It's just not fair."

"You weren't supposed to be listening."

Bella put her hands on her hips. "And you're not supposed to keep secrets. Now, I need to get on, I said I'd be at me mam's by now."

~

WITH HER HAT FIXED, Bella reached for her coat, and turned to speak to William-Wetherby. "I won't be long, but have you got everything you need?"

William-Wetherby glanced at the newspaper and the pot of tea by his side. "I think so. Don't forget to go to the library for those books, I'm bored to tears if I've nothing to entertain me except the newspaper."

"Of course I won't." She was turning towards the front door when Mrs Booth came in.

"Oh good, you're ready," Mrs Booth said.

Bella picked up her shopping bag. "Yes, I'm sorry I'm late, but I was going to walk to you."

Mrs Booth went to the front window and glanced out. "I know, but I want to go the other way around. Have you noticed some strange men hanging around the corner near me for the last week or so? I'd rather not walk past them."

Bella followed her mam's gaze. "He's different to the one I saw the other day. What do you think they're doing?"

Mrs Booth shrugged. "I've no idea."

"Do you think we should tell the police ...?" Bella turned towards William-Wetherby but stopped when she saw the expression on his face. "What's the matter?"

"What do they look like?" he asked.

Bella glanced back out of the window. "A bit nondescript really. That fellow's average height, brown hair, our sort of age ..."

"Is he alone?"

"He is now, but there were two of them earlier," Mrs Booth said.

William-Wetherby closed his eyes as a deep sigh left his lips. "Can you pass me the writing paper? If you give me a few minutes, I'll write to the chief and you can drop it into Prescot Street on your way out."

"Do you think it's something to do with us?" Bella's eyes were wide.

"I've no idea, but I'd like them to come and investigate." He nodded towards his leg. "After this, I'm not taking any chances."

Chapter Seventy-Two

Bella peered through the crack in the front door before opening it to let Chief Inspector Adams inside.

"Good afternoon, sir." William-Wetherby pushed himself up, resting on his crutches.

"I'd say you're making progress," the chief said.

"Slowly," William-Wetherby said. "I still can't put any weight on the leg, but I've mastered the crutches and so I can manage about the house ... just."

"And you've had the cast off your leg."

"Only last week. It's made life easier, but the doctor said the bone's still weak. Learning how to walk again is going to take time."

The chief grimaced. "Unfortunately, time is the one thing we haven't got. I've been told you must return to work before the end of the year. We've made a position for you writing up the cases for the CID lads, but you'll need to be at Cheapside by the twenty-first of December if you want to continue getting paid."

William-Wetherby stared at his superior. "That's less than two weeks away, I won't be walking by then."

"They're the terms I've been given by the head constable. I pushed to give you as long as possible, but time is running out."

Bella had remained in the background, but took a step forward. "Excuse me, sir, but what would happen if my husband was unable to return to work by that date?"

The chief sucked air through his teeth. "Difficult to say other than he'd have his wage stopped. I'd like to think we'd hold a job open for him but I can't guarantee it."

"But you wouldn't make a decision immediately?" William-Wetherby said.

"I don't know." The chief studied him. "If you're not able to work on the twenty-first, I'll require a letter from you explaining why. I'll use that to go back to the head constable."

William-Wetherby nodded. "Thank you, sir."

"There was one other thing," the chief said. "We've been watching the men on the street corner. We believe they are connected to the Birmingham gang, although we can't be certain."

"Have you spoken to them?"

"We have, but each time they claim to be waiting for friends. We've been tailing them and occasionally one of them will take a train out of Liverpool that goes through Birmingham. We alerted the Birmingham force, but they've been unable to pick anyone up at the other end."

William-Wetherby sighed and sat back down. "They're watching me to make sure I don't do anything. I didn't tell anyone at the time, but when Tommy Hudson shot me, he said he'd lost two and a half years of his life and a lot of money because of me. Do you think he's checking up to make sure I don't recover too quickly?"

The chief shook his head. "I suspect your imagination is getting the better of you. The sooner you're back at work the better."

"But why else would they be there ... and then go to Birmingham?"

"Given that they come from Birmingham it isn't unreasonable."

"I still don't think it's right. Couldn't someone go on the same train and follow them?"

The chief stared at William-Wetherby. "As you're well aware, we cannot conduct business on another constabulary's area. I'll write to my counterpart in Birmingham again, but I would say you should forget about them and concentrate on getting yourself walking."

Once William-Wetherby and Bella were alone, he reached for the newspaper.

"He doesn't know what he's talking about. Of course they're watching us. Why else would they be there?"

Bella went to the window. "What do we do?"

"We're moving house. I'm not staying around here for them to intimidate us."

"Where will we go ... and what about me mam? I'm not leaving her again."

William-Wetherby looked up from the paper and stared at Bella. "No, we can't leave her. It would be too easy for them to find us again if she's still here."

"What do you mean?" Bella's eyes were wide.

"If she comes to visit us or you come here, the men could easily follow either one of you. She'll have to come with us." William-Wetherby turned back to the newspaper, studying the houses for rent.

"Where will we go?" Bella asked. "It can't be too far away."

"We need to find somewhere with two houses close to each other. There's nothing in here tonight but I'll keep looking. I'm not sure how we'll do it but we need to move without them seeing us. I want to be rid of these villains once and for all."

. . .

THE LETTER to the chief had taken William-Wetherby two weeks to perfect but as he reread it, he was satisfied it said everything he wanted to say. He wanted to stay with the police and he was keen to be part of the CID, but because he was still unable to walk, he regretted he would be unable to return to work for the foreseeable future. He was disappointed that the head constable underestimated his injuries and planned to stop his wage when his situation was a direct result of police work. Had he stayed in the police accommodation until the Birmingham gang had been recaptured, he would still be there and wouldn't have seen his family for months, something that he hoped they would agree was unacceptable.

Giving it a final read-through, he put it in an envelope and sealed it before Bella could read it. He had no intention of leaving the force and once they were away from this house, he hoped she'd see sense. Leaving the letter on the table, he pushed himself up and grabbed his crutches. He was by the window when Bella came downstairs.

"Is there anyone there?"

William-Wetherby shook his head. "It's getting too dark to see, but I don't think so. No one's been there all day."

"They could have gone back to Birmingham for Christmas."

"I hope so, it'll make our lives a lot easier if they have. Is everything packed upstairs?"

"Yes, we're all done and I've put George to bed so he's not too tired. I'm going to me mam's to see how she's doing. The boys were actually being helpful this afternoon and Fred should be home now. He wouldn't let anyone touch the things in the scullery until he got home."

William-Wetherby checked his pocket watch. "The carriages won't be here for a couple of hours, so they've time yet. I'll try and make a pot of tea while you're out, I need to do something to keep me occupied."

As six o'clock approached William-Wetherby opened the front door and took his first tentative steps outside. Peering into the darkness, he shivered. There was no sign of the strangers but with a heavy frost expected overnight, it was hardly surprising. He turned his attention to the other end of the street; he needed the landlord here so he could give him the keys and be away as soon as possible. He manoeuvred his crutches back inside the front door, but as he stepped over the threshold, he heard the sound of a horse and carriage. *Right, let's get everyone loading these things up.*

It took over three hours to deliver all the crates and furniture to the new houses on Molyneux Road and as he shut the door behind the last of the drivers William-Wetherby breathed a sigh of relief. The pain in his thigh was causing his whole leg to throb and he needed to sit down.

"Come and settle yourself by the fire." Bella took his arm as he manoeuvred down the hall towards the back room. "I've got it nice and warm in here."

After the freezing temperatures outside, the heat hit him but he didn't mind. It was like being back in the house he'd lived in in Handsworth, only smaller. Much smaller.

"Is there a cup of tea going?" he asked.

"Yes, there's one coming. We've still so much to do, but it'll have to wait until tomorrow. I'm exhausted. Me and Mam got all the beds made up and put some water bottles in to air them, that's all we need for tonight."

"Does your mam like it?"

Bella's face lit up. "Like it? She loves it, and Fred's in his element with the size of the kitchen."

William-Wetherby closed his eyes. The kitchen was a fraction of the size of his father's house in Handsworth, but he supposed it was twice the size of the scullery in Martensen Street. Fred had never known anything else.

Bella put a cup of tea by his side. "And we can't get much closer to each other without moving in together. We still can't believe it. What were the chances of getting two houses like this, next door to each other? Edward and Albert are happy too, having a room to themselves and I won't have to worry about them waking George when they go to bed."

William-Wetherby smiled as Bella sat opposite him but her eyes became serious.

"Did you write that letter to the chief about your job?"

The smile disappeared from William-Wetherby's lips. "I did. I dropped it into Prescot Street while we were on our way around here and so the chief should see it tomorrow."

"How will we manage?"

"Don't worry, I wouldn't have brought us here if we couldn't afford it. I've still got a lot of Mr Wetherby's money. We've only spent it on medical bills and so it should last until I can go back to work."

"I hope so," Bella said. "Now we're here, I don't want to move again."

Chapter Seventy-Three

William-Wetherby stood by the window of their new front room and peered out. They'd been there for a month and so far they hadn't seen anything to suggest the gang from Birmingham had been able to find them. Admittedly, they'd had Christmas during that time, but the New Year was now three weeks old and there had been no sign of them. With a sigh of relief, he glanced at the clock on the mantelpiece. Bella would be back from the shops soon, he needed to get out of here. The front room was for special occasions only. As he reached the hall, the postman pushed several letters through the door. William-Wetherby smiled at the man's consideration; he always left them caught in the letter box, which saved him the trouble of bending down.

Collecting the mail he went into the back room and sat down. Nothing but a couple of bills and the long-awaited letter from the police. He tore open the envelope but as he read he rubbed his hand over his face. The head constable was only prepared to hold a job open for another two months. *Damn man. Let him take a shot to the leg and see how quickly he recovers.* He moved his hand to his right thigh and rubbed the wounded area. It was still too painful to put any weight on and other than moving around the house, he hadn't done any walking on it. He needed to get himself out.

With the letter back in its envelope, he heard the front door open and watched Bella push the baby carriage into the hall.

"My, it's cold out today. I'm glad I don't have to go out again."

William-Wetherby's shoulders slumped.

"What's the matter?" Bella walked to the fireplace to warm her hands.

"I was hoping we might be able to go for a short walk this afternoon. Just up and down the road."

Bella raised an eyebrow. "What's brought this on?"

"I need to practise walking again. It's six months since the shooting and I should be more active than I am."

Bella's eyes narrowed. "Have you heard from the police?"

William-Wetherby waved his letter at her. "This came this morning. They'll only keep a job open for me until the twentieth of March. If I'm not back by then, I'll have to resign."

"I thought you were going to tell them you weren't going back; I've told you I don't want you working there again."

"What else can I do with my leg like this? Even if I go back to being a clerk, most of the jobs are at the docks, and I can't walk that far every day. Not at the moment anyway. Taking a desk job at Prescot Street is as good as it's going to get."

"And all Tommy Hudson needs to do is send his men to stand outside each police station and within days he'll know where we live again. Can't you see that?"

William-Wetherby rested his head on the back of the chair and closed his eyes. *She's right.* "Well, what do you suggest? Wherever I work, I'll have to walk past the top of Prescot Street. Do you want me out of work indefinitely?"

"Of course not, but ... I don't know. Do you think Tommy Hudson will keep this up for two and a half years to make up for the time he was in prison?"

William-Wetherby shrugged. "I hope not. If I don't earn any money for another two years, we'll be on the streets. Mr Wetherby's money won't last that long."

Bella sighed and took a seat opposite him. "How long do you think it will last?"

"At the rate we're going through it, I'd say another year, if we're careful."

Bella shook her head. "The boys are growing so fast though. We managed without buying them new school uniforms last year, but Edward changes school this year, we won't be able to avoid it."

"To think I've given over twelve years to the police, working more hours than most and going above and beyond the call of duty and this is how they treat me. Even if I take the desk job, they won't pay me the same wage I was earning before. Any way you look at it, it's not ideal."

"You need to forget about the police and do something for yourself. I'll help you with your walking, but only if you promise me it won't be so you can go back to them. Will you do that?"

William-Wetherby nodded. He'd agree to anything if it meant walking unaided again.

Chapter Seventy-Four

Wilillam-Wetherby sat across the table from the head constable and watched as he signed the certificate on his desk confirming that on this day, he, William-Wetherby Jackson, had resigned from Liverpool City Police. As a statement of fact, it was true, he had arrived at Cheapside this morning with his letter of resignation, but this wasn't how he'd wanted his career to end. He had wanted to continue; to be a chief inspector possibly a chief superintendent one day, but Tommy Hudson, and the man sitting before him, had put an end to that.

"There you are, Mr Jackson." There was no hint of emotion in the head constable's face and William-Wetherby hesitated to take the certificate from him.

"Thank you, sir.

William-Wetherby folded the document and slipped it into his inside pocket.

When he reached the reception area, Bella was waiting for him.

"Did he accept your resignation?"

"He did, without a hint of regret. I hope I never have to come into contact with him again."

"I hope so too. We'll have you walking again soon and find you a job where you don't have to work all the hours God sends."

WINTER WAS GRADUALLY RELENTING and blossoms were appearing on the trees, and as they approached home, William-Wetherby let go of Bella's arm and walked the last ten yards back to the house with only one walking stick for support. Despite the practice he'd been putting in, it didn't feel like he was making any progress, but it had to be better than doing nothing.

As he lowered himself into the chair, his right hand shook from gripping the walking stick so tightly. "Is this ever going to get any easier?"

"I'd say we moved a little faster today." Bella retrieved the letters from the letter box and joined her husband in the back room. "You've one here from Charles. What's he got to say?"

William-Wetherby read the letter before wiping the back of his hand across his eyes. "Bad news I'm afraid. Sid, my old friend from Birmingham, died earlier this week. Poor Sid. I know we hadn't seen each other for years, but I often thought of him. I wouldn't have got through the time with Father without him."

"That's terrible. Was he the same age as you?"

William-Wetherby's eyebrows drew closer together as he thought. "He was a few years older than me, he must have been about forty, perhaps forty-one. Not old enough to die."

"What was it?"

"According to the doctor, his years of drinking had damaged his liver and in the end, it stopped working." William-Wetherby shook his head. "The funeral's on Friday and Charles thinks I should go. He says he's asked our cousin Henry if I'm invited and I am."

"Henry? He's Uncle William's son, isn't he ... and wasn't Sid Mr Wetherby's nephew?" The lines on Bella's forehead deepened. "That means the Wetherbys will be there. I don't think so ..."

"Sid was my friend. Uncle William might be there, but I won't let him stop me paying my last respects."

"What about Sid's mam? Didn't Charles say she's angry with you for what happened to Sid?"

"Maybe she is, but one of the reasons was because she thought I had a life of luxury here while Sid was suffering. If she knows the truth and sees me like this, she might think again."

"But you can't walk. How will you get there?"

William-Wetherby stared up at his wife, his dark eyes moist. "Will you come with me?"

≈

Birmingham, Warwickshire.

WILLIAM-WETHERBY HELD onto the arm of his wife as they inched their way to the exit of the railway station. As soon as they stepped outside he took a deep breath and broke into a fit of coughing. Spring might be in the air but so was all the smoke from the nearby factories. How had he forgotten how bad the air was down here?

Bella guided him to one of the pillars leading from the station. "You wait here while I find us a carriage ... and mind the bags."

He watched as Bella jostled with the crowd. *She shouldn't have to do this.* He put his weight onto his leg and screwed up his face as the pain radiated from the wound. *If I do that often enough, it'll get more bearable.*

It was turned four o'clock before they arrived in Small Heath and Charles was at the door to greet them.

"You made it."

"We did, but I need to sit down." William-Wetherby handed his hat to the maid before Bella helped him off with his coat.

"Are you on your own?" Bella asked as they went into the back room.

"I am. Rose's sister, Daisy, is in the throes of giving birth and so Rose has gone to sit with her mother. Don't worry though, she's left us something to eat."

"A cup of tea will do me," William-Wetherby said.

"Or a nip of brandy ... that'll help your leg."

William-Wetherby rolled his eyes. "If you insist, I'll give it a try. We don't keep the stuff at home."

Once the maid had served the tea, William-Wetherby studied his brother.

"So what's all this with Henry? You seem very friendly all of a sudden."

"I am, he's a decent chap."

"He's Uncle William's son!"

Charles laughed. "And he doesn't like his father any more than we do. I bumped into him the other week while he was collecting his rents and we had quite a chat. He told me his mother is having a house built for him next door to theirs."

William-Wetherby raised an eyebrow. "I thought he lived in that mansion with Uncle William. Isn't that big enough?"

"Apparently not. He said that since his wife had their daughter, Aunt Olivia and Uncle William are always interfering."

"Why doesn't he move away? He can't be short of money."

"I think he would, but Aunt Olivia commissioned an architect to design this house and so he hasn't got much choice at the moment. Can you believe it'll have five reception rooms, eight bedrooms, two bathrooms and quarters for the servants?"

William-Wetherby sighed. "Yes, I can and I don't suppose I'd complain if someone else was paying for it."

"I'm sure I wouldn't, but Henry isn't affected by money in the way the rest of them are. I'll introduce you at the funeral."

Chapter Seventy-Five

William-Wetherby's brow creased as he walked into the near empty church. Where was everyone? The Sid he remembered had always been popular, but he could count the number of friends present on his fingers. Was this what drinking had done to Sid's life?

He faced the front of the church as the organ started up, signalling the arrival of the funeral party. Sid's brother Sam comforted Mrs Storey as they walked the length of the church and took their seats at the front. Beside them were Sid's sister and her husband. He'd never really known them. Bringing up the rear was Uncle William, his arrogant stride and expensive tailcoat making him look more like an undertaker than a mourner.

The service was short and as they made their way to the local tavern, Henry joined them.

"Thank you for coming." He offered his hand to William-Wetherby. "I'm sure Mrs Storey will be pleased you're here. It was one of her biggest fears that no one would turn up."

Henry spoke with sincerity and William-Wetherby couldn't fathom how this young man was related to his uncle.

"He was a good friend ... before I was sent away. I'd no idea he'd fallen on hard times until much later."

"My grandfather was unduly harsh with him in my opinion, but Father wasn't much better." Henry glanced towards William Junior. "I don't know what Sid ever did to upset him."

William-Wetherby sighed. "He helped me out when I needed him. That was his only crime."

With the food served and the plates cleared away, William-Wetherby pushed himself up from his seat and hobbled over to the table where Sid's brother and sister were comforting their mother.

"Good afternoon, Mrs Storey. Do you mind if I join you?"

William-Wetherby couldn't judge Mrs Storey's facial expression through her thick mourning veil, but he breathed a sigh of relief when she nodded her consent.

"I was sorry to hear about Sid, he was a good man."

Mrs Storey reached under her veil with a handkerchief. "He was once."

"I don't even know how to apologise to you for what happened. With the exception of Mr Wetherby's funeral, the last time I saw him was the day I left Birmingham ... as Mr Wetherby had ordered me to do. That morning, he came to wave me off and as far as I was concerned he was going back to work for Mr Wetherby."

"Perhaps if you'd written to him ..."

William-Wetherby's brow furrowed. "I did to start with but with the exception of one letter and a Christmas card, I never received any other replies. That was one of the reasons I stopped. It's difficult having a one-sided conversation."

"You're lying. He only received a single letter from you and got it into his head that you'd settled down to a happy life in Liverpool and forgotten about him."

William-Wetherby sat up straight. "I'm sorry, Mrs Storey; I

don't know how to respond to that. I can't prove it, but I must have written half a dozen letters before I finally stopped. My life of luxury was living in a temperance hotel in one of the roughest parts of Liverpool, sharing a room with an old sailor. I was there for a year and sent the last letter before I left telling him of my new address."

"Well, he didn't get them." Even though he couldn't see them, William-Wetherby felt Mrs Storey's eyes boring into him. "My brother was on good terms with the postman at the time and I even asked him to check that we were receiving all our mail."

"Your brother ... you mean Mr Wetherby? He was friendly with the postman?" William-Wetherby shook his head. "I'm sorry, Mrs Storey, I know you've been fond of his memory since he died, but Mr Wetherby hated me. If he'd seen a letter with a Liverpool postmark, he wouldn't have passed it on."

"Now you're talking nonsense. He only visited the house once or twice a week. The postman called most days."

"It wouldn't have taken much to ask the postman to hold back any letters with a Liverpool postmark. With the exception of the time he wanted me out of your house, Mr Wetherby never called more than once or twice a month."

"I don't know what you're saying, but I don't like your tone." Mrs Storey straightened in her chair.

"I'm not saying anything, although I will say this. Once I left Birmingham, my lifeline was getting letters from anyone who cared to write. I wrote to Eleanor every week, I wrote to Charles and Aunt Mary-Ann nearly as often. I even got a few letters to Margaret and Florence in Wetherby House. If what you're saying is true, Sid was the only one who didn't get anything from me. You can draw your own conclusions, Mrs Storey, call me a liar if you like, but I think the decline of your son was more to do with Mr Wetherby than me." William-

Wetherby turned to look for Charles. "I'm sorry to have troubled you, if you'll excuse me ..."

William-Wetherby winced as he pushed himself up and headed towards Charles and Henry.

"There you are," Charles said. "Have you made your peace with Mrs Storey?"

William-Wetherby sighed and checked his pocket watch. "She doesn't believe me; I think it's time we were leaving."

"My, that's an old pocket watch." William-Wetherby flinched at the sound of William Junior's voice to his right-hand side.

"It was my father's. I keep it for sentimental reasons."

William Junior smirked. "Of course you do. I believe you've settled in Liverpool now. I had expected you to come back to Birmingham once Father died."

"Why would I do that when I have a wife and three sons in Liverpool? They more than make up for anything I left here. I should thank your father for that."

William Junior knocked one of William-Wetherby's crutches with his foot. "I heard you were involved in a shooting ... someone came and tracked you down, did they?"

William-Wetherby frowned. "How did you know that?"

"It helps to keep in with the chief constable. He picks up these snippets of information and keeps me informed of anything interesting."

"And is that all I am? A snippet of information? It's cost me my livelihood, not to mention my health."

William Junior raised an eyebrow. "It's cost you your livelihood? Does that mean you're no longer in the police?"

"Yes, it does and so you needn't waste your time reporting me to the police for being out of the Liverpool area."

Henry glared at his father. "You're unbelievable. Don't you have other guests to talk to?"

William Junior turned on his heel. "I'm sure I can find someone more entertaining."

Once his father was out of earshot, Henry turned to William-Wetherby. "So, what will you do now?"

"I need to learn to walk again first and then I'll see."

"Are you all right for money?" Henry asked. "I don't have much that isn't tied up in investments, but let me know if I can help."

William-Wetherby studied his cousin. "Thank you, I appreciate it. Hopefully I won't need anything. I still have some of your grandfather's money and hope to be working again before it runs out."

"Well, you know where I am if you change your mind ... and don't mind Father, what he doesn't know, he can't worry about."

William-Wetherby shifted his crutches. "Thank you. Will you excuse me, I need to sit down." He headed towards the table Bella occupied with Rose, but as he passed Mrs Storey's table, she motioned for him to stop.

"I want to apologise." She fidgeted with a handkerchief in her hands. "I've been thinking about what you said, and you may be right. My brother rarely did anything unless he benefitted from it and there were times he would call at the house for no apparent reason. It makes sense now."

"I can only say yet again how sorry I am, Mrs Storey. I just wish Sid had lived to find out."

Chapter Seventy-Six

Liverpool, Lancashire

With the front door open to let a breeze through the house, William-Wetherby could hear the boys playing in the street, but he wasn't paying attention. He lifted his head from his hands and looked again at the numbers in the book in front of him. It was only six months since he'd left his job with the police; they shouldn't have gone through their savings so fast. He'd been so careful but the medical bills had cost more than he'd thought and he was still buying laudanum to help him sleep.

"What's the matter?" Bella said as she put a pot of tea on the table.

William-Wetherby gazed at her, but his words stuck in his throat as Bella picked the book from the table.

"We're running out of money?" Bella asked.

William-Wetherby nodded. "I've let you down, I've let you all down. I thought I'd be working again by now but this leg just won't mend."

"How long will our money last?"

William-Wetherby shrugged. "Another couple of months at best."

Bella sat beside him. "That'll take us to winter; we'll need more coal by then. What will we do?"

"I'll have to find a job."

"Doing what?"

William-Wetherby squeezed his eyes together. "I don't know, but I'm not going the way of my father. There's got to be something I can do."

"What about Henry? Didn't you say he'd help?"

"He did, but I've got my pride."

"Pride won't put a roof over our heads."

"Do you think I don't know that?" William-Wetherby glared at his wife. "I'll sort something out, please give me a chance."

BELLA SAT in the front room of Mrs Booth's house, George on the floor beside her and a hat on a mannequin in front of her.

"Doesn't William-Wetherby wonder why you're spending so much time around here?" Mrs Booth asked.

"I don't think he misses me. For the last couple of weeks he's been sitting with his head in the newspaper most mornings and writing for jobs in the afternoon."

"But he's had no success?"

Bella shook her head. "No. That's why I'm making hats again, not that they'll make much money."

"Why do men have so much pride?"

Bella stopped what she was doing. "Don't say anything to him, but I've written to Eleanor and told her what's happening. I asked if she could get Charles to speak to Henry. After all, he did offer to help and if William-Wetherby won't ask, I will."

"I've obviously never seen how they live in Birmingham, but I imagine he's upset about all the money in the family when you're scrimping and saving."

Bella returned to her work. "I try not to think about it. If things hadn't been as they were, William-Wetherby would never have come to Liverpool and so I can't be bitter. It'd be nice if they'd have a little sympathy for us though."

"When did you write to Eleanor?"

"A couple of days ago. I'm hoping I'll hear back from her any day now."

THE POSTMAN HAD BEEN by the time Bella got home. She took the letters from the door and scanned them before slipping an envelope from Eleanor into her pocket.

"Have you had any success this morning?" she asked William-Wetherby as she walked into the back room and handed him the remaining letters.

"No." He threw the newspaper onto the chair beside him. "Why do so many jobs require you to be physically fit? Even to be a clerk, you can't have anything wrong with you. I could do their bookkeeping without any problem, but because one of my legs doesn't work as well as it should, I'm not even considered. I imagine these are all letters telling me I'm not wanted."

Bella took a deep breath. "Something will turn up."

When she was alone in the kitchen, Bella pulled the letter from her pocket and prised the envelope open. As she pulled out the letter, a five-pound note fell into her hands. *A five-pound note! What on earth do I do with this?* She glanced at the letter and read that Eleanor had passed the message on to Charles, but her eyes were pulled back to the note in her hands. She'd never seen one before.

Bella's thoughts were disturbed as William-Wetherby shouted her from the back room. "Will dinner be ready soon?"

Stuffing the letter and money back into her pocket she returned to the back room. "Yes, give me a minute. Let me set the table before I shout the boys. What's your rush?"

"I need this leg working. We're going to walk into town this afternoon and I'm not stopping until we reach the docks."

Bella hesitated. "I was going to go back to me mam's ..."

William-Wetherby glared at her. "What's so important that you're around there all the time? You should be more concerned about helping me and not just sitting next door drinking tea."

"I don't sit ... Yes, of course, I'm sorry. Let me pop next door and tell her I won't be in after dinner."

As Bella walked back into her mam's house Mrs Booth looked up from the dining table.

"That was quick. Have you had your dinner?"

"No, not yet, I've come to tell you that William-Wetherby wants to walk into town this afternoon."

"That'll take you hours."

"I know, but he's getting fed up with everyone turning him down because of his leg ... I've got to help him."

"Of course you have. The hat will wait."

Bella nodded. "That's not the only reason I'm here. I got this in the post from Eleanor." Bella pulled out the five-pound note and put it on the table. "What do I do with it?"

Mrs Booth picked it up and examined both sides. "I've never seen one of these before."

"Me neither and not many around here will have done either. I can't go waltzing into the shop with it."

"You'll need to take it to the bank and ask if they'll change it for some coins."

Bella put her hand to her chest. "Me ... go to the bank? Will they even serve me?"

"I've no idea ... I've never been in. If you're going into town this afternoon why don't you ask William-Wetherby to do it?"

Bella shook her head. "I didn't tell him I wrote to Eleanor, he may not be happy with me."

"Well, with the way things are, I would say he should be pleased to have this much money. Beggars can't be choosers."

Bella sighed. "You're right, but I think I'll wait until he's in a better mood. We've got enough money to pay the rent for another couple of weeks so there's no rush."

WITH THE FIRST hints of autumn in the air, Bella fastened off the end of her thread and secured her needle in the pincushion before looking at Mrs Booth who sat opposite her.

"That'll do for now, I'd better go and make dinner."

"What time will you be back? Will William-Wetherby want to go for a walk again?"

Bella shrugged. "He's still not recovered after the exertions of last week. We hadn't got to the railway station before he was struggling but he wouldn't stop and take a carriage. He can be so stubborn at times."

"At least he's trying, many folks would use it as an excuse never to work again."

"You're right of course. I'll see you later."

Bella let herself into her own house and walked straight to the back room. "Right, let me get some ... What's the matter?"

William-Wetherby's face was like thunder. "This is what's the matter." He waved a letter in the air."

Bella's stomach lurched. "W-what is it?"

"It's a letter from Charles telling me he's sorry about the money situation and that in addition to the five pounds he's sent, he's asked Henry to send me some too."

Bella's smile flickered on her lips. "But that's good, isn't it?"

"No, it isn't. Have you any idea how hard it is to feel like a failure without your wife spreading gossip around the rest of the family?"

"I wasn't spreading gossip. You said yourself a few weeks ago that the money would only last a couple of months at best. We've got three sons and I have no intention of not being able to feed them or keep a roof over their heads for the sake of your pride."

"Why didn't you ask me about it? How foolish do you think it makes me look when you're begging for handouts?"

"I didn't mention it because I knew this was how you'd react. Henry told you earlier in the year that he'd help you out if you asked. Why is it so hard?"

William-Wetherby screwed up the letter and threw it into the unlit fire. "Because I'm supposed to provide for you. God, I'm such a failure."

Bella picked the letter up and uncrumpled it. "What are you thinking of? There's a five-pound note in here. I'm glad the fire's not lit."

William-Wetherby said nothing but put his head back on the chair and closed his eyes.

"You need to write to Charles and thank him. It's very generous ... Oh, and we need to go to the bank to change these for coins."

William-Wetherby stared at her. "These?"

Bella flushed. "Eleanor sent one last week. I didn't know what to do with it, but me mam thought I should go to the bank."

"Your mam! Is there anyone you haven't spoken to about this? Do you want everyone to think I'm a fool?"

Bella knelt beside him. "You're not a fool. It's because you did such a good job in the police that you were unfairly targeted. It's not your fault you can't walk. We're going to get you mended, but in the meantime, this will help." She held up the five-pound note. "We've got ten pounds now that we wouldn't have had. It should last us into next year and we need to pray that something turns up before it runs out."

Chapter Seventy-Seven

William-Wetherby pushed himself up from the chair beside the fireplace and walked to the front door. The postman had delivered more letters than usual and most were bills. He returned to the back room to open them.

Dear Mr Jackson ... the outstanding balance is £1 3s 6d; Dear Mr Jackson ... the current debt is 18s 9d; Dear Mr Jackson ... you owe £3 4s 10d ...

He threw them onto the table. How had he amassed bills of over five pounds when the money Henry had sent had only just disappeared? He hadn't expected such generosity, but on top of the money from Charles and Eleanor, Henry's money had lasted nine months but now even that was depleted. He kicked out at the dining table but bent double as a pain shot through his leg. Damn thing; he'd had enough of it. He was going to do something about this.

Once dinner was over, William-Wetherby waited for Bella to go next door, before he made his way to the front door. At least they lived on the street corner and he could disappear without her seeing him from the window. He paused as soon as he rounded the corner and looked both ways for a carriage. Although he wasn't going far, he couldn't do it on his own.

Ten minutes later, he climbed from a carriage and handed a penny to the driver. "Can you come back in half an hour?"

The driver nodded and left William-Wetherby to stare at the front of Prescot Street police station. Taking a deep breath he straightened his back as best he could and headed into the building. The sergeant on the desk had been a constable when he'd left.

"Good afternoon, Officer. Who's in charge here nowadays?"

"Good afternoon, sir, it's good to see you back. It's Chief Inspector Shaw."

Chief Inspector Shaw. He was only an inspector when I left ... and he hadn't been in the job as long as me. "Is he available?"

"Let me check, sir. Take a seat."

William-Wetherby glanced around the white, tiled walls and wooden floors. The place hadn't changed in the last year, only the officers. *To think I could have been a chief inspector by now.*

"Mr Jackson." Chief Inspector Shaw came out of an office and extended his hand to William-Wetherby. "Come on in. What can I do for you?"

William-Wetherby hobbled behind the chief and accepted the chair he offered. "Thank you for seeing me ... and congratulations on the promotion. I'm sure it was deserved."

The chief smiled. "Chief Inspector Adams was moved up to Bootle last month and so I was given the nod. I'm still getting used to it to be honest."

"Well, I'll come to the point. Since I left here, I've missed the police work. My leg's on the mend but obviously not enough to be walking the street. I wondered if you have any clerks jobs going. I'd be happy to take anything."

The chief studied him. "You were always good at detective

work as I remember. Let me speak to the super and see if we can find something for you, it's a shame to waste you if you want to come back. Give me a couple of days and I'll see what I can do."

WHEN WILLIAM-WETHERBY ARRIVED HOME, Bella was waiting for him. "Where on earth have you been? I've been worried sick."

"I went out about a job."

"Why didn't you tell me? I'd have come with you. Did you get it?"

"They're going to let me know in the next couple of days."

"That sounds promising." She nodded towards his leg. "It didn't put them off?"

"No, I don't think so."

Bella's smile grew. "That's good. Where is it?"

William-Wetherby avoided her gaze as he took his seat. "With the police."

"The police?" Bella's mouth dropped. "You promised you'd finished with them."

"And I would have done if anyone else would have given me a job, but the truth is, they're the only ones who'll have me and I'm not turning them down when we don't even have the money for tonight's rent."

Bella stopped what she was doing. "We can't pay the rent? How's that happened?"

"I don't know. I thought we had enough, but it's disappeared quicker than I expected."

"Well, what are we going to do?"

William-Wetherby glanced at the clock. "The landlord won't be here for another hour. Could your mam lend it to us ... just until I get the job?"

"She's got her own to pay and Fred doesn't give her much

... but I'll ask. If she's got it, she'll lend it to us but we can't keep on borrowing from her. What about going back to Charles?"

"He's given me enough, I can't keep going back to him either."

William-Wetherby put his head in his hands as he waited for the landlord to call. When the inevitable knock on the door came, his stomach churned. He shouldn't be letting Bella do this.

"I'm sorry to tell you that I don't have it all this week," Bella said.

The landlord's voice was harsh. "That's not good enough, I've got a living to make; I need that money."

"I have some of it." He imagined Bella fumbling with the loose change. "Will you take this for now and we'll have the rest by next week? My husband's been ill and hasn't been able to work. He's on the mend now and hopes to be working again by next week."

There was a pause before the landlord spoke. "One week, but I'm not a charity. If the money's not here by next Thursday, you're out."

"Thank you, don't worry, we'll have it for you." The front door closed almost before Bella finished her words.

"What did you tell him that for?" William-Wetherby said.

"I had to say something. Did you want him to throw us out tonight?"

"He won't throw us out, not yet. We've been here eighteen months and this is the first time we've missed a payment."

Bella slumped into the chair opposite him. "You didn't see the look on his face. We're going to have to come up with the money for next week."

. . .

WITH BELLA once again next door, William-Wetherby smiled as he collected the mail from the back of the door. No bills today but there were two from the police. He limped back to his seat and tore open the first envelope as soon as he was settled. A smile spread across his lips. *They've arrested Tommy Hudson and two of his gang.* Did that mean he no longer had to look around every corner when he went out? He continued reading. They had enough evidence to put them inside for the next five years. He leaned his head back on the chair and let out a long sigh. What a relief ... for the next five years, at least.

With his smile fixed to his lips, he opened the second letter. *They have a job for me, too.* He slapped his hand on the arm of the chair but slowly the smile fell from his lips. They don't want me until the end of next month ... *I can't manage for another five weeks.* He read the letter again. The job sounded ideal, writing up the case notes for the CID with an opportunity to discuss ideas ... but not for over a month. They'd given no indication of how much he'd earn either. He'd have to write and ask if he could start sooner, what difference would a month make to them?

He was about to push himself up from his chair when the front door opened and Bella walked in.

"You look pleased with yourself," he said.

"I am. I sold a couple of hats this morning and so we'll have enough money to pay the rent this week. I've a couple more that'll be ready next week too."

William-Wetherby raised an eyebrow. "I thought you didn't have enough money to buy any more materials?"

Bella turned from him and began to set the table. "Me mam found some bits and bobs in her wardrobe that I could use."

"How much did you get for them?"

"Enough."

"You don't make more than a couple of shillings on a hat. That won't pay the rent."

"It'll give us enough until you sort yourself out. Have you heard about that job yet?"

"I have," William-Wetherby relaxed back into the chair. "I've been offered it."

Bella stopped what she was doing. "When do you start?"

"The letter says the end of next month, but I'm going to see if I can start sooner. Aren't you pleased?"

"Yes, of course, but you know I don't want you to go back to the police. Please say you'll keep looking for something else."

The lines on William-Wetherby's forehead deepened. "I thought you'd be happy that we'd be able to pay the rent again. What's up with you? We won't be able to rely on your hats."

Bella said nothing as she moved towards the kitchen but William-Wetherby pushed himself up and grabbed her wrist. "Not so fast." He took hold of her left hand. "What have you done with your ring?"

Bella glanced at her third finger. "I-I must have left it upstairs."

"Don't lie to me, Bella." His eyes narrowed. "Have you pawned it?"

Bella pulled her hand away. "Only until you start work. What good is it to me, if we can't pay the rent?"

"But that ring's special."

"My family are special and as much as I love the ring, having somewhere to live is more important."

Chapter Seventy-Eight

Bella stood with tears in her eyes as William-Wetherby closed the door on the landlord. The money from the ring had paid the rent for the last four weeks and he was due to start work next week, but it hadn't prevented them sending the landlord away empty-handed.

"What are we going to do?" Bella's voice squeaked through her tears.

William-Wetherby stepped forward to wrap his arms around her. "I don't know."

"We should have gone back to Charles or Eleanor again. They'd be horrified if they could see us now."

"They've been more than generous; I couldn't ask for more."

"But what about the bailiffs? Do you think he means it when he says he'll send them around?"

"I don't know." William-Wetherby rested his brow on the top of Bella's head. "Now I've told him I'm starting work again, I hope he'll give me more time."

The sound of rattling on the front door caused them both to straighten up.

"Mam, are you in there?" It was Edward. "Why's the door locked?"

Bella wiped her eyes with a handkerchief. "What do we tell them? They're bound to ask why I've been crying."

William-Wetherby coughed to clear his throat. "We don't tell them anything. You go and make a cup of tea and I'll send them straight upstairs."

As she cleared the breakfast table the following morning, Bella gasped at the sound of hammering on the front door.

"Who's that?" Her eyes were wide as she stared at William Wetherby. "They're going to break the door down if they don't stop."

William-Wetherby pushed himself up from the chair by the fire. "I think that's their plan."

"Do you think it's the bailiffs?" Bella's voice squeaked. "Have they come to throw us out?"

"Calm down." William-Wetherby walked to the hall. "If it is, they're going to have to break the door down. I'm not letting them in."

"What's that noise?" Edward shouted from upstairs.

"We don't know," William-Wetherby said. "You stay in your bedroom and keep the other two with you."

Seconds later, a crashing sound ripped through the house as the front door was torn from its hinges. As silence descended, a stranger stepped through the opening and placed the door against the wall before walking into the back room.

"Mr Jackson? I'm from the bailiffs' office and on behalf of the owner of this property we've come to reclaim it and sufficient contents to cover the rent arrears owed to him."

"You can't do that. This is our home," William-Wetherby said.

"If you can't pay the rent, you can't stay."

Bella stepped forward. "Please, sir, we have three sons; you can't make them homeless."

"I'm sorry, Mrs Jackson. We're only carrying out our instructions. If you can't give me the sum of four pounds, three shillings and sixpence, I have no choice in asking you to leave the premises with immediate effect."

Bella stared at the bailiff but was distracted by a loud gasp from the stairs.

"They're going to throw us out?" Edward studied his parents. "Don't they know Dad was in the police and it's not his fault he can't work?"

Bella stared at her son and noticed Albert and George behind him, their eyes wide.

"I told you to stay upstairs." William-Wetherby's voice filled the house.

"No, leave them," Bella said. "Go around to Granny's and we'll come and fetch you when all this is over."

"I need my trains if ..."

"No, please leave everything. Nothing's going to happen to your trains. Go and see Granny and tell her we'll be around soon."

Once the boys had gone, the bailiff nodded to the two men beside him. "Start collecting up the saleable furniture."

"No, please." Bella sobbed. "At least let us collect up our personal possessions ... the children's toys ..."

"It gives me no pleasure to do this, especially under the circumstances, but I'm only doing my job." He held up his hand as the men moved towards the stairs. "I'll give you five minutes to collect up the things you need."

TEN MINUTES LATER, with her arms full of clothes, toys and her prized photographs, Bella kicked on her mam's front door until it opened. As soon as she saw Mrs Booth she collapsed onto the floor, tears streaming down her cheeks.

"The bailiffs ..."

"I know," Mrs Booth said. "Edward told me."

"He shouldn't have seen it, none of them should."

"Where's William-Wetherby? Is he coming?"

Bella nodded. "He's trying to bring some more things. What are we going to do, Mam? We won't be able to hold our heads up again."

Mrs Booth helped her daughter from the floor. "Come and sit down and I'll make a cup of tea."

"Where will we even sleep? We've lost the beds as well as everything else."

"Calm down. You can stay here for as long as you need to. We've enough bedrooms."

"But we can't pay you ..."

"You don't need to. We have Fred's wage for now and once William-Wetherby's working again, we'll have more money than we know what to do with."

"But ... but ..." Bella's words were broken up by her sobs. "Tell me this isn't happening." She buried her face in a handkerchief, but looked up when William-Wetherby joined them; his face was white.

"I think that's it. Even if the bailiffs gave us more time, I couldn't have moved the bigger items."

"Put everything on the floor and have a seat," Mrs Booth said. "I'll go and see the boys."

"Did you see everyone watching out their windows?" Bella said once they were alone. "I feel ashamed."

"You've nothing to be ashamed of, it's all my fault ... but I'll make it up to you. I promise."

Chapter Seventy-Nine

Birmingham, Warwickshire

With spring making way for summer, Charles would have liked to walk home from work, but he knew the folly of ignoring an order from his sister to visit. He sighed as he stared out of the window of Mr Keen's carriage.

"Are you sure Eleanor didn't say why she wanted to see me?" It was the third time he'd asked his brother-in-law the same question.

"No, I'm telling you," Mr Keen said. "Once I got home last night she hardly said a word to me. I asked her what was up, but all she said was that she needed to speak to you."

As the carriage pulled into the driveway, Charles leaned forward and opened the door.

"Let's get this over with; Rose will be expecting me."

As soon as the maid opened the front door, Charles saw Eleanor step into the hall, relief washing over her face."

"Thank goodness you're here." She ushered him into the back room and closed the door before the maid or Mr Keen could follow them. "I've not known what to do with myself all day."

"Isn't Mr Keen ...?"

"No." Eleanor held a hand to her chest. "This is private. We have a problem and I don't know what to do about it."

Charles took a seat. "What sort of a problem?"

Eleanor screwed her eyes together as if holding back her tears. "I had a letter from Hannah in Margate yesterday ... it's Florence."

Charles rolled his eyes. "What's she been up to?"

Eleanor studied her brother and took a deep breath. "She's in the family way."

Charles's mouth dropped open, while his mind processed what he'd heard. "She can't be," he finally managed. "She's not married."

Eleanor took Hannah's letter from the pocket of her dress. "Read it for yourself."

DEAREST ELEANOR

It is with sadness that I write with unfortunate news. I have been remarking for several months that Florence hasn't been her usual self. She's been full of sickness, but wouldn't let me mention it to you or call a doctor. She seemed to be recovering well until she recently suffered a heavy cold and I needed to call the doctor. Please brace yourself for a shock, but while he was examining her he found her to be with child.

To say we were all shocked is an understatement but the diagnosis sent Florence into one of her fits of hysteria. I'm afraid the doctor had to sedate her for over a week until he was able to reduce the dose of the medication. The doctor believes she is almost halfway through her time, and the baby can be expected in November.

I am sorry to share such terrible news in this way, and I feel

413

sure you will have many questions, but even now, two weeks after we heard the news, I delayed writing to you in the hope that Florence would inform us of the father. Unfortunately, any mention of the 'act' is met with further hysteria. She is clearly unable to work and Mr Goodwood insists she must leave Margate before she brings shame on the whole family.

For the next few weeks we expect her condition to remain private, but I ask for your prompt response as to where we should send her before she disgraces us all.

CHARLES LOOKED up from the letter and stared at Eleanor. "They want to send her here? But ... but they can't. Everyone knows her; do they want to bring disgrace on us? Mr Goodwood should have been keeping an eye on her, not letting her go and do ... this." He slapped his hand across the letter as he spoke.

"But what do we do with her? I'm sure Mr Keen won't want her here, but you're the man of your house and with no children's minds to sully, could you have her?"

"We couldn't possibly. With all the connections Aunt Mary-Ann and Rose have we'd be putting them in a terrible position." Charles stood up and paced the room. "Are we the only two who know ... other than the Goodwoods?"

Eleanor nodded. "I would imagine so. I can't imagine Hannah will be keen to tell anyone else."

"What about her mother?"

"Aunt Adelaide?" Eleanor paled before she shook her head. "She wouldn't, not with the age of her and with Aunt Martha dying last year. The shock could kill her."

"At least that's something. Aunt Mary-Ann would be bound to find out otherwise."

"But what do we do with her?"

"What about Margaret?" Charles said. "She lives on a farm

in the middle of nowhere. Could we send her there? It would be less of a journey for Florence."

Eleanor shook her head. "I had a letter from her last week telling me she's in the family way again, so we can't push Florence on her." Eleanor watched as Charles lifted his eyes to the ceiling, cursing under his breath. "We're going to have to tell William-Wetherby. He'll be furious. Do you think we could send her to Liverpool?"

Charles put his head in his hands. "As much as I'd love to, I don't know how we can. They're still living with Mrs Booth; seven of them in that little house."

"I thought they'd moved to a bigger house."

"They have but it's still a squeeze."

Eleanor sighed and picked up the letter again. "As head of the family, we still need to tell him. Is there anywhere in Liverpool they could send her?"

Charles shrugged. "I've no idea. Will you write? You're so much better at it than me."

"I'll do it as soon as you've gone, but in the meantime, not a word to anyone."

"Don't worry, nobody's going to hear this from me."

Chapter Eighty

Liverpool, Lancashire

William-Wetherby sat at the dining table with Fred as Bella and Mrs Booth cleared away the dinner plates.

"What will you do this afternoon with no football to go to?" William-Wetherby asked.

"I'm taking me barrow into town to sell the pies and cakes I've made."

William-Wetherby laughed. "You won't reach the police station before they're all gone."

"I hope you're right, Mr Jackson, it'll save me legs, but you have to have a goal to aim for." Fred stood up from the table and collected his hat. "Would you care to walk with me?"

"I wish I could, but the leg's not up to it yet. Maybe next time."

"As you wish, I'll see you later."

As Fred walked to the door, the post landed on the doormat.

"I'll take that." Bella took it from Fred but paused before

she walked back into the living room. "There's a letter here from Eleanor but it's addressed to you and marked 'Private'. What can be so important?"

William-Wetherby took it from her and waited for her to go back to the kitchen before opening it. He hadn't reached halfway down the page before the blood drained from his face. *His little sister? How could she?*

Bella returned to the living room with a stack of plates but stopped when she saw her husband. "What's the matter? You've gone white."

William-Wetherby folded up the letter and stared at Bella.

"Let me see." Bella reached for the letter.

"No, you can't ... it's private." William-Wetherby pushed the letter into his inside pocket. *I can't share this shame with anyone.* "I'm going to the pub. They have a darts challenge on a Saturday afternoon."

By the time he got home that evening, the table had been set for tea and Fred was back from his travels.

"You were right, Mr Jackson." Fred smiled at William-Wetherby. "I sold the lot before I reached Prescot Street. I'm going to need a bigger oven ... and kitchen."

William-Wetherby stared at Fred.

"The pies."

"Yes, of course. I'm not surprised, they're the best in Liverpool. Did you leave some here for tea?"

"Of course he did." Mrs Booth put a selection of pastries on the table. "You seem preoccupied. Is everything all right?"

No, everything's not all right. "Yes, why shouldn't it be?"

"He got a letter shortly after you left this afternoon and he's not been the same since," Mrs Booth told Fred. "You should know by now that we're all family, you can trust us with anything."

"Leave him, Mam. He'll tell us when he's ready." Bella placed a pot of tea on the table.

"I need to write back to Eleanor after tea, she asked me to reply by return."

"What did you go to the pub for? You'd have made the last post if you'd written straight away, now it won't go until Monday morning."

"Because I didn't know what to say. Can we drop the subject? Are the boys joining us for tea or can we start without them?"

With the tea dishes cleared away and the family dispersed, William-Wetherby found the writing set and settled down at the table. Even now after he'd had hours to think about it, he still didn't know what to say. Perhaps he should tell her he had no suggestions. The most obvious solution was that she move in with Charles, but he couldn't put such a burden on his brother ... or Rose. How would she feel to have an illegitimate child born in her house when she hadn't been able to deliver one herself? Although, wait a minute, that could be the solution ... and they wouldn't have Mr Wetherby interfering this time.

With his letter written, William-Wetherby leaned back in his chair and smiled. Florence could be hidden away with Charles until such time Rose could take the child from her and pass it off as her own. The family resemblance should mean there'd be no questions about the parentage and then Florence could disappear as discreetly as she arrived.

"You look pleased with yourself," Bella said as she stood up to go to the kitchen.

"I'm not sure pleased is the right word, but I hope I've helped Eleanor with her problem. I must post this letter." William-Wetherby went for his hat. "I might pop in for a quick one on the way, don't wait up."

. . .

WILLIAM-WETHERBY DIDN'T KNOW how a letter could arrive in Birmingham and another one return to Liverpool so quickly, but as he sat at the dining table, his face was red with rage. Why was Charles being so obstructive? All he needed to do was put Florence in one of his spare rooms and no one would be any the wiser. By the sound of it, he hadn't even asked Rose about them having the child.

"What's up with you?" Bella asked.

"There are times I want to shake Charles. Eleanor has a problem but Charles won't even consider my solution."

"Was he the solution?" Bella raised an eyebrow but didn't wait for his answer. "If Eleanor's got a problem and you want Charles to help out, it's perhaps no surprise he's less keen on the idea than you. Is there anything we can do?"

"No."

Bella nodded and walked away. "What about Margaret or Florence?"

"What about Florence?"

"Nothing, I just wondered if they could help."

"Florence has done more than enough," William-Wetherby muttered under his breath.

"Listen, me mam's going to be out for at least another hour and Fred won't be back until teatime, tell me what's going on and I might be able to help."

William-Wetherby shook his head. "Eleanor's sworn me to secrecy."

"I don't care, I'm not just anyone. We haven't kept secrets from each other for the last fifteen years. I don't like the idea that Eleanor is doing this to you now."

"She has her reasons."

"Whether she does or she doesn't, it's clearly something you've not stopped thinking about all week. Besides, Eleanor needn't know you've told me."

William-Wetherby sighed as he studied his wife. If anyone

would understand, it would be her. He stood up and put his hand in his pocket. "This is the letter she sent me last week."

Bella took the letter from him and read it slowly. "Poor Florence."

"What do you mean, 'poor Florence'? She has no one to blame but herself."

Bella put her hands on her hips as she glared at her husband. "Have we not had this conversation often enough? We don't know that Florence has done anything wrong."

"She must have."

"No she mustn't. If someone decided to overpower her and have their way with her, there'd have been nothing she could do about it."

"If someone overcame her, why doesn't she say so? She won't tell anyone who the father is, which makes it sound like she's protecting someone, perhaps someone she cares for."

"Because she cares for someone doesn't mean she agreed to this. If the man cared anything for her, he should be marrying her, not leaving her to sort this out on her own."

"Whether it's her fault or not, she's brought shame on the family and Charles and Eleanor don't want to be associated with her. I suggested Charles take her in and he and Rose could raise the child as their own, but he won't hear of it."

Bella shook her head. "Your family have known privileges most others can only dream of and yet when one of you gets into trouble you turn your backs on them because of what people will think. If that's what money does to you, then I'm glad we don't have any."

"It's not like that."

"Well, that's how it looks to me. You've no idea what the poor girl's going through, all you're bothered about is what it'll do to your reputations. Given that none of you have an ounce of compassion for her, I'll invite her here and me and me Mam can look after her."

"Here? We've got seven people here as it is, where will she sleep?"

"We'll sort something out. We're not going to let her feel like a pariah when she may be perfectly innocent."

"I don't know ..."

"I'm not asking for permission, I'm telling you. Either you write to Eleanor and tell her or I will."

Chapter Eighty-One

B ella and Mrs Booth waited on the concourse of the railway station for the train to arrive from London. It was the first time Florence had travelled without spending time in Birmingham, but she'd had little choice.

"She'll be exhausted when she arrives," Mrs Booth said.

"She will. I can't thank Fred enough for giving us the money for a carriage. He's a good lad."

"Hardly a lad any more, but he's got more reason than most to have sympathy with our young guest. We all have, it's such a shame William-Wetherby doesn't see things the same."

"He's getting better," Bella said. "He'll come around once she's here."

At precisely four o'clock, the train from London pulled up alongside the platform and Bella watched Florence walk down the platform towards them.

"She looks dejected, bless her." Bella waved as Florence scanned the platform in front of her. With a small smile she waved back and walked towards them.

"Thank you for having me." Florence's voice was almost lost amongst the noise of the steam engines.

Bella linked her arm. "You're more than welcome. Now let's take you home. You'll be fine once you've had a cup of tea."

"Is William-Wetherby angry with me?"

"He wasn't happy, but he knows it wasn't necessarily your fault. He won't shout at you."

Florence squeezed Bella's arm. "Why are you the only people who're kind to me? Even Eleanor doesn't want to see me."

"Because we don't have anyone to impress," Mrs Booth said.

BELLA USHERED Florence into the back room where William-Wetherby was waiting for them.

"It's not showing yet then," he said as he got to his feet.

"No ... not when I've got my coat on."

"Is that why you're wearing it?" Bella smiled. "I did think you must be warm in this weather. Let me take it for you."

Florence pulled her coat around her. "No, I'm fine." She glanced at her brother. "Thank you for having me. I thought I'd end up in the workhouse."

William-Wetherby studied his shoes.

"We would never let that happen," Bella said. "For the time being this is your home. You'll be in the small front room with me mam."

Florence gazed around the room as tears formed in her eyes. "You're so short of space and yet you agreed to have me? I didn't think anyone cared for me that much."

Bella put her arms around her sister-in-law. "You're with family now, of course we care for you."

Florence buried her head in Bella's shoulder, moving only to wipe her tears.

"I don't deserve you," she said finally.

Bella took her hand. "Come on, no more of this now. You're safe here."

Florence smiled and glanced at Bella's hand. "Where's your ring?"

Bella shifted in her seat but said nothing.

"It's in the jewellers," William-Wetherby said. "We'll have it back soon."

Florence's brow furrowed. "What was wrong with it? It always looked perfect to me."

"Nothing ..." Bella's voice was faint.

Florence's frown deepened as she glanced between her brother and his wife. "Do you need some money to get it back?"

"It's fine, we're saving up." William-Wetherby's voice was stern.

For the first time since she'd arrived, Florence smiled. "I can help you. I've still got some of the money from Mr Wetherby and Mr Goodwood gave me some money before I left Margate ... to make sure I was cared for. You can have it all."

"That's very sweet," Bella said. "But we can't take your money."

"But you must. I can't live here without paying my keep. Tell me how much you want and we'll go and fetch the ring tomorrow."

～

Birmingham, Warwickshire.

CHARLES JUMPED from the carriage outside Eleanor's house before turning to help Rose down the steps.

"It's so much easier getting in and out of carriages with these newer skirts," Rose said. "I can actually see my feet."

"You'll be causing men to have accidents showing so much ankle."

Rose laughed as she put her arm through his. "You have to move with the times. I'm sure you don't want me looking old-fashioned next to everyone else."

Charles scowled. "It doesn't seem right, that's all." He knocked on the front door and waited until they were shown into the back room where Eleanor and Mr Keen waited for them.

"Are the children not here?" Rose said. "I haven't seen them for such a long time."

Eleanor laughed. "You saw them last week. They're out playing somewhere, which I'm glad about because we need to talk."

Rose glanced at Charles. "That sounds serious."

"It is." Eleanor paused as the maid brought in a tray bearing cups, a pot of tea and a selection of cakes. Once the door closed, Eleanor faced her brother.

"Have you said anything to Rose yet?"

"You told me not to."

"Very well, I suppose it's time we did some explaining." She turned to her husband. "I know you've been aware that something's been going on, but Charles and I were too embarrassed to share our secret with anyone outside the family. Until now, the only people who know are the two of us, William-Wetherby and Bella."

"Why do they know and I don't?" Rose pouted as she picked up her tea.

Eleanor sighed. "Because William-Wetherby did us all a great favour. We learned a couple of months ago that Florence is in the family way."

Rose gasped. "No!"

"Yes, and as you can imagine, if word gets out it has the potential to bring shame on the whole family. For obvious reasons, Charles and I agreed that she couldn't stay with either of us, but William-Wetherby was prepared to accept her in Liverpool."

"I suppose he has no reputation to uphold while he's away," Mr Keen said.

"Thank you, dear, that's enough. Firstly, I wanted to report that I received a letter from Bella earlier this week saying that Florence had arrived safely, and although she's subdued, she's settling in well."

"So why did we need a meeting?" Charles asked.

"Because Bella put something in her letter we need to discuss. While everything is satisfactorily discreet for now, Bella mentioned that Florence is looking forward to the baby being born. What happens if she wants to keep it? We can't have her coming back to Birmingham with a baby, even if it is only for a visit. What do we do?" She gave her brother a knowing look.

Charles's brow furrowed. "Has William-Wetherby said Florence and the baby can't stay with them?"

"Not in so many words but think about it. They have a house full of people and the baby's due in a couple of months. Once it starts growing up they won't be able to manage."

Charles studied Rose before he took her hand. "William-Wetherby did have a suggestion, but I don't know what you'll think of it. He wondered if we might like to raise the child as our own."

"Us!" Rose's eyes were wide. "How would we do that? With the new style of dresses, it would be obvious to anyone that I'm not carrying a child, and what would I say to Mother?"

"If we found a solution to those problems, would you like to raise the child as your own?" Eleanor said.

Rose held Charles's gaze. "Do you think we could? Would

folks think it strange that we suddenly have a child after twelve years of marriage?"

Eleanor interrupted. "What if you move house? Come and live around here. That way you'd be closer to Aunt Mary-Ann too. If you arrive with a baby no one will be any the wiser."

Charles stared at his sister. "We could move, but I'd rather stay closer to where we are now."

"Either way, if we can work through the practicalities, shall I tell William-Wetherby that you'll have the child?"

Charles noticed the hope in Rose's eyes. "Yes, please do. I'd better start looking for somewhere else to live."

Chapter Eighty-Two

Liverpool, Lancashire

Bella pushed herself up from her knees and picked up her bucket, the cleaning done for another day. She stepped over the newly scrubbed front doorstep and walked down the hall.

"You don't look comfortable there," she said to Florence as she went into the back room. "Is everything all right?"

"I've got something sticking in my ribs and I can't shift it."

"It's probably the baby's foot, let me help you up. A walk around the room may help."

Once on her feet, Florence followed Bella into the kitchen. "What happens when the baby's ready to be born?"

Bella studied her sister-in-law. "You'll find out soon enough. You'll start feeling some pains around your belly. Once that starts, tell me and we'll get you into bed."

"But then what happens? How does it come out?"

What do I say? Bella opened a drawer and fished around for a spoon she didn't need. "Your body changes and lets it out when it's ready. Don't worry about it yet, you've got another month or so to go."

Florence held her hands to her lower back. "I wish it would hurry up. I'm looking forward to seeing it. To think I can have someone of my own to love and who'll love me back."

"You have people who love you ... and what about the baby's dad? Will you see him again?"

The pupils of Florence's eyes dilated and Bella watched as she put a hand to her chest as if to calm her breathing.

"No, don't make me talk about him ... I can't talk about him. It would ruin everything."

Bella's eyes narrowed. "What do you mean? He's already ruined everything for you."

"Nooo..." Florence closed her eyes and put her hands over her ears. "I won't talk about it, you can't make me."

Bella pulled Florence's hands back to her sides. "It's all right, I won't make you if you don't want to. I was only trying to help."

Florence shook her head. "Nobody can help ... I have to forget about him. This is my life now and nothing can change that."

THE BOYS HADN'T ARRIVED home from school by the time William-Wetherby joined Bella and Mrs Booth in the back room.

"You're home early."

William-Wetherby went into the hall and peered into the kitchen. "Where's Florence?"

"She's gone for a lie-down."

"Good." William-Wetherby closed the door to the back room. "I need to talk to you about the baby before Fred and the boys come home. I told them at work I was seeing the doctor."

"What's the matter?" Bella put down her knitting as William-Wetherby sat opposite her.

"I had a letter earlier in the week confirming that Charles and Rose are going to have the baby once it's born. We need to work out the best way to get it to Birmingham."

Bella stared from her husband to her mam and back again. "Has anyone asked Florence about this?"

William-Wetherby's brow furrowed. "It's not up to Florence. She can't keep it herself and Charles is expecting it."

"Not up to Florence? It's her baby!"

"A baby she should never have had and which will bring shame on the whole family if we don't do something about it. At least this way she'll still see the child. Do you want us to send it to the workhouse?"

"No I don't!" Bella was on her feet.

Mrs Booth stood beside her. "Florence sees this child as the only thing in the world that will love her and you're going to take it from her."

"Well, she should have thought of that before she had it out of wedlock. This isn't some romantic story in a book, it affects us all and she can't take care of the child herself."

"She can if people are willing to help her." Mrs Booth straightened in her chair.

"Well, tell me where she'll live. She can't stay here, and she'll need money if she goes anywhere else."

"We used her money when she first arrived." Bella glanced at the ring now sitting proudly on her finger. "We'll have to give it back to her."

"Don't be ridiculous, where will we find that much from?"

"That doesn't matter. If she stays around here, we'll take care of her," Mrs Booth said.

"Stays around here?"

"Why not?" Mrs Booth collected up her knitting. "We can find her a wedding ring cheap enough, find her a room to live in and tell the neighbours her husband's at sea. It's not hard."

William-Wetherby opened his mouth to speak but Bella glared at him. "We are not taking Florence's baby from her unless she wants us to. I can't believe all this has been planned without a word to her."

"We can't change things now. Charles is about to move house and Rose is already knitting for it."

"What do you think we're doing?" Bella pointed to the knitting resting on the arm of her chair.

"The baby's not staying here and that's the end of it." William-Wetherby headed for the door. "I'm going to the tavern, don't bother waiting for me for tea."

Chapter Eighty-Three

The clouds had been thick in the sky all day and Bella reached up to switch on the gas lamp earlier than she would have liked.

"Another winter on its way," she said to Mrs Booth.

"At least we're all comfortable now, this time last year you'd only just moved in."

Bella nodded but remained silent when she heard a noise.

"Bella, Mrs Booth." Florence's shrill voice filtered down the stairs. "Come quickly."

Bella threw her knitting onto the chair and raced up the stairs; Mrs Booth was close behind.

"What is it?" Bella asked Florence.

Florence's face creased as a contraction took hold of her. "Everything hurts. Every few minutes I'm getting these pains."

Mrs Booth sat on the bed next to her. "It sounds like the baby's coming. Can you take some deep breaths and try to stay calm?"

Florence's eyes were wide. "The doctor said it wouldn't be here until next month. Is this what happened to Aunt Charlotte? Her baby died."

"No, it's not the same." Bella smoothed the hair back from Florence's face. "Her baby came out much sooner. Your baby will be fine. I'll go and fetch the midwife and she'll help you. You stay there and do as Mam tells you."

Unsure whether Florence was listening, Bella left the room and hurried downstairs. As she reached for her coat, William-Wetherby arrived home.

"The baby's coming," she said. "Me mam's with Florence and I'm going for the midwife. Keep the boys down here if they come in, I'll be back soon."

AFTER A NIGHT WATCHING OVER FLORENCE, Bella stumbled down the stairs and into the living room.

"Mam, what's going on?" Edward said. "Aunty Florence kept us awake all night."

Bella went to the kitchen and put the kettle on. "She didn't do it on purpose. She'll be fine soon."

"Who's that other lady?"

"She's here to help Aunty Florence. She'll be gone by the time you're home from school." Bella placed the bread and butter on the table.

"I'm too tired to go," Albert said. "The teacher will cane me if I fall asleep."

"Once you've had some breakfast, you'll be fine. Has Dad gone?"

"He said he had to be in work early," Edward said. "I reckon he wanted to go for a sleep."

"I'm sorry, but we'll all have an early night tonight to make up for it. Now hurry up."

Once she'd seen the boys out, Bella leaned back against the wall and yawned. *Why was something so natural so difficult?* With a sigh, she pushed herself upright and went back upstairs. The midwife looked as tired as she felt, but she examined Florence, almost willing the baby to appear.

"Come on, push, you're almost there."

"No, I can't." Florence lay on the bed, her back arched. "Let me die, I can't do this."

Mrs Booth wiped Florence's face with a cloth. "You can, come on, a few pushes and the baby will be out."

"No ... God's punishing me ... Tell him to have mercy." Florence let out a loud cry as another contraction tore through her body.

"That's it," the midwife said. "Another one of them and the baby's head will be out."

"No ... I can't ... I won't ... you can't make me ... Stop ... make this stop ..."

Florence let out another scream and Bella smiled at the relief on the midwife's face.

"You're nearly there, one more push and you'll have a baby."

Finally, as the midwife cradled a baby girl in her arms Bella propped Florence up on her pillows.

"You've done it, I knew you could." The midwife leaned forward to pass the baby to Florence.

"Get it away from me." Florence glared at the baby. "She's the devil."

Bella took the baby from the midwife. "No she's not, you have a daughter. Look at her, she's beautiful."

Florence lay back and screwed her eyes shut. "Beautiful? How can anything beautiful cause so much pain? She's my punishment. God sent her because I sinned ... God needs to cleanse her."

"She needs to rest," the midwife said. "She's exhausted and doesn't know what she's saying. We need to wrap the baby up and get some milk into her. By the looks of her, she arrived early. Take her downstairs and I'll make Florence comfortable before I join you."

WITH DINNER TIME APPROACHING, Bella popped her head into Florence's bedroom and spoke to Mrs Booth.

"Is she showing any signs of waking up?"

"I think so, she's been restless this last ten minutes or so."

As they spoke, Florence's eyes flickered open.

"You're awake," Mrs Booth said. "I was beginning to think the sleeping draught would never wear off. Let me help you sit up, Bella has something for you."

Once Florence was sitting comfortably, Bella placed her daughter in her arms.

"Look at her." Florence smiled as she reached for a hand. "She's tiny, but the most perfect thing I've ever seen. She's going to have everything she ever wants, a mother who won't leave her, pretty dresses, no bossy men. Can I take her out and show her to everyone?"

"Perhaps not today, it's only been two days since you delivered her, you need to recover."

"But I feel wonderful ... never better." Florence's eyes sparkled.

"The baby needs looking after too." Mrs Booth said. "Why don't you try and feed her? We've been giving her bottles since she was born but a mother's milk is best."

Florence's eyes flicked between the two women. "How do I do that?"

Mrs Booth perched on the side of the bed. "Let me help you." She moved to open the front of Florence's nightgown.

"No! What are you doing?" Florence pulled her clothes to her chest.

"That's how you feed a baby. Can you feel a fullness in your chest? That's milk."

Florence's eyes were wide. "No. No one's violating me ever again."

"It's nothing of the sort," Bella said. "It's natural."

Florence pushed the baby away. "Get her away from me."

Bella glanced at her mam as she picked up the baby. "You need to feed her. It's the only way she'll grow."

"You did this to me on purpose. I won't do it, you can't make me."

"Florence, we're not making you do anything. We can give her another bottle if you're not ready," Bella said.

"She's not speaking to us." Mrs Booth waved her hand in front of Florence's face. "She's in a trance."

Mrs Booth took Florence's arm and shook it but Florence continued to stare. "I'm going for a walk and you can't stop me. I shouldn't be in bed at this time of the day."

Florence pushed Mrs Booth out of the way before pulling the bedcovers back and swinging her legs out of the bed.

Mrs Booth caught hold of her shoulders and pushed her back. "Florence, listen to me. You need to stay here."

"But I have so much to do. I must buy clothes for the baby, and a carriage, and she needs something to eat." Florence's eyes were bright as she faced Mrs Booth. "Do you think she'll like bread?"

Mrs Booth ran her hand over Florence's head. "No, she needs milk and we have some. You need to rest."

Florence nodded and closed her eyes as Mrs Booth turned to Bella. "We need a doctor. Give me the baby and go and fetch him ... quickly."

The doctor arrived within quarter of an hour and once he'd given Florence a sedative, he let himself into the back room where Bella and Mrs Booth waited with the baby.

"I would say it's a reaction to the birth," the doctor said. "With more rest she should recover. I've given her another sleeping draught and I'll see her again tomorrow. How's the baby?"

"We're doing the best we can for her, but we're not sure she's suckling properly."

The doctor took the child from the cot. "She's smaller than I'd like. Has Miss Jackson tried feeding her?"

Bella shook her head. "She's refused so far."

"You may need to give her milk from a spoon until she's able to take the bottle. I suggest you persevere with Miss Jackson though. Being so small, the child needs to be nursed properly."

"Thank you, Doctor, we will." Mrs Booth stood up to let him out. As she was closing the door, William-Wetherby rounded the corner.

"Was that the doctor?" William-Wetherby's brow furrowed. "We can't afford him."

"We had a problem with Florence that we couldn't deal with ourselves."

William-Wetherby groaned. "That's all we need."

Bella waited for him to sit down before she described Florence's behaviour.

"We have to get the baby to Charles while she's like this and hope she forgets all about it," William-Wetherby said.

"We can't do that. The child needs nursing. You can't take her away yet."

"You've said yourself, Florence won't nurse her. If you're feeding her with a bottle, I'm sure Rose can do the same thing."

"But Florence wants so much for that child. It's the only thing she's got."

"What she wants and what she can provide are two completely different things. Charles can give the baby far more. If we move her now, while Florence has no idea what's happening, it may be for the best. We can always tell her Rose is looking after her for the time being."

Bella dropped a kiss onto the bundle in her arms. "Poor little mite hasn't even got a name yet. We need to register her and Florence won't be able to do it. What shall we call her?"

William-Wetherby gazed at his niece. "I'll leave it for you to decide, but do it this afternoon. I'll send a telegram to Charles and tell him I'm taking her to Birmingham tomorrow."

Chapter Eighty-Four

Birmingham, Warwickshire

As the cool October wind blew through the railway station, William-Wetherby tucked the blankets around the bundle in the baby carriage before him. Charles should be here by now, but there was no sign of him. He made his way to the entrance and peered into the crowds. *Come on, where are you?*

After what seemed an eternity, and with the child stirring from her sleep, William-Wetherby breathed a sigh of relief.

"Where've you been?"

"It was a bit short notice. I had a meeting with some buyers that I couldn't cancel. Why the hurry?"

"Florence has had a funny turn. Apparently, the birth was difficult and she didn't cope well with it."

Charles shook his head. "We shouldn't be surprised, but how on earth do we fit a baby carriage in there?" He stared at the carriage he'd just climbed from.

"I didn't think of that, but I couldn't have managed without it. Give me the baby and you'll have to fit it in."

When they were finally squeezed into the carriage, Charles studied the child in his arms. "Rose is so looking forward to seeing her; I promised we'd take her to register the birth tomorrow. Not that she's decided on a name yet."

"We've done it."

"You've done it? Why? We were going to register her with our names so that no one would ever find out."

William-Wetherby shrugged. "I didn't think of that. Bella wanted to make sure it was done but I'm sure it doesn't matter. No one ever looks at birth certificates. She chose a name for you, Grace ... and at least she's a Jackson."

"Who did she put as the father?"

William-Wetherby handed the birth certificate to his brother. "She didn't. Just keep this safe and no one will ever know."

When they reached Charles's new house, William-Wetherby stayed in the background as his brother handed the baby over to Rose.

"She's tiny," Rose said. "Welcome home, my baby. You're going to be so happy here."

Grace squirmed as she fought the blanket that bound her.

"She's probably hungry," William-Wetherby said. "There's a bottle in the bag with a bit of milk in, but Bella's been feeding her from a spoon. The doctor said that because she was early, she's not able to take a bottle yet. I tried to feed her myself on the train, but she didn't want it. You can imagine the looks I got."

Charles laughed. "Well, I'm glad you did. We hadn't thought of getting anything like that."

"You've got a lot to learn." William-Wetherby followed his brother's lead and went upstairs.

"It's as well you're staying the week; you can show us how it's done."

"I don't know what to do, Bella did all that. I expected Aunt Mary-Ann to be here; I'm sure she'll help."

"She won't," Rose said. "She says Florence is a disgrace to the family and we shouldn't have encouraged her by taking the baby."

"Having the baby isn't encouraging her, it's giving the baby the best chance of a good life. I'm sure she'll come around once she sees her."

Rose's hair shielded her face as she stroked a finger down Grace's cheek. "She says she won't cross our threshold again. It looks like I've gained a daughter but lost a mother."

William-Wetherby fidgeted with the bottle of milk in his hands. "I'm sorry. I never meant that to happen."

"It's not your fault," Charles said. "Times are changing and she's not ready for it."

"I'll go and see her. This child needs special care until she's old enough to suckle. Bella and her mam were managing, but you've no experience. I'll be in serious trouble at home if anything happens to her."

Chapter Eighty-Five

Bella paced the living room as she waited for William-Wetherby to arrive home. She knew it was a long journey to Birmingham, but why had he chosen to stay for so long? As four o'clock approached, the front door opened and she darted into the hall with a finger on her lips to direct him into the back room.

"What's the matter?" William-Wetherby hadn't had time to take his coat off.

"It's Florence. Something's wrong with her but we can't afford to call the doctor out again."

"What's up?"

"I don't know. Sometimes she's fine, if not a bit loud, and she's making plans for everything she's going to do with Grace. At other times, it's more of a worry. It's as if she's in a trance ... except, well, this may sound strange, but she's talking to people. When she's like that, she shouts at us if we speak to her, saying we're interrupting her friends. The other day she asked me whether I could hear them talking."

"Has she missed Grace?"

"No, that's the other strange thing. Even though she talks

442

about her incessantly, she never asks to see her. It's as if she thinks she's already with her."

William-Wetherby ran his hands across his face. "It doesn't sound the same, but Mother had spells where she would lock herself into her own world and not speak to anyone for hours. My father ended up sending her to the asylum."

Bella felt the bile rising in her throat. "We can't do that to Florence. We're the only family she's got."

"We haven't got the money either …"

Bella took William-Wetherby's hands in hers. "We're trying to help her, but what else can we do?"

"Let me see if I can talk some sense into her. Perhaps it's time she was out of bed. It is almost two weeks since she had the baby."

WILLIAM-WETHERBY CREPT upstairs and knocked on Florence's bedroom door.

"Florence, can I come in?"

"Excuse me a minute," he heard Florence say. "Who's there?"

William-Wetherby pushed on the door before stepping into the room to see Florence sitting up in bed. "It's only me, who's that you're talking to?"

Florence's brow furrowed. "Can't you see her? It's Mother."

William-Wetherby hesitated. "Florence, there's no one there."

"Don't be so rude, of course she's there. Look." Florence pointed to the bottom of the bed. "She says you're looking tired and that you need to take care of yourself. Didn't you hear her?"

"No, I didn't."

Florence held her hand up to silence him before letting out a deafening laugh. "I thought so too."

"Stop this, Florence." William-Wetherby took his sister's hand. "There's no one there."

Florence ignored him. "You must bring Father next time you visit. He promised to see me, but was always too busy ..."

William-Wetherby stared at his sister, her long fair hair tied in a plait that fell over her shoulder. What had happened to her? Florence ignored him and after a minute he returned downstairs.

Bella glanced up as he rejoined her. "How is she?"

"Just like you said." He sighed as he sat down. "She was having a conversation with Mother ... convinced she was in the room."

"What do we do?"

William-Wetherby shrugged. "I've no idea; I don't remember Mother being like that. Let's give it a few days and see if she improves. She's not doing any harm."

"I suppose not. How was your trip anyway? Has Grace settled in?"

William-Wetherby shook his head. "Not as well as she should have. She wouldn't take the bottle you gave me and Aunt Mary-Ann refuses to have anything to do with her. By the second day we had to ask Eleanor to come over and show us what we were doing wrong."

"Didn't you feed her from the spoon?"

"Rose tried, but it was going everywhere and so she decided to try the bottle again."

"I told you she wouldn't take it." Bella put her hand to her head. "I should have gone with you. The poor child should be here with Florence. I should never have let you take her away so soon."

"We had to do it. You know Florence couldn't look after her."

"But me and me mam could have and better than Rose is by the sound of it. It'll break my heart if anything happens to her."

"Nothing's going to happen to her."

"You'd better be right. You'll have to contact Charles in a few days and if Rose is still struggling, we need to go and bring Grace back."

WITH EVERYONE except Fred sitting around the table for tea, the silence was shattered as the front door slammed shut. Everyone froze before Bella jumped from her seat.

"Florence!"

She dashed upstairs to check the bedroom. William-Wetherby was waiting in the hall when she returned.

"She's gone, her bed's empty." Bella stepped out into the street. "She could have slipped down any of the side streets."

William-Wetherby grabbed for his hat.

"Don't be silly, you won't catch her." Bella raced down the road staring down each side street as she passed. When she reached the top of the fourth road she saw Florence skipping down the middle of the road in her nightdress.

"Florence, come back. Where are you going?"

When Florence failed to stop, Bella increased her speed until she was able to grab her by the shoulder.

"What are you doing? Look at you, you haven't even got any shoes on."

"But I've so much to do." Florence's voice echoed around the houses and Bella noticed some of the curtains twitching. "I need to buy the baby some clothes ... some nappies and dresses. I haven't done nearly enough knitting and I need some more wool. And she needs food ... she must be hungry by now."

445

"Florence, she's fine. Everything's fine. We've sorted her out."

"Mother told me I had to take care of her ... I haven't done anything. I can't stay in bed all day when I've so much to do. I'll need to clean the street before she can play out."

"Florence, stop. You have to come home. You're not dressed ... and you have no money."

Florence glanced down at her nightdress before staring back at Bella. "Why am I dressed like this? I need to go home. Come on, hurry up, I've got too much to do."

She retraced her steps, muttering to herself as she went. As soon as they reached the house, Florence went into the back room.

"Am I too late?" Florence stared at Mrs Booth as she tidied away the dishes. "I've got so much to do, I must have forgotten the time."

"No, you're fine." Mrs Booth held out a chair as Bella encouraged her to sit down. "We saved something for you. Sit down and get your breath back."

Bella stared at her sons as they sat with their mouths open. "You three, you've got half an hour before it gets dark, off you go."

William-Wetherby took the seat next to his sister and held her hand. "You don't have to do everything on your own. We're here to help. Promise me you won't run off again. What if we hadn't found you?"

"But you're not doing anything. You were sitting here laughing when my baby needs everything. I have to do every-thing." Her eyes darted around the room. "This room needs cleaning, she can't play in all this dirt."

"There's no dirt in this house, young lady." Mrs Booth placed her hands on her hips.

"But there is, look." Florence was on her hands and knees pointing to the corner of the room.

"Florence, come and sit down. You need to eat." William-Wetherby pulled his sister to her feet before turning to Bella. "Keep an eye on her and I'll go and fetch the doctor. Talking to imaginary friends is one thing, this is quite another."

Chapter Eighty-Six

Five o'clock was a time of day William-Wetherby had grown to enjoy. Since taking the job as a clerk a year earlier, he had finished work promptly and walked the short distance home looking forward to his tea being on the table. But not any more. Over the last two weeks, every day brought a greater sense of dread. Having worked as a police officer for so many years, he thought he was prepared for most things, but he had never encountered anything like his sister. They'd taken to locking the doors at all times, and Bella and Mrs Booth were struggling to cope with her.

When he got home, he paused and took a deep breath before knocking on the door. Bella let him in.

"How is she?"

Bella smiled. "She's been completely normal today. Quite like her old self."

William-Wetherby let out a sigh of relief.

"The problem is, she remembers everything she's done or tried to do, and she's horrified. She hasn't stopped thanking me for locking her in."

"Do you think that's it then? Has she asked about the baby?"

"She did, and I told her that while she was ill Charles and Rose were looking after her. She took it quite well, and was actually grateful to them. She has asked to see her though."

William-Wetherby nodded and was about to go into the living room, when Bella held him back. "One other thing, there's a letter for you from Charles. It might be worth seeing what he has to say before you talk to Florence."

After greeting Mrs Booth and his sister, William-Wetherby took his seat at the table and picked up the letter. Before he reached the end, he closed his eyes and put his hand to his head.

"What's the matter?" Florence asked. "Have you had some bad news?"

"N-no ... everything's fine; just some news from work. Will you excuse me?" William-Wetherby pushed himself up and went into the kitchen, shutting the door behind him.

Bella followed him. "What's up? You never shut that door."

William-Wetherby pinched the bridge of his nose before handing his wife the letter.

"Oh my ..." Bella put a hand to her chest as she stared at her husband. "How did that happen?"

William-Wetherby shook his head. "I've no idea, but Charles sounds distraught."

"Never mind Charles, what about Rose ... not to mention Florence? How do we tell her her daughter's died?"

William-Wetherby shook his head. "I've no idea but I suggest for now, we don't. It could set her back weeks."

Tears filled Bella's eyes. "We should never have sent her away. If we'd have kept her here and persuaded Florence to feed her, maybe she'd still be alive."

"You can't say that. You know how Florence has been and

the letter says she died of heart failure. We couldn't have done anything about that."

"It says something else too," Bella turned back to the letter and sounded out the words. "Mar ... as ... mus. What's that?"

William-Wetherby took Bella in his arms and let his cheek rest on her head, the image of Arthur's undernourished body vivid his mind. *How could this have happened again?* "I don't know, I've never heard it before." *I can't tell her he starved to death.*

"Could it have been because she wasn't feeding properly? It must have been. Charles says Rose is devastated and is blaming herself. Why would she do that if it couldn't be helped?"

"You can't say that."

"They're not short of money, why didn't they call a doctor?" Tears rolled down Bella's cheeks.

"You can't blame them, I'm sure they didn't do it on purpose."

"They're having the funeral tomorrow and we won't even be able to go."

"Funerals are no place for ladies, especially not the funerals of babies and children. Now, dry your eyes. We have to go back into the living room but we can't tell Florence what's happened, not as she is. Let her think Grace is still with Charles ... for the time being at least."

AFTER AN UNEASY NIGHT'S SLEEP, Bella was on her hands and knees cleaning the kitchen floor when Florence joined her.

"Good morning." Bella smiled at her sister-in-law. "You look happy today and you're dressed."

"We've got things to do," Florence said. "I've been thinking; it's Christmas in little over a month. We have to make the Christmas cake and pudding before it's too late. Don't worry, I'll help you."

"They're done, me and Mam did them a couple of weeks ago, when you were in bed."

"You did them without me?"

"You weren't well if you remember and they needed doing."

"But I need to do something." Florence's lips quivered. "It won't be Christmas if I don't make a cake. I need to go and buy the ingredients."

Bella took Florence's arm. "There's still plenty to do, but not yet. We haven't started the mince pies or any of the other cakes. You can help with them."

"Pies, yes. You must tell Fred not to make any; I'll do them. I need the ingredients. Where's the shopping basket?"

"Mam's taken it with her, she's at the shops now. You can do some baking this afternoon if you like."

"Yes, I will." Florence's eyes darted around the kitchen. "We need to clean the place from top to bottom. I'll start with the cupboards, empty them out and wash everything. The floor will need doing again, there are footprints on it."

"We only cleaned the cupboards last week. There's no need."

Florence glared at Bella.

"But if you want to do them, please do. It won't hurt to do them twice."

The smile returned to Florence's lips as she pushed Bella from the kitchen and closed the door. "Leave it to me."

Bella retreated to the back room. *I can't deal with this.*

When she returned from the shops, Mrs Booth stopped in the doorway of the back room. "What's this? Time off at eleven o'clock in the morning?"

Bella sighed. "I can't get in the kitchen. Florence wants to do some baking but the place has to be spotless before she starts."

"I'd better not go in with this lot then." Mrs Booth nodded at her shopping bags.

"I'd take a seat and wait. Is there anything in those bags to give William-Wetherby for his dinner? I don't suppose I'll be able to make anything before he comes home."

When he arrived home, William-Wetherby sat down to some cold meat, cheese and bread.

"What's going on? This is more like tea."

Bella shook her head. "Florence hasn't let us into the kitchen for the last two hours. She was acting perfectly normal when she came down and had got herself dressed and replaited her hair; but then she got all these ideas ... She's wearing me out."

"Should I go and see what she's doing?" William-Wetherby asked.

"No, leave her. She's quiet and out of the way, the longer it stays that way, the better."

As he was finishing his food there was a shriek from the kitchen followed by uncontrollable laughter.

Bella closed her eyes and took a deep breath. "What's she done now?"

William-Wetherby went into the hall and knocked on the kitchen door. "Is everything all right, Florence? I'm about to go back to work and I haven't seen you."

As he waited, the door opened and Florence stood before him covered in flour.

"Good God; what have you done?"

Florence let out another high-pitched shriek. "The flour went everywhere. Look at the kitchen, it's like it's been snowing."

Bella joined them and pushed open the door to see that Florence wasn't exaggerating. "How did that happen?"

Florence shrugged her shoulders and burst out laughing. "It went ... poof." She clapped her hands together.

"Are you going to tidy it up so that Bella can come in?" William-Wetherby spoke to his sister as if she was a child and Florence's shoulders sagged.

"I'd only just cleaned it ... but I can do it again." The smile was back on her face.

Bella returned to her seat. "We have to do something with her. Either that or I won't be held responsible for anything I do."

Chapter Eighty-Seven

William-Wetherby studied his sister as she stared out of the window of the carriage with her hands on her lap. She appeared oblivious to her surroundings and hadn't asked where they were going. The journey to Mill Road had taken less than ten minutes but William-Wetherby shivered as he glanced up at the formidable, red-brick façade of the hospital that had once been the workhouse.

Florence let her brother help her down from the carriage and followed him into the reception area where a neatly dressed young woman greeted them.

"Good morning," William-Wetherby said. "My sister needs help. Could we see a doctor?"

The receptionist studied Florence before she nodded and led them to a large waiting area. "Take a seat and a doctor will call her for examination."

William-Wetherby glanced at Florence before looking back at the receptionist. "She is prone to rather hysterical behaviour. How long will we have to wait?"

"We have to wait?" Florence's hands twitched as she

glanced around her. "We haven't got time to wait, I have to get out of here."

Florence brushed past her brother before he caught hold of her arm and pulled her back.

"Come here, we have to wait."

"No."

"I'll find a doctor who can see her immediately." The receptionist disappeared into a room and returned with a doctor.

"What's the problem?" the doctor asked as they were ushered into the office.

"This is my sister, Miss Florence Jackson. My wife and I are no longer able to take care of her."

Florence sat in silence while William-Wetherby explained her recent behaviour.

"Has anything happened to have caused this change?" he asked.

William-Wetherby glanced at Florence before answering. *She needs help, there's no point hiding anything.* "Nearly two months ago, she gave birth to an illegitimate baby girl. That was the start of it."

"Are you aware who the father is?"

"No ... she refuses to say."

"I see. So where is the child now?"

William-Wetherby shifted in his seat and glanced at Florence. "I can't say."

"But it's being cared for?" The doctor raised an eyebrow.

"In a manner of speaking. Will you be able to admit her, Doctor? She's calm at the moment but when she has her bursts of energy we're at a loss for what to do with her."

"I'll need to examine her first. Tell me, do you have any history of insanity in the family?"

How do I answer that? Mother may have been in an asylum, but she wasn't insane. "Not as far as I'm aware."

The doctor nodded. "All right. Let me examine the patient and I'll call you back in."

As William-Wetherby left the room, Florence was talking to someone, but he didn't think it was the doctor. *Maybe that'll convince him.*

William-Wetherby waited in the empty room for quarter of an hour before the doctor called him back in.

"Mr Jackson, I can confirm that your sister is gravely ill and requires urgent medical attention. I would suggest we admit her for a minimum of two weeks before we make a firm assessment. Once I've taken her personal details, and yours as well, you'll be free to go and I'll write to you with an update on her progress."

William-Wetherby breathed a heavy sigh. "Thank you, that's such a relief. Did you hear that, Florence? The doctor's going to let you stay here while he makes you well again."

Florence smiled. "And then can we be a family again?"

"Yes, we can. Once you're better, you can come home and it will be like old times."

A FEW DAYS BEFORE CHRISTMAS, William-Wetherby arrived home from work, his coat dripping from the rain. He handed it to Bella for her to dry in front of the fire.

"You were unlucky with the weather," Bella said as he took a seat at the table. "It's been fine all morning. There's a letter here for you, it looks like it's from the hospital."

"Let's see what they've got to say." He opened the letter and read it to himself before sitting back in the chair. "They want to see me. The doctor says her behaviour is still erratic and she can't come home in her current condition."

"So she won't be home for Christmas? Haven't they been able to do anything to help her?"

William-Wetherby folded up the letter. "It doesn't sound

like it. I'll try and finish work early this afternoon and call in on my way home."

At half past five, William-Wetherby sat outside the doctor's office waiting to be called in. There were several others before him and it was turned six o'clock before it was his turn.

"Mr Jackson, the doctor will see you now." A nurse held open the door and showed him in.

"Thank you for coming." The doctor extended his hand. "You're here about Florence Jackson, is that right?"

"Yes, Doctor."

The doctor sighed. "I must admit this is a challenging case. We believe she's developed a psychosis as a result of the traumatic birth of her daughter."

William-Wetherby stared at the doctor with a blank expression.

The doctor gave a sympathetic smile. "She's basically lost touch with reality and is living in a make-believe world."

"Can't you snap her out of it?"

"It's not that simple. When she sees people or places, they're real to her, as real as you or I, and she can't understand why we can't see them."

"But where does her energy come from? Is that part of the condition?"

The doctor nodded. "It can be attributed to a traumatic experience. Sleep and rest is often the best remedy, but with your sister we've tried a variety of treatments and nothing works for more than a few days. Some days she's calm and polite but other days, it's as if demons possess her and the only way to control her is with restraints."

"Do you think you'll be able to help if you keep her here a bit longer?"

The doctor sucked air through his teeth. "It's difficult to

say, but I suspect she may benefit from more specialised help than we can give her."

"More specialised help. What does that mean?"

"It means that unless she improves I'll have to certify her as a lunatic and send her to an asylum."

"A lunatic? But she isn't. She's a sweet person who needs help."

"And that's exactly what she'll receive if we can send her to the asylum."

William-Wetherby's brow furrowed. "But there isn't an asylum around here. Where would she go?"

"The nearest is in a place called Rainhill. The train to Manchester passes through the local station."

"But you can't send her so far away." William-Wetherby perched on the edge of his seat as he searched for the right words. "We can't afford to visit her all the way out there and she needs people around her; she needs her family. Can't she stay here?"

The doctor nodded. "I'm not a heartless man, Mr Jackson, and I do want the best for my patients. We can delay her certification until the New Year to give her a chance to recover. I'll also allow weekly visits now she's settled."

William-Wetherby smiled. "Thank you, Doctor. I'm sure she just needs more time."

Chapter Eighty-Eight

Villiam-Wetherby stood by the door of the carriage and offered Bella his hand as she climbed down. She studied the five-storey Adelphi Hotel before them.

"I didn't think I'd ever come to such a grand place for afternoon tea," Bella said. "I hope my clothes aren't too shabby."

William-Wetherby glanced at her smart new overcoat. "You look wonderful, stop worrying."

As they entered the central court of the hotel, Charles stood up to greet them.

"How was the journey?" William-Wetherby shook hands with his brother before he leaned over the chair to kiss Eleanor's cheek.

"As good as can be expected," Charles said.

"How's Rose?" Bella asked.

"She's coping, but some days are better than others. Thankfully she's made amends with her mother and she's staying there while I'm away. I didn't know, but apparently Aunt Mary-Ann had a baby son who died."

Bella nodded. "She told me about it once."

Charles raised an eyebrow. "Well, hearing about Grace brought back a wave of painful memories and she couldn't stay away. She's been taking care of Rose ever since."

"That's a relief," Bella said.

"It is, but it doesn't help us with Florence."

"No." Eleanor dismissed the waitress as she spoke. "Is Florence so bad that she needs to go in an asylum? After what happened to Mother, I don't want her going near one."

Bella glanced at her husband as he chose his words.

"I don't want to send her to the asylum any more than you, but she's far worse than Mother ever was. She's had several episodes where she sees people and hears voices. She swears they're in the room with her and sits talking to them."

"It might not be normal, but is it a reason to be sent to an asylum?" Charles asked.

"That was my immediate thought. She's quite manageable when she's like that and I thought it would pass, but it's when she comes back into the real world that the problems start. Mania, the doctor called it, and you can't control her. She never stops talking, always planning to do something or other for the baby or Bella."

"The baby?" Eleanor raised an eyebrow at her brother. "Haven't you told her?"

William-Wetherby shook his head. "We couldn't, not as she's been and she hasn't missed her. It's as if she thinks she's still with her ... in an imaginary way ... and we couldn't bring ourselves to do it."

"So haven't the doctors at the infirmary been able to do anything with her?" Charles asked.

"They're at a loss and say she needs specialist treatment. All they can do, and all we could do when she was at home, is lock her in to make sure she doesn't escape. Before she was admitted, we found her walking the streets one evening in her nightdress with no shoes on. The final straw for the infirmary was one day last week when she threatened to throw herself out of the window if they wouldn't let her go shopping."

"She doesn't even like shopping."

"She's developed an obsession with it," Bella said. "I tried to distract her, but you've no idea."

"So it's settled?" Eleanor said.

"The doctor has applied to a magistrate for a certificate to have her sent to the asylum in Rainhill. Fortunately, we'll be able to take the train to visit her."

"Does Florence know?"

"The doctor's going to tell her today. He should have done it by the time we get there."

THE DOCTOR WAS ready for them when they arrived and he showed them into his office.

"Please take a seat." He indicated the row of chairs on the opposite side of the desk from his. "This morning I received the signed order committing Miss Florence Jackson to the care of Rainhill Lunatic Asylum."

"When will she be transferred?" William-Wetherby asked.

"This afternoon. The nurses here are unable to guarantee her safety and so it's in her best interests if the move takes place as soon as possible."

"Does she know what's happening?" Eleanor asked.

The doctor nodded. "We believe so. She was quite lucid this morning when I spoke to her and I asked a nurse to put on her outdoor clothes ready for your visit. Before we go to see her, however, I do have one concern. Mr Jackson, prior to her admission, she lived with you in Molyneux Road, is that correct?"

"Yes, Doctor. I gave you all the details when I brought her in."

"You also said that she originates from Birmingham. How long has she been in Liverpool?"

William-Wetherby turned to Bella for an answer.

"She moved here in July last year, so just over six months ago."

"And did she live in Birmingham prior to that?"

William-Wetherby shook his head. "She left Birmingham when she was eighteen or nineteen and moved first to Oxford before going to Margate in Kent."

"So she's been out of Birmingham for over ten years?"

"I suppose she has. Does it matter?" Charles asked.

"It might. Given her most recent address, the Liverpool Union will pay for her stay in the asylum, but if she needs long-term care, we may have to move her."

"Back to Birmingham?" Charles said.

The doctor shook his head. "No. Since she's been away for more than ten years, we may have to send her back to Margate … or wherever the nearest asylum is."

"You can't do that," Eleanor said. "She'd have no one to visit her."

Charles put his hand on his sister's shoulder. "I'm sure it won't come to that; she'll be out in a couple of months."

Eleanor nodded, but William-Wetherby noticed a flicker of concern in the doctor's eyes. Before he could speak, the doctor stood up.

"Shall we go and wish her a safe journey. Her train is at five o'clock so we don't have much time."

The doctor unlocked the door to the room where Florence was being held, and he gestured for William-Wetherby to lead the group in. As soon as he stepped over the threshold, Florence bounced towards him, throwing her arms around his neck.

"You came. You all came." She smiled at the group. "You were nearly late though, I'm about to go out. They said they're taking me to another hospital, but I'm going to persuade them to take me shopping first. I met a couple of women visiting one of the imbeciles the other day and they wore the most marvellous dresses. I'd like one for myself. I haven't got anything pretty to wear at the moment. Bella, don't you look lovely ..."

"Miss Jackson, please. Can you pause to take a breath?" The doctor led Florence to the chair in the corner of the room. "Your brothers and sisters have come to say farewell and to let you know they'll come and visit you once you settle in your new home. You'll like that, won't you?"

"If you come all at once, we can have a party." Florence's eyes sparkled as she clapped her hands. "It'll be something to save my new dress for. There might even be dancing."

Charles turned towards his brother. "For the love of God, when did this happen?"

The doctor replied in a low voice. "When she arrived here, she had periods of quiet, when the hallucinations took over her mind. She hasn't had one for over a week but she hasn't been quiet since."

"Will they be able to cure her in Rainhill?"

"I can't say, but they have doctors more familiar with this condition; she'll be in the best place."

At half past four there was a knock on the door and two burly men and a nurse walked into the room.

"It's time to go now, Miss Jackson." The doctor helped her up. "Say goodbye for now, you'll see everyone soon."

Florence threw herself at everyone, squeezing them tightly. "I wish you were coming with me."

Eleanor wiped her eyes. "We'll visit as soon as we can and you can tell us about your new ... home."

"I will." Florence beamed. "But first we must go shopping."

As the doctor led Florence from the room, Eleanor sat

down and buried her head in her hands. "You didn't warn me she was that bad. I thought she'd be like Mother, quiet and thoughtful. What happened to her?"

Bella was on the chair next to her sister-in-law. "We did the best we could, but even the doctors have struggled. We promise we'll visit her and bring her home as soon as we can."

WITH THE SUN disappearing behind the buildings, William-Wetherby led the family out of the hospital towards a waiting carriage.

"What time are you leaving in the morning?" he asked.

"Ten o'clock," Charles said. "Mr Keen doesn't like us both disappearing at the same time."

"I suppose not. We must come to you next time, if I can get long enough off work. They've been quite understanding these last few weeks, but they'll expect me to make up the time now Florence has left."

Charles climbed into the carriage. "I didn't tell you, I bumped into Henry the other week. He told me Uncle William's had enough of pretending to work and he's closed down the business."

William-Wetherby raised an eyebrow. "I thought Henry was running it?"

Charles smirked. "No. He'd had enough of living and working so close to Uncle William and so he's packing up the family and moving to London. Apparently, they had a huge argument, and Henry told Uncle William that if he wanted to keep the business running, he'd have to start doing some work himself."

William-Wetherby grinned. "Marvellous, I wish I could have been there to see it."

"That wasn't all. Uncle William threatened to exclude him from his will but Henry reminded him that he'd inherited a sizable amount from Mr Wetherby and that he could keep his money. Henry said his father's face was so red he thought it would explode."

William-Wetherby laughed. "With the money he's got, I don't suppose Henry needs to work. Why didn't Uncle William sell the business as a going concern though?"

Charles shrugged. "With his excellent management skills, I think he's run it into the ground. It wasn't worth selling. He's renting the building to another firm and is planning on living off the money from his property portfolio."

William-Wetherby relaxed back into his seat and studied his wife and sister sitting opposite. "You know, I wouldn't swap with Uncle William for the world. Despite everything, we still have each other and we have the children. He's ended up with nothing except Aunt Olivia and a house they must rattle around in."

It was Eleanor's turn to grin. "Aunt Olivia's not there most of the time. She's friendly with Aunt Charlotte and they're involved with so many organisations I doubt she sees much of Uncle William."

William-Wetherby smiled. "He may have more money than most people could dream of, but the reality is, he's got nothing. I hope he's happy."

Epilogue

Three years later

As the train pulled into Birmingham New Street, William-Wetherby leaned out of the train window to see Charles on the platform waiting for him.

"We need to hurry," Charles said. "The train to London leaves in five minutes."

"I can't move that quickly," William-Wetherby said. "You go on ahead and hold the door open. I'll follow you."

By the time William-Wetherby caught up with his brother, clouds of steam bellowed from the train's engine and he climbed on board seconds before the engine pulled away.

"In here," Charles said. "I reserved a compartment for us."

William-Wetherby collapsed onto the seat. "Happy New Year to you. Business must be going well."

"We can't complain. Since we moved into making water tanks, we've had a number of big orders. We're hiring more men."

William-Wetherby laughed. "If it wasn't for this leg, I'd have come and worked for you years ago. Still, at least Edward and Albert are working now and contributing to the house-keeping."

"Has Fred made his fortune yet pushing his barrow around Liverpool?"

"Don't laugh," William-Wetherby said. "He's still doing his bookkeeping during the day, but he's a master confectioner now. He's so busy, I offered to be his chief salesman, but at the moment he could sell more than he makes so he doesn't need me."

Charles smirked back at his brother. "And there was us thinking he'd grow out of it and find a proper job."

"Don't ever say that to him, he's deadly serious and has great plans for the future. He works hard and deserves his success. Not that it's stopped him finding a lady to walk out with."

"Good for him, and at least you're back on your feet."

"I think we can say we're over the worst. We have our own house again and Bella's finally happy that I have a job as a salesman rather than with the police. I don't suppose we'll ever be wealthy, but as long as we can pay the rent and feed ourselves, I'll be happy."

Charles nodded. "This situation with Florence makes you realise how fortunate we are. I can't understand why the doctors couldn't do anything for her."

William-Wetherby sighed. "I know, I feel we've all let her down."

"You couldn't keep visiting her once she'd been moved to Kent, none of us could."

"And that's what was so sad. When she was in Rainhill she was always happy to see us. Always fussing about doing something or other and she never stopped talking, but she always had a smile on her face."

"It's a shame she couldn't have a family of her own. Did she ever mention anything about the baby's father?"

William-Wetherby shook his head. "Not to me. Bella asked her once but she became hysterical and all she would say was that it would ruin everything if she told anyone. It sounded like she was protecting someone, but why she would do that, I've no idea."

"So, what are we going to do when we finally make it to Kent?"

"I've no idea. The doctor's letter sounded urgent, but I don't know if we'll be comforting her or burying her."

"It could be both."

The two men stared out of the window as the green fields of England sped by until the landscape began to change.

"We must be coming into London," William-Wetherby said. "How many more trains do we need to catch?"

"Only one. I've decided we'll take a carriage across London, I don't have any desire to be driven underground on these new trains. From what I've heard it sounds positively terrifying."

William-Wetherby smiled. "That's a relief, I wasn't looking forward to it myself. Did you book a hotel?"

"I did. We'll go straight there once the train pulls into the station."

AROUND NOON the next day the carriage that had collected them from the local railway station in Chartham pulled up before the grand entrance of the asylum.

"It's like a stately home." William-Wetherby glanced up at the stone entrance flanked on both sides by walls of red brick and stone. "Much more inviting than Winson Green ever was."

They walked into the reception to find a nurse sitting at a desk to welcome them.

"We're here to see Miss Florence Jackson," Charles said. "We believe we're expected."

The nurse checked her notes. "Ah yes, if you'll follow me. Miss Jackson is on one of our outside wards. The doctor will speak to you as soon as he can."

As they were led into a small whitewashed office, a doctor gestured to some chairs. "Take a seat, gentlemen. I'll take you to Miss Jackson shortly, but I have to warn you she's in a grave condition. Unfortunately, she contracted tuberculosis, consumption if you prefer, sometime last year and since October, she's been steadily worsening. We don't expect her to be with us much longer."

"Is there nothing that can be done?" William-Wetherby asked.

"I'm afraid not. We subjected her to fresh air almost from the start, leaving windows open when they would normally be closed, but she succumbed to it. It's as if she lost the will to fight."

"Can we see her?"

The doctor nodded. "Come with me."

William-Wetherby shivered as they walked across a courtyard.

"We've had to isolate her from the other patients," the doctor explained. "We're learning that the disease can be transmitted from patient to patient and so we'd advise you to keep a handkerchief over your nose and mouth while you're with her. Avoid any physical contact too, to be on the safe side."

A knot tightened in William-Wetherby's stomach as the doctor led them into a room containing a single bed. Their youngest sister lay covered to her neck with a starched sheet topped with neatly folded grey blankets, her long plait resting over her left shoulder. He glanced around as Charles took the seat on the opposite side of the bed and the doctor backed out of the room and left them alone.

"Florence, can you hear me? It's me, Charles. William-Wetherby's here too."

For a moment there was no movement but then Florence's eyes flicked open.

"You came." The exertion forced her to cough and William-Wetherby held a cloth to her mouth as blood trickled from it.

"We wanted to see you. The doctor said you weren't well."

Florence moved her head slowly from side to side, but didn't speak.

"You rest." William-Wetherby wiped his hand on his trousers. "Let us do the talking. I've got so much to tell you about the boys. They're growing up quickly and they've missed having you around ..."

As William-Wetherby continued to speak of his sons, the doctor came back into the room.

"That's enough for one day, she tires easily. Call again at the same time tomorrow if you wish, but don't forget to wash your hands on the way out. We advise all visitors to do that nowadays."

WHEN WILLIAM-WETHERBY and Charles returned to the asylum, the doctor was waiting for them in the reception. They hesitated when they saw him.

"Has she gone?" William-Wetherby's voice was hoarse.

The doctor nodded and led them into an office. "I'm sorry to tell you that Miss Jackson passed away at ten past eleven yesterday evening. I would suggest that your visit gave her the peace she needed to depart."

William-Wetherby wiped the back of a finger across his eyes. "Such a shame. She didn't deserve to die here, all alone."

"She wasn't entirely alone. There was another man who

called to visit her about once a month. He said he was a relative. Mr Goodwood. Do you know him?"

"We do. He was married to one of our father's cousins. Florence worked for him when she lived down here."

"That explains a lot. She was always happy to see him but would never talk about him. He called last week and asked me to write if anything happened to her. Would you have any objection to me doing so? He was also interested in her funeral arrangements."

William-Wetherby turned to Charles, the lines on his brow deep. "Where do we bury her? Could we take her back to Birmingham?"

Charles let out a loud sigh. "I wish we could, but I've no idea whether the trains would carry a coffin, and even if they do, it'll be expensive."

William-Wetherby turned to the doctor. "Is there a church in Chartham we can approach?"

"As you are both unfamiliar with the area, may I suggest she be buried in the asylum's graveyard?"

"No." Charles was on his feet. "She should never have been here and we don't want to leave her here as a permanent reminder of these last few years."

The doctor paused. "Perhaps the church at Chartham will be most suitable then."

"When can you release the body?" William-Wetherby asked.

"We'd like to perform a post-mortem tomorrow, if you're agreeable."

"No." William-Wetherby shook his head. "You're not violating her any more. You know she died of consumption so I don't see the need. Hasn't she suffered enough?"

The doctor sighed. "If we could take samples of her lungs ... and brain, we may be able to understand more about the conditions she suffered."

William-Wetherby was on his feet. "I'm sorry, Doctor, but no. It's time to let her rest in peace. My brother and I will go to the church and arrange for the vicar to bury her at his earliest convenience. Can I ask the local undertakers to call and collect the body?"

The doctor sighed again. "If you wish. The body will be ready for collection any time after midday tomorrow."

THEY'D HAD to wait for three days but finally, with the winter sun shining on them, William-Wetherby and Charles walked behind the coffin as it was carried the short distance from the undertakers to the church. As they reached the doors, the figure of Mr Goodwood stepped out to greet them.

"Thank you for inviting me," Mr Goodwood said. "I wanted to pay my last respects."

William-Wetherby nodded and continued walking into the church, where the vicar was waiting for them. With only the four of them in church, plus the pallbearers, the vicar read through the service before motioning to the men to take the coffin out to the churchyard.

Once the body was committed to the ground the three men turned to leave.

"Will you join us for a bite to eat, Mr Goodwood?" William-Wetherby asked.

"Thank you, I'd like that. It's a long drive back to Margate and I need something to settle me, she was a special person, your sister."

"You visited her in the asylum though. She wasn't the same person we all knew."

Mr Goodwood smiled. "She wasn't, but she was still full of fun and mischief, almost like a child. Certainly more like the young girl who came to work for me all those years ago, rather than the one who left."

As they took their seats in the tavern, William-Wetherby turned to Mr Goodwood. "What do you know about the events that put her in the family way?"

Mr Goodwood took a large mouthful of the ale Charles put in front of him. "Nothing."

"Didn't you see her with anyone? She'd been attacked once before, if you remember. Did she arrive home distressed as she had done before?"

Mr Goodwood stared at the floor and shook his head. "No, nothing." He took another mouthful of ale. "Actually, if you'll excuse me, I'd better be going. It'll be dark by the time I get home. It was nice to meet you both again."

William-Wetherby watched their guest leave before he spoke. "What's he hiding?"

Charles shrugged. "Either he knows who it was, and won't say ... or it was him."

William-Wetherby nodded. "That's what I thought. Do we go after him?"

Charles studied his ale before answering. "I'd like to, but what good would it do? It won't bring her back. Whatever the truth, let it be."

THE JOURNEY back to Liverpool took two days and when William-Wetherby finally arrived at Lime Street Station, Bella was waiting for him on the concourse. He hurried towards her. "What's the matter?"

"Does anything have to be the matter for me to want to see my husband?" She snuggled herself into his arm. "I got your letter this morning and thought you might like the company. Did you see her before she died?"

As they made their way home, William-Wetherby told her of the week's events.

"So, do you think the uncle was the baby's father?" Bella asked as they approached the house.

"I don't suppose we'll ever know for sure, but it makes sense. Florence said it would ruin everything if she told us who he was and that would certainly apply to him."

"It would also explain why he gave her so much money to leave. To cover his guilty conscience. He should be locked up, in my opinion." Bella pushed open the front door of their new house. "Me mam's here. She should have George in bed by now. The other two will be out."

"Mrs Booth." William-Wetherby nodded towards his mother-in-law as he walked into the back room.

"I'm so sorry," Mrs Booth said.

"I think we all are. At least she looked peaceful at the end and by all accounts she wasn't unhappy where she was."

"Still, she was no age."

"Thirty-three." William-Wetherby took a seat by the fire and rested his head on the back of the chair.

"Tragic." Mrs Booth stood up. "I'm sure you'd like to be alone and so I'll be off. There's a cup of tea in the pot."

As the front door closed, William-Wetherby reached out his hand to Bella and she took it as she knelt on the floor by his side.

"You look like you could do with more than a cup of tea."

"In a minute." He turned his head to study his wife. "I'm sorry I was ever angry with you for helping women like Florence. I understand now how helpless they are. Thank you." He kissed her hand.

Bella gave a weak smile. "You came from a different world, I'm just sorry it was such a hard lesson."

William-Wetherby stared at the ceiling. "I don't suppose there are many happy endings when something like that happens."

"I can think of one." Bella pushed herself up and went to the sideboard. "Fred. He'll do well for himself."

William-Wetherby took the glass of whisky she offered him. "That's all down to you and your mam. He couldn't have done it without you."

"I don't know," Bella said. "All we did was put a roof over his head."

"You did much more than that ... You did much more than that for me too. I love you, Bella Jackson."

Bella laughed as she wiped a tear from her eye. "Don't go all soft on me now. In case you didn't know, it wasn't your money I wanted when you first came to Martensen Street. I've loved you since that first day and as long as I've got you and the boys I'll be happy." She raised her glass. "Good health, William-Wetherby."

～

Thank you for reading *Different World*.
I hope you enjoyed it.
If you did, I'd be delighted if you'd share your thoughts and
leave a review on Amazon

～

I'd love to keep in touch with you!
I send out regular newsletters with details of new releases and
information relating to The *Ambition & Destiny* Series.

By signing up for the newsletter you'll also get a FREE digital
copy of *Condemned by Fate*, a short story prequel to the series.

To get your copy and keep in touch, visit:
www.vlmcbeath.com

Author's Note and Acknowledgements

When I was growing up in Liverpool (a great-granddaughter of ancestors characterised by William-Wetherby and Bella), none of the family thought to question why our immediate family were the only ones with our surname listed in the telephone directory. We also didn't question why there were a lot of people with the same surname located in and around Birmingham. We just accepted it as one of those things.

It wasn't even the reason I began researching my family history. That started because of rumours we had heard and from snippets gleaned from my grandad. He wsas the youngest son of Bella and William-Wetherby and although he was very young at the time, the shame of their eviction, because they couldn't pay the rent, never left him. In later life, even when times were hard, he would often say that we (as a nation) didn't know how well off we were.

Even though my grandad was aware of some of the events in *Different World*, I don't believe he had any idea of what had led up to them. In fact, until I started this family history research, none of my living relatives had any idea of what had gone before. The only thing we had heard was that the family had once been wealthy and that there was 'a young woman' in Birmingham who had our money. We assumed at the time that the money had passed out of the family as a result of the death of a grandmother and the subsequent remarriage and death of the grandfather.

We now know that Charlotte ended up with the bulk of the money but given it was Mr Wetherby who made the fortune, and the fact that he was a step-father/-grandfather and not directly related, perhaps we shouldn't be surprised. What was more disturbing was the fact that he chose to actively disinherit our side of the family. Why he did that I'll never know, but some sort of family feud / breakdown seems the most likely explanation.

So what happened after the end of the story? Unfortunately for William-Wetherby and Bella, their happy ever after was short-lived. Approximately, one year after Florence's death, William-Wetherby was diagnosed with tuberculosis and he died later that year. He was forty-three years old.

Bella continued to live with her sons, around the corner from her mam and Fred, but sadly there was one more tragedy for the family. With the start of the First World War, her eldest son signed up for the British Army but in September 1917 he was killed on the fields of Flanders in Belgium.

Fortunately, neither of the younger sons were involved in the war and subsequently both married and between them gave my great-grandparents three grandchildren, seven great-grandchildren and, at the time of writing, eight great-great-grandchildren.

Fred remained a lifelong friend of the family and despite becoming a self-made millionaire; he never forgot his roots and visited Bella every week until her death in 1958.

As for Mr Wetherby's fortune, it appears that much of it didn't stay in the family for long. He left most of his assets in trust funds with strict instructions as to what should happen to them on subsequent deaths. This, however, didn't seem to happen and I suspect the trusts were dissolved shortly after his death.

Charlotte never had any children and on her death in 1937, she left everything to her husband Mr Mountford. He died two years later, leaving his substantial fortune to his brother. The brother subsequently died leaving everything to his second wife.

Henry received a sizable inheritance from Mr Wetherby and this money probably stayed in the family and subsequently passed to his descendants. Henry's rift with William Junior, however, seems real. As was stated in the story, he did move to London and there is no evidence to suggest he returned to Birmingham. His mother died about ten years after the end of the story and left money for him and his daughter in her will. Within a year of his wife's death, however, William Junior married a woman twenty-four years younger than him. On the day of the wedding, he signed a new will leaving everything to her. He died two years later. Despite the money he'd received from Mr Wetherby, however, the sum William Junior left amounted to less than £3,000 (approximately £150,000 in 2017).

So that draws to a close the story I wanted to tell. It's been a fascinating journey with many eye-opening moments and a great deal of sadness. The challenges, obstacles and hardships our Victorian ancestors faced puts many of our modern-day problems into perspective.

Once again I couldn't have done it without help and support from my family and friends. As ever, special thanks must go to my husband Stuart for all his help, both domestically and with checking the final draft. Thanks also go to Rachel for helping me polish the near final version.

I would also like to thank Wendy and Susan for their wonderful editing support. They have helped me make these books what they are and helped improve my grammar and writing style at the same time. Finally, I would like to thank my mum, dad and brother-in-law Dave for their continuing support.

I have been asked if there will be any further books in the series. I do have a couple of ideas for associated books and so it is possible. At this stage it is too early to say for sure, but please keep in touch by signing up to my newsletter, or following me via any of the links below, and you'll be the first to hear.

Thank you for reading.
Val.

Also by VL McBeath

The *Windsor Street Family Saga*
The full series:

Part 1: *The Sailor's Promise*

(an introductory novella)

Part 2: *The Wife's Dilemma*

Part 3: *The Stewardess's Journey*

Part 4: *The Captain's Order*

Part 5: *The Companion's Secret*

Part 6: *The Mother's Confession*

Part 7: *The Daughter's Defiance*

The *Ambition & Destiny* Series
The full series:

Short Story Prequel: *Condemned by Fate*

Part 1: *Hooks & Eyes*

Part 2: *Less Than Equals*

Part 3: *When Time Runs Out*

Part 4: *Only One Winner*

Part 5: *Different World*

A standalone novel: *The Young Widow*

Eliza Thomson Investigates

A Deadly Tonic (A Novella)

Murder in Moreton

Death of an Honourable Gent

Dying for a Garden Party

A Scottish Fling

The Palace Murder

Death by the Sea

A Christmas Murder

To find out more about visit VL McBeath's website at:

https://www.valmcbeath.com/

About the Author

Val started researching her family tree back in 2008. At that time, she had no idea what she would find or where it would lead. By 2010, Val had discovered a story so compelling she was inspired to turn it into a novel. Initially writing for herself, the story grew beyond anything she ever imagined.

Prior to writing, Val trained as a scientist and has worked in the pharmaceutical industry for many years. In 2012, she set up her own consultancy business, and currently splits her time between business and writing.

Born and raised in Liverpool (UK), Val now lives in Cheshire with her husband, youngest daughter and a cat. In addition to family history, her interests include rock music and Liverpool Football Club.

For further information about The *Ambition & Destiny* Series, Victorian History or Val's experiences as she wrote the book, visit her website at: vlmcbeath.com

Follow me

at:

Website:
https://valmcbeath.com

Facebook:
https://www.facebook.com/VLMcBeath

Amazon:
https://www.amazon.com/VL-McBeath/e/B01N2TJWEX/

BookBub:
https://www.bookbub.com/authors/vl-mcbeath

Printed in Great Britain
by Amazon

39049449R00283